D0553155

The
Double

ANN GOSSLIN

Legend Press Ltd, 51 Gower Street, London, WC1E 6HJ
info@legend-paperbooks.co.uk | www.legendpress.co.uk

Contents © Ann Gosslin 2021
The right of the above author to be identified as the author of this work has
been asserted in accordance with the Copyright, Designs and Patents Act
1988. British Library Cataloguing in Publication Data available.

Print ISBN 978-1-80031-9-370
Ebook ISBN 978-1-80031-9-387
Set in Times. Printing Managed by Jellyfish Solutions Ltd
Cover design by Rose Cooper | www.rosecooper.com

All characters, other than those clearly in the public domain, and place
names, other than those well-established such as towns and cities, are
fictitious and any resemblance is purely coincidental.

All rights reserved. No part of this publication may be reproduced, stored
in or introduced into a retrieval system, or transmitted, in any form, or by
any means electronic, mechanical, photocopying, recording or otherwise,
without the prior permission of the publisher. Any person who commits any
unauthorised act in relation to this publication may be liable to criminal
prosecution and civil claims for damages.

Ann Gosslin was born and raised in New England in the US, and moved overseas after leaving university. Having held several full-time roles in the pharmaceutical industry, with stints as a teacher and translator in Europe, Asia, and Africa, she currently works as a freelancer and lives in Switzerland.

Ann's debut novel, *The Shadow Bird*, was published by Legend Press in 2020.

Visit Ann
www.anngosslin.com

Follow her
@GosslinAnn

The first rule is to keep an untroubled spirit. The second is to look things in the face and know them for what they are.

Marcus Aurelius

People only see what they are prepared to see.

Ralph Waldo Emerson

1

Rosenborg Castle
Copenhagen, Denmark
22 October 2008

When a man in ceremonial dress announced his name, Vidor rose from his seat and approached the stage. Polite applause and a blaze of flashbulbs accompanied his journey up the steps. Blinded by the cameras, he briefly stumbled as a wave of nausea threatened to derail his progress towards the dais and the beaming man awaiting him.

Having rushed to the airport to catch his flight to Copenhagen, and too nervous to eat, he'd consumed nothing since breakfast. That single whisky on the plane to calm his nerves had left a burning sensation in his gut. The big day had come, the pinnacle of his career, yet here he was, unsteady on his feet and afraid of passing out.

His Royal Highness, the Crown Prince of Denmark, resplendent in gold epaulettes and a blue silk sash, smiled at him as he approached the dais. He touched his breast pocket to make sure he hadn't left his notes on the kitchen table. Winner of the Søgaard Prize for Excellence and Innovation in Neuroscience. Quite a feather for his cap. Perhaps next

7

year it would be the Nobel. With his name in the history books, no one would doubt him then.

In the great hall, where the air was thick with the odour of too many bodies, he found it difficult to breathe. But he remembered to smile as the Crown Prince placed a gold medal around his neck, and a brass plaque was thrust into his arms. They shook hands and together turned towards the rows of heads, faceless in the muted light, while the media pack snapped away in a frenzy of popping flashbulbs. 'Over here! Give us a smile.'

He flinched in the bright lights and shuffled his notes, frowning through a brief moment of confusion – *why was he here?* – before launching into his prepared remarks. He began with Newton's famous quote about standing on the shoulders of giants, sure to be a crowd pleaser. But his words stalled and juddered as he thanked his colleagues and students, pausing to remind the esteemed members of the audience about the slow and painstaking nature of scientific progress. One step forward, two steps back. He meant to offer them a pithy line, frequently quoted in his field, but couldn't locate the phrase in his notes. Did he not write it down?

Sweat streamed from his brow. Before him, the disembodied heads expanded to ghoulish proportions, then receded like deflating balloons. He struggled to read his notes, and when he looked up, he spotted a man slipping through the doors and taking a place at the back of the hall. Arms crossed, jutting chin. A sinister, jeering figure, with black eyes that glowed like embers.

Blood rushed to his face. *Him again.* How dare he? Choking with rage, a strangled cry escaped his lips.

'Monster. Traitor! You're supposed to be dead.'

Blind with fury, Vidor leapt from the stage and raced down the aisle to lunge for the intruder's throat. The satisfying crack of the man's skull hitting the stone floor gave him a brief moment of pleasure.

Amidst the rising tide of chaos and clamour, someone wrenched his arm back. A sharp cry, a stab of pain. Darkness fell upon him like a shroud.

2

Clinique Les Hirondelles
Saint-Odile, Switzerland
23 October 2008

Ten minutes past the hour, and Gessen's first patient of
the day had failed to appear. After a night of broken sleep,
he'd opened his eyes in the waning darkness, trying to hold
onto the remnants of a dream. Lost in a forest, obscured by
shadows, he'd thrashed for what seemed like hours through
the deepening gloom. Only to stumble through a hedge of
thorns, scratched and bleeding, to find the ruins of a once
glorious city, razed to the ground.

A classic anxiety dream, Gessen mused. Brought on, no
doubt, by yesterday's report from his accountant on the dire
state of the clinic's finances. But he had no time to worry
about money today. As always, his attention was focused on
the individuals in his care, and this particular patient, an angry
young man admitted against his will, was proving to be a
difficult nut to crack. After six weeks of little progress, their
treatment sessions had turned into a battlefield.

He stood and scanned the grounds, as if Ismail might
be lurking in the garden outside his window. The cobalt

sky shimmered with that peculiar, scintillating light of the high mountains. But there was no sign of a furtive young man crossing the vast lawn between the stone manor and the precipitous slope to the valley below. Though ringed by treacherous peaks, the great bowl of open space and crystalline air seemed to reassure him: *All will be well.*

A shadow darkened a corner of the box hedge. Gessen blinked and it was gone. He buzzed Ursula, but when no reply came, he hurried off and nearly collided with her in the hall outside his office. Her face was taut with worry, and strands of pale hair hung loose from a metal clip.

'Ismail's gone missing.' Her eyes flicked to the window. 'He was at breakfast this morning, but now nobody can find him.'

Dread pooled in his gut. Losing a patient was his worst nightmare, but Ismail had to be somewhere on the grounds. If he'd breached the boundary, his wrist monitor would have triggered an alarm. Gessen hurried down the hallway, with Ursula close behind. 'Have you looked everywhere?'

'We checked the obvious places,' she said. 'But if he's trying to elude us he could be anywhere.'

True. The clinic's extensive grounds and gardens offered any number of places to hide. The patients' wrist monitors, while a useful tool for tracking their movements, weren't accurate enough to pinpoint their exact coordinates at any given moment. They would have to fan out and look for him. He rubbed his temples. Though nothing about this was funny, he could picture Ismail contriving his vanishing act as a wonderful joke. What fun to lead the staff on a merry goose chase while he hid at the back of a wardrobe like a naughty child. Except he wasn't a child, even if he acted like one at times. A spoiled and entitled young man, furious at having his freedom curtailed.

As they stood on a hillock behind the manor house, Gessen scrutinised the grounds. 'Have you informed Security?'

'Not yet.' Ursula bit her lip. 'I suppose I should have, but I wanted to tell you first.'

They hurried along the gravel path that led to the men's residences, while Gessen peered left and right at the masses of shrubbery and small stands of pine. He should have cleared all that out years ago. With so many places to hide, Ismail could be anywhere.

'Let's split up,' he said. 'I'll check his chalet, while you organise the house attendants to search the grounds.' As Ursula headed back to inform the staff, his mind raced ahead. Where could the boy be? Cameras studded the property. Any one of them should have picked up Ismail's movements. Time to alert Security. Sweat dampened his collar as he punched the number into his phone. Before anyone picked up, he spotted a figure, some fifty metres away, slipping through the hedge. His heart lurched with relief, and he texted Ursula: *Found him.*

Spurred on by a rush of adrenaline, Gessen crashed through the shrubbery and into the hushed atmosphere of the Zen garden. Normally, his favourite place in the grounds, painstakingly constructed with exotic flora and statuary shipped from Japan. But with his heart hammering against his ribs, it was impossible to appreciate the elements of stillness and ease. A movement in the far side of the garden caught his eye. A slender figure heading towards a gap in the hedge.

'Ismail!'

The boy hesitated. When he turned, his dark eyes blazed with scorn. Weak with relief, Gessen struggled to stay calm. 'We've been looking for you.'

Ismail folded his arms. 'And now you've found me.' He waited while Gessen trotted over, as if this infuriating lad were in charge and his doctor was nothing more than a well-trained lackey. Ismail patted his pockets for the cigarettes he wouldn't find. Though he'd been offered nicotine patches, he complained bitterly that not only was he robbed of his freedom, but also one of his greatest pleasures. What was next? Coffee? Food and water?

'I'm just glad to see you're all right,' Gessen said, chest

heaving, as he tried to project a professionalism he didn't feel. What he felt like doing was giving the lad a good thrashing.

'Why wouldn't I be?' Ismail brushed a dried leaf from his sleeve. 'What are you doing out here, anyway? Don't we have a session or something?' He turned on his heel and headed across the lawn in the direction of the manor house.

Gessen followed doggedly behind, reluctant to say anything more lest he set the boy off. His heart ticked oddly as he tried to keep up. A close call. Not something he wished to repeat. And where, during all the excitement, was Ismail's personal bodyguard? A man named Sendak, courtesy of Ismail's father, whom Gessen passed off to the staff as a new groundsman. Wasn't the man paid to keep Ismail out of harm's way? After this latest show of rebellion, it might be best to have someone on his own payroll to watch Ismail around the clock. A glorified minder, as a backup to the useless bodyguard. Another expense he couldn't afford.

* * *

Seated across from Ismail in one of the suede wingback chairs in his office, he waited for his headstrong patient to say something in his defence.

'I'm here to help you,' Gessen said, as the minutes dragged on, 'but I can only do that if you meet me halfway.'

Ismail spread his fingers and made a show of examining his nails. 'And how do you suggest I do that?'

Only the very wealthy, Gessen mused, could be so coolly self-assured. He suspected it was a pose, though there was no doubt Ismail was suffering. Anxiety and depression topped the list. Exacerbated, surely, by the ongoing stand-off with his father, a wealthy diplomat and business tycoon, with an explosive temper, if the rumours were true. To complicate matters, Ismail now had two men to rebel against, both of whom stood in the way of his only desire: a swift return to Oxford and the 'unsuitable attachment' awaiting him there.

A pretty, socially ambitious girl, apparently, whom the father was anxious to keep away from his son.

Gessen leaned forward, hoping to make eye contact. 'Talk to me.'

Ismail raised an eyebrow. 'I'd rather not.' With a look of distaste he scanned the room. 'Why isn't there a single bloody clock in this pimped-up prison of yours?'

'Is there somewhere you have to be?' Gessen suppressed a smile. The boy certainly had a way with words. A brilliant student in his last year at Oxford, he'd been headed for a first-class degree in biomedical engineering, until his plans were derailed in the wake of a suicide attempt. A bid for his father's attention, Gessen believed, rather than a true desire to die, but that didn't mean he could take any chances. Not with a patient like this, trapped by family decrees and fighting for personal autonomy. After graduating, Ismail had planned to take a year off and travel with his girlfriend before returning to England to study medicine. That is, until his father swooped in and scuppered his plans.

Ismail slid onto his tailbone and closed his eyes. A segue to his usual modus operandi, refusing to speak. Since Gessen couldn't force him to talk, their sessions often ended in a stalemate. Mute patience on one side, seething resentment on the other, with Gessen obliged to travel the thin line between silence and a restrained monologue. Tossing titbits into the void about how important it was for Ismail to work through not only the impasse with his father, but the storm of emotions roiling in his heart.

But he might as well be talking to a stone. Worn out by his troubled sleep and the panic over the boy's disappearance, Gessen folded his hands in his lap and listened to Ismail breathe. As the silence stretched into minutes, his mind wandered to a small item in the newspaper he'd seen at breakfast. An acclaimed Cambridge University neuroscientist, who was in Copenhagen to receive an international prize, had gone berserk and attacked a man in the audience.

As he pictured the scene, Gessen puzzled over the drama. Had the scientist known the man he attacked, or did a random stranger trigger a momentary psychosis? A memory kindled, a buried injury revealed. Gessen's speciality, the rupture of the psychic wound, ossified through time, yet festering still. In a man like Professor Kiraly, an award-winning Cambridge don at the pinnacle of his career, it was intriguing to imagine what that wound might be.

Ismail sighed noisily and rose to his feet. 'Are we done here?'

Gessen felt a surge of paternal empathy. How easily he recalled the passions of youth. The fierce desire to set fire to the world and fashion it anew. *We don't choose our families.* A sentiment he'd shared with Ismail at the start of his therapy. *Parents and siblings are thrust upon us. There's no running away, so we must learn to deal with them as best we can.* But convincing Ismail to make friends with his anger was no simple matter. Whether the boy liked it or not, they had a long road ahead of them.

A blood vessel beat in Ismail's neck and his dark eyes flashed. A good thing his father was safely in Geneva, Gessen thought. Such anger, if not held in check, could escalate to catastrophic proportions.

'In the time remaining today, I'd like to explore in more depth your relationship with your father.' He gestured at Ismail to retake his seat. 'Why don't we start with your very first memory and go from there.'

3

Their hour together, like all the others, ground to a halt and ended in deadlock. As Gessen paged the house attendant to escort Ismail to his room, he studied the boy's impassive face with a twinge of sympathy. Poor lad. Never truly alone, from the moment of his birth, nor free to choose his own path in life. Watched over with anticipation and dread, like the only son of an ailing king, waiting to fulfil a destiny long etched in stone. Speaking of which, Ismail's private bodyguard must be somewhere close by, though the man had a knack for remaining in the shadows.

His next patient wasn't until three, and Gessen welcomed the thought of spending a few hours alone in his private quarters. An underground passage connecting the stone manor house to his cosy chalet allowed him to come and go without being observed by the patients, though there were fewer than usual these days. Equipped to treat twelve full-time residents, the clinic was down to five. The first time since launching his ambitious enterprise nearly a dozen years ago that he'd had so few patients in his care. No wonder his accountant was nervous. Gessen rarely thought about the money side of things, but he couldn't ignore the fact that he would soon be operating at a loss.

Inside his chalet, cleverly screened from the other buildings by a copse of trees, light poured in through the large windows. Fernanda, the corgi and beagle mix he'd rescued from a kill shelter in Spain, wagged her tail in greeting, then rushed across the room to fetch a well-chewed orange ball and drop it at Gessen's feet. He tossed the ball and smiled as she raced to catch it. She could do this for hours, and after a long day of attending to the needs of others, the joy in the eyes of this little dog, saved from a miserable death, never failed to brighten his mood.

He stroked Fernanda's silky ears and let her out into the fenced garden to lie in the sun. Placed squarely in the middle of the kitchen table, the accountant's report was like a reproach. The three-pronged warning loud and clear: admit more patients, raise fees, or cut operating costs. Only the first was an attractive option.

Next to one item, a quarterly donation to a charity in Warsaw, his accountant had scribbled a remark in red ink. *Is this necessary? Consider dropping it.* Ever the diplomat, what his accountant meant was: axe this immediately and save yourself a boatload of money. But Gessen had no intention of changing a thing. Not even when the world's financial markets were toppling like dominoes. Sending money to the Varem Heym Foundation was non-negotiable.

He closed the report and looked out through the sliding glass door to the terrace, neatly framed by a hedge of Japanese hawthorn. He dropped into a chair and studied the line of jagged peaks to the east. In certain lights they resembled the massive teeth of a Jurassic reptile.

Perched high above a forested valley in the Bernese Oberland, the former retreat of an eccentric 1920s industrialist who'd lost everything in the crash had been transformed into the clinic's main building. A folly of turrets and parapets, acres of parquet, and a soaring tower with a bird's-eye view of the grounds. Surrounded by quintessentially Swiss chalets for the patients and staff, the whole set-up might have been plucked straight from a fairy tale.

Fifteen years ago, when he'd had no money for such an enterprise, the idea of starting his own clinic was just a pipe dream. But after a former patient died of cancer, he was shocked to learn she'd left him the bulk of her fortune. The poor woman suffered from a recurrent somatic disorder, resulting in paralysis and extreme distress. She'd seen a dozen specialists to no avail, until at last, under Gessen's ministrations, she was able to resume her old life. While under his care, though she'd talked extensively about herself, he'd had no idea she stood at the helm of a vast fortune.

In her will, she made it clear he should use the money to establish a private clinic, where he could help lift others out of the terrible mental and physical anguish that had beset her in midlife. Along with a considerable sum of money, the bequest included the manor house and surrounding property that would become the heart of the clinic.

Over the years, with a seemingly endless stream of funds at his disposal to create a bucolic respite from the world, he'd been profligate to the point of irresponsibility. What did he care about money? Mental health was the holy grail, and on many occasions he would waive the fees for patients who couldn't pay, or reduced the costs for others.

But as the reputation of the clinic's facilities and storybook setting grew, the thorny psychiatric cases he'd sought to treat had somehow transformed into the wealthy and bored who found their way to his door. He welcomed a few of these individuals, seeking nothing more than relief from their malaise, though always with a twinge of guilt, as a way of injecting some much-needed cash into the clinic's depleted coffers. He justified this treachery so that those truly in need, but unable to pay, would benefit from his skill as a clinician of the mind. Now, according to the grim reckoning of his accountant, and having taken a major hit in the global financial crash, the hour had arrived to pay the piper.

He poured himself a coffee and opened the *Berner Zeitung* to read again the news item about the Cambridge don in

Copenhagen. It was only three lines and gave no details, but one of the London papers online provided a more tantalising summary:

Copenhagen, 23 October 2008 – The winner of the 2008 Søgaard Prize for Excellence and Innovation in Neuroscience, Professor Vidor Kiraly OBE, of Cambridge University, United Kingdom, was taken to hospital yesterday following an incident at the awards ceremony at Rosenborg Castle. Honoured for his pioneering work on sensory integration and pattern recognition in the human brain, Kiraly was in the Danish capital to accept the prestigious award from his Royal Highness, the Crown Prince of Denmark. According to eyewitnesses, Kiraly displayed signs of agitation during his acceptance speech and began to shout in a foreign language at a man at the back of the hall. Before anyone could stop him, Kiraly rushed off the stage and knocked the man to the floor. Though Kiraly was largely incoherent at the time of the attack, a member of the audience identified two of the words he shouted as 'monster' and 'dead'. Medics arrived promptly on the scene and administered a sedative before transporting Kiraly to a local hospital. The man who was attacked appeared to be seriously injured and was taken away by ambulance. No further information on the victim's condition, or Professor Kiraly's whereabouts, is available at this time.

Gessen clicked on other links about the incident, including a video taken during the ceremony. The video started mid-sentence, as an elegant man announced Professor Kiraly's name. Clad in a grey suit with an expensive sheen, Kiraly mounted the stage, his eyes shadowed, and his dark hair, touched with silver at the temples, swept back. A gold signet ring on his left hand caught the light.

The Crown Prince of Denmark, resplendent in full dress uniform, strode forth and presented Kiraly with a medal and a brass plaque. Polite applause, a burst of flashbulbs. Kiraly flinched at the lights as he stepped up to the dais and leaned into the microphone, thanking the committee and his Danish hosts, noting how pleased he was to be back in the Danish capital, home to his favourite philosopher, Søren Kierkegaard. He said a few words in what Gessen took to be Danish, eliciting from the audience – and the Prince – a ripple of laughter.

Two minutes into his prepared speech, beaded with perspiration, Kiraly paused to look at the audience. As the blood drained from his face, followed by a flush of anger, he raised his fist in the air and shouted something Gessen couldn't make out, before rushing down the steps and into the aisle. The camera panned jerkily to a man at the back of the hall, elegant in a pin-striped suit and horn-rimmed glasses, his leonine head adorned with a white mane of hair. Kiraly raced down the aisle and launched himself at the man, shouting something in a language Gessen assumed was Hungarian.

Two security guards grappled Kiraly to the ground. Another man, perhaps one of the organisers, rushed over to assist. As Kiraly's face was pushed against the floor, his eyes flicked with terror, before a hand swam up to the camera lens and the film cut out.

Gessen stared at the darkened screen, his heart bumping against his ribs. In need of air, he raised the blinds and flung open the window, hoping the sight of the high mountains and vast bowl of open space would settle his churning thoughts.

The raw fury in Kiraly's face. So unexpected in such an elegantly dressed and courtly Cambridge don. Why the explosive rage, and at that particular man? Was it someone Kiraly knew, or believed he did? It didn't make sense. Gessen's first thought was amok syndrome. From the Malay word for 'rampage', the rare, delusional condition was characterised by non-premeditated violent or homicidal rage against another person or persons. He'd never seen a real case up close, but it had fascinated him since his medical school days. Often accompanied by amnesia or exhaustion, an individual afflicted with amok syndrome might be driven to psychotic rage by something as trivial as a perceived insult.

He had some experience with similar bizarre disorders. Years ago, he'd treated a young boy with lycanthropy, a rare delusion that one was turning into an animal, such as a wolf. In the case of Gessen's patient, it wasn't a wolf but a lynx. The boy was from Romania and, according to his mother, he was frightened by a lynx as a toddler, and had acted strange ever since. Then there was the woman from Korea whom he'd diagnosed with *shin-byung*, a delusional disorder with symptoms of anxiety, dizziness, and gastrointestinal complaints. The patient believed she was possessed by ancestral spirits and such was her distress that even now, six years later, he could recall the terror in her eyes and her piercing screams.

An older woman with Capgras was a particularly heartbreaking case, one of his first as a trainee doctor in Zurich. A truly bizarre disorder, also known as imposter syndrome, in which family members or friends appear either as strangers or are mistaken for each other. The woman had become convinced her husband of thirty-five years was her long-deceased father and refused to let him sleep in her bed. Diagnosed with atypical psychosis, she only recovered after spending several weeks at a psychiatric facility in the high mountains near the Austrian border.

It was that case that sparked the idea of setting up his own clinic where patients, traumatised by the bright lights, harsh buzzers, and rattling meal carts of the typical psychiatric ward, could heal in an environment of peace and natural beauty. Though at the time he'd had only his dreams, but no money to turn them into reality, a few years later, when the patient he rescued from somaticised paralysis had passed away, he'd used her generous bequest to make the clinic a reality. But the unusual and intractable cases had waned in number, and his only interesting patient from a medical perspective was a woman with Munchausen's. If this Professor Kiraly was truly suffering from something like amok syndrome, possibly complicated by childhood trauma, it would present Gessen with the biggest challenge he'd encountered in years.

He closed his laptop and stood at the window to breathe in the sun-warmed air, filled with the dried grass and red-berry scent of early autumn. If Kiraly were to become his patient, and Gessen was successful in treating him, he would not only cure a world-class scientist from a serious psychiatric affliction, but it might give a tremendous boost to his flagging energy and the declining fortunes of the clinic.

Not that he could ever reveal to the public that Kiraly was his patient. An anonymised case study would be the only outlet to publicise his role. But surely the grateful professor, returned to health and exonerated from any charges lodged against him, would be delighted to give credit where credit was due. Perhaps extol the excellence of his doctor and the clinic's staff, and spread a little gold dust in his wake.

4

'Vidor Kiraly?' The voice of Gessen's friend, a soft-spoken Berliner who worked at a clinic in Copenhagen, echoed down the line. 'Oh, yes. The whole city's talking about him. Poor man. What a spectacular fall from grace. I believe he was taken to Bispebjerg Hospital. Give me a minute to make some calls, and I'll get back to you.'

He was halfway through his second cup of coffee when his friend rang back. Kiraly was indeed at Bispebjerg. Refusing treatment and adamantly against a transfer to an NHS hospital in London. No family or next of kin, apparently. And no emergency contact provided, so they didn't know whom to call.

No family or close friends? Surprising in such a high-profile, successful man, but that could work in Gessen's favour. He thanked his friend and considered his next move. With nowhere else to go, perhaps Professor Kiraly would be willing to come to him? The remote location and superb facilities at Les Hirondelles might be inducement enough.

As he studied the dregs of the strong Turkish coffee he drank in the mornings, Gessen was struck by a memory from his boyhood, how he'd been lured during a visit to a provincial fair into a shadowy tent by a woman with crow-black hair who promised to read his fortune in the tea leaves. Past, present, and future. *Come, my boy, don't be afraid.*

He'd shivered at the idea, but before he could pull away, she prepared the leaves and bent her head over the cup. In a thick accent, she spoke of a dark knight, a monstrous secret, a gold ring. Admonishing him with a stern frown, after she'd taken his money, to beware his second Saturn return. Whatever that was. Even as a boy he'd known it was nonsense, though shivers had travelled down his arms, and for several days afterwards he suffered from a strange fever and bouts of dizziness.

Later in life, after her prophecies came true, he wondered how she'd known. Had she seen something in his face or a shadow in his eyes? A glimpse, perhaps, of the fatal flaw he himself knew nothing of. On some days, while working with a particularly difficult patient, trying to understand the trauma in their past by the signposts of the present, Gessen's thoughts would return to the fortune teller, who'd frightened him by the urgency of her words, wondering if their different means of divination, one mystical, the other grounded in science, were simply opposite sides of the same coin.

After several attempts he got Kiraly's attending physician on the phone and made his proposition. If Kiraly were willing, Gessen would cover the costs of his transfer and treatment at his private clinic in the Bernese Oberland. Top-notch facilities and stellar psychiatric care, guaranteed.

'I know who you are,' said the woman in lightly accented English. 'I've read your case studies on trauma and somatisation. Very compelling, and a particular interest of mine. Though he's stable now, Professor Kiraly continues to insist there's nothing wrong with him and is threatening to leave the hospital against medical advice.'

Gessen jotted a few notes. 'I'll have my assistant email a copy of our brochure. Perhaps our tranquil setting and extensive range of facilities will be inducement enough for Professor Kiraly to agree to therapy.'

He ended the call and buzzed Mathilde to have her forward the clinic's information straight away. His mind was already leaping ahead. If Kiraly agreed to the transfer, he would send Ursula to Copenhagen to accompany him on the trip to Saint-Odile. A skilled clinical psychologist, Ursula would be furious if she suspected he was using her as a lure. But it certainly didn't hurt that along with a keen analytical mind and excellent language skills, she was blessed with a quiet grace and winning smile. Something about this case suggested that a male doctor, appearing at Kiraly's bedside to offer a solution to his problem, might be contentious, even threatening. With Les Hirondelles as an enticement and Ursula as his ambassador, Gessen might persuade Kiraly to seek relief from his affliction where others had failed.

5

Far below, lights spring on in the gathering dusk. Cowbells sound a mournful note as an ancient herder leads his charges down the mountain. The peaks, craggy indeed, are dusted with a layer of snow that turns to peach – no, scratch that – *turns to… apricot as the light fades. Alpine serenity. Tout est parfait…*

Vidor groaned and tossed the notebook on the bench. Penning such drivel had given him a throbbing headache. But the delightful Dr Lindstrom, who possessed not only an engaging mind but also the face of a Botticelli angel, had encouraged him to write down his thoughts, or whatever else came to mind. So why not oblige?

At the back of the notebook he'd begun a sketch of the grounds and flipped to the page to add a few more details to his map. Once, as a young boy on a family outing to the countryside near Budapest, he had wandered away and got lost in a forest so dense that little light reached the ground. A terrifying experience he'd no wish to repeat. Ever after, upon finding himself in a new place, it was his habit to sketch out the terrain. Entrances and exits. Landmarks and escape routes. Places of seclusion, should he wish to be alone.

A hundred paces from the high front gate to his assigned living quarters, and another eighty or so to the stone manor house at the centre of the grounds. An architectural mishmash of turrets, peaked roofs, and mullioned windows. Some long-dead industrialist's idea of a castle in the sky. It amused him to imagine the Herculean effort it must have taken to haul all that stone up the mountain. Only one way up and one way down, according to the info-packet in his room, with the single-carriage funicular their only link to civilisation. A creaky toy-sized train he couldn't remember boarding.

Perched high above the valley and ringed by jagged peaks, when the snows came they would be cut off from the world. He couldn't help thinking it was a precarious location for a clinic, though he was familiar with the nineteenth-century vogue of establishing sanatoriums high in the mountains for the healing effects of the crystalline air. In an emergency, rescue by helicopter would be the only way out. Not that he would be here long enough to witness any of the infamous winter storms. After a week or so of rest at someone else's expense – and who could say no to that? – he would return to his tidy house and bustling lab in Cambridge and pick up his life where he left off.

An attendant with an unruly thatch of ginger hair appeared from behind the boxwood hedge to announce it was time for Movement & Meditation. Had two days passed already? According to Dr Lindstrom, he'd been here a solid week. Though fuzzy on the details, he was brought to this place after suffering an accident of some kind in Copenhagen. An ischaemic attack from overexcitement, perhaps. Or a minor cerebral haemorrhage. That would account for the amnesia. But Dr Lindstrom assured him he was not to worry. All would be explained when he met with the clinic's director. Her eyes had shone when she spoke the man's name. Whoever the mysterious Dr Gessen was, she was clearly an acolyte.

Worse than the confusion about the exact details of his arrival, he had lost all sense of time. Along with his belt and shoelaces, they'd taken away his wristwatch and without it he was lost at sea. No timepiece or calendar to order his days. Only at the sun's zenith could he guess with some certainty the position of the clock. Not even a sundial graced the grounds. With his days largely empty, but for the meals in the dining hall and the twice-weekly regimen of quasi-Eastern folderol the staff called 'M&M', a time-killing activity cooked up no doubt by the elusive Dr Gessen, the hours seemed to contract and expand in baffling ways.

He dropped his notebook in the canvas satchel the clinic had provided and followed the attendant to a round building with a thatched roof. His guide had a nervous, twitchy air. Another of Dr Gessen's many disciples, Vidor supposed. The longer they made him wait to meet this mysterious character the more his impatience grew.

* * *

In the north turret of the manor house, Gessen adjusted the focus on the binoculars until his newest patient swam into view. Seated on a bench next to the bronze statue of swallows in flight, Vidor Kiraly emanated an air of ennui as he scribbled in a notebook. Twice he looked up to gaze at the high peaks across the valley.

He'd been observing Kiraly from a distance since the day he arrived, and yet Gessen still didn't know what to make of him. Each observation was coloured by the fear that Kiraly might rampage again, though he'd yet to note anything alarming in the man's behaviour. According to the staff, Kiraly was as placid and obedient as a well-trained beagle. Having agreed to cover the costs of his stay, a charitable act he could ill afford, Gessen tried to quell the nagging feeling he had embarked on a fool's errand.

As with all new patients, Ursula was in charge of Vidor's

care during the settling-in period. He'd discovered early on, after a few false starts and one minor disaster, that the treatment phase proceeded more smoothly when patients were allowed time to adjust before starting on the arduous work of excavating the mind. Once they discovered that the clinic was more like a high-end resort than the nightmarish facilities of their imagination, or popularised in films, they dropped their guard and gladly abided by the rules.

But Vidor Kiraly wasn't just any patient. Gessen would never be so crass as to shout it from the rooftops, but the presence of such an illustrious figure was a coup for the clinic, not to mention a boost to Gessen's reputation as a skilled healer of intractable disorders. Now that Kiraly was here, however, with no hint of anything amiss, Gessen wondered if he hadn't misinterpreted the case.

Amok syndrome. What was he thinking? It was exceedingly rare, with the majority of reported cases confined to the peoples of the Malay Peninsula. As a medical student he'd been advised to think 'horses not zebras', upon hearing the gallop of hooves. A caution conveniently forgotten in his zeal to take on Kiraly's case. Had he presumed that one-in-a million zebra as a salve to his ego? The chance to cure a rare delusional disorder might just be wishful thinking.

More likely, Kiraly's outburst was simply a matter of an overworked academic flying into a temper at the sight of someone he'd thought had come to taunt him. An old foe, perhaps, or a schoolboy nemesis. Academia was littered with such rivalries. But after reviewing again the photos of Vidor at the ceremony, the police report, and his chart notes with the tantalising words, *amnesia* and *possible fugue state* – catnip to Gessen – he changed his mind. Some variety of psychotic delusion was surely at play.

Then there was the other thing that had niggled at him ever since he'd first viewed Kiraly through the binoculars. Something in the man's face or posture stirred to life a glimmer from the past. Though he was sure he'd never met Kiraly before, a certain look about his eyes and the slope of his forehead was familiar. The ghost, perhaps, of a memory from a long-ago sighting in a Paris cafe. Or a brief encounter while passing through the train station in Geneva. Though he seldom thought about his youth, now decades in the past, he never forgot a face.

As he lowered the binoculars, he felt a prickle of shame for spying on a man who believed he was alone. Seated cross-legged on the polished teak floor, he closed his eyes and tried to still his mind with a few moments of meditation. Except for a small round cushion and a bronze statue of the Buddha by the window, the room was bare. Years ago, he'd carried that statue, a gift from a Tibetan monastery and wrapped in layers of sackcloth, all the way back to Switzerland. The trip to Tibet was a desperate attempt to find solace during a dark period in his life, after he'd stumbled upon the truth about his parents in a cache of documents concealed in the attic.

As a young boy, he'd been abandoned by his mother, who failed to return from a trip to the village market, leaving him to be raised by the people they were staying with in Switzerland, who later adopted him as their own. It was his mother's gold wedding ring he'd been after, set with a row of tiny diamonds, to present to the woman he wished to marry. But having unwittingly discovered some unsavoury details about his past that were meant to stay hidden, he'd plunged into a black hole of despair, nearly impossible to escape.

In Tibet, he'd hoped to find comfort in the stark beauty of that sacred land. But not even the old monk, who radiated a beatific peace and acceptance of all that is, could help him. Having failed to find the consolation he'd sought in the Himalayas, the experience resulted in one good thing: it started him on the path of his life's work.

He closed his eyes and tried to still his mind, but the face of Vidor Kiraly infiltrated his thoughts. Tomorrow, his therapy would begin in earnest, and as Gessen slowly picked apart the threads of Kiraly's life, perhaps the troubling feeling that they had crossed paths before would be put to rest.

6

In the silence of the meditation hall, Vidor joined the circle of three women and two men seated on floor cushions, backs straight, their hands folded like obedient children. He had already endured two of these idiotic sessions and resented spending another hour of his life at a third. At least he could console himself with the pleasures of allowing his mind to wander when it was meant to be still. Perhaps have a bit of fun with the clinic's cardinal rule: patients were known by their first names only.

He smiled at the thought. If no one knew who he was, he could be anyone he chose. Today, the spurned lover of a Montenegrin beauty. Tomorrow, the deposed monarch of an obscure mountain kingdom. Perhaps, even, a celebrated brain scientist and OBE. He chuckled. Why not? Who would know the difference? The staff were on to him, he supposed, though they hadn't let on. The counsellor's primary job, apparently, was to smile and nod. Perhaps intervene should any tensions arise.

Vidor couldn't imagine what type of tension that might be. Not when the patients seemed as docile as lambs. No doubt due to the cocktail of pharmaceuticals they were fed each morning after breakfast. Well versed in neuropharmacology, Vidor could rattle off the drug names like a child chanting a nursery rhyme. Even so, he could sense the traces of madness beneath the drug-induced calm.

The leader of today's session was a soft-voiced, fussy gentleman about Vidor's age, though his phlegmatic manner and mournful brown eyes made him seem older, like an elderly basset hound. The patients perched awkwardly on their round cushions, a posture that led to a dull ache in Vidor's spine. As his lumbar sounded the alarm, he cursed himself for agreeing to come here. Though he'd been given little choice in the matter, to even suggest he needed the services of a psychiatrist was a grave misunderstanding. He'd give this Dr Gessen another week. Two at the most. In the meantime, he'd continue to make use of the admittedly excellent facilities before cutting the bonds of captivity and boarding a plane to London.

After leading them through a series of stretches and breathing exercises, Jean-Claude suggested they try a mindfulness exercise. 'If any thoughts or emotions arise,' he intoned, 'imagine they are clouds drifting on the wind, or leaves floating down a river. Refrain from becoming attached. Let them drift.'

Vidor suppressed a groan. Clouds, leaves? How poetic. But the hippocampus had a mind of its own and was not easily fooled. He wondered how much Jean-Claude was being paid to come up with this nonsense. During the long minutes of fidgeting and sighs, Vidor was less conscious of drifting clouds than a rumbling of gastric juices. When the heavyset woman to his left peeked at him through a fringe of dark hair, he looked away. He wasn't here to socialise, and the very thought of some unhappy soul laying claim to his attention made him want to flee.

The warm air was putting him to sleep. Vidor stood and opened a window, but as soon as he sat down again, the heavyset woman leapt up and shut it with a bang. 'I have a horror of draughts,' she said to no one in particular. The look on her sour face presented less an impression of illness than abandonment. Perhaps her husband had run off with his Scandinavian mistress and she'd come here to lick her wounds.

They moved on to the sharing part of the session. When Jean-Claude asked who would like to start, the woman shot her hand in the air.

'Wonderful. Please go ahead, Babette, we're all ears.'

In accented English, she related the story of a summer holiday in Bavaria when she was eleven years old, and how she had become separated from her parents during an outing at some ancient castle.

Vidor tuned out at that point, as she had told a similar tale at the previous session. Separation and abandonment. Childhood fears and confusion. Didn't they all have some version of the same story? At least she hadn't yanked up her blouse, like the last time, to show everyone the surgical scars that criss-crossed her abdomen.

Jean-Claude turned next to Vidor, his doleful eyes telegraphing encouragement. Vidor squirmed, but as long as he was stuck here, he might as well have a bit of fun. So he delivered a tale about a trip to the Hungarian countryside when he was a child, just before his family escaped the Soviet aggression and fled to France. A true story, actually, though he'd been tempted to invent some nonsense to please his audience. It was a memory he was particularly fond of, so why not let Jean-Claude and the others imagine him as an excitable boy of five, rather than the gentleman with the greying hair who sat awkwardly amongst them on these ridiculous cushions.

It was the height of apple-picking season when we left the city for the fresh air of the countryside. As I rode through the orchard on my father's shoulders in the amber light, I reached up to pluck a bright red fruit from the tangle of gnarled branches. Even after all these years, I can still feel the grip of my father's strong hands on my knees, holding me steady as I grabbed the coveted apple. When I offered it to him, he'd laughed, and said it was mine for the keeping, so I polished it on my shirt and bit into it with a satisfying crunch. Never before or since has an apple tasted as sweet.

A slim young man with dark, liquid eyes, whom Vidor privately called the Emirati Prince, let out a groan. But Jean-Claude reminded them that opening their hearts was an important part of healing. Bottled-up feelings, often festering for years, must be allowed to escape into the air. He cradled a brass bowl in his hand and struck it with a wooden mallet. When the high, clear note died away, he spread his arms and beamed at them. *I embrace you, I embrace you all.*

Vidor had a vision of the group as actors in a play and Jean-Claude as their director. When the curtain fell on their tableau, surely he would drop all this 'clouds and leaves' nonsense and scuttle back to his room to light a contraband cigarette, relieved to have escaped their greedy attentions.

Across from him, an older woman, with an air of hauteur, held tightly to a black handbag as she rose to her feet. Vidor turned to see the Emirati Prince smirking at him. A vein pulsed in Vidor's temple, and he clenched his jaw. Good grief, would this session never end? Every cell in his body urged him to flee. *Run, run.* But where could he go? As far as he could make out, he was a prisoner here.

7

Gessen's pulse quickened at the sight of a letter from the Bispebjerg Hospital in Copenhagen, balanced on the stack of morning mail.

Dr Anton Gessen, MD
Clinique Les Hirondelles
Saint-Odile, Switzerland

4 November 2008

Dear Dr Gessen,
I am writing to provide an update on the status of Mr Tobias Nielsen, aged 71, who was admitted to Bispebjerg Hospital on the evening of 22 October of this year, in serious but stable condition, following an assault that took place at Rosenborg Castle.

At the time of admission, Mr Nielsen was non-responsive, with a superficial head laceration and a contusion to the left temple. When he regained consciousness (about two hours later), we recorded a Glasgow Coma Scale score of 13. He was held for observation for two days before being released into the care of his daughter.

Three days later, after complaining of headache and

nausea, he was readmitted to the ward. A CAT scan revealed an intracerebral haemorrhage in the posterior fossa. Following surgery to repair the bleed, Mr Nielsen lapsed into a coma, with a GCS of 4. During the subsequent days, his condition continued to deteriorate.

This morning, at 6.32, Mr Nielsen was pronounced dead.

It is my understanding that the man who attacked Mr Nielsen is receiving psychiatric treatment at your clinic in Saint-Odile, Switzerland. Since this case now concerns a capital offence under Danish law, I expect the municipal authorities will shortly bring charges against Mr Kiraly for either grievous bodily harm or manslaughter.

If Mr Kiraly is charged in absentia, and his case is considered a forensic one, the courts will likely allow Mr Kiraly to continue his treatment at your clinic, pending a diagnosis. Under Danish Penal Code 69 (see enclosed), he would need to receive a diagnosis of 'diminished responsibility' or 'temporary psychosis' to continue receiving medical treatment at a recognised facility. Otherwise, Mr Kiraly will be subject to sentencing under Danish criminal law.

I hope I have sufficiently informed you of the circumstances to date. I have passed your contact details to the metropolitan police in Copenhagen, and they may be in contact with you for additional information.

Cordially yours,
Henrik Larssen, MD
Bispebjerg Hospital, Copenhagen

Gessen smoothed out the letter and placed it in Vidor's file, absently lining up the stack of documents as he digested this turn of events. Bad news, indeed. Not only for Mr Nielsen and his family, of course, but for Vidor, as well. Proving diminished responsibility would not be easy now. Not when he had pages of case notes from Ursula's sessions with Vidor describing his insistence that he was perfectly fine, and that

35

the attack on Mr Nielsen was an unfortunate consequence of low blood sugar and nervous exhaustion.

Such a flimsy defence would not keep Vidor out of prison. The psychotic rage observed in amok syndrome might work as a diagnosis, though Gessen had little to base it on. If Vidor's violent outburst was due to something organic, like temporal lobe epilepsy, he could build a case around that, though Vidor had no history of seizures. Vidor's only hope was to stop pretending he was fine and allow his doctors to explore his past, something he'd adamantly resisted with Ursula. Of particular interest to Gessen was the repressed trauma that surely lurked below the surface of Vidor's polished demeanour. Time was of the essence, and if his unwilling patient refused to cooperate, Vidor was looking at a murder charge.

* * *

Gessen stood in the centre of the Persian carpet, scanning the contents of his office to confirm that everything was in order. The polished mahogany desk was free of paperwork, and the dove-grey curtains were drawn against the morning sun. Between the two wingback chairs, a potted yellow orchid lent a tropical note to the otherwise neutral decor. On the far wall, the single piece of artwork, a watercolour of mountains and sky, was intentionally bland. The work of turning inward to excavate the mind required minimal distraction.

A knock on the door, and Vidor was ushered inside by his personal attendant, a bright-eyed young man from Krakow, fresh from his trainee programme in Bern.

'Professor Kiraly.' Gessen crossed the room to offer his hand. 'I am Dr Gessen. Welcome to Les Hirondelles.'

Vidor's grip was dry and cool, and Gessen studied his face, hoping for a spark of recognition from either one of them. But now that he'd seen Vidor up close, it was clear they were strangers to each other. Had he imagined it, that flicker of familiarity? He gestured to one of the chairs.

'I trust you've settled in by now,' he said, sitting opposite Vidor, 'and I apologise for not meeting with you earlier. I find our guests feel more comfortable when given a chance to settle in before starting treatment.' He waited in the silence. 'I presume Dr Lindstrom explained that to you when you arrived.'

He had assigned Vidor the Adagio Suite in Chalet Est, the largest on the grounds where Vidor could, if he chose, watch the sun rise over the mountains. The dawn at Les Hirondelles was a moment of sublime splendour, if one rose early enough to take it in.

Vidor examined the objects in the room, starting with the row of books on the shelf behind Gessen's desk and coming to rest on the orchid on the table. 'I've settled in quite nicely, thank you,' he said, his voice laced with irony. 'If I didn't know better, I might believe I'd been spirited away to an exclusive resort for the idle rich.'

'Spirited away?'

'Didn't your Dr Lindstrom tell you?' Vidor discreetly coughed. 'I have no memory of my arrival here. I woke to find myself in one of your chalets wearing strange clothes.' He gestured at the loose blue tunic and tan trousers. 'My wallet and wristwatch were gone.' He paused. 'My passport, as well.'

Gessen suppressed a flicker of surprise. He stood to retrieve the file on his desk and extracted two sheets of paper. The clinic's admissions form and a document from the hospital in Copenhagen confirming the transfer to Les Hirondelles. 'That's your signature, isn't it?'

Vidor blinked at the papers and shook his head. His air of befuddlement seemed genuine. 'I don't remember signing these.' He handed them back. 'Dr Lindstrom mentioned something about an incident in Copenhagen. But whatever it was, I feel perfectly fine now.' He smacked his chest in a parody of health.

Gessen eyed his patient with interest. Unless he was lying,

Vidor appeared to be suffering from retrograde amnesia. Not unusual following a trauma, but the fact that he claimed no memory of his arrival, while appearing completely lucid, was odd. 'Why don't you tell me what you do remember?'

'Could we have some air in here?' Vidor tugged at his collar. 'It's very stuffy.'

Gessen opened the window. A gust of wind with a hint of dying leaves ruffled the papers on his desk. Vidor leaned forward and sucked the fresh air into his lungs.

'Would you like to lie down?'

'No, I'm perfectly well.'

'Let's start with Copenhagen.' He returned to his seat and picked up his pen. Vidor's pallor was worrisome, and Gessen wondered if he might faint. 'What were you doing in the city?'

'I was there to receive an award.'

Gessen pointed to the documents on the table. 'How did you end up in hospital?'

'I suppose I must have passed out.' Vidor's eyes shifted to the window. 'I remember rushing to Heathrow to catch my flight. There was no time to eat anything before boarding. In fact, I'd had nothing since breakfast, and that was just coffee and a roll. I was met at the airport in Copenhagen and driven straight to the venue. *Rosen...* something.' He frowned at a dark speck on his sleeve. 'I remember seeing the Crown Prince. A handsome man. Rather impressive in his full regalia. My name was announced.' He paused. 'I climbed up to the dais.'

'And after that?' Gessen tried not to stare, but he wanted to catch every flicker of the eyes or twitch of skin.

'After that... nothing.' Vidor straightened his shoulders. 'Until I woke up here.'

Very odd indeed, Gessen mused. He scratched a note on his pad. From a clinical perspective, Ursula's account of meeting Vidor in Copenhagen and organising his transfer to Les Hirondelles was unremarkable. According to her description of the trip, the patient had been lucid, cooperative, even friendly. Relieved, by all accounts, to be discharged from the hospital in Copenhagen. 'Very charming' were the words she used. Where had those memories gone? Though perhaps they'd never been stored. Lost to time in the aftermath of damage to the brain. A minor bleed, perhaps, or a seizure.

'According to eyewitness reports,' Gessen said, consulting the file, 'you attacked a man at the back of the lecture hall. He was badly injured and taken to hospital by ambulance.' For now, Gessen would not tell Vidor the man had died. It would only make things worse, and as Vidor's doctor, his first job was to address two questions: what caused him to attack a stranger, and what was the chance he would do it again?

'Attacked a man—?' Vidor leapt clumsily to his feet. 'Preposterous. I've never harmed anyone in my life.'

Faced with Vidor's sudden anger and spluttering denials, Gessen felt again a wave of déjà vu. A conviction, stronger now, that the two of them had met before. There was that medical conference on Neurology and Psychiatry in Paris a few years back. Could they have passed each other in the congress centre or stood in the same queue at the coffee bar?

Gessen had downloaded from the internet the scant information on Vidor he could find. A refugee from the 1956 Hungarian uprising, who'd spent his childhood in Paris before moving to the UK to attend university. Gessen had lived in Paris during his student years at the Sorbonne. Their paths could have crossed while Vidor was in the city between terms. A student cafe, a film festival, or simply passing each other in the street. Whatever it was, he couldn't shake the feeling they had met somewhere before.

'Please sit down, Vidor.' Gessen smiled, hoping to return their discussion to an even keel. 'You don't mind if I call you Vidor, do you? It will facilitate our work together if I can address you by your first name.'

'Our work together?'

In the silence that followed, Vidor fiddled with the black plastic strap on his wrist. Ursula would have explained it was an electronic monitoring device required of all the patients, but perhaps that detail, along with his other memories, had failed to stick.

He met Gessen's eyes. 'Am I a prisoner here?'

'A prisoner? Whatever gave you that idea?'

Vidor pointed at the black wrist monitor and his clinic-issued clothing.

'The monitor is for your own safety. Heart rate, blood pressure, and sleeping patterns are transmitted electronically to your personal medical file. And the clothing… Is it not to your liking? In the many years I've been running this clinic, I've found that it's easier for our patients to access their true selves when the need to cover and adorn their bodies is taken out of the equation. So much of our energy goes into the presentation we create for public view, wouldn't you agree? Soon, you'll appreciate the chance to strip all that away. The only personal item we allow patients to wear during their stay is their wedding ring.' Gessen nodded at the gold signet ring on Vidor's left hand. 'Though I understand in your case…?' He raised his eyebrows. 'I only mention it because you didn't provide us with an emergency contact.'

Vidor stiffened.

Gessen could imagine his thoughts, that neither his marital status, nor the provenance of his ring was anyone's business.

'Since I feel perfectly fine,' Vidor said, in a clipped voice, 'when will I be discharged? With a department to manage and a lab to run, I don't have time to faff about in the Swiss mountains.'

As the silence grew, Gessen decided to call his bluff. 'If you're not satisfied with our services, Professor Kiraly, you're of course free to go at any time.' He abruptly stood. 'I'll have our admissions coordinator arrange for a car to take you to Spiez. From there, you can get a direct train to Bern or Geneva.'

'I'm free to go?' Vidor's face brightened.

'You have always been free to leave.' In an attitude of dismissal, Gessen turned to pull a binder from the shelf.

'In that case, I'll be ready in thirty minutes.'

The sky had grown steadily darker, and a thunderclap punctuated the stillness. Fat raindrops clattered against the glass like a fistful of stones. Gessen hurried to shut the window. He'd been too intent on registering the nuances of Vidor's facial tics to notice the change in the weather.

'Before you go, you should know, however, that while you're free to leave my clinic, resuming your old life will not be simple.' He drew close to the glass to track the storm's path as it swept across the valley. Rain pummelled the hills, and the wind thrashed the pines. 'In all likelihood you'll be charged with a serious crime,' Gessen said, keeping his back turned. 'Assault and battery, at the very least.'

He pivoted and caught the look of confusion on Vidor's face. In time, Gessen would have to reveal the extent of the bad news. But if Vidor knew that he'd killed the man in Copenhagen, before Gessen could properly evaluate his case, he might be tempted to fake symptoms of psychosis as a means of claiming diminished responsibility.

'Reinstatement of your position at the college is contingent upon my advice that you're well enough to resume your duties.' He moved to the desk and consulted Vidor's file. 'Since I most certainly cannot give such assurance to your Chancellor, you'll have to find another way into his good graces. Would you like to see the letter?' Gessen held up a sheet of ivory writing paper, with the gold crest of the university engraved on top.

Vidor's face flushed. 'I've got a lab to run and a grant proposal to write. Does he expect me to lounge around here in these glorified pyjamas while my rivals snatch a key breakthrough from under my nose?'

Gessen removed his glasses and rubbed his eyes. Some patients needed more time than others to accept they were ill. Getting to that point was often akin to hauling a bucket of rocks up a mountain. One arduous step at a time. 'It's not only your Chancellor keeping you here. There's the more serious matter of the assault charge. There'll be an arraignment as soon as you're released.'

'Assault?' Vidor's fury collapsed like a dead balloon. 'But how can I be held responsible for something I can't remember?'

'So you claim. But that won't hold up in a court of law.' Gessen waited for this to sink in. 'You need a doctor – a psychiatrist – to argue that you were not yourself at the time of the attack, and that your act of violence was due to diminished responsibility.' He laced his fingers together. 'As I've said, you're free to go whenever you wish. But I hope you'll see the value of staying on here.'

Rain lashed the windows. Far below, in the windswept valley, all was grey. For a moment Gessen had a vision of himself and Vidor as two strangers set adrift in a leaky boat, foundering at sea. He pressed a button on his phone to summon the attendant.

'Take some time to think about it,' Gessen said, noting the aggrieved look in Vidor's eyes. 'If you do decide to stay, I should warn you that our work together won't be easy, and the outcome far from certain. Much will depend on you.'

8

Sheltering under the umbrella of a young man from Eritrea, who appeared to be one of his personal minders, Vidor retrieved from his inside pocket the scrap of paper he'd found next to his plate at breakfast.

In the middle of the journey of our life, I found myself in a dark wood, for the straightforward path was lost. It is a hard thing to speak of – how wild, harsh and impenetrable that wood was – that the very thought of it renews my fear. – Dante, The Divine Comedy.

Vidor crumpled the scrap in his fist and tossed it in the shrubbery. If this was Gessen's idea of a joke, it was anything but funny. The man was a charlatan. Feeding off the pain of the poor souls who washed up on his doorstep. *Lost in the woods, my eye.*

Anxious to escape his faithful attendant, who likely reported to Gessen in minute detail anything he said or did, Vidor ran up the steps of the chalet and slipped past the bearded chap at the front desk, with his nose stuck in a magazine, and into the common room. Empty, thank god. At least there was that. The last thing Vidor wanted was to be forced into small talk with the Emirati Prince while making a cup of tea. Something about the boy's absurdly misplaced hauteur got under his skin.

On the wall near the tea and coffee station, four botanical

prints provided the only bright spot in the otherwise featureless decor. He leaned in close to read the names. *Hornbeam, brimstone butterfly, candle snuff fungus, witch hazel.* Brimstone butterfly. Candle snuff fungus? You couldn't make this stuff up. If the prints were meant to be cheery, they sadly missed the mark.

The third inmate in the shared chalet was a weedy sort who never seemed to leave his room. At least he was quiet in his habits. Vidor tiptoed across the parquet flooring and pressed his ear against the door. Water running in the bathroom. Poor chap. Probably washing his hands again. Vidor could picture the phrase *an unhealthy obsession with germs* scrawled in the man's patient file. How many hours of the day did he spend washing his hands?

The few times Vidor had seen him, scurrying from the chalet to the main building, he wore a surgical mask, and hopped along the slate path in an awkward gait to avoid touching any patches of grass. His meals, brought to his room on a tray by an attendant, were wrapped in plastic, having been nuked into oblivion, Vidor surmised, in a microwave. Before stepping away from the door, Vidor coughed twice. Mean and petty to be sure, but his first meeting with Gessen, and the shock of learning that quitting this place had consequences, had put him in a sour mood.

He hurried into his own suite and firmly shut the door. A pity there was no lock, a fact he found disturbing. He'd never been able to sleep properly in a room without a bolt on the door. But the information binder on the desk explained it was clinic policy for safety reasons, assuring him that *the front desk is staffed round the clock for your comfort and safety.* As if that was supposed to make him feel better. Each night, before going to bed, he took the precaution of pushing the heavy leather armchair against the door. He'd always been a light sleeper, so if someone tried to come in, at least the noise would wake him.

Relieved to be alone, he noisily expelled the air from his

lungs. Peace at last. He dropped his satchel on the floor and stretched out on the bed. For a place that was essentially a hospital, the room was a pleasant surprise. A far cry from the scuffed linoleum flooring and metal-frame beds one might expect. Separate bedroom and living spaces, kitted out with sumptuous linens and furnishings, and a large bathroom done up in polished limestone. Though trapped here against his will, it would do nicely for the brief time he planned to stay.

On the wall opposite the bed, two paintings were hung, side by side. The one on the left, a watercolour seascape of a clutch of sandpipers – ten in total – chasing their shadows at the water's edge. The other, a desert scene in gleaming oils, had a darker palette. Red rocks and blistering sands stretched to the horizon, seemingly empty. But if he squinted, he could just make out the hazy outline of a camel caravan, like a mirage floating on the horizon.

Vidor pressed his ear to the wall behind the bed. No sounds came from the other room, though at night he could sometimes hear the Emirati Prince, muttering and pacing, his bare feet slapping against the parquet. Not much else to do at night here if one couldn't sleep. No internet or television or radio, nothing to distract them from the hamster cage of their thoughts.

A weariness fell over him like a shroud. While he could find no fault with the amenities, it was the free-floating unease of being a prisoner that made his heart tick oddly. All the luxuries in the world couldn't make up for the fact that he was trapped inside the perimeter fence. Forced to undergo who knew how many more interrogations by this Dr Gessen. A man who appeared to enjoy the power of having Vidor's fate in his hands.

The hourglass in his brain, that inexorable taskmaster, ticked away the minutes. How long would it be, before they let him go?

9

Gessen cleared his throat and posed the question again. It shouldn't be this difficult to extract an answer, but however many times he asked Vidor about his family, the man spun and wove like a matador, shutting down in anger if Gessen even hinted there had been discord of any kind.

A vein pulsed in Vidor's throat. 'My father was a hero, and my mother a saint,' he said, biting off each word. 'You may doubt all you want, but that's the truth.'

Gessen held up his hands, palms out. 'I don't dispute your description of their characters. But it would help to know more about your relationship with them. Jean-Claude tells me that in one of your Movement & Meditation sessions you mentioned a visit to an apple orchard. How you rode on your father's shoulders and plucked apples from the trees. It sounds like a wonderful memory. Why don't you share something similar with me? Or a few details, perhaps, about your early days in Paris.'

They were fifteen minutes into a game of chess. A tactic Gessen had hit upon after their last fruitless session as a means of tricking Vidor into revealing a snippet of memory from one part of his brain, while concentrating on the game with another.

The mountains, shrouded in mist, were framed by the half-drawn curtains. Earlier, Mathilde had brought in a tray of coffee and pastries and set them on the table. A homely touch designed to induce Gessen's patient to drop his guard.

Vidor swooped in to capture Gessen's queen. 'Check.' His smile was triumphant. 'You want a memory? All right.' He stared into the distance, as if trying to conjure the perfect anecdote to get Gessen off his back. 'My first memory of Paris was the sound of the dustmen in our street.' He sipped his coffee and examined the chessboard. 'Our flat was on the first floor and with the windows open we could hear everything that went on in our little quarter. The greengrocer stacking the wooden crates on the shelves outside his shop. The knife sharpener pushing his bicycle with its squeaky wheel. Cats mewing around the fishmonger. It was a typical Parisian street.'

He looked at Gessen and sighed. 'I assume you know the city? Though there weren't so many cars in those days, and in our working-class neighbourhood, none of the elegance that people associate with Paris today.'

Gessen waited, his eyes on the chessboard.

'Most of our neighbours were immigrants. Hungarian émigrés like us, along with Russians and Armenians, and other foreigners whose origins I wasn't aware of. I was a child. Everything was new, everything was strange. But I do remember, after a time, being happy.' He briefly closed his eyes. 'Except for one thing.' Leaning over the board, Vidor deftly executed the *en passant* move to evade capture of his pawn. 'In our haste to get away, I was forced to leave a treasured toy behind. A tin soldier, of no value to anyone but me. I wept, heartbroken, until my mother promised she'd buy me a new one as soon as we were settled.'

Gessen let this sink in before moving his bishop to the only possible square, though it was clear he was cornered. 'It sounds like you made a lucky escape,' he said, avoiding Vidor's eye. 'All of you safe and sound in a new city.'

Vidor sighed. 'My parents were happy to find a place of refuge, and we made a good life for ourselves.'

A pleasant enough story, but Gessen didn't believe it for a

minute. Any kind of move involved a level of disquiet, ranging from mild to the traumatic. Even more so when a family, running for their lives, was forced to leave behind everything they knew and loved. He studied Vidor intently under lowered lids as he waited for him to expand on the story, but Vidor, having claimed Gessen's king with a crow of triumph, had shut the door on that particular moment in his past.

* * *

A week later, six intensive sessions had come and gone, and Gessen's desperation to crack the mystery of Vidor's affliction was growing by the hour. With surprising skill – or was it cunning? – Vidor had stymied every effort to unpeel the layers of his life. Time for a new strategy. For today's session, rather than meet with Vidor in the clinical setting of his office, Gessen invited him into the adjoining sitting room. The intimate atmosphere and sumptuous furnishings in the style of a London club might just coax Vidor out of the defensive posture of a patient and into the belief he was Gessen's equal. Two men sitting by the fire, talking about their lives.

In the glow from the flames, the two leather armchairs gleamed like chestnuts. On the far wall, framed oil paintings of the Matterhorn and the Eiger, subtly lit, created an atmosphere of intimacy.

Gessen noted Vidor's surprise at the richness of the room's decor, and the sense, easy to presume, that a butler might appear at any moment bearing brandy and cigars. Which was exactly the point, to lull Vidor into a state of relaxation. In their previous sessions, Vidor had visibly stiffened when Gessen pressed him to talk about his family. Even now, despite the cosy setting, his neck and shoulders were tense, alert to whatever traps Gessen might have in store for him.

He motioned at the chessboard by the fire. 'Shall we?' As they settled in their chairs, he engaged in a few pleasantries about the weather and general queries about Vidor's comfort before segueing smoothly into the pressing matter at hand. 'We touched on your father the last time we spoke. He sounds like an interesting man,' Gessen said. 'Why don't you tell me more about him?'

Vidor, his attention on the board, moved his pawn to e6, exposing his queen. A surprising move, but Gessen had learned to expect nothing but surprises from this puzzle of a man.

'I told you about my father the last time.'

'Ah, yes. The courageous man who led his wife and children to safety. An upstanding member of the Hungarian émigré community in Paris. Loving husband and father.'

Vidor's expression soured. 'Are you suggesting none of that is true? That all this time I've been lying?'

Gessen moved his pawn to f4. A deliberate mistake. If Vidor spotted it, in another two moves he would be in checkmate.

'Not at all,' Gessen said. 'But the past can be a slippery thing, and as we grow older, we sometimes create stories to fit an idealised version of it.' He met Vidor's eyes. 'I wouldn't call it lying, but it's a natural, human instinct to protect ourselves from difficult truths or sad memories. In the short term, it can feel like a valid strategy. The problem is, those painful parts of our story never go away. They slumber in the deep caverns of the mind, until something happens, usually a shock of some kind, and they bubble to the surface. That's when the real trouble begins.'

'Caverns of the mind?' Vidor raised his eyebrows. 'How poetic. Though I can only assume you're referring to the hippocampus and the amygdala.'

Gessen chose to ignore this. He had no desire to go head to head with Vidor on the anatomy of the brain. He was less concerned about the 'where' of trauma than the 'why'. 'Tell me more about the toy soldier you were forced to leave behind when your family fled Budapest.'

'I was a child.' He exhaled noisily. 'The toy was important

to me. I don't see how that has any bearing on my life today. Do you think I've been pining after that ridiculous toy soldier for the past fifty years? As I grew older and understood the gravity of our situation, I was grateful we'd all got out alive.'

Silence filled the room.

Gessen waited for Vidor to puncture the dead air with a pithy utterance, but he wasn't one to chat. They might sit like this for days and Vidor wouldn't blink. In the hearth, a burning log collapsed into coals, sending up a shower of sparks. Every hour with Vidor, Gessen mused, was like trying to scale a tower of glass. With no way to get a purchase, he kept sliding to the ground. At this rate, with Vidor stonewalling at every turn, it could take years to make a breakthrough. Neither of them had that kind of time.

It wasn't in Gessen's nature to go rogue and do something unethical, but the previous afternoon, after mentioning his frustration to Ursula, she had floated an interesting idea. It skirted the edge of what he could live with in good conscience, but her suggestion was an excellent one. Brilliant, in fact, and he'd promised her he would give it some thought.

Vidor stood and approached the hearth, where he picked up the iron poker and prodded the coals. 'Are we done here? I'd like to go back to my room.'

'Why don't you tell me about a time your father disappointed you.'

Vidor stared into the flames. 'He never disappointed me. My father was peerless.'

'All young children revere their fathers.' Gessen considered his next words, well aware of their portent. 'When we're small, our fathers are indeed gods. All knowing, all powerful. After about the age of nine or ten, however,' Gessen said, lacing his fingers together, 'that belief begins to fade, until it is replaced with a more realistic view. The father loses his godlike power and is seen for what he is: human, and thus fallible. A hard truth to learn as a child, but an important one.'

'My father was a god to me,' Vidor countered, turning to face him, 'right up until the day he died.'

'And when was that?'

Vidor focused on a spot behind Gessen's left shoulder. 'In nineteen... I was twenty-six, so, it would have been 1976. No, 1977, rather.' He scratched the side of his neck. 'I'd been living in England for several years at the time but made frequent trips across the Channel. We were always close, my father and I, with none of the rivalry you often find between fathers and sons.'

'What do you mean by rivalry?' Gessen waited, alert to every twitch and flicker. Vidor tightened his jaw. If he grew angry enough, something of substance might finally burst forth.

'Competition, of course,' Vidor said, relaxing his shoulders. 'The son coming up from behind. The father sensing his power diminish with age. It's all over the Greek myths. Surely you've heard of Oedipus?'

Gessen acknowledged the joke with a smile. 'I might have come across the name.' He sipped from a glass of water and studied the chessboard before making a move. 'It sounds very cosy, your family life. I can picture you at home with your mother and sisters. Your father at his work, out in the world. Comfortably settled into your new life, after the terrible trauma you'd suffered.'

The sound of cowbells, very faint, came through the window, opened a crack to freshen the air. Vidor returned to his chair and frowned at the chessboard, as if he had forgotten their game and only now realised that he was in peril. Having taken Vidor's queen and in a position to topple his king, Gessen leaned over the board until their faces were close, so close that Gessen could smell the peppermint on Vidor's breath from the tea he'd drunk.

'That's a very charming story.' Gessen moved his knight into position and tapped Vidor's king. 'But I don't believe a single word you've said.' He held his opponent's gaze. 'Checkmate.'

10

As Vidor rounded a corner of the path through the Zen garden, he came upon a girl he'd never seen before, occupying his bench by the fountain. It wasn't his personal bench, of course, but ever since his arrival he'd considered it his own. Each day, after breakfast, he would sit in this particular spot in a secluded corner of the garden, notebook in hand, to jot down ideas for an article he planned to write on the neural circuitry of grapheme-colour synaesthesia.

The girl's hair, the colour of summer wheat, framed her thin face. Her arms were clasped across her abdomen, and her shoulders hunched, as if trying to take up as little space as possible. She must be new. Unless she was visiting one of the patients here, though it was his understanding that visitors were discouraged, if not outright forbidden.

She dabbed her nose with a tissue and dashed the tears from her eyes. Should he slip away? He always felt crippled in the presence of a crying female. So many ways it could go wrong. Once, he'd made the mistake of patting a young student on the shoulder when she came to his office in floods of tears over a failed exam, but the glare she gave him made it clear his paternal overture might be construed as assault.

If he sat next to her, chances were high he would scare her away. In her place, he certainly wouldn't want some stranger – a malodorous creep, for all she knew – disturbing his solitude. Poor thing. She was clearly suffering.

Still, it was his bench, and he planted himself on the far end, half turned away from the girl to give her privacy. Far below, the valley, at the height of autumnal splendour, glowed in the morning sun. The trees, half stripped of their golden foliage, swayed in the breeze. A throng of brown cows, enjoying the last mild days before the winter set in, dotted the hillsides. A slice of pastoral simplicity, frozen in time. Not the view one would expect from a psychiatric hospital, but perhaps that was the charm of a madhouse set amongst remote mountain peaks. He had hoped to be gone by now, but Gessen was proving to be a formidable adversary, impervious to deflection or charm.

At the flicker of movement to his right, he risked a sideways glance. The girl, tearing at the skin on her thumb, winced when she drew blood. He coughed discreetly. 'Are you visiting someone?'

She turned her face, blotchy and red-eyed, in his direction.

'What?' She blinked. 'Oh, I didn't see you there.' She waved her hand above her head. 'Away with the fairies, as my gran says.' She sniffled and blew her nose. 'And I'm not crying, either, if that's what you're thinking. It's just hay fever.'

An English girl. The sound of her accent – London, if he wasn't mistaken – triggered a rush of homesickness. How he longed to go back. His snug house, just a short stroll to the college. The book-lined study he kept neat as a pin. His tidy garden. He wondered, with a pang, how his students were getting on without him. Or what his housekeeper thought about his disappearance. Two days ago, he'd posted a letter to Magda to let her know he was fine, and to carry on with her regular duties while he was away.

'Don't let me disturb you,' he said, as she shifted on the bench, 'I was just admiring the view.'

She examined him with the penetrating gaze of the young, though her eyes had gone misty again. Medicated to the gills like the rest of them, he supposed. He'd balked at swallowing the prescribed tablets himself, having never taken anything stronger than an aspirin before. One blue and white pill was for depression, the other two for anxiety. Anxious he might be, considering the circumstances, but he wasn't depressed. He had a right to refuse the tablets, but the dispensary nurse, whose manner was kind, strongly urged him to follow doctor's orders.

The girl sighed and studied her nails, bitten to the quick like a child's. How terrible to be so young and so sad. Perhaps he could jolly her out of her mood. 'Which part of England are you from?'

'London.' She tugged the sleeves of her cardigan over her wrists. 'But I'm at university now.'

'Not Cambridge by any chance?'

'Oxford.' She pushed a loose strand of hair from her forehead. 'Pembroke College.'

Clever girl. He should have guessed. 'And what are you studying at Oxford?'

'Philosophy and French.'

An interesting combination. Though he couldn't help wondering what she planned to do with her degree. There wasn't much call for philosophers these days.

'You can't study the great philosophers in translation,' she said, as if guessing his thoughts, 'and I already know German.' She plucked at a thread on her sleeve. 'My dad says I should study something more practical. He's always banging on about job prospects. He works in the City and thinks philosophy is a ridiculous waste of time. It doesn't help that he's American. Always focused on the money angle.'

A Yank father in finance. He could imagine how that might be a challenge to a sensitive girl, and he couldn't help but wonder how she'd ended up in a place like this. Perhaps a boyfriend had broken her heart, and she'd done something stupid. An overdose of pills? No scars on her wrists that he could see, but he'd witnessed enough romantic angst amongst the shifting sea of undergraduates at St Catharine's to know that a dramatic gesture could take any number of forms. Or perhaps love had nothing to do with it. An overdose of philosophy could just as easily be at the root of her sorrow. Kierkegaard, that gloomy Dane, and certainly not his favourite philosopher as he'd professed in Copenhagen, would drive anyone to despair.

'I was looking at the fish in that pond over there,' she said, pointing at the shallow, rock-filled pool a few metres away. 'One of them looks different than yesterday. Do you think they can change colour, like chameleons?'

Vidor considered this. He'd never taken much interest in the fishpond. 'Possibly,' he said, 'though I'm not a specialist in fish. It's probably your eyes playing tricks on you.'

'Tricks?' She showed a spark of life. 'Why would they do that?'

He plucked a dried blossom from a nearby bush and crumpled it in his hand. 'It's not our eyes that see, but our brain. What we take to be reality, or a true representation of the world,' he said, gesturing at the valley below, 'is nothing but a construction of the visual cortex.'

She gave him an odd look. 'That can't be right. When I close my eyes, I see nothing, when I open them, the world appears. What I see…' she pointed at the bronze fountain, 'you see too, right?'

Rather than reply, he tore a blank page from his notebook and drew two small circles a few inches apart. He held it up to her. 'How many circles do you see?'

'Two, of course. How many do you see?'

He smiled. 'Hold the paper in front of you and cover your left eye. How many circles do you see now?'

'Two.'

'Now, focus on the left circle with your right eye, and slowly bring the paper closer to your face. How many circles do you see?'

'One.' She wrinkled her brow. 'How does that work?'

A sense of triumph flushed his cheeks. Was that all it took

to cheer her up, a silly optical illusion? He was surprised she'd never come across it before.

'Our eyes have a blind spot,' he said, making a rapid sketch of the human eye. 'At the point on the retina where the optic nerve enters, there are no photoreceptors. So the brain fills in the blank space with its best guess, using information from the surrounding image. When the circle on the right entered the blind spot of your right eye, your brain filled it in with the white of the paper. Everything we see,' he said, shifting into full lecture mode, 'is a construction of the brain. It creates an image based on the electrical signals it receives from the photoreceptors on the retina. Since there are variants in our photoreceptors based on our DNA, it's possible that what you see and what I see is not exactly the same. For example, if we were to look at the same red carnation, your perception of "red" might be different to mine.'

A shadow crossed the girl's face, and her eyes took on a panicky look. A mood shift, difficult to parse. Had he cast a pall over what was meant to be a moment of wonder?

'*All that we see or seem is but a dream within a dream*,' she murmured.

He gave her a questioning look.

'My grandmother had a thing for Edgar Allan Poe. I'd never understood that line before.'

Tears welled in her eyes, and he waited for her to say more, but nothing disturbed the silence except the rustle of a Japanese maple, its few remaining leaves, the colour of dried blood, trembling in the breeze. He looked at the girl in alarm and mumbled some excuse before slipping away. What had he done? A place this fraught with fragile minds and delicate sensibilities had no room, apparently, for disturbing facts about the universe, or the byzantine workings of the brain. From now on, he would keep his thoughts to himself.

11

Vidor blinked at the sight of Dr Lindstrom seated in one of Gessen's wingback chairs. Had he stumbled into the wrong room? He'd been feeling out of sorts since breakfast, queasy and unsettled as if he'd eaten a plate of bad eggs. It didn't help his feeling of unease that on his way over to the main building, the weedy man who shared his chalet passed him on the footpath, his head wrapped in a bandage, seeping blood.

'Where is Dr Gessen?'

'He was called away on other business, so you'll have your session with me today.' She smiled warmly. 'I hope that's all right with you.'

Dr Lindstrom eyed him over a pair of horn-rimmed spectacles that did nothing to hide her pretty features. It might be easier, Vidor mused, to bare his soul to an older woman. One in possession of a greater store of well-honed wisdom than this fresh-faced girl. Not that he had any intention of baring anything, but he doubted this young doctor knew much about the trials of life.

A tiny red light winked at him from a panel on the wall. 'Am I being recorded?'

'Dr Gessen asked me to tape our session while he was away.' She scratched a note on a yellow pad. 'I was just about to mention it.'

This was a new development. 'Don't you need my permission to do that?'

'Of course we do. Patient rights are paramount here.' She made another note. 'You signed a release on admission allowing us to record your sessions as needed. But rest assured,' she smiled again, 'all recordings are strictly confidential, to be viewed only by Dr Gessen and myself.'

As with the other documents, he had no memory of signing a release form. Nothing at all of being admitted. Impossible to accept that such a large swathe of his memory had been erased. Or the events never stored at all. Unless they were lying to him.

She opened a file with his name, *Kiraly, V.*, clearly labelled at the top, and extracted a single sheet of paper.

'That's your signature, isn't it?' As she passed him the document, he felt a flutter of déjà vu. Hadn't Gessen recently asked him the same question about another set of forms? Deprived of his normal routines, his presence and personhood had grown warped and hazy. Vidor studied the loops and slashes of the name. The jagged V, the K like a claw. It looked like his signature, but it could easily have been forged.

'I don't remember signing this.'

'I can assure you that you did. I handled your admission, and you signed this in my presence.' Her eyes, a disconcerting cobalt blue, were fixed on his. 'You're ill, Mr Kiraly,' she said, her voice softening. 'But we're here to help you. If you would only trust us, things could go much more smoothly.'

Trust? Not something that came easily to him, and he hadn't a clue what approach might work in this case. A paternal stance, a charm offensive? Her stern expression and buttoned-up manner made it clear she would brook no impertinence.

'For our session today, I'd like to conduct a word association exercise.' She beckoned for him to follow her into a different adjoining room, not the elegant sitting room as he'd hoped. This room was quite small in size and sparsely furnished with a straight-back chair and a chaise longue, upholstered in black leather. Here, at last, was the infamous couch. Did this mean he'd advanced to a new level, or that he'd gone back a step? As he eyed the set-up with a prickle of anxiety, he imagined the ghost of Freud – or was it Jung? – gazing smugly upon him.

She waited as he lay down and crossed his arms over his chest. 'Before we begin, could you tell me which language you prefer? I've got assessments in French and Hungarian, as well as English. Usually, we find that the patient's native tongue is best, but in your case…'

'English, if you please. I've spoken almost nothing else for forty years.'

A whisper of shuffled paper. 'Here's how it works: I'm going to read out a series of words, and after each word I say, you tell me the first word that comes to mind. Don't think about your answer. Just say the first thing that pops into your head. The whole exercise should take about fifteen to twenty minutes.'

Her skirt rustled as she settled into the chair behind his head. On the wall, an abstract painting in soft pastels hung directly in his line of sight. Perfectly innocuous, exceedingly bland. Something one might find at the dentist or in a mid-class hotel room in Leeds.

'Ready?' Dr Lindstrom cleared her throat and began. 'Water.'

He scrunched his brow, wondering if there was a way to game this thing. 'Wet.'

'Blank.'

'Paper.'

'Iron.'

'Magnet.' A spot on his left foot itched. This was ridiculous, being reduced to a lab rat. Though it was probably no worse than the sensory integration experiments he put his test subjects through. Asking them to identify a scent or sound while he flashed a series of words or colours on a screen, their scalps studded with electrodes. But such experiments were meant to elucidate key neural pathways in the brain. This ludicrous exercise felt like two children playing a game of pat-a-cake.

'Broken.'

Fatigue weighed down his limbs. 'Bones.'

'Father.'

'Gone.'

On and on they went through the list of words. There was no rhyme or reason to them, no pattern he could discern, though he'd always been more of a numbers person. Analysing data was his strong suit. The gears in his parietal and frontal lobes clicking into place as he worked through a series of equations and algorithms. But as his muscles relaxed, he gave himself over to the sound of Dr Lindstrom's well-modulated voice and lilting accent, until the rhythm of the words took on the cadence of a lullaby. Never a good sleeper, he could imagine sinking into a deep slumber, her cool fingers soothing his brow. Not a lover's touch, but a maternal one. His own mother had been dead for thirty-five years, but in Dr Lindstrom's soothing voice she seemed to rise again.

'Dry.'

'Desert.'

'Bird.'

'Caged.'

On and on, until it felt as though they'd been trapped in the little room for days. As fatigue turned to exhaustion – when had he ever felt this tired? – the painting on the wall appeared to take on a three-dimensional form. An oblong shape pushed out from the canvas and beckoned to him. *A portal.* His body slipped its bonds and levitated above the couch for a few moments before floating towards the aperture, just large enough for him to slip through.

On the other side, he caught a glimpse of paradise. That enchanting word, Persian for garden, and the paradise arrayed before him was indeed an enticing garden of delights, shimmering and dancing in the sun. He closed his eyes and breathed in the scent of orange blossoms and rose petals, rejoicing in the sound of water splashing in a fountain. A dark-haired woman in a white robe appeared from behind a pomegranate tree and held out a slender hand. Her green eyes beckoned. *Come.*

In a strangled voice he called out *Ummi!* and stumbled forward to meet her.

'Mr Kiraly?'

Dr Lindstrom leaned over him, peering into his face with a frown. 'Are you all right?'

He struggled to sit and fell back. 'I'm sorry, what? I must have… nodded off.' He squeezed his head in his hands.

'It is rather warm in here.' She touched his shoulder. 'Let me get you a glass of water.'

Her face swam in and out of his line of vision. Water, yes. His throat was inexplicably parched and his head ached terribly, as if he'd been travelling through a scorching desert under the noonday sun. She unfastened the shutters and opened the window to let in the mountain air, damp and cool as water from a spring. When he looked at the painting, the blood still pounding in his chest, it was flat and innocuous. Nothing but a few lines slashed in chalk. The garden of earthly delights was gone.

12

As he waited on the platform at the tiny station in Saint-Odile, Gessen studied the printed itinerary provided by his assistant. Assuming no delays, he should arrive in London shortly after midday. In his carry-on bag, he'd tucked the folder of Vidor's case notes to review on the trip, though doubtful he'd find anything he hadn't spotted before.

He'd gone over the transcripts from Vidor's sessions a dozen times. Searching for clues or a break in the rambling narrative where Vidor betrayed himself in a lie. But each retelling of his family history spooled out like finely spun thread. Too smooth, Gessen felt, his fingers tingling like antennae, each time he listened to the polished replies. On Vidor's home ground, with any luck, he might dig up something to shatter the illusion of the perfect life his patient insisted upon.

* * *

A ray of sun broke through the clouds as the taxi turned into Camden Road, a tidy street of terraced houses, and slowed to a stop in front of number 29. The white paint on the window frames was showing signs of age, but otherwise the Georgian house, with its glossy black shutters and bright red door, looked well cared for. In a round clay pot on the doorstep, a profusion of orange and yellow asters bloomed, and the box hedge bordering the front garden was trimmed with surgical precision. Someone must be looking after the place while Vidor was gone.

A striped cat with protruding hip bones and a feral look lurked in a corner of the garden, its yellow eyes narrowed in suspicion as Gessen passed through the front gate. He wondered if this was the cat Vidor mentioned in the letter he'd written to a woman named Magdalena Bartosz. It was clinic policy to have a quick look through any patient's letters before they were posted from the village. A breach of privacy that made Gessen uneasy, but he'd been forced to institute the practice a few years ago when a written cry for help from a Russian oligarch's son brought a SWAT team to the clinic's front gates.

He brushed a bit of lint from the lapel of his coat before mounting the steps and pressing the bell. Schools would be out for the day, but there were no sounds of children in the road. Nothing but the twitter of sparrows and the faint hum of tyres on a distant street. When no one answered, he pressed the bell again. Such was the scarcity of knowledge about Vidor's life, Gessen had no idea whether or not he lived alone. The seconds ticked past, and as he turned away, disappointed to have struck out so soon, the door swung open. A solidly built woman with dyed blonde hair coiled in a bun, appeared in the doorway.

'Is this the home of Professor Vidor Kiraly?'

She crossed her arms with a proprietary air. 'And who might you be?'

'My apologies, madam, for not introducing myself.' He made a slight bow. 'My name is Dr Anton Gessen. Professor Kiraly is currently under my care, and I was hoping to have a quick look at his home and surroundings.' Natural habitat was the more accurate term, but that might sound eccentric to this suspicious woman. Even though it felt like it at times, Vidor wasn't a forest creature he was studying in the wild.

'Does Professor Kiraly know you are here?'

He hesitated. 'I have his blessing to look around.' A half lie. Surely if he'd asked, Vidor would have consented. But he couldn't worry about that now.

Her stern expression relaxed. 'In that case, you may come in, Dr…?'

'Gessen.'

She stood aside and invited him through. 'I've been so worried about Vid— um, Professor Kiraly, I mean.' Her cheeks reddened. 'Nearly a month since his collapse and not a word. I telephoned the college, but they will not tell me anything. Confidential, they said, and I am not anyone. Not family, I mean.' She blushed again. 'Only the housekeeper.'

Her English, though fluent, was marked by a distinctive accent. Polish would be his first guess. Or perhaps Romanian.

As he stepped into the hall, she grew flustered. 'I am Mrs Bartosz.' She extended her hand. 'Magda. I don't know where my manners are. Would you like tea? I have only just now put the kettle on.' She ushered him into a sunny kitchen with two large sash windows overlooking the garden. The cat slunk in behind them, and Magda clapped her hands. 'Scat,' she said, chasing it out the back door. 'Professor Kiraly loathes that animal. I don't mind it myself, but he is always threatening to put poison out if it keeps coming into the garden.'

Interesting, Gessen thought. In his letter to Magda, Vidor had written, *Don't forget to feed the cat*. If he didn't tread carefully, she might grow suspicious and clam up.

'Cats give him the… how is it called? The willies?' Magda was saying. 'Not just this one. All cats.' She shook her head as one might when speaking of a misguided child. 'He thinks they have… secret knowledge, like mysteries of the universe, maybe. And if cats had thumbs like people,' she waggled her hands, 'they would rule the world. *Szalony*. No?' She tapped her forehead, though her smile was quickly followed by a frown. 'What kind of doctor did you say you are?'

Gessen met her eye. 'The ordinary kind.'

'That's all right then.' She flushed. 'I thought maybe you were one of those, you know,' she twirled her finger by her ear, 'and here I am saying that Professor Kiraly is not right in the head.' As she talked, she set the tea things on the table. 'You do not mind if we sit here? Or maybe in the garden, if it's not too cold? When Professor Kiraly isn't here...' her voice trailed off. 'He is fussy about his things, so when I finish cleaning, I have my tea in the kitchen.'

She sat heavily in the chair and poured out two cups. He hadn't noticed before, but the kitchen was spotless. The counters, cooker, and fridge all gleamed as if new. Not a smudge or a fingerprint.

'This is a lovely home.' Gessen stirred sugar in his tea. 'To be honest, I was expecting the charming but chaotic household of a man who spends all his time in the lab, or with his nose in a book. Forgive me for prying, but do you live in?'

She clattered her cup in the saucer. 'I am not a live-in housekeeper, no. But I come every day after Professor Kiraly leaves for the college. I clear the breakfast dishes and tidy up. On Tuesdays and Thursdays, I am here all day to do the whole house. Top to bottom. He likes a clean house. Everything in its place. Not so strange in someone like him, no?' She leaned in and whispered. 'A brain scientist. Very organised, very neat.' She smiled shyly. 'Not that I understand what he does.' She lowered her voice again. 'But I hear he is like... genius, you know? Such an honour, his prize.' Her face clouded over. 'A shame what happened. Poor man. Too much excitement, maybe? Too many people. Cameras flashing. Bright light gives him headache. Did he tell you?'

Bright light, headaches. Gessen made a mental note to look more closely at possible epilepsy. When he'd finished his tea, he pushed back his chair and moved to the window. 'Lovely garden. Is that your handiwork, as well?'

'Oh, no. I know nothing about flowers... except... to look at them. A man comes once a week to tidy the garden and fix anything broken. I think maybe Professor Kiraly's mind is too much on his work to think about the business of living.' She gestured at the room. 'He does know you are here?' A frown creased her forehead. 'A very private man. I do not like to think you come here without his permission.'

He assured her once more of his good intentions. After she filled the sink with water to soak the dishes, she dried her hands and turned to face him. 'You are a nice man, I think, so maybe I tell you this. A letter came from him a few days ago. He said he was fine, and I must not worry, except... ' She plucked the yellowed leaves from a potted geranium and dropped them in the bin. 'Before this trouble... he sometimes said things like how the Russians want to kidnap him. Silly, no? If he is ever in danger, he said he will send me a note with secret message. Anything about a cat means he's been kidnapped.' She straightened the kitchen chairs. 'So I can't help but worry...'

Gessen tried to keep a straight face. If he smiled at such foolishness, she would likely march him to the door. But he wasn't surprised. Mild paranoia in someone like Vidor, who appeared to have repressed an enormous swathe of his psyche, was not unusual.

He made a slight bow. 'I will do my very best to get Professor Kiraly back on his feet.'

Magda folded the tea towel and hung it over the sink. 'I show you the rest of the house, then, though there is not much to see. Many years before this, I was housekeeper for another professor. His wife was artist of some kind, and the house was...' she waved her hands. 'How do you say, a shambles? So stressy for me. I never knew what they want, with everything higgledy-piggledy. Books everywhere, big round cushions for sitting on floor. No telly. The man would not allow it. And the children... *oof*... like wild animals.'

In Vidor's house, chaos was not an issue. Neat as a pin, quiet as a sepulchre. Spare, minimalist furnishings in the lounge. Plain wooden floors and slatted blinds on the windows. A taupe sofa and matching armchairs. Nothing on the walls except for two black-and-white photographs of marshland, geese flying overhead. No bevelled mirrors or crystal chandeliers. Not a single silk lampshade or porcelain tchotchke. For some reason, he'd imagined Vidor's tastes would be more epicurean. The little he'd mentioned of family life in Budapest hinted at servants, velvet settees, crystal decanters, a grand piano. All left behind in the scramble to flee the Soviet tanks.

He left Magda in the kitchen and climbed the stairs to find more of the cheap flat-pack furniture in the bedroom, decorated in the style of a Marriott off the motorway, circa 1984. Beige curtains. A carpet the texture and colour of porridge. On the nightstand, a travel-sized clock ticked the minutes away. The only odd note was the heavy brass bolt fixed to the inside of the door. Did Vidor lock himself in at night? Against what, or whom? The neighbourhood seemed innocuous enough. It wasn't as if bands of thieves and cutthroats were menacing this quiet corner of Cambridge.

He stepped into the bathroom to peek in the medicine cabinet. So much you could learn about a person by what they kept in there and how it was arranged. A steel razor and packet of extra blades. A bar of yellow soap from a Cambridge shop, still wrapped in paper. Gessen lifted it to his nose and sniffed. A faint scent of sandalwood and myrrh, reminiscent of an Eastern bazaar. A glass and toothbrush. A bottle of aspirin. No other drugs that he could see.

He pulled open the curtains and looked down into the garden where the feral cat was sunning itself on the flagstones. Gessen turned away to examine the room, so silent he could almost hear the house settling on its foundation. The abode of a solitary man, alone in the world. No photos of family, at least none that he'd seen. No evidence of the four sisters, or the beloved mother and heroic father. What of them? Their likenesses must be immortalised somewhere. Perhaps in a photo album tucked away in a cupboard. Or had a family rupture occurred sometime in the past? Vidor once let slip that his eldest sister had emigrated to North America long ago, but it wasn't clear whether he'd meant the States or Canada.

His father was long dead, apparently, if Vidor had told the truth. And if his mother were still alive, she'd be in her late eighties, at least. Vidor alone, *tout seul*, as if he'd sprung from the bowels of the earth, with no ancestors or history behind him.

When he pushed open the door of Vidor's study, he stopped dead. In contrast to the rest of the house, it looked as though a cyclone had blown through. Books and paperwork were spilled across the desk in a chaotic jumble. An open drawer was bursting with folders and thick with papers. A quick search through the files revealed nothing of interest. At the sound of a creak on the stairs he yanked his hand away, slicing his thumb on a jagged piece of metal. Blood flowed from the cut, but with nothing else to staunch the bleeding he hastily pressed a Post-It note against the wound.

As he backed out of the room, a square of stiff paper stuck behind the bookcase caught his eye, and he crouched down to tease it out. A snapshot, yellowed with age, of a small boy in leather sandals and short pants standing on an outcrop of reddish stone, squinting in the sun. Vidor as a child? Then why tuck it away in such an odd place?

With a start of recognition, it reminded him of a similar photo of a boy he'd found while snooping in his father's study, having come across a jumble of black-and-white prints shoved in a drawer. As an excitable five-year-old boy, he'd been thrilled to uncover that cache of photos. So mysterious and alien, the desolate landscape, compared to the dappled sunlight and flowering trees of his own neighbourhood. In some of the photos, grey-faced women and children huddled in the sooty light, posed against a series of low buildings in the background.

Innocent of their nature, he'd been captivated by these tableaux, as he gazed into the eyes of the children, sensing that the pictures were old, and that the children would be all grown up then. He'd pocketed one of the photos, that of a boy his age, in short pants and with grubby knees. Dark hair and vacant eyes. He had the snapshot still, if for nothing other than a reminder to keep the memory of that nameless boy alive.

Magda marched into the room, arms crossed over her bosom, severe as the guard at a sacred temple. 'Professor Kiraly does not allow anyone in here.'

He hid the photo behind his back. 'Is it always this untidy?'

She shook her head. 'I have never seen it like this before. Mostly, it is very neat. But the day he leave to accept his prize, he turned this room upside down looking for something. His plane ticket, I think, or maybe his speech? Later, on his way out the door, all in a fluster, he says something about a notebook with a dark green cover. If I find it, I am to take it home with me for safekeeping.' She looked around at the mess. 'I never did find the green notebook, and it gives me much pain to see his things like this. But God help me if I touch anything.' She made the sign of the cross. 'He would have my head on a plate.'

Gessen backed away, hoping she wouldn't notice him tucking the photo into his back pocket, or the bleeding cut on his thumb. 'Please don't think I was snooping,' he said, stepping into the hall. 'I'm merely trying to get a sense of Professor Kiraly's life before his collapse. We don't know what's wrong with him yet. Or why he hurt that man in Copenhagen, but certain details about a person's life can provide important clues.'

'What kind of clues?' Her pencilled brows rose.

'Diet, daily habits, medications. Potential allergens or toxins. He doesn't keep any poisons in the garden shed that you know of?'

'Poison?' She shook her head, looking chastened. The mention of poison always did the trick, though she'd already let slip Vidor's threat to exterminate the cat.

'What about health problems. Did he ever talk about feeling unwell?'

A twitch about the eyes.

'So you were worried about him, before his collapse?'

'Oh, no. He was in fine shape.' It had grown uncomfortably warm in the narrow hallway, and she pulled a tissue from her sleeve to dab her face.

When they returned to the safe ground of the kitchen, Magda's relief was palpable. They stood awkwardly for a moment before Gessen said, 'You've been very helpful, Mrs Bartosz.' He noted the tense set of her shoulders, the nervous flick of her eyes. She was hiding something. If only he had more time, he might get her to open up, perhaps spill the secrets only a housekeeper knew. But if he didn't leave now, he'd be late for his appointment at the college with one of Vidor's students. Perhaps this Farzan Rahimi would be more forthcoming.

13

For such a glorious day, unusually warm for mid-November, the quadrangle at St Catharine's College was oddly deserted. A trio of sparrows pecking at the gravel provided the only sign of life. Though not the type to yearn for idle pursuits, Gessen felt a sudden desire to hire a punt and drift down the Cam through the falling leaves and dappled sunshine.

It was far too lovely to sit inside a stuffy office and interrogate some unwitting student about the minutiae of Vidor's life. But duty called and having stopped at the Porter's Lodge to announce himself, he couldn't back out now. Mr Rahimi was expecting him any moment. He checked his watch. Vidor should be in his session with Ursula now and he wondered how she was getting on. Ursula excelled at drawing out even the most obstinate patient. Under her skilled ministrations, Vidor might finally loosen the stranglehold on his thoughts.

He headed across the wide expanse of lawn to the opposite corner of the quadrangle. Inside the vast hall, he paused to breathe in the stone-cooled air, his mind flitting briefly to his own student days at the Sorbonne. A different place and time, but the cool and musty atmosphere, suffused with the weight of history, smelled oddly the same.

Up two flights of stairs and down a long dim passage, he

paused to check the names on the doors as his feet tapped on the floor, polished by years of academics pacing the halls, and with centuries of intellectual sweat and toil steeped into the wood. He knocked on a closed door and waited, but all was silent. Pushing it ajar, he peeked in to see a thin young man hunched over a computer terminal, eyes fixed on the screen, furiously typing.

'Mr Rahimi?'

The man jumped like a scalded cat.

Gessen stepped inside and introduced himself. 'I didn't mean to startle you.'

Mr Rahimi pushed the hair off his forehead and blinked. 'Not at all.' He rose from the chair and studied Gessen with his dark, intelligent eyes. 'I was lost in my work.'

Gessen smiled. 'Of course you were.' He took in Mr Rahimi's slight form and the bluish tinge under his eyes. Didn't they feed them at the college? Or perhaps his meagre bursary obliged him to live on tea and stale buns. His mind rushed ahead to fill in the blanks. A bad habit, difficult to break, of assigning an imagined life to someone that probably had little to do with their real one.

'It's no problem, I knew you were coming. And please call me Farzan.'

An international student, hailing from Iran, his perfectly enunciated English was tinged with an Edwardian lilt.

'Shall we go to a cafe?' Farzan grabbed his jacket from a hook on the wall. 'Much nicer than sitting in this stuffy room.'

Indeed, the little office was cramped and dark. This wasn't a social call, but it would be a shame to waste the mild weather. 'Lead the way.'

Their footsteps echoed as they clattered down the stairs and into the sunshine. Gessen had never been to Cambridge, and everywhere he looked he saw something to please the eye. The autumnal sun glazed the magnificent stonework, and the neatly clipped lawns, an enchanting emerald green, appealed to his sense of beauty and order. He could understand why

Vidor had chosen to spend his entire academic career here. Undergraduate, graduate, lecturer, professor. It would be difficult to move away from hallowed grounds such as these, with their hidden quads and sacred halls, steeped in history. Though an unwavering commitment to a single place, Gessen reminded himself, could also be a sign of rigidity or fear of change.

As he followed Farzan out of the cloistered quadrangle and into the town, he couldn't help but wonder about the nature of the gossip circulating amongst Vidor's students and colleagues. The words 'nervous breakdown' were surely being bandied about. A nonsense term in medical circles, but a handy description when speaking to a layperson. He glanced at the young man by his side, brow furrowed, head bent, likely devising an algorithm to explain the impenetrable processes governing the brain. More philosopher than scientist, Gessen held fast to his belief that the human mind, unfathomable in its mystery, would forever resist being described by a series of equations.

They threaded their way through a busy street thronging with shoppers and students weaving like mad on their bicycles, before ducking into another courtyard where their footsteps rang out pleasingly on the stone. Tables were set out in a sunny corner, perhaps for the last time this year, before the cold weather drove everyone indoors. The tables were empty, except for the one closest to the cafe where a girl in a long skirt and knitted cardigan was bent over a book, oblivious to their presence.

'What can I get you?' Gessen asked.

'No, you are my guest.' Farzan's voice was firm. 'They have excellent coffee here. Or tea, if you'd prefer.'

Though a confirmed coffee drinker, Gessen decided on tea. After the two cups of excellent tea he'd drunk at Vidor's kitchen table, it seemed unwise to make the switch to a more bitter brew.

While Farzan ducked inside to get their drinks, Gessen

surreptitiously studied the girl at the table nearby. Intent on her book, she hadn't looked up when he and Farzan approached. If he were a young girl, dreaming away the afternoon, he might have been dazzled by Farzan's film star looks, but she clearly had more serious pursuits on her mind. He tried, and failed, to catch the title of her book.

Farzan returned with a pot of tea and a plate of biscuits and scones. All very English, as one might expect, but now that they were out of the lab and in the fresh air, Farzan's nervousness had only grown. When he picked up his cup, his hand shook, and his eyes flicked worriedly at the girl seated a few metres away. Twice he turned his head to glance behind him.

'It's terrible what happened to Professor Kiraly,' he said, stirring sugar in his tea. 'Everyone is worried about him.' Farzan scanned Gessen's face as if hoping to find clues to the fate of his advisor.

Had Farzan seen the video of Vidor's very public breakdown? Probably everyone in the college had seen it by now. It was a terrible violation, and he cursed the person who'd posted it online. Privacy was becoming a thing of the past. What kind of world was it when you couldn't fall apart without the whole of humanity watching?

'He's doing well,' Gessen said, mindful of doctor–patient confidentiality.

'Will he be returning to the college soon?'

Gessen poured a splash of milk in his tea. 'Difficult to say, I'm afraid, but it's important that Professor Kiraly not feel pressured to return to his normal duties until he's ready.'

A thick-chested man, solid as a tank, in mirrored sunglasses and a beige windbreaker headed towards them. Farzan stiffened, like a concerned fox, ready to bolt.

Gessen studied him over the rim of his teacup. 'Forgive me for prying,' he said, 'but are you feeling all right?'

'Yes, I'm fine, it's just that lately…' He rubbed his palms on his jeans. 'I've been feeling rather spooked.' He turned to look behind him. 'A bit paranoid, I know. But after what happened to Hisham…' His voice trailed off.

The man in the beige jacket, who'd paused to peer in the teashop window, ambled down the street and turned the corner. Farzan, visibly relieved, picked up a half-eaten scone, only to set it down again. His elbow knocked a teaspoon off the table and the sound of it hitting the pavement was like a shot.

Gessen studied Farzan's face over the rim of his cup. What was he afraid of? He patted his mouth with a napkin. 'Who's Hisham?'

'Another graduate student in the department. A nice guy. About eight months ago, he disappeared.' He absently tore a paper napkin into shreds. 'We were friends, but since he worked in a competing lab, Professor Kiraly didn't like us talking to each other. He was afraid Hisham would pump me for information.'

'What kind of information?'

'Details about our lab's recent data. But we never talked about our work. I knew better than that. I didn't even know the research project Hisham was busy with. In the past couple of years, the work we were doing in Professor Kiraly's lab was garnering all kinds of praise, and after learning he'd won the Søgaard Prize, a prestigious award worth a million in cash, he got really paranoid that another lab would steal our data and publish it first.'

Gessen ears pricked up. 'Does that happen often?'

'Not often.' Farzan poured more tea into his cup. 'But you do have to be careful. There's a lot of pressure for funding, and some of these top brain researchers are like rock stars, you know? At least in our field.'

Gessen spread strawberry jam on another scone and took a bite. Heaven. How he'd like to eat the entire pot with a spoon, just like a child. On the ground between the tables, a group of sparrows pecked at the crumbs on the cobblestones. 'And how are you faring in Professor Kiraly's absence?' He couldn't help but wonder about the boy's emotional state. Though Farzan wasn't his patient, he seemed distressed about something. 'Do you go home often?'

Farzan looked startled. 'You mean to Iran?' He shook his head. 'No, never. I can never go back.' He fumbled in his jacket pocket and pulled out a packet of cigarettes. 'You don't mind, do you?' He lit one and turned his head to exhale a stream of smoke.

The poor boy's face was stiff with fright.

'I did something stupid before I left. It's nothing, really, but in Iran it's punishable by death. I thought as long as I was here, I would be safe, but after the thing with Hisham…'

Gessen waited, but Farzan fell silent. 'What thing?'

Farzan took a drag from his cigarette. 'Like I said, he disappeared. I thought he might have been deported back home to Iraq, even though he'd received his notice of leave to remain, but the Home Office had no information on him. So I figured he'd been either kidnapped or killed, maybe by someone with a vendetta against the Kurds. But six months after he disappeared, I got an email from him with a photo of a mosque in the background. He said he'd returned home to Kurdistan in northern Iraq, and everything was fine. Sorry that he'd left in such a hurry and didn't say goodbye. Something about a family matter or his mother being sick.' He raised his head and looked Gessen in the eye. 'But I don't think Hisham sent that email.'

'Why would you think that?' As Gessen studied the tremor in Farzan's hand, the ghost of his old terror came flooding back. The wild hammering on the door late at night. The frantic flight to Switzerland by boat and train, all under the cover of darkness. His mother's sudden disappearance on a rainy afternoon, not long after he'd been told his father wouldn't be joining them.

'We had a code word,' Farzan said. 'Something we came up with one night at the pub. Hisham wasn't used to alcohol, so he was a bit, you know, loopy.' He waggled his head. 'His idea was that if one of us ever vanished, we should use a code word to signal we were in trouble, and another one that meant we were safe.' He stubbed out his cigarette. 'Mountain meant safe. Rock meant danger. I picked the danger word based on the name of a legendary bird in ancient Persia. So huge it could carry off an elephant in its talons. Terrified me as a child.'

The girl at the next table closed her book and stood. As she tucked the paperback into her bag and buttoned her cardigan, Farzan grew silent and followed her movements with his eyes.

Gessen drank the last of his tea and shivered in his thin jacket. The sun had gone behind a bank of clouds, and a chill wind chased bits of paper across the pavement. 'What do you think happened to your friend?'

Farzan lit another cigarette. 'I suspect he was being followed. Someone broke into his flat while he was out and searched through his things. Nothing was taken, but...' A breeze whipped his hair, and he stood to zip up his jacket. 'There's something else. Not long after Hisham disappeared, his computer was infected by a virus and all his data – three years of work – were gone. Poof, just like that.' He snapped his fingers. 'Apparently, nothing was backed up on an external drive or saved on the server.'

He exhaled a great plume of smoke. 'The thing that bothers me most is that our code word meaning all was well didn't appear in his email. Hisham's not a British citizen, so the Home Office wouldn't look into it. I called all the airlines to find out if he'd boarded a flight to Baghdad, but of course they wouldn't tell me anything. Who am I? Not family, just a friend.' He tamped out his cigarette and flicked it away. 'Someone else sent that message. Someone who wanted him out of the picture for good.'

Farzan gazed across the courtyard as if looking for a sign in the blocks of stone. 'You asked me what I think happened to my friend?' He looked straight into Gessen's eyes. 'I think Hisham is dead.'

14

Paris, France
September 1968

A lorry scoured by burning sands; a boat rocking in the wind; a night train trundling through the darkened countryside. Wind, sand, stars… on his journey to another world.

On the sleeper train he shares a compartment with four other students on their way to the capital. They disembark at first light, and he walks through the vaulted station, nearly empty at that hour, dull-witted and stiff-limbed from the long journey that began in a dust-choked village and ended in the shining city of his dreams.

His heart sings as he walks out of the Gare de Lyon and stumbles into the morning sunshine. Taxi touts vie for his attention, 'Taxi, monsieur?' But he shakes his head and drags his luggage towards the Métro. It would be nice to get his first look at the city by taxicab, but his bursary, while generous, won't pay for such luxuries. Later, he'll explore on foot, radiating out from the Latin Quarter where his student flat is located, in an ever-widening arc, following the snail-like spiral of the arrondissements, all the way to the twentieth.

He's been studying a map of the city for weeks and

when he closes his eyes, he can picture the neighbourhoods and landmarks in his head. Tour Eiffel, Arc de Triomphe, Montparnasse, Notre-Dame. Every one of these splendid architectural gems, gloriously here, on his doorstep, waiting to be discovered. For the first time in his life he understands what it means to be free. No more skulking about the menacing alleys, or dodging shadows under a brutal sun. No one knows him here. Cloaked by a glorious anonymity, he can wander the streets unmolested and alone.

A few days later, still buzzing with the newness of his surroundings, he passes a cafe where tables crowd the pavement under a row of linden trees. A girl, sitting with two others, calls him over. 'Have a drink with us, why don't you?' He freezes, terrified, but the girl's smile and bright flaxen hair have a hypnotising effect on his fear. Before he knows it, he's joined their table, and a glass of wine appears. He's never drunk alcohol before, and the sharp taste comes as a shock.

With its dark berry colour, he thought that wine would be sweeter, like nectar. But the second sip is better and the next one better still. And there he is, drinking a goblet of wine in the golden light, a true Frenchman at last. The spirits loosen his tongue, and their free-ranging talk slips and glides over the usual subjects: films and books and favourite authors. The girl with the flaxen hair, the one from Norway, smiles at him over the rim of her glass, while the dark-haired girl lights a slim cigarette and playfully blows smoke in his eyes.

'So, where are you from?'

He squirms. Should he tell them the truth? He has nothing to hide. And yet he hesitates, wondering if his newfound friends will look badly upon him, once he reveals his colonial origins. But the alcohol has made him reckless, and at the cusp of new beginnings, he is anxious to start off on the right foot, and to be honest and forthright in all things. So he tells them he is from the desert land across the water, a vast and unknowable place of dark shadows and blazing light.

The blonde girl has gone pale. Realising his mistake he tries to improve the mood by raising his glass in an awkward toast. *Santé*. But the air around them has thickened into silence, and the moment is lost. When the girl looks at him, her eyes are wide with shock. To her friends she cries, *Allons-y*, grabs her bag and hurries away.

A wave of shame crashes over him. What does she take him for, some kind of monster? Will he never escape the ruinous bonds that lash him to his fate?

15

Clinique Les Hirondelles
Saint-Odile, Switzerland
18 November 2008

After an excellent luncheon of poached lake perch in lemon butter sauce and parsley potatoes, Vidor settled into a lounge chair in a corner of the rock garden with a view across the valley. A breeze carrying the sharp scent of pines from a nearby copse riffled the pages of his notebook. The only bright spot left in the garden was a spray of faded pink flowers from the rambling thyme clinging to the stones. Wrapped in a wool blanket against the chill, and sated from the noonday meal, he closed his eyes and prepared to doze. An excellent repast, though a glass of chilled Pouilly-Fuissé would have been a welcome addition. A pity alcohol was forbidden. Even the coffee, he suspected, was cut with decaf.

When a blast of gunfire rent the air, Vidor leapt from his seat, heart thumping. What was that? Another two shots followed in quick succession, and he flinched at the sound. Were they under attack? But the sharp reports, still ringing in his ears, appeared to be echoes from across the valley. Was it hunting season? He'd heard one of the staff mention it. The government-sanctioned culling of deer and chamois. Vidor loathed blood sports of any kind, and he felt a sudden kinship with those innocent and terrified creatures, gunned down for sport.

Jumpy from the gunfire, his nerves refused to settle until several minutes had passed. In the quiet hour after lunch they were supposed to turn their thoughts inward. A time for meditating or writing in their journals, as if they were adherents of a religious order, where talking was frowned upon and silence king.

Through half-closed lids, he caught sight of that rather odd, older woman, keeping a tight hold on her handbag as she lurked near the sculpture of two entwined fish at the edge of the Zen garden. He closed his eyes, hoping she would go away, but at the sounds of rustling foliage, he peeked through narrowed lids to see her making a beeline in his direction. The clasp of the quilted black bag slung over her arm winked in a shaft of sunlight. He feigned sleep, but she stealthily advanced, a cat stalking its prey. *Oh, dear God.* Apparently, she was about to speak.

Annoyed at being driven from his chosen spot, he gathered his things. In spite of being held here against his will, he'd grown fond of this corner of the Zen garden. So charming and harmonious in its carefully wrought perfection, it might have been airlifted straight from Kyoto. As he made his escape, she called out. '*Excusez-moi, jeune homme.*' Her tone was imperious.

'I beg your pardon, madam.' He suppressed a sigh. 'Do you wish to speak to me?'

She cast him an odd look. 'Well, I'm not addressing the elves now, am I?' She perched on a nearby bench and patted the space beside her. 'You interest me.' She glanced at the ring on his left hand. 'Does your wife know you've got a roving eye? I've seen the way you look at that pretty young doctor. Passes herself off as Swedish, but take it from me, she's a Swiss girl, born and bred. The youngest daughter of an excellent family.' She lowered her voice to a whisper. 'Though, *entre nous*, I happen to know she was once a patient here.'

Vidor took a step backwards, anxious to put some distance between himself and the woman he'd seen before from afar, but never spoken to. With a distinctively mad look in her eyes, she might just qualify as the looniest of the patients so far. For a brief moment, he wondered how she would fare as a test subject in his lab. Did she perceive the world in the same way as a normal person? Was her idea of green and purple identical to his? In those lacquered and heavily bejewelled fingers, did a rose petal feel rough or smooth? If only he could pop her into a functional MRI machine and get a peek at her brain.

'I'm afraid I have an urgent appointment,' he said, 'so I'll wish you a *bonne journée*, madam.'

'Wait.' Her hand snaked out and grabbed his wrist. 'I've been longing to have a conversation with you. You seem halfway intelligent, unlike most of the feeble-minded fools who end up here.' She snorted. 'Top-notch accommodation, five-star ambience. That's what it says in the brochure, doesn't it? But this place doesn't hold a candle to the Beau Rivage. At least, not how it was in my day.'

'I'm afraid I don't know it.' He tried to extricate his arm, but she had a grip like a raptor.

'The Imperial Suite.' She winked. 'That's where my husband, Maximillian, and I would spend our summers until his health failed.' She placed a hand on her breastbone and sighed. 'May he rest in peace.'

Even in the bright afternoon sun, Vidor could scarcely detect a line on her face, though she must be in her late sixties. She probably had regular injections of one of those chemical polymers that provided the illusion of youth. But nothing could disguise the prominent veins and liver spots on her hands. And where was the sense in trying to turn back time? She wasn't fooling anyone. But what did he know? It was harder for women, he supposed, to relinquish the glow of youth.

As a young lad, still in his teens, he remembered surprising his mother in the entry hall of their flat in Paris. She had just celebrated her fifty-second birthday and was standing in front of the big gilt mirror, pulling at the skin by her eyes. When she caught him staring, she smiled sadly. 'Silly, isn't it?' she'd said. 'When we have so much to be thankful for, but a woman's vanity…' She shook her head. 'It's not easy to let go. We're born, we age, we die. It all happens so fast.' She clasped him by the shoulders and kissed his forehead. 'My dear boy, you will take care of me when I'm old, won't you?'

Naturally, he'd said yes, and he would have, but the chance never came. Five years after he'd seen her at the mirror, she was diagnosed with an aggressive blood cancer and dead within the year. In a strange way, it might have been a mixed blessing. A celebrated beauty in her youth, she had dreaded the idea of growing old, and turning into one of the wrinkled crones who'd stalked the folktales of her childhood. In sympathy with his mother, a flash of pity for this woman, who'd accosted him in the garden, or any woman who'd been cast aside when her looks started to go, softened his heart.

The woman glanced to her right and left before opening the clasp of her bag. She reached in as if to retrieve something from its depths, a pen perhaps or a lipstick, but her hand stayed inside, and she leaned close to whisper something he couldn't hear. What the devil did she have in there? A kitten, a mouse? Or perhaps it was a doll she took for a real child, similar to a case he'd read in the newspaper once about a distraught woman in Cornwall.

A cloud blocked the sun, and as he looked at the dark peaks, jutting into the air like dragon's teeth, an inexplicable terror squeezed his throat.

And this, the naked countenance of earth, on which I gaze, even these primeval mountains teach the adverting mind.

The glaciers creep like snakes that watch their prey, from their far fountains, slow rolling on; there, many a precipice…

'Are you talking to me?' Her eyes, yellow-flecked like tourmaline, latched onto his.

Had he spoken aloud? He shifted his legs. 'I was merely reciting a few lines of Shelley.'

She pursed her lips. 'Shirley?' A shaft of sunlight pierced the clouds and danced off her rings, ruby and emerald solitaires, big as robin's eggs. He wondered why she'd been allowed to keep them.

'I don't believe we've met properly. My name is Vidor Kir— , uh, just Vidor, and you are?'

'Madame du Chevalier. *Enchantée.*' She extended her hand to be kissed. 'Though that isn't the name I was born with,' she said with a sly wink. 'I acquired it when I went on the stage. But there's no need for us to be formal. You may call me Hélène.'

The stage? He stifled the urge to laugh.

'I can see you're intrigued, so I will tell you. I was a dancer.' Her flirtatious smile lit up her face. 'Trained with Balanchine, you know. Though after I tired of the ballet, I did a stint in musical theatre in London's West End before moving abroad. Though you can't tell in these trousers,' she winked again, 'I have a great set of gams.'

He smiled to be polite, but his puzzlement grew. He'd had the idea she was French, but her accent had a slight English intonation. Or was it American? Is that how she'd acquired it, during her time abroad? Or was this merely a flight of fancy, the product of a diseased brain, where each day she donned a new role. Perhaps, when he saw her again, she would introduce herself as the reincarnated daughter of Isis.

She turned her back to whisper into the bag again. He hoped whatever was in there was not actually alive, or anything that slithered. A shiver coursed through his chest. Ever since finding a poisonous snake curled on his bed as a child, he'd had a morbid fear of them. Let Freud have a field day with the sexual connotations, but snakes were vile and terrifying creatures, that's all there was to it.

He shifted to the left, preparing to make his exit, when a shadow fell across the lawn. Vidor flinched. He'd thought they were alone, but the Emirati Prince loomed close and slunk past without acknowledgment. As he skirted the bench, he turned his face away from the valley and the mountains beyond. Being from a flat, desert country, navigating such vertiginous heights must be nerve-wracking. Two acrophobics in the Swiss Alps. Who'd have thought they'd have something in common?

As the boy passed behind them, he leaned in close, and Vidor caught a whiff of his aftershave. '*Salaam alaikum, Saidi.*'

Vidor jerked away. 'What's that?'

'You heard me.' He glanced at Hélène before bending close to Vidor's ear. '*Arak lahiqaan.*' A breathy whisper, the flash of white teeth.

Good day, sir… See you later. The words rose like a bubble from the murk. How did he know what they meant?

'You talk in your sleep, my friend.' The boy laughed and slipped away.

* * *

With mild alarm, Gessen observed through his high-powered binoculars Vidor and Hélène chatting together in the Zen garden. He couldn't hear what they were saying, of course, but he could tell by the sly look on her face that she was up to her old mischief. Hélène liked to indulge in a bit of harmless fun, but he might need to have a stern word with her if he thought she was crossing the line. Vidor's case was too delicate for anyone to interfere in his recovery. With an hour to go until their next session, he still had time to clear his desk of the towering pile of mail, financial reports, and forms requiring his signature.

As he sifted through the stack, an envelope postmarked from the UK, and addressed in carefully rounded letters, caught his eye.

Dear Dr Gessen,

You asked me to write if I think of anything that might be useful to you in helping Professor Kiraly return to health. During our short time together, I was not comfortable to reveal certain things. I do not have anything to hide, but some things are private, even shameful, and I could not say them to you while we drank tea together at Professor Kiraly's kitchen table. So, I am writing now, and hope it will help you in some way.

For as long as I have been working for Professor Kiraly (eight years this December), he has suffered with strange headaches and sometimes sleepwalking. Once or twice I see him staring out the window for several minutes. When I tried to get his attention, it was like he wasn't there. When under much stress, he will talk in his sleep in a strange language that I think must be Hungarian, though I do not know a single word of that tongue myself.

Perhaps you are wondering how I know these things about my employer? This is the part I was not able to say to your face, but the truth is that Professor Kiraly and I have another relationship besides housekeeper and employer. I have never given this other relationship a name, so I am not sure what to call myself. Not a mistress, I do not think, since Professor Kiraly is not married, and we do not hurt anyone. 'Girlfriend' or 'love interest' are also not good for a woman of my age, and I cannot claim that love is involved. Perhaps 'lady friend' is the best way to label me, if you feel a need to do that. I will explain now, and you can decide.

Every Saturday evening, unless he is travelling, Professor Kiraly arrives at my flat at six o'clock and rings the bell. When I open the door, a kind of... play acting begins. He is my gentleman caller and I am his...

lady friend. He calls me Maggie and I call him Vida (his childhood nickname). We eat the dinner I make and drink a bottle of wine and then we climb the stairs to my bedroom, where we undress and have… I blush to tell you, but a smart man like you will know what I mean.

Afterwards, he likes me to sing or read to him. Sometimes, after he falls asleep, he says things in his language, sometimes shouting. Maybe nonsense, who knows? One or maybe two times he has shouted something that sounded like 'Abby'. Perhaps a sister's name, or an old lover? I do not think he has ever married. One time I wake in the night to find him gone, poof! But he'd left his shoes behind. Another time, I find him stumbling around the front garden, and I must lead him back to bed. Poor man was sobbing like a child. Sunday mornings, he is early riser and leaves the flat before I go downstairs.

When I next see him at his home, I am again his housekeeper, Mrs Bartosz and he is Professor Kiraly. I have never told anyone about this before. The first time he suggested we have dinner at my flat, I did not know what would happen. But I am not a girl, or a dimwit either, so I do not think he is interested only in my pierogi, or my conversation. It is maybe not nice for his privacy to write this, but you seem like a nice man, so I tell you.

When Professor Kiraly is at my home on Saturday evening, he is like a different man, not Professor Kiraly at all. Sometimes he is sad and scared. Almost like a child. I know not much about his life, only that he and his family flee the troubles in Hungary and settle in Paris. I hope it is not wrong for me to write to you. I am very fond of Professor Kiraly and wish you good luck in helping him to feel better soon.

Sincerely yours,
Mrs Magdalena Bartosz

Gessen swivelled in the chair to face the mountains as he digested this not insignificant addition to the meagre storehouse of what he knew about Vidor. Though he hadn't expected to receive the letter, Mrs Bartosz's confession wasn't a complete surprise. During his visit to Vidor's home, it was clear she was holding something back. Perhaps out of loyalty to her employer. Or an immigrant's fear of being ousted from the country.

That she was his mistress, in addition to his housekeeper, while a titillating detail, wasn't as interesting as the bit about his behaviour: sleepwalking, sobbing in the garden, nocturnal shouting, possible trance states. Not to mention the headaches. Symptoms that could point to a neurological disorder, such as temporal or frontal lobe epilepsy, possibly exacerbated by repressed childhood trauma. Both disorders were associated with psychosis and defensive aggression in the face of a threat.

She had certainly spilled the beans, Mrs Bartosz, as everything she wrote contradicted Vidor's earlier claim that he was a sound sleeper and in excellent health.

'Thank you, Mrs Bartosz,' he said aloud, sending her a note of gratitude through the airwaves, before folding up the letter and locking it in his desk drawer. At long last, he was getting somewhere.

16

Through the window, Gessen studied the heavy clouds massing above the high peaks. So far, they'd only had a few flurries, but it wouldn't be long before the first heavy snowfall of the year arrived in a fury of white, each storm bringing with it the threat – or promise, depending on one's mood – of being cut off from the world.

He had arranged a meeting with Ursula and took the seat across from her at the table in his office. An exemplary clinical psychologist, she had joined his staff seven years ago, following her doctoral studies in Bern. They made a good team, perfectly in sync with each other's approach to patient care. But last Monday, after arriving at the clinic from her flat in Spiez, where she lived at the weekends when not on call, he'd noticed a ring on her left hand. A band of white gold adorned with three square-cut diamonds. His heart sank when he saw it. She looked radiant, and he was happy for her, of course. But any day now, he expected Ursula to announce she was leaving.

He poured out two coffees and handed her a cup. 'How did he seem while I was away?'

'Vidor Kiraly?' She dropped her pen and focused on the wall behind his head.

He could practically hear the gears of her finely tuned mind clicking into place.

'Watchful and alert are the words that come to mind.' Her eyes met his. 'He was curious about where you were and what I might have in store for him, as if the two of us, you and I, that is,' she said, 'were laying some kind of trap.'

He wouldn't be wrong there. The weaving of psychological snares, so subtle as to be undetectable, was Ursula's speciality. Gessen smiled. 'Did you catch anything?'

'Possibly.' She flipped open her notebook. 'There was an odd moment during the word association exercise when his eyes glazed over, as if he'd gone into a trance. Then he pointed at the painting on the wall and cried out.' She tucked a stray lock of hair behind her ear. 'I can show you the tape, if you'd like.'

'A trance?' He made a note.

'First time I've seen anything like it,' Ursula said, 'though it could be he dozed off and had a few seconds of REM sleep before waking again.'

This was a new development. Had Vidor accessed a repressed memory during the exercise? It wouldn't have taken more than twenty minutes. Not enough time to reach REM sleep – the realm of dreams and out-of-body sensations – though it was possible. 'I'll have a look at the tape.' He stood. 'And thank you again for holding the fort while I was gone. I wouldn't know what to do without you.' He avoided looking at her ring. If she was planning on resigning, he would hear about it soon enough.

After Ursula left his office, he spent a few moments in silent meditation before returning to his desk to cast an eye over the logbook to see how his other patients had fared in his absence. It wasn't often that he was away from the clinic, but on the few occasions he'd had to travel to a medical conference or provide a consultation in Zurich or Basel or Bern, he'd always felt comfortable leaving things in Ursula's capable hands.

While Gessen was nosing around Cambridge, Vidor, according to the log, had passed an unremarkable two days. Mornings were spent in his room, afternoons in the Zen garden. In the session with Ursula on the first day of his absence, exactly the time he was poking around Vidor's study, Vidor had apparently undergone some kind of transient attack. Perhaps he had sensed Gessen rifling through his things and experienced something akin to a telepathic seizure at the very moment Gessen discovered the photo of the small boy stuck behind the bookcase. There was no way to ask Vidor about the photo, though, without revealing that he'd gone through his personal things. A breach of privacy that would shatter any trust he'd managed to build so far.

He bent his head over the logbook. On the second day of Gessen's absence, Vidor had headed over to the front gate, where he remained for nearly twenty minutes. Doing what, it was impossible to say. Looking for a way out? Or checking to see if his doctor had returned from wherever he'd gone?

* * *

In the free hour before his session with Ismail Mahmoud, Gessen played the video of Ursula's session with Vidor, listening impassively for a few minutes before turning up the volume and zooming in on his face. *Broken, bones. Father, gone. Dry, desert.* Nothing particularly remarkable there. Except maybe that bit about the father.

Though he was not as convinced as Ursula about the utility of word association results, as an addition to Vidor's other assessments, they might provide a key piece of the puzzle.

Close to the end of the session, Vidor's expression abruptly changed, and his voice took on a different timbre. Slight, but it was there. He flicked his right ear twice, and opened his eyes wide, as he stretched his hand towards the painting and cried out. On the tape, Ursula's voice was tinged with concern. *Are you all right?* Gessen reset the video and played it again. That ear flick looked familiar. He'd seen it before, but where? In a session, or was it…?

He opened Vidor's file and clicked on the video from Copenhagen, creating a split screen so he could view both videos at the same time, frame by frame. There was Vidor, mounting the dais, accepting the plaque from the Crown Prince, turning to the lectern to face the audience. And there it was, the ear flick, followed by a flash of anger as Vidor flushed red and began to shout. Gessen closed his eyes. That odd little tic had unlocked something in his brain. *Rewind, go back*. He'd seen that gesture before.

17

With deliberate care, Vidor unfolded the linen napkin and placed it on his lap. He was alone in the dining room and looking forward to a solitary breakfast when he spotted the English girl stepping through the door and heading his way. He was in no mood to chat, having awoken with the odd sense that, during the night, he had travelled a long distance through rocky and treacherous terrain.

While dressing, and groggy with fatigue, he'd been startled by a sharp knock on the bedroom wall, followed by a series of staccato raps. What had that idiot boy been doing? Probably sending cryptic messages as another way to insult him. The rage he felt left him so dizzy and weak he'd been forced to drop his head between his knees.

The English girl waved as she walked past, though her eyes looked vague. Since their conversation by the fishpond, she'd cut her long hair short, and it fluffed about her ears like a blown dandelion. She perched on the empty seat next to him. The breakfast buffet offered a sumptuous spread, but the only thing on her plate was two pieces of wheat toast, thinly spread with butter. He eyed her new haircut with a twinge of alarm. Easier to manage, or had she chopped it off in a moment of distress? He hoped he hadn't traumatised the poor girl.

She bit off a piece of toast. 'I know who you are.' She gave him a quick sidelong glance.

A muscle twitched in his jaw. She couldn't possibly know such a thing. Or was the sad-girl demeanour an act, and she truly was mad? 'I'm sorry, what?' A chill passed through him, and he glanced at the gloomy skies through the window. How quickly the weather changed in the mountains.

'My name's Libby,' she said. 'I don't think I mentioned it before.' She pulled her cardigan tight around her thin chest and hugged her arms. 'Anyway, I have a friend at St Catharine's. She said one of her professors had a crack-up while getting some award.' She nibbled her toast. 'It's you, isn't it?'

The back of Vidor's neck tingled. Though well known in the rarefied world of neuroscience, it had never occurred to him that anyone here, especially this slip of a girl, would possibly know who he was. Perhaps his recent ground-breaking work, celebrated enough to capture the million-euro Søgaard Prize, had catapulted him into the public sphere.

'Funny, you'd be here.' She scratched her wrist hard, until pink welts rose on her skin. 'There was an article in the newspaper.' She looked at him sadly. 'And some moron posted a video online, though you probably haven't seen it.' She tilted her chin at the empty room. 'Can you believe this place? No phones. No internet or newspapers. Crazy, right? Do they really think that locking us away from the real world is a good idea?' She'd taken off her cardigan and gooseflesh stippled her arms. 'And what happens when we get out? We'll be like baby mice, unprepared for the onslaught that awaits us.' She flung out her hand, knocking over a full glass of water, staring blankly, as it flooded the tablecloth and dripped onto the floor.

Vidor was disturbed by the naked quality of her distress. They weren't supposed to ask, but if he did, he wondered if she would tell him why she was here.

'Don't worry.' She abruptly stood and leaned in close until her warm breath tickled his ear. 'Your secret is safe with me.'

On the way back to his room, Vidor paused to examine the jagged line of the mountains rising above the valley, only to be seized by an attack of vertigo as the world revolved under his feet. On the other side of the gardens, screened by a wall of shrubbery, lay the vast bowl of open space. Strange that there wasn't a sturdier fence to protect them from their baser impulses. As long as he could remember, Vidor had loathed standing on any kind of high place, be it cliff, bridge, or parapet. Terrified of the siren call of the infinite ether, *l'appel du vide*. Not that he harboured a wish to die, but the compulsion to launch his body into the tantalising emptiness might someday prove too much.

Sweat broke out on his brow as he stumbled up the steps of his chalet. The bearded attendant at the front desk glanced up as he hurried past and pushed open the door to his room. Alone at last.

Except he wasn't.

A man was sitting on his bed. Dark hair, blue shirt, slip-on shoes. A flash of rage stabbed him in the chest. 'What are you doing? Get out of my room.' When Vidor raised his fist in the air, the man copied him in perfect synchrony. It was like looking in a mirror. The face, so familiar, jeered at him.

'Get out.' Vidor launched himself at the intruder and fell flat on the empty bed. No one was there, nothing at all but a figment of his imagination. Had he gone mad? He held his head and groaned. It was this wretched place, with its cabal of doctors and attendants, all conspiring to drive him to the brink of lunacy. They wouldn't stop until he was reduced to a gibbering creature, shrivelled and pale, chained to the wall of a dank bunker deep in the mountains. He had to get out. But who would help him? His pulse slowed as the surge of adrenaline waned. Dr Lindstrom seemed sympathetic. It was Gessen who was keeping him here against his will. Today, he would devise a plan. Tomorrow, he would beg Dr Lindstrom to help him escape.

18

'Did you have a mishap with the gardening shears?' Vidor dropped into the chair opposite Gessen's desk.

'What?' He frowned. 'Oh that, it's nothing.' He'd forgotten about the plaster on his thumb. It should have healed by now, but the nasty cut he'd acquired while poking around Vidor's study was taking an inordinate amount of time to heal.

He followed Vidor's gaze as he took note of the recent additions to his office. Green and gold paisley cushions on the chair in the corner. A row of fossil ammonites on the bookshelf, flaunting their perfect spiralled symmetry. That morning, he'd brought in a few specimens from his collection at home, thinking they might make a good conversation piece.

'I see you're admiring my ammonites,' Gessen said. 'Fascinating, aren't they?' He paused. 'Until I was lured away by the call of medicine, I began my studies in mathematics and wrote a thesis on Fibonacci spirals in nature. A lovely sequence. Do you know it?'

Vidor's shocked expression turned quickly to suspicion. 'Of course I know it. It is deeply embedded in my bones.' He tapped his sternum. 'I, too, wrote a thesis on the Fibonacci sequence as an undergraduate.'

'Did you? How strange.' Once again, Gessen had the unsettling feeling that he and Vidor, following their separate journeys from birth, had landed on the opposite sides of the same coin. 'And where did you write your thesis, in Paris?'

'Cambridge.' His voice was flat. 'As I told you several times already, I left for England soon after earning my baccalaureate.'

Gessen waited for him to fill the silence, but Vidor remained mute. 'Do you mind if I put on some music?' He rose from the chair. 'I find it helps to settle the mind.' He pressed a button on the remote and adjusted the volume as the opening notes of a Bach violin concerto filled the room. 'Close your eyes,' he said, lowering the lights. 'Allow the music to fill your senses.'

Fibonacci spirals, Bach. What next, chanting and crystals? Gessen was rapidly running out of ideas. With a murder charge hanging over Vidor's head, there was no time to waste. But getting at the root of the problem was impossible, as long as he failed to discover the crack in Vidor's defences. How could he possibly prove amok syndrome, or any other form of temporary psychosis, with no evidence of festering trauma to work with? Vidor's toxicology screen in Copenhagen was clear, so he couldn't point to mind-altering drugs as a mitigating factor.

Even his blood glucose levels, which Vidor insisted was the real cause of the attack, had been perfectly normal. His EEG checked out as well, though a single recording wasn't sufficient to rule out temporal lobe epilepsy. He could schedule a longer EEG and try to induce a seizure with flashing lights. But such assessments took time, and Vidor's extended stay, with no ground gained, was costing Gessen money he could ill afford.

He closed his eyes and allowed the music to wash over him. The last time he'd heard this piece live was at a concert hall in Florence. After stumbling upon the file of documents that revealed the terrible history of his mother and father, both long dead, he'd tried to outrun the pain by travelling to Tibet, before circling back to Europe by way of Italy. He'd begun his journey in a tiny village in Sicily, before drifting northward, accompanied at times by a ghostly companion he could only assume was a delusion created by his exhausted mind. Or perhaps a spectral presence, as suggested by an old woman he'd met on a mountain trail. Mostly benevolent, and believed to accompany those on the brink of death.

After he'd reached Florence and was sitting in the darkened concert hall as the final notes of Bach's violin concerto in E major faded away, the idea of becoming a psychiatrist floated into his head. If he could dedicate his life to helping others heal from trauma and the terrible weight of the past, it might provide him with a tiny measure of redemption.

Through half-closed lids, he studied Vidor's bored expression, as if trying to parse the thoughts of an unfamiliar life-form.

'Lovely, isn't it,' Gessen murmured. 'Stirs the soul.' When he switched off the music, the air in the room hummed with the last vibrations of the strings.

'Are you going to ask me about my dreams now? Whatever programme you have in mind,' Vidor said, 'could you please step up the pace so I can get back home. Every day I'm not in my office, or the classroom, or the lab is a day wasted.' He gave Gessen a thin-lipped smile.

An email from Ursula earlier in the day was evidence of Vidor's growing desperation. Just after breakfast, he'd cornered her on the way to her office and begged her to have him released. She promised to speak to Gessen on his behalf, hoping to calm him down, but it was clear Vidor's frustration had reached a tipping point. And a desperate man, feeling caged, might resort to rash behaviour. In the coming days, he would have to be carefully watched.

Gessen waited for Vidor to finish. 'Rest assured,' he said, 'discussion of your dreams is not on the agenda. Not yet, anyway.' He smiled. 'Now, I'd like you to turn your attention to the past.' Gessen met Vidor's eyes. 'You want to go home? Then no more dodging the ball. Today, you're going to tell me about your father. I suggest you start with your very first memory, and then go from there.'

19

Another dead end. With Vidor continuing to stonewall, short of strapping his patient down and threatening him with shock therapy, what could Gessen do? But each time he suggested there might have been friction between father and son, Vidor countered with another saccharine tale of paternal heroism, and how the man had surely taken his rightful place in the pantheon, alongside the other gods.

Gessen paged through his notes. Could the trauma have originated from someone else? Another family member, a neighbour, a friend. Or was he simply grasping at straws, and there was truly nothing to uncover? A case of Gessen's own traumatic history colouring his judgement.

When Mathilde came into the room with his coffee and the day's mail, he leapt up to take the tray, welcoming the distraction.

'Shall I light the fire in the sitting room?' she asked. 'It's chilly today.'

The thermometer outside the window hovered just above zero. Chilly indeed. 'Thank you, Mathilde. If it's not too much trouble.'

'Not in the least, and it will do you good to sit by the fire. If you don't mind my saying, you look terribly worn out. When was the last time you took a proper holiday?'

He smiled. She knew the answer as well as he did. 'Two years ago?'

'More like seven.' She lingered in the doorway, her usually brisk expression softening. 'If you're not careful, you'll end up on the other side of that desk.'

She might be right. Yesterday, he'd been overwhelmed by desire to run away, to escape his fractious patients and gnawing worry about the fate of the clinic. It was true he hadn't had a holiday in ages, and he sometimes dreamed of sprouting wings and flying over the Alps to the warmer climes of Italy.

Years ago, not long after finishing his studies at the Sorbonne, he'd read a newspaper article about the plight of the swallows in Switzerland, too exhausted and hungry to make their migratory flight to the other side of the Alps. The weather so harsh that the exhausted birds were being gathered up in cages and flown in aeroplanes to their winter feeding grounds in sunny Ticino. The favourite bird of his first and only love, and the clinic's namesake. At the time he'd wondered, with a pang of sadness, if Sophie might have read the same article, and imagining her gratitude at the quirky generosity of the Swiss. Transporting the birds over the very mountains he could see outside his window, because they were unable to make the journey on their own.

He met Mathilde's questioning glance and suppressed his habitual response. It was their old argument. Though a good ten years his junior, she'd been his faithful aide-de-camp for many years, and her maternal chiding was woven into their dynamic. 'By the way,' he hesitated, 'has Ursula said anything to you?'

'What about?' Her look was inscrutable.

Their usual game of don't ask, don't tell.

'You mean that ring on her finger?' Her look was sympathetic. 'I wouldn't worry. She'll tell you when she's ready.'

He considered asking her to join him for coffee, but she

had her own work to do and he couldn't keep putting off the business of the day. Seated by the fire, he poured out the coffee and sifted through his stack of mail, pausing at a letter postmarked Toronto. In the search for Vidor's family, he'd written to a number of women in Canada and the US, after Vidor let drop that one of his sisters had emigrated to North America. Though his letter campaign felt like trying to hit a target with a fistful of pebbles, perhaps he'd struck the bullseye on the first attempt. He slit open the envelope and smoothed the letter on his knee.

Toronto, Canada
20 November 2008

Dear Dr Gessen,
My apologies for the delay in replying to your letter of 12 November. I was out of the country for several weeks, and only returned the day before yesterday to a chilly house and a stack of mail teetering on the table in the front hall.
At first, I couldn't make any sense of your letter and assumed there must be some mistake. Crossed wires, you might call it, or perhaps simply a question of one of those computer searches gone wrong. It happens quite often these days, I understand, what with old classmates and former lovers anxious to rekindle memories best left in the past where they belong. When I read your letter, my first thought was that I didn't know anyone named Vidor Kiraly.
As to the matter of that gentleman being a relation of mine, I could by some stretch of the imagination accept that your Mr Kiraly was a distant cousin from the old country looking to reconnect. Vidor is certainly a common name in Hungary, as is the family name Kiraly (and my middle name, if that's of interest), but my family name is Molnar (Miller in English, so you

can imagine how many of us there are). I didn't change it when I married my late husband. Quite a modern thing to do in those days, but I was a bit of a rebel in my youth and with my husband having a plain old Anglo-Saxon name, I didn't care to lose the part of my heritage I held so dear. I have fond memories of my early life in Budapest – I was fourteen when we emigrated to France – and it was part of family lore that, no matter where fate took us, we would always be proud Magyars.

But after tucking your letter into a drawer in the writing desk where I pay my bills, I thought nothing more of it until yesterday, while walking on the old bridle path through a lovely wood. Out of nowhere, it struck me that the Vidor Kiraly you mentioned could indeed be someone my family knew, and the mix-up due to my brother's name being Vida, a variant of Vidor. Your Vidor would be the right age to have been a friend of my brother. He was always known as Vida, though his full name was Vidor Péter Molnar. Péter was my mother's name before she married. It was a common practice to use the mother's family name as a child's middle name.

Even so, the person you're looking for couldn't possibly be my brother. He died of virulent meningitis at the age of twelve. A terrible tragedy for my family. My mother took to her bed and stayed there for months. So long ago it was, but the memory of that terrible time has stayed with me, just as clear as if it happened last week. Strange to think that if Vida had lived, he'd be in his late fifties now.

I'm sorry I couldn't be of any more help to you. I emigrated to Canada almost forty years ago and am as settled here as anywhere on this green earth. With each passing year, my former life seems to fade into the mists. He was a lovely boy, our Vida. It gives me comfort to think that his brief time on earth might be preserved, like a butterfly under glass, in someone else's memory.

The rain is coming down in buckets. I must sign off now and hurry to shut the windows.

Yours sincerely,
Anna Kiraly Molnar

Gessen tucked the letter into Vidor's ever-growing file. A pity. But nothing ventured, nothing gained. What he should do was ask Vidor point blank where his sisters were living. But he doubted Vidor would be so forthcoming. Not when it was obvious Gessen wanted to contact his family members to dig up salacious details on Vidor's life.

If he didn't make any progress in the next few sessions, he would have to pull out his trump card. Inform Vidor that the man he attacked in Copenhagen had subsequently died, and that his own life and liberty were on the line. It was a risky tactic, so he would have to tread carefully. Vidor might fabricate a horrific event from his past that resulted in chronic post-traumatic stress. Or he could easily fake additional episodes of psychosis, muddying the waters even more. Whatever trauma Vidor came up with would be difficult to corroborate, and where would that leave him? Colluding with Vidor, intentionally or not, to have him absolved of the crime of killing an innocent man.

If he wanted to get anywhere, he would have to do some more sleuthing into Vidor's past on his own. The next obvious place was Paris. Vidor's home after the flight from Budapest, and though decades had passed since he moved away, if Gessen were lucky, he might find someone who'd known Vidor as a child.

Gessen hated being away from the clinic, even under the best of circumstances. It didn't help that he was currently at loggerheads with Ismail. Someone needed to rein the boy in before he did anything stupid. And only yesterday, his

Munchausen's patient had managed to land herself in the infirmary. Though her personal attendant swore she watched Babette like a hawk, she'd somehow found time to swallow a handful of gravel, necessitating an emergency endoscopy. A crude form of self-harm, at best, but it got her the thing she craved most: a great deal of fuss, and the staff attending to her every need. Before Gessen went anywhere, he would have to scold Hélène, once again, about yanking Vidor's chain. While it might seem amusing, she was making a difficult situation worse.

Ursula would have to handle all this, and more, during the few days he would be away. At least she'd agreed, if reluctantly, to his latest plan to get Vidor to talk. Hopefully, upon his return, he'd have something to work with. Heavy snows were forecast in the coming days. He studied the darkening sky, beset with misgivings, and hoping the trip to Paris wouldn't turn out to be another dead end.

20

When had he last been in Paris? Years ago, it must be now, when he was invited to give the keynote lecture at a conference at the Palais des Congrès. Late spring it was, with the horse chestnut trees flaunting their pink and cream blossoms in a frothy mass along the Seine, as the city hummed with the portent of summer. Now, in late November, the trees' blossoms were long gone, and an amber light shone on the dying leaves as he trod along a gravel path in the Jardin du Luxembourg.

He exited the park at the Odéon gate and checked his watch, pleased to see there was enough time to pass through the gardens of the Cluny Museum, though not enough to duck inside to view the tapestries. During his first year at the Sorbonne, in thrall to the city's delights, he liked to sit in a quiet corner of the garden, amongst the flowers and bees, with a book open on his lap. Forty years later, the thrill Paris once gave him flickered to life.

Such was his affection for the city of his youth that he'd even considered bringing Fernanda along, simply for the joy of watching her explore the park. As he scuffed his feet through the falling leaves, he imagined her bounding up to the other dogs, out for a morning stroll, when the air was crisp and mist hung in the boughs. But he'd thought better of it, and just as well. This wasn't a holiday, and he was obliged to direct his energy towards solving the mystery of Vidor Kiraly.

With any luck, and a little prodding, the city would reveal the information he sought.

Having a few minutes to spare on his way to see Bertrand, a school chum from his Sorbonne days, he swung by the magnificent library's reading room. With its ornate, blue-painted ceiling and subterranean light, it had been his favourite place to study. Between lectures, he would sit at the end of a highly polished table, breathing in the hush, as he turned over the pages of his philosophy texts. While this trip visit to Paris was a fact-finding mission about Vidor's past, and not a trip down memory lane, as long as he was in the city, it wouldn't hurt to visit some of his old haunts.

The air vibrated with the hush of intense concentration, as rows of students pored over their books. It was here, seated at a table in the back, that he'd first spotted Sophie, her cloud of golden hair creating a halo of light in the dense atmosphere. *This time of year it was, or close enough.* Early December, just before the end of term, and the library was heavy with the smell of damp wool. She'd worn a sweater the colour of the evening sky, and a red scarf looped around her neck. Flustered, he'd knocked a book to the floor, and when she looked up their eyes met. A flash of recognition like a jolt of electricity.

C'est toi. There you are. It was the girl who'd been drifting through his dreams of late, though he couldn't fathom who she might be, or why she'd infiltrated his slumber. Nearly forty years ago, yet the pain had never left him. The story of their love contained in the simple words, *if only... Si seulement.* The two saddest words in any language. If only he didn't feel things so strongly. If only he had been the son of a different man, she would have been his wife.

Gessen blinked, and the vision was gone. Across the years Sophie had lived on in his imagination as a young woman, though she'd be nearly sixty now. Married, surely, perhaps a grandmother. A wave of regret passed over him like a fog. How young he'd been, how delirious with heartache. Begging her to run away with him, to Canada or America or New Zealand. Anywhere they could start a new life, far from the curse of history.

He should have known that no matter where he turned, there was no escaping the poisonous legacy in his blood. After he'd smashed their dreams to bits, with no explanation for his behaviour, her parents had whisked a heartbroken Sophie away to their country house in Normandy. When she returned to the university in the autumn, thin and lifeless, she met with him once at a nearby cafe, her speech wooden, her eyes flat. He refused to tell her the real reason he'd broken their engagement, having vowed to tell no one about his past. But he couldn't bear the idea of her believing he was a cad. So he told her a watered-down version of the truth, clasping her hand as he whispered the vile story in her ear. She'd said it didn't matter to her, that love conquered all. But that wasn't the point. It mattered to him, and after his wrenching split from Sophie, he'd made a solemn vow to never marry, to never have children. He would be the end of the line.

* * *

By the time Gessen reached his friend's office, he was a few minutes late, and a student with scraggly hair and a wild look in his eye was just coming through the door. The boy could have been Gessen's twin, forty years ago, his mind teeming, the thirst for knowledge unquenchable. He knocked and pushed open the door.

'Anton.' Bertrand sprang from behind his desk and kissed Gessen noisily on both cheeks. 'It's been too long.'

'Indeed, it has.' Bertrand had scarcely changed, though. Still thin as a wire, and vibrant as ever. Only the greying hair at his temples betrayed his age.

Bertrand moved a stack of papers from a chair. 'Please have a seat. I just need to send a couple of emails.' He removed his glasses and rubbed his eyes. 'Wretched admin, I'll never get used to it.'

Gessen scanned the bookshelf while he waited. How

different his life would have turned out if he'd stuck with his youthful plan to study philosophy and mathematics instead of switching to medicine. Even now, he kept a much-thumbed edition of Marcus Aurelius's *Meditations* in the top drawer of his desk. Often turning to it after a difficult day or a particularly trying session with a patient.

The clatter of the keyboard, a long, drawn-out sigh. '*Fini.*' Bertrand pushed his chair back and stood. 'Let's have a coffee somewhere.' He grabbed his jacket from a hook by the door. 'I'd like to escape before some student bumbles in with yet another complaint.' He hustled Gessen into the hall. 'I don't remember being so spoiled at that age. We just got on with things, didn't we?' He flung his arm around Gessen's shoulders. 'All fired up, weren't we? With our fierce desire to burn down the world and create a new one from the ashes.'

Out on the pavement, Bertrand hesitated. 'Shall we go to our usual place, for old time's sake? It's been tarted up a bit, but the coffee's still good.'

Bertrand strode across the boulevard, talking over his shoulder as Gessen tried to match his loping stride. He couldn't help but smile. Here they were again. Tall, lanky Bertrand striding ahead, with Gessen trotting behind, like a younger brother trying to keep up.

At this time of day, just after four, the cafe was quiet. The marble-topped tables looked improbably the same, and the waiters still wore waistcoats and imperious expressions. But the rack of newspapers was gone, and the once plain walls were stencilled in a design of silvery-blue filigree. A group of students clustered around a table in the back corner, intent on their conversation. Two women, probably tourists, judging by the shopping bags at their feet, occupied the table by the window.

When their coffee was set in front of them, with a pleasing click of porcelain against stone, Gessen breathed in the steam before stirring sugar in his cup. After a minute or two of exchanging pleasantries and asking about each other's lives, he brought up the reason he'd come to the city.

'I've been working with a new patient,' he said. 'Quite an unusual case. Though I'm having trouble getting him to cooperate in his own treatment.'

Bertrand studied Gessen over the rim of his coffee cup, eyebrows raised, but said nothing. Gessen could practically hear the comforting whir of his friend's thoughts.

'It appears to be a case of either severely repressed trauma, or even a split identity. Though such cases are exceedingly rare.' He knocked back his coffee. 'And it's not an easy disorder to make sense of, under any circumstances.' After a pause, Gessen continued. 'He seems to have suffered a temporary psychosis and attacked a stranger unprovoked. I've been working with him for nearly a month, and even though the man is in serious trouble, he's resisted our every attempt to help him.'

Bertrand ran his hand through his thatch of hair. 'Do you remember your Socrates? "Sometimes you put walls up, not to keep people out, but to see who cares enough to break them down."'

It was a quote Gessen vaguely remembered from their student days. Very apropos, and so like Bertrand to have a suggestion at the ready.

'The thing is,' he said, trying to put his thoughts into words, 'I keep having the sense that I've met the patient before.' His attention was distracted by the sound of laughter from the student table. 'He grew up in Paris, and it isn't farfetched to imagine I might have bumped into him somewhere, perhaps in one of the cafes by the Sorbonne – even this one – though he claims it's unlikely. He says he left for Cambridge about the same time I arrived in the city.'

'Someone you knew?' Bertrand signalled the waiter for another round of espressos. 'How strange the wheels of fate. Fontaine would have been pleased.'

'That he grew up in Paris and left for England at eighteen appears to be the case.' Gessen flicked a crumb from the table. 'But he has this odd tic. Once or twice, while we were in session and I was pushing him to tell me about his father, he reached

110

up absently and flicked his ear, like this.' Gessen demonstrated. 'While I was on the train, I was thinking about my first weeks at the Sorbonne and I remembered this student in one of my philosophy lectures who always sat at the back of the room. Once, I came in late and took a seat behind him. I noticed he wasn't taking any notes, but when another student interrupted the lecturer and launched into a heated argument his shoulders tensed, and he flicked his ear. Exactly like my patient.'

'The plot thickens.' Bertrand's face grew animated. 'The Case of the Nervous Tic. Perhaps your patient has a doppelgänger. The mysterious double we're all supposed to have, somewhere. Or, maybe it's an Ankou.'

'On cue?' Once again, Bertrand had lost him.

'In Breton mythology, the Ankou is the servant of Death. Or henchman, if you prefer, and is sometimes described as the personification of another's soul. A skeletal or shadowy figure who assists in the collection of the dead.' Bertrand paused to sip his coffee. 'For the one who hears it, the cart's squeaking wheel is thought to be a harbinger of death.'

Gessen felt a chill. 'I'm fairly sure my patient is alive.' He smiled at his friend.

Bertrand's gaze grew filmy as if he were receding into the past, then snapped back as he cocked his head to eavesdrop on the two American tourists complaining about the rudeness of the French. 'What makes you think that boy and your patient are the same person?'

Gessen stared at the dregs of his coffee, hoping to overcome the onerous fatigue he couldn't seem to shake. 'I can't put my finger on it. But there's something about his eyes that keeps troubling me. It could just be coincidence. Or an uncanny double, as you say.'

Bertrand patted Gessen on the arm. 'I've got an appointment with a student in thirty minutes, but why don't we meet later for dinner? My wife has a mind like a steel trap. Eveline might remember your mysterious boy.'

21

When he entered Bertrand's flat at half past six, Eveline had yet to arrive. As fellow international students at the Sorbonne, Gessen had only a brief acquaintance with the girl who would later become his friend's wife. While Bertrand poured him an aperitif, he filled Gessen in on the intervening years. After earning a dual degree in French Literature and Biology, Eveline went on to medical school and had made a career in infectious diseases.

At a quarter to seven she breezed through the door of the flat, a graceful woman with ash blonde hair and intelligent green eyes. In her fine wool trousers and dove-grey blouse, crisply pressed, it was difficult to picture her coming straight from a laboratory. She greeted her husband before turning to Gessen with a curious gaze. In manner and dress, she seemed more French than the French. Impossible to believe she hailed from a tiny village in Dorset. Not only did she speak like a native, but she'd also captured the expressions and body language of a born and bred *Parisienne*.

As she leaned in to kiss her husband and whisper something in his ear, Gessen felt the pang of everything he'd lost. Would he and Sophie have had such a life? A light-filled flat in Saint-Germain-des-Prés, two successful children, and a coterie of friends?

'Lovely to meet you properly at last,' Eveline said, fetching wine glasses from the cupboard. 'Funny we were in the same year at university and never got to know each other.'

Bertrand opened a bottle of Châteauneuf-du-Pape and set it on the counter to breathe, while Eveline placed a wedge of brie and glass bowl of olives on a platter. Gessen hung back. 'May I help in any way?'

'Absolutely not.' She smiled. 'You're our guest.' She shooed the two men into the salon.

All it took was a few minutes of reminiscing for the years to fall away, and they were students once again, with their talk ranging from books and music to politics and travel. It was the type of free-flowing conversation Gessen rarely had time for in his monastic existence in the mountains. But he waited until they'd finished their dinner, a delicious boeuf bourguignon, and were sipping Cointreau on the dark green sofa in the salon before broaching the topic of his mystery boy to Eveline. Such was the pleasure of their reunion, after so many years, it seemed gauche to throw cold water on their lively conversation. But he had little time to waste. Did Eveline remember an international student who'd attended the university in 1968 and '69, and then disappeared? Darkish hair, grey-green eyes. Rather slight in stature.

She pursed her lips. 'Possibly, though there weren't too many of us that year, were there? Forty or forty-five perhaps?' She smiled. 'I haven't thought about my student days in years.' She set her glass on the table. 'If you'll excuse me for a minute, I believe I have some old photos stashed away.'

Only after Eveline had gone to search her office did Gessen remember to ask Bertrand about their children.

'Fine, fine,' Bertrand said, topping up Gessen's glass. 'Henri is in his final year at Sciences Po and Amélie is doing a two-year graduate course in America.' He pointed to a row of photos on the credenza. 'There they are, all grown up.'

Gessen raised his glass, *Santé*, as the two old friends made the rueful smile of those entering the final third of their lives.

Eveline returned, brandishing a thick photo album above her head. 'Voila! I knew I had this somewhere.'

Bertrand cocked an eyebrow at Gessen. 'Lucky for you my wife is sentimental. Not to mention an incorrigible packrat. I chucked all my old stuff years ago.'

'Touché, *mon amour*.' Eveline blew him a kiss. 'But when we find Anton's mystery lad, who'll be laughing then?' She squeezed in next to Gessen on the sofa and placed the open album on her lap. 'That's me,' she said, pointing to a skinny girl in a purple-and-green knit dress with a black beret set jauntily on her blonde hair. 'Can you believe the beret? I thought it would make me fit in somehow, but of course no one was wearing them in 1968. Except for old men. I'm sure my fellow students had a massive giggle at my expense.'

She flipped through the pages of photos, mainly variations of Eveline and her friends, or snaps of Paris monuments and street scenes. 'This might be useful.' She drew closer to the lamp. 'It was taken at the introductory reception for international students. There were only eleven girls in our year, I believe. The dark-haired girl next to me was from Chile. Teresa, I think her name was. And that's you, right?' She passed the album to Gessen.

He stared at his own face, pasty and thin, and winced at the untidy mass of wavy hair, bell bottom denims and loud plaid shirt. How ridiculously young he was. Barely cooked, though his mind had been on fire, desperate to inhale great gulps of knowledge, like a starving man stuffing himself with delicacies. Still innocent, when the photo was taken, of the secret that would send him to the brink of hell.

He scanned the faces of the other boys, hoping one of them would spark something in his brain. That they all looked nearly identical didn't help. Those wide-lapelled shirts and dungarees, the same mop of straggly hair. Mick Jagger look-alikes.

In the third row, on the left, a boy looking away from the camera seemed vaguely familiar. During his first year at the

Sorbonne, Gessen had known all these students, at least by sight. But never a social butterfly, he'd attended at most one or two of the get-togethers for the foreign students. Painfully shy in those days, he was interested in books and learning, not parties. He flipped the page.

Eveline leaned against his shoulder. 'I think that's the end-of-term party for the first years. I didn't go to any more after that, mostly because I wanted to fit in, not be set apart as a foreign student.'

The light was poor and most of the students in the photo appeared loopy with drink or exhaustion from having survived exam week. Had he gone to that party? He couldn't remember now. His first year was a blur, arriving in the city full of hope, only to feel like a fish out of water amongst the sophisticated French. It hadn't helped that he was out of sorts, having left Switzerland rather abruptly. After arguing with his adoptive parents about their reluctance to talk about his real mother and father, or how he'd come to live with them.

But in this shot, there was one boy who could be the same as in the group photo, the one who'd turned his face away from the camera. In the party photo, the boy's gaze was directed at something behind the person taking the picture. With his hair pushed back, and his face turned away, the line of his forehead was clear, as was the shape of his nose. Was this the boy he was thinking of, the one who flicked his ear in the lecture hall?

He tapped the photo. 'Do you remember him?'

Eveline squinted. 'I think so. A bit of an odd duck, if I recall. Attended a couple of parties, but didn't mingle much and didn't drink. That stuck out, considering the rest of us were quaffing the free wine as if dying of thirst.'

'Do you recall his name?'

She pushed her hair off her face and closed her eyes. He waited. 'Something with an M perhaps or an N? Michael, or Nico? Wait!' Her eyes flew open. 'He spoke French.' She shook her head and laughed. 'But we all did, of course, some

with atrocious accents…' She squeezed her eyes shut. 'M…
Mikhail, maybe? He could have been Russian. Give me a
minute… No, it's gone.'

A heaviness fell over him. Just as he feared. Too far in
the past, and the boy too inconspicuous to have made an
impression.

At Eveline's suggestion, they went out for dessert and
espresso at a bistro down the street. Pleasant as the evening
was, Gessen sensed he was beginning to wear out his welcome.
It was nearly eleven and Eveline's eyes showed signs of
fatigue. When they'd finished their crème brûlée, Bertrand
set his fork on his plate and pushed back his chair. Sadly, their
time together was drawing to a close. At the corner they would
part, Gessen to his hotel, his friends to their flat.

Bertrand held his wife's elbow as they passed along the
pavement, quiet now that the blustery weather had forced all
but the intrepid indoors. The wind rattled the branches of the
lindens overhead. The chilly air was damp with impending rain.

As Bertrand steered them along a narrow street, they
passed a Vietnamese restaurant and a Lebanese takeaway.
In an alley by a sushi place, two yellow-eyed cats waited
for scraps. Eveline stopped short, and Gessen nearly bumped
into her.

'I remember now.' She turned, her eyes shining. 'Milen.
That was the boy's name. Not Michael or Mikhail, but Milen.
I'm pretty sure of it. It just popped into my head. I've been
thinking of that party ever since we left the flat, and I could
see it like a film in my head. That boy skulking in the corner,
so shy and awkward he was practically feral. I think he might
have been from Albania, or maybe Malta? Someone tossed
a crumpled paper cup in his direction and shouted his name.
Milen. *Attention*! Or something like that.'

Milen. It didn't quite ring a bell, but it was a start.

Her forehead crinkled in a frown. 'Does that help? Maybe
if I had more details…'

'It certainly does,' Gessen said. Impulsively, he leaned in

and kissed her on the cheek. 'I'm sorry to be so mysterious. I would tell you more if I could, but doctor–patient confidentiality prevents me from saying too much. If it turns out that my suspicions are right, this Milen person could provide a clue.'

'A high-profile case, is it?' Bertrand gave him a questioning glance.

Had he said that, or was his friend fishing for more? Bertrand loved a good story. When Gessen didn't respond, he pressed him again. 'What makes you suspect your patient could be the boy from the Sorbonne?'

'I'm not sure, exactly.' He hesitated. 'It's just a hunch.'

When Bertrand paused to look into a shop window, Eveline leaned in close and touched his arm. 'It's Vidor Kiraly, isn't it?' She met his eyes.

Gessen's thoughts spun. How could she possibly have guessed?

'Sorry, I know it's confidential, but Bertrand mentioned your high-profile patient had attacked a stranger unprovoked.' She lowered her voice. 'It's all anyone can talk about in the lab, so I put two and two together.' Eveline glanced behind her. 'We've never met, but I do have a story about him that might help your case. Last year, just before the Nobel Prizes were announced, a bunch of us were sitting around trying to guess who might be tipped for the prize in Medicine or Physiology when Kiraly's name came up.

'Everyone was sure he would win. I can only imagine how disappointed he was not to get the call, but then he won the Søgaard, which is the next best thing, though I imagine it might have felt like a consolation prize.' She looked behind her again. Bertrand had pulled out a notebook and was jotting something down. 'We were at a cafe having drinks after work, so you might want to take this with a grain of salt, but a visiting scientist from Budapest said flat out that Kiraly wasn't Hungarian. He'd met him at a conference in Berlin, apparently, and said that while Kiraly's mastery of Hungarian was excellent, he would bet a whole stack of money that it wasn't his mother tongue.'

Gessen stared at her. Not his mother tongue? 'Perhaps, after forty years in England, I can only imagine that…'

Eveline shook her head. 'You wouldn't forget key expressions or idioms or tonal inflections. Look at me, I've spoken French exclusively since I was nineteen, but when I visit my family in the UK, no one would suspect I spoke anything other than English.' She gave him a steady look. 'It's something to think about anyway.' As Bertrand approached, she brought a finger to her lips. 'Mum's the word.'

After thanking his friends for their hospitality, Gessen turned in the direction of his hotel, his head buzzing with wine and the shock of Eveline's pronouncement. But if Vidor wasn't Hungarian, then where did he come from? It wasn't illegal to change one's name or adopt a nationality not one's own. But what might have spurred Vidor to do so? In his own case, Gessen was not his birth name, either. He had acquired it later from his adoptive father. Though now a Swiss national, he'd been born overseas. The change in paperwork orchestrated by his mother, shortly before she disappeared.

Whatever the case, it fit with his own suspicions that Vidor at one time could have gone by another name or hailed from a different background. But why the switch, and when was it made? Whatever Vidor's name might once have been, the puzzle remained. When – or how – had the transformation from a socially awkward student, possibly named Milen, to the worldly Vidor Kiraly taken place?

22

A shadow covered the sun, and Vidor looked up to see the Emirati Prince, not two metres away, blocking his light. Libby stood by his side, so close they were nearly touching. She shaded her eyes with her hand as they watched a group of attendants huddled in the distance. Around them quivered an air of alarm.

'I bet one of the patients has escaped,' Ismail said. His cut-glass accent pierced the thin air. Educated abroad, it would seem, old-school style. Probably to prepare him for the rigours of running one of those tiny oil kingdoms built on a bed of shifting sands.

'Who's escaped?' Vidor couldn't help but interrupt. He didn't like the look that boy was giving Libby, or the way they were standing with their shoulders practically touching. The attendants were doing a poor job of being discreet as they stooped to peep in the shrubbery.

'The woman with the handbag would be my guess.' Ismail turned to scrutinise the nervous staff. 'I've seen her talking to whatever it is she carries around in that bag… gives me the creeps.' He bumped Libby with his shoulder. 'You haven't got any fags, have you? Bloody rules. I'd kill for a smoke.'

Libby smiled at Vidor. She seemed happier than the last time he saw her, though he hoped she wasn't falling for this playboy. A lad like that would snap her heart in two. And how would heartbreak help her recover from whatever sadness had brought her here?

So, Hélène had done a runner? He suppressed a smile. The old girl was wilier than he'd thought. But where could she have gone? The only way off the mountain was the funicular, and the operator wouldn't have taken her down without a pass. He hoped she hadn't flung herself off an escarpment, though it was unlikely. And what of the handbag? Would she have taken it with her? He hadn't thought she'd be one to flout the rules, but what did he know? Behind those placid, yellow-flecked eyes might lurk a mind like a well-oiled machine.

If only he had the good sense – or courage – to slip away, consequences be damned. In his session yesterday with Dr Lindstrom, he had once again begged her for help, pleading to the point of humiliation that she convince Gessen he should be allowed to return to his life. An uncharacteristic outburst of anger at a stranger, in a long and blameless life, was not reason enough to keep him locked up. He had even confessed to her his greatest fear: that Gessen had no intention of letting him go, and that he would be a prisoner here for ever.

With a deep sense of foreboding, he hauled himself from the chair and headed towards his chalet.

'Hey, wait up. You're Victor, right?'

He returned Ismail's smile with a flat stare. 'Vidor.'

'Well, Vidor, Libby and I have a bet going about where you're from.'

She swatted his arm. 'No, we don't.' She appealed to Vidor. 'He's just kidding.'

'So, tell us who's right. My guess is Afghanistan. Or maybe Iran.'

Vidor's heart flipped. *Afghanistan.* Whatever gave him that idea? 'If you must know,' he said stiffly, 'I'm a full-blood Hungarian. My family are Magyars from centuries back. Though we might, like so many,' he said, trying to take the edge off his annoyance, 'have a little Genghis Khan mixed in.'

'So, I was right, then.' Ismail cocked an eyebrow. 'Wasn't he a Persian bloke?'

Too clever by half. His monthly allowance was probably more than the GDP of some African countries. 'And you? I take it you're from where… Dubai, or is it Kuwait?' Normally, it took a great deal to ruffle him, but something about the boy got under his skin.

Ismail stuffed his hands in the pockets of his coat and winked at Libby. 'I mostly grew up here.' He pointed his chin towards the horizon. 'Geneva. My father's a diplomat. But I went to school in England.' He gazed at Vidor with those inscrutable eyes. 'So where did you learn to speak Arabic, then?'

What was the lad going on about? In a nervous gesture, Vidor reached up and flicked his ear. 'I speak several languages, but Arabic isn't one of them.'

'Is that so? *Umuk majnuna, wa abuk khinzir.*'

The hard consonants pierced his skull, and he sucked in his breath. Though he couldn't understand their meaning, the words were clearly an insult. Something about his father being a pig… though how would he know that?

Ismail laughed as Libby tugged his arm, leaving Vidor to wrestle with the mysterious rage coiled in his chest. *How dare he show up here to taunt me?*

23

With little more than a sketch of Vidor's history to work with, Gessen's only option was to seek out anyone who might have known him as a child. There must be someone residing in the vast city of Paris who remembered the Kiraly family in the late fifties and sixties. At the entrance to the Métro at Saint-Germain-des-Prés, he sent a quick text to Ursula: *Staying in Paris one more day. Call if you need anything.*

As he rumbled under the city, he tried to boost his spirits with the hope that buried deep in the municipal archives was a record of the Kiraly family's address. His online search had revealed that some 12,000 Hungarian immigrants were living in Paris in the late sixties. If luck was on his side, there wouldn't be too many Kiralys amongst them.

According to Vidor's somewhat vague recollections, his family had lived in a few different flats in the early years, before settling into their permanent home just after his tenth birthday. Vidor claimed he couldn't remember the exact address, though he did mention it was within walking distance of the catacombs. A frightening place to a young boy with a lively imagination, so he would go around the long way to avoid the entrance, especially after a school friend told him there were more skeletons of the dead lying under the city than people walking the streets above. In a rare moment of candour, Vidor had openly admitted to Gessen a horror of enclosed spaces and a fear of being buried alive.

A chilly rain splattered the pavement as his taxi pulled up to the *mairie* in the fourteenth arrondissement. A stone's throw from the entrance to the catacombs, it was as good a place as any to start. Deaths, marriages, and births would all be recorded here, probably going back to the early days of the Republic. The woman behind the desk gave him the once-over with a jaundiced eye before disappearing into a back room and returning with a printout of the records from 1956 to 1970. He perched on a wooden chair while she went through the names. Kiraly? She pursed her mouth and squinted in the dim light. The beads on her necklace swung as she bent over the files.

He breathed in the damp air, suffused with centuries of facts and figures on the living and the dead. But it wasn't in vain. Seven families named Kiraly were listed as living in the quarter in that fourteen-year period. He paid the fee to receive a copy of the records and tucked it in his bag. He would look at them more closely in the pleasant surroundings of a cafe, rather than the chilly atmosphere of the *mairie*'s record room under the gaze of its sour-faced guardian.

* * *

The rain was slowing to a drizzle as he hunched his shoulders and headed towards the first address on his list, the rue Boulard, where a woman whose maiden name was Kiraly had once lived. She might be one of Vidor's four sisters. The dates were right, given that the eldest sister was seventeen when he was six, and the youngest was ten. Had Vidor been the much wanted and long-awaited son, or a surprise baby – pleasant or otherwise? The answer to that question could make a world of difference. In the course of his career, he'd seen far too often the disturbing results of growing up as an unwanted child.

He pressed the bell and, after stepping inside, he explained the situation to the *gardienne*, a crusty old woman who announced, with a measure of pride, that she'd held her post for forty-three years. A Hungarian family named Kiraly had indeed resided in the top-floor flat, but there were only two daughters, and no sons. He crossed the name off his list and headed out into the cold drizzle to the next address, where an unmarried woman with the surname Kiraly had lived from 1963 to '69. As he rounded the corner, a chilly wind buffeted his face and he squinted to locate the number of the building. When he pressed the bell, no one answered. The third address was another dead end. The rain was coming down hard now, and he was about to call it a day when, three blocks from the Métro, he stumbled upon the next address on his list, close to the entrance of the catacombs.

The *gardienne*, her eyes cloudy with cataracts, didn't remember any Kiralys, but she suggested he try the flat on the top floor, where the resident widow had lived since the early sixties. If anyone knew the history of the building, it was Madame Joubert. The *gardienne* would ring to ask if she was accepting callers.

He waited in the stuffy room, the air thick with the scent of lemon drops and stewed tea. A tabby cat lay curled on a crocheted cushion. A single teacup and saucer sat next to an ancient electric tea kettle. When the *gardienne* hung up the phone, she fixed him with a gelid eye. 'She's willing to see you. But she doesn't get many visitors these days, so mind you don't tire her out.' She waved her hand towards the hall. 'The lift is at the back. Sixth floor.' She crossed her arms and waited, as if expecting something more. Was she worried – or hoping – he was some kind of blackguard? A murderer, perhaps. Or a thief, at the very least. A little excitement to liven up her day. He bowed and wished her a *bon après-midi*.

The lift, no bigger than a coffin, rattled and jerked its way to the sixth floor. It opened with a metallic groan, and he stepped into the hallway. The faded maroon carpet smelled of dust. He knocked on the door to number 15 and waited. From the *gardienne*'s description he had the impression that Madame Joubert was a bed-ridden recluse, but the woman who opened the door had a gleam in her eyes and an impish smile.

'Ah, Monsieur. Do come in.' She led him into the salon and offered him a chair by the window. 'I'd just put the kettle on for tea when Madame Dubonnet telephoned to say I had a gentleman caller. I hope she didn't give you any trouble. Rather an ogress, that one.' She winked. 'Or would you prefer an aperitif? My son-in-law sent me a bottle of a delicious *eau de vie* last month. Peach, I believe. It might make for a little taste of summer on this dreadful day.'

Gessen said he would have whatever she was having. So she vanished into the kitchen and returned in a moment with a tea tray. He leapt up to help her, but she shook her head. 'I'm not as decrepit as all that. It's only when I sit too long that my bones freeze up.'

She set the tray on the table and settled into a brocade armchair. Her fine, candy floss hair was coiled in a loose chignon. A jewelled brooch in the shape of a chameleon glinted on the collar of her blouse.

'Unusual, isn't it?' she said, catching his gaze. 'My late husband had it made for me. When the children were grown, I returned to school to study biology, and later on I trained to be a docent in herpetology at the Parc Zoologique. I was keen to study for an advanced degree earlier in my life, but my father was dead set against his only daughter tramping about the countryside in search of snakes and salamanders.'

At the mention of snakes, Gessen nervously eyed the terrarium on the window ledge.

She followed his gaze. 'No snakes over there, if you're wondering. I keep them in another room.' Her eyes crinkled with mirth. 'So many people are terrified of them.'

He swallowed. Snakes in the flat? Since he was a child, he'd had an atavistic fear of anything reptilian. Especially snakes.

'Just a couple of ordinary garden toads,' she said, pointing at the ledge by the window. 'Tristan and Isolde. Come spring,

I'll release them into a quiet corner of the Bois de Boulogne, but for now they make for very pleasant company.'

As intrigued as Gessen was by a woman who kept garden toads named Tristan and Isolde, he was afraid she might hold him captive for hours with her tales of amphibian delights. Best to get straight to the point, and then be on his way.

He bit into one of the tea cakes. Of course, it would be a madeleine. But no Proustian wave of memories coursed through his mind. Just thoughts of the matter at hand: to confirm Vidor's story of his flight from Hungary as a child.

'I'm looking for information about someone who used to live in this building,' Gessen said, setting his teacup on the table. 'According to civil records, a family named Kiraly lived here in the late fifties. If it's the one I'm looking for, they would have had four daughters and a son. The *gardienne* mentioned you were living here during that time.'

'Indeed I was.' She dabbed her lips with a tissue. 'I've been here for decades, though I spent my girlhood in Provence. My husband and I met during the war.' Her eyes clouded and she picked at a loose thread on the chair cushion. 'I sometimes wish I'd been born after it was all over, if only to be spared from the horror, but when we first came to Paris, the city was still recovering from the cataclysm. My husband found a cheap flat down the street from what had been the Gestapo's headquarters, during the occupation, but I couldn't bear to live there.'

She shivered violently, as if hearing the cries of the tortured. 'Flats were a bit more expensive in this *quartier*, but part of this street had been damaged in the fighting, and in this building the upper-floor flats were empty. We took this one because it had the best light. My husband was a talented artist and he had the idea of taking up his painting again, but he never managed it.' She lifted her teacup to her lips and set it down again. 'The poor man fell into a paralysing depression. At one point, things were so bad I suggested we emigrate to Canada, or even New Zealand, to start over. But he didn't believe in running away. So we stayed. But the seeds of flight were sown in the next generation. All three of our children live overseas. Two in Montreal, one in London.'

She shook herself from her reverie. 'I'm so sorry. Kiraly, did you say? What kind of name is that, Russian?'

'Hungarian.'

As she turned to look out the window, a shadow crossed her face. 'If I recall correctly, a Hungarian family did live on the first floor. But I don't believe their name was Kiraly. Something that started with an S, if memory serves. I didn't know them well, only to nod to in the vestibule.' She rubbed her forehead. 'S... something. Soros, perhaps?' She squeezed her eyes shut. 'Once or twice a piece of their mail was delivered to me by mistake. I can just about see the name on the envelope. Sov... something.' Her eyes snapped open. 'Sovàny. *C'est ça*. A Jewish family, I believe. One of the few who escaped the camps.' Her lids fluttered and she dabbed her mouth with a napkin. 'One time, when I took one of the letters down to her, Mrs Sovàny invited me in for tea. I declined, however, as I could hear a heated argument going on at the back of the flat. It sounded like two of the children were quarrelling, a boy and a girl.'

'So, there was a boy?' Gessen's ears pricked up.

'Yes, I believe so.'

'Do you remember his name?'

She shook her head. 'A slight boy, if I'm not mistaken. Hair the colour of horse chestnuts.' She fiddled with the chameleon brooch. 'I'm sorry I'm not much help to you.' Her eyes filmed over. 'It was so long ago.'

He assured her she'd been a great help, indeed, and thanked her for her time. To show his appreciation for inviting him into her home, he forced himself to approach the terrarium to admire Tristan and Isolde, though the creatures' warty skin and oddly intelligent eyes gave him gooseflesh. Ever since he was a child, following a nasty incident with a garden snake, he'd been wary of reptiles, even the supposedly benign ones.

Another dead end was his first thought, as he exited the building. Though it might be a lead, after all. The name wasn't right, but the presence of a Hungarian family in the flat might be a thread he could follow. His futile search, thus far, through the rain-swept streets had stripped him of whatever energy he'd felt when he'd boarded the train for Paris in the predawn darkness. But he still had three more addresses on his list. One of them might be the very one he was looking for.

24

Paris, France
October 1968

The party is already in full swing by the time he slinks through
the door at twenty past seven. His plan is to make a brief
appearance, mingle for a few minutes if absolutely necessary,
then slip away. He didn't want to come at all, but when his
roommate arrived home with yet another girl in tow, it seemed
best to make himself scarce.

The invitation for the party arrived last week at his student
flat. A heavy white card, engraved with black calligraphy,
requested the pleasure of his company at a reception for the
first-year foreign students. The dress code stipulated jackets
and ties for the boys, dresses for the girls. Wearing a jacket
and tie to lectures had been done away with as part of the
student unrest in May. But for a formal soiree, it made sense
not to appear in sloppy jeans and a ripped T-shirt.

In a borrowed suit jacket and burgundy tie, slightly frayed
at the ends, he slides his hand along the sweeping balustrade.
As he ascends the winding staircase, his palms prickle with
sweat. Classical music filters into the hall. A faculty member
with a beard and black-rimmed glasses is in the middle of

a speech when he ducks into the grand salon and finds an empty place at the back, trying not to gawp at the grandeur of the sculpted ceiling and gold filigree. Tuxedoed waiters circulate with trays of drinks and hors d'oeuvres, under a blaze of lights from the crystal chandeliers. His terror mounts as he scans the clusters of students deep in conversation, pausing from their animated chatter to drink from their wine glasses. He hangs back on the sidelines, waiting for the right moment to slip out the door. When a waiter passes him with a tray, he accepts a glass of sparkling water, only to discover he's chosen champagne by mistake. He holds it awkwardly in his hands.

The odour pricks his nostrils, and when he ventures a sip, the taste is pleasantly sweet. After drinking half, his limbs feel lighter and his jaw loosens. Though it's only the second time he's drunk liquor in his life, he's heard about alcohol being a social lubricant. Now he understands. He twirls the empty glass in his hand and smiles. Only to look away nervously as he catches sight of a girl staring at him. Her long, dark hair is brushed back from her forehead and held by a clip. The green-and-orange paisley dress reveals a great deal of leg. Is she about to come over? He feels a flash of panic.

If she asks, he will tell her his name is Manuel and that he hails from a village in southern Spain. After the humiliation during his first week in Paris, when those three girls invited him to join them for a drink, he's sworn off telling anyone his real name or where he is from. His Spanish is rusty, which might give him away, but they're supposed to speak French together anyway.

A blonde girl in a blue dress and string of white beads keeps looking his way. She's about to head over when a plump boy with dark, springy hair smoothed down with pomade hijacks her attention. Another girl, sporting a black beret and dressed in a lumpy crocheted vest over a short green skirt, casts him a friendly glance. One oddball to another is how he interprets it. But he's too afraid to talk to her. His hands are sweaty, the necktie too tight. What he wants most is to flee.

Misfit that he is, what is he doing here, anyway? Why had he ever thought he had the right to be in this gilded room, an impoverished boy from a backwards country, stranded amongst the gilt and crystal? A peasant whose origins would be exposed the moment he opened his mouth. The girl in the black beret looks too smart to fall for his claim of Spanish heritage. Maybe, if he's lucky, no one will ask. It's not as if they're wearing nametags with their personal histories branded in ink.

Manuel. He practises the name under his breath. She's coming his way, and he panics. *Breathe*, he counsels himself. *Breathe and you'll be fine. Manuel.* He tries out the sound on an exhalation of breath. Here she comes. He remembers to smile. *Je m'appelle Manuel. Enchanté de faire ta connaissance.*

25

Clinique Les Hirondelles
Saint-Odile, Switzerland
27 November 2008

A heavy snowfall, the first of the season, had blanketed the valley in a layer of white. Vidor dragged his feet behind the fidgety lad who escorted him to the arts building on the other side of the Zen garden. After depositing him at the door like an unwanted package, the attendant gave him an odd look and scuttled away.

The air inside the brightly lit room smelled of chalk and turpentine. He'd never had art at school, and no memory of making mud pies or finger-painting as a child. For as long as he could remember, it was the world of chemistry and biology, and the workings of the brain that set his curiosity on fire. Numbers and patterns, the circuitry of perception. And the sheer wonder of the neuronal axon potential, without which complex life forms would not exist. Across the room on a low shelf, a row of seashells and fossils and minerals glinted in the morning light.

Neither Gessen nor Dr Lindstrom had explained how art therapy might improve his mental health. Whatever it took to get back home, he was willing to try. With an extensive report on his current research findings due at the Worthington Foundation by mid-December, he could only hope that Farzan, or one of his other graduate students, had taken over the task. If he missed the deadline, he could lose millions in funding. Surely that man he'd attacked in Copenhagen had been back home for weeks now, and no harm done. So why shouldn't he return to his work as if nothing had happened? In his absence, that idiot Dodson was surely plotting to usurp Vidor's position as department chair. A young Machiavelli, not to mention a whiny bastard. Just the thought of that man running rampant over his domain made the bile rise in his throat.

* * *

A woman in a hand-knit sweater the colour of dried leaves appeared from the depths of a supply cupboard. 'You are Vidor, yes?' She strode forward and clasped his hand. 'I am Isabelle. Welcome.' Her red-and-orange embroidered skirt swished around her legs. Gold earrings swung in her ears.

'Beautiful, isn't it?' She gestured at the window. 'Wonderful light. A good day to make art. Come.' She took his arm and led him to a large table by the window. In the currents of air he caught a whiff of her perfume. A musky odour of cardamom and cloves that made his head spin. An exotic scent… he'd smelled it before, but where? An old-world fragrance, reminiscent of incense, or something from an Asian bazaar.

Last night he'd slept badly, having been woken from uneasy dreams by someone banging on the door to his room. He'd stumbled out of bed in terror, but when he opened the door, no one was there. A full moon was shining in the black sky, and he stepped onto the terrace in his slippers to listen. Nothing but the rustle of small creatures in the underbrush, and the mournful hoot of an owl. Before crawling back to bed he counted, three times, the sandpipers in the painting on the wall, each time coming up with only nine birds. Where was the tenth? He woke in the morning, bleary with fatigue, only to find to his consternation that ten birds skittered along the sand in the receding tide. It was this place. If he wasn't mad before, he would be soon if he didn't find a way to break free. As long as that damn watercolour in his room played tricks with his mind, the last thing he wanted was to create a painting of his own.

'Vidor?'

Her eyes, amber and gold, like a lynx, swam into view. 'Would you like a glass of water. Or perhaps some tea? I always keep a kettle going.' She nipped into the anteroom and returned a moment later with two steaming mugs. 'My own secret blend, a recipe from my village. Mountain herbs picked by hand. Very calming.' She handed him a mug. 'Now, tell me about yourself.' They settled onto high wooden stools in front of an easel. 'Have you ever made art? Painting and sketching, perhaps. Or maybe something with clay?'

Her expression was so earnest, he was ashamed to admit he was absolutely rubbish at creative expression and had never so much as doodled with a pencil during a department meeting.

'Don't worry. Anyone can make art.' She tapped her sternum. 'We all have a Michelangelo inside.' On the table she placed a pad of heavy paper and a number of implements. Pencils, chalk, brushes, finger-paints. 'Are you right-handed?' He nodded. 'Then I suggest you try drawing with your left hand to start. But first, we do some breathing and visualisation exercises. This wakes up the right side of your brain, you see?' She tapped her head and smiled. 'Then I'll leave you alone to make your art.'

She slipped behind him, 'May I?' and pressed her right hand on his abdomen and the left on the small of his back. 'Eyes closed. Deep breaths.' He closed his eyes and breathed in the scent of her perfume. But as his lungs filled with air, a familiar darkness descended, followed by a whoosh and a whisper, like bats at dusk. His knees sagged.

'That's right. Deep breaths, in and out. Picture your diaphragm, how it pushes the air out of your lungs. Feel the oxygen flooding into each of your cells. Breath is life. Never forget this. Without breath, we die.'

Vidor breathed in, breathed out, feeling absurd. But the weight of her hand on his belly was comforting, and at last the rustle and chatter in his head began to recede. In spite of the calming effect of this silly exercise, he had little belief it would provide him with the artistic impulse he lacked. If a Michelangelo was indeed coiled inside him like a snail, they had yet to meet.

The clouds broke, and sunlight streamed into the room, that diamond-sharp light so peculiar to the Alps, though a close cousin to the intense shimmer of the high desert. A camel caravan, plodding through the dunes, flashed before his eyes. But that was absurd. He'd never been to the desert. A city boy, he'd known little of life outside the bustle and noise of the streets. Women laden with purchases from the market stalls. Dusty alleys. The clatter of donkeys' hooves on the sun-baked stones. He closed his eyes. No, that couldn't be right. There were no donkeys in Budapest. It was the old familiar dream come to life. The strange nocturnal visitation he'd been having off and on for years. A desert plain baking in the noonday sun. A flat blue sea winking on the horizon. Wooden carts rattling through the streets, sour with dung and sweat, punctuated by a melodious wail, summoning the workers from the fields as the sun slipped below the mountains.

He rubbed his eyes and blinked to find himself alone in the room. When he turned to the easel, he started. A drawing, executed in chalk, aglow with the shades of ochre and umber. To the left, the sea was a hard slash of blue on the horizon. To the right, a range of sand-coloured hills faded into the distance. A lone figure, head bent, his face in shadow, gazed at the sea. What was this? He picked it up, intending to tear it into pieces when Isabelle appeared from nowhere and plucked it from his hands.

'Let me have a look. Why, it's wonderful.' She beamed, as if he were a child who'd made a handprint in clay.

Vidor squeezed the bridge of his nose. 'I don't…' He had no memory of making the sketch. And where did such a scene come from? 'I've never been to the desert.'

'When the muse awakens… ' She gave him a mischievous look. The beads on her necklace clacked as she pinned his drawing to the wall. 'You do not mind? When the sky is grey, your beautiful drawing will remind me of a holiday I once made to the Sinai many years ago. We rode camels in the desert with a Bedouin as our guide and slept under the stars. In the morning, the sand glowed like gold in the rising sun. Just like your painting.'

Hampered by a strange paralysis in his limbs, Vidor struggled to suck oxygen into his lungs. The scent of paint and turpentine was making him ill.

'You come back on Thursday, yes?'

He nodded dumbly without thinking. When was Thursday? What was today? A sharp pain stabbed his temple. One of his blinding headaches was coming on, and he hurried away to his room, where he could lie down in the dark and shut out the world.

* * *

Halfway to Montreux, Gessen gazed out the window at the clouds on the horizon as he mulled over his conversation with Madame Joubert. Another false lead, apparently, and without a new one, the trail had run cold. Perhaps Vidor had lied, and he hadn't lived anywhere near the catacombs as a child. It would have amused him to send his doctor off on a wild goose chase, though Vidor couldn't possibly know that he'd gone to Paris.

His phone beeped. Ursula. He took the call with a flicker of unease. She never rang during the rare times he was away, preferring he believe she could handle any situation on her own.

'I'm on the train. Is everything all right?' Her sharp intake of breath sounded loud in his ear.

'I'm afraid there's a bit of an issue.' Her voice broke up as they passed through a tunnel, and he strained to decipher her words. 'Nothing to panic about,' she said, 'but… I thought you should know that Ismail appears to have gone missing again. At first, I thought he was up to his old tricks, but when he didn't show up for lunch, I had the attendants do a quick search of the grounds. I checked with Thierry to see if he might have taken Ismail down to the village in the funicular, but he said not. So he must be here somewhere.'

Her voice was edged with panic, and Gessen willed himself to breathe.

'We didn't want to alarm the patients,' she said, 'but I did make a few discreet inquiries. He seemed perfectly fine during our session yesterday afternoon. But nobody's seen him today since breakfast. Mr Sendak is in a state.'

Gessen's heart flipped. Once again, Ismail had given his private bodyguard the slip. How could this have happened? After that earlier scare, when they thought he'd gone missing, the security around Ismail had been sharply increased, with a rota of attendants keeping an eye on him round the clock.

Perhaps the lad was just jerking his chain. Giving his bodyguard the slip again to show he was nobody's fool. He must have suspected from the start that Sendak had been hired by his father to keep him on a short leash. A source of bitter resentment. Imprisoned on all sides, was how Ismail described it. Accusing Gessen of siding with his father in a ploy to keep him trapped in the mountains. Presumably for a great wad of cash – his father's usual form of bait – when there wasn't a thing wrong with him. He'd practically spit the words in Gessen's face, during the first of these painful conversations. The desire to choose his own path in life, Ismail fumed, rather than take over the reins of his father's hateful business, was not a mental illness.

'I'll be there in two hours. Ismail couldn't have got very

far, so try not to worry. And get Mr Sendak to help you. That's what he's paid for.'

Gessen dropped the phone on the empty seat beside him, then picked it up again to call his head of Security. A former officer in the Swiss Army, Walter Keller was a model of discretion and calm. But after speaking with him, an attack of anxiety cramped Gessen's gut and he bent double from the pain. Three years ago, following the escape of a patient with Susto syndrome, a woman in a constant state of terror from her disturbing condition, he'd made extensive changes to the clinic's security protocol. The electronic wristbands, concealed CCTV cameras, and hidden sensors studding the perimeter provided round-the-clock surveillance, while maintaining an illusion, however minor, of the freedom to come and go.

Tilda, the woman with Susto, had been a model patient for nearly six months, when she gave her minder the slip one afternoon and failed to return from the village. Though she'd acted up in minor ways before, it was nothing too serious. Little rebellions to assert her independence. Sending food back to the kitchen, claiming it tasted funny, or leaving her bed to wander the grounds after dark in a filmy nightdress, frightening the more fragile patients.

But the situation with Ismail was different. Tilda, in spite of her shenanigans, knew she was ill and accepted that staying at the clinic was her best hope for recovery. A disordered mind would not do one's bidding at the snap of a finger, like a well-trained collie. It took time to unravel the tangled knot of years. Time and patience.

And in Ismail's case, he was suffering from more than a spell of depression. Incandescent with fury, from the day he arrived, he'd been looking for ways to escape. To return to his studies and the girl waiting for him, though he'd never mentioned her specifically in their sessions together. Ismail might not realise it, but Gessen was on his side. In the course of Ismail's therapy, he hoped to give the young man the tools needed to stand up to his father. Not as a rebellious son intent on vanquishing a monstrous patriarch, but as a man in his own right, with agency and autonomy. A delicate needle to thread. If only Ismail would be patient and give his treatment the time it deserved.

But now he was missing. Gessen cursed himself under his breath for leaving the clinic twice in the space of two weeks. All in a futile search to dig up Vidor's past. A disastrous mistake to let his personal feelings interfere with professional judgement. Now it was time to pay the piper. He was a bloody fool for chasing after some imagined mystery that lived in his head. What was the chance that the boy he'd known in Paris had anything to do with Vidor at all? In his ceaseless quest to heal the unease over his own feelings of guilt and exile, he was all too easily drawn into the shadowy corners of others like him. Misfits and loners, hobbled by a dark history.

* * *

Ursula met him at the funicular, her face nearly hidden under the hood of her parka. As they walked towards the clinic's gates, his shoulders hunched against the biting wind, he could sense her growing panic.

'Ismail was fine during our session yesterday,' she said. 'He was telling me about his first days in England, and how entranced he'd been by the college and the green fields of Oxfordshire. He spent a good ten minutes talking about those green fields, and how he'd taught himself to ride a bicycle, so he could cycle in the lanes.' She stopped to catch her breath. 'It was while cycling on a towpath along the Thames, his first spring at Oxford, that he realised he could never take over the mantel he'd been groomed for since birth. And that his destiny was to spend the rest of his days in England. At that moment, he told me, all thoughts of Cairo, and whatever pleasures it might once have held, vanished like smoke.'

'So, you think he's run away?'

In an attempt to map all the possibilities, Gessen's mind galloped ahead as the two of them trudged towards the gates. He was winded by the walk, his leg muscles trembling, as if in the short space of time since Ursula's call, he'd aged twenty years.

'Run away?' She blinked twice. 'He must have. But if that was his plan, he won't get very far. Not without any money.'

'Unless he got a message out,' Gessen countered. 'And someone's waiting for him in the village.'

Ursula gnawed on the end of her thumb. 'We looked there, and Thierry said he hadn't taken anyone down the mountain today in the funicular.'

They passed through the clinic's gate and Gessen paused, trying to quell the buzz of anxiety under his skin. 'He could have hiked down the mountain. It wouldn't be easy, but he's young and fit.' He glanced around. No one was about, though it was a fine day, clear and cold, with a hard metallic sun. 'Where is everyone?'

A worry line appeared between Ursula's eyes. 'In their rooms, I suppose, or the wellness pavilion? I didn't want to alarm anyone, so I thought it best if the patients went about their usual routines.'

Gessen pictured the staff, at the behest of his security team, poking about the shrubbery as if looking for a lost cat. They rounded a corner by the yew hedge and nearly bumped into Libby.

'Oh, hello.' Her voice rang out. 'You haven't seen Ismail, have you? We were supposed to meet in the fitness centre. He wanted to show me a routine that would strengthen my bad knee.'

Gessen's smile snapped into place. 'Dr Lindstrom just told me he's not feeling well and is spending the day in his room.'

She stared at him. 'That's funny. He seemed fine this morning.'

'You saw him this morning?'

'At breakfast.' Her gaze shifted between the two of them. 'Is something wrong?'

'A minor stomach bug. I have no doubt he'll be back on his feet by tomorrow.' Gessen took hold of Ursula's elbow and steered her towards his office where they could speak privately and devise a plan. He turned back to see Libby staring after them. She was a smart girl. They couldn't keep Ismail's absence from the patients for much longer. By the time they reached the main building, clouds had moved in. Soon it would be dark.

He shut the door to his office and studied the view from the window. Four sparrows pecked at the frozen ground. Odd to see them at this time of year. But no signs of a slender, dark-haired man skulking in the shadows. Where was he? The temperature was dropping fast. Clouds were mustering in the high peaks and snow was predicted by nightfall.

'If we don't find him in the next hour,' he said, turning to face Ursula, 'we'll have to alert the authorities.'

26

Four o'clock arrived, with still no sign of Ismail. Gessen's dread rose as the minutes ticked away. They couldn't wait any longer. It would soon be dark, and the absence of a signal from Ismail's wrist monitor was a bad sign. Either he was too far away and out of range, or he'd fallen into one of the many crevasses that ringed the valley. That Ismail was lying bruised and bloodied at the bottom of a ravine didn't bear thinking about.

When Gessen first acquired the property, it was apparent from the surveyor's report that the grounds contained several potentially hazardous areas. But long before he enrolled his first patient, every precaution was taken to prevent a serious mishap. In his twelve years of running the clinic, not a single patient had been injured – with the exception of the odd bump or bruise. But an excellent safety record didn't mean that Ismail wasn't lying wounded – or dead – at the bottom of a drop-off.

From the privacy of his office, he telephoned the local police, who informed him they would coordinate the search with Mountain Rescue. As Gessen hung up the phone, a pain stabbed his gut. Time was of the essence. Darkness was moving in and the temperature falling. With the ever-deepening layers of snow in the mountains, if they didn't find him soon, Ismail would die of exposure. Gessen sank into the chair. How did he slip away? It was nearly impossible for someone on the staff not to know where a patient was at any given moment of the day or night.

Nearly. That nebulous word held such immense room for error that his hands shook. To the casual observer, the pastoral setting and open spaces of the clinic grounds belied the fact that it was a virtual prison. A carefully designed set-up that monitored his patients' every move, while giving the impression of boundless freedom.

He pulled on his coat and headed to the chalet that housed his security team. They'd already viewed the tapes from the cameras and found nothing of concern, but he wanted to see the footage himself. Icy pellets of snow fell from the sky, and a chilly mist shrouded the valley. It would be snowing hard in the mountains.

Walter Keller, his head of Security, greeted Gessen with a grim look. In the operations room, they scanned the sixteen screens with views of the property. There were no cameras in the patients' rooms, but every other square millimetre of the grounds was covered.

Gessen leaned close to the console and studied the footage. Left to right, up and down, starting from the moment he'd left for Paris. There was Ismail leaving the main building after breakfast and heading towards his chalet, dressed in a dark jacket but minus the red knitted cap that all patients were obliged to wear outdoors. A minor rebellion that may have proved fatal. Fifty minutes later, he showed up in the northeast corner of the Zen garden, where he sat on a bench and stared into the distance.

'Wait, what was that?' Gessen pointed to camera number nine, and the entrance to the path into a copse of pines on the northern boundary. The recording appeared to judder for a moment and then reset.

'Oh, that.' Keller consulted the logbook on his desk. 'There was a brief malfunction in that camera for about forty seconds. But it came right back online.'

Forty seconds? Plenty of time for a man to disappear. 'How did that happen?'

'No idea. None of the other cameras were affected. It could have been a power surge, or moisture in the casing. Marco went out there to have a look, but didn't find any evidence of tampering.'

Gessen sank into a chair. How convenient that one of the cameras malfunctioned on the very day a patient slipped his tether. Coincidence? Or had someone interfered with the system? He closed his eyes as another pain cramped his gut. The day before Ismail was admitted, the entire staff had received a special briefing. Everyone knew that, security-wise, he was a sensitive case, and they'd been advised to take every precaution.

How was he going to tell Mr Mahmoud, a powerful and imperious man, accustomed to top-notch, impeccable service, that he'd lost his son? After the many assurances he'd given him that the clinic – even in the absence of razor wire – was as secure as any high-risk facility. Mr Mahmoud had specifically chosen Les Hirondelles. Not just for Gessen's excellent psychiatric pedigree, but due to his absolute faith in Swiss ingenuity and technology. The man had entrusted him with his son's life, and Gessen had let him down in the worst possible way.

As he turned away from the bank of screens, a familiar childhood terror flooded his limbs. The frantic drive through the night, as he lay hidden under a blanket in the back seat. Boarding a ship with his mother under the cover of darkness, where she held tight to his wrist as the harbour receded on the horizon. No explanation given for why they were leaving his father and older sisters behind.

Not long after settling in a tiny village in Switzerland, and his mother failed to return from a trip to the local market, he'd been told to consider their host family as his own. He'd struggled for years to accept his new name, and to pay heed to the warning to tell no one about his mother or his previous life. In this atmosphere of secrecy and lies, he learned to say nothing about where he'd come from, and to shrink himself down to a wisp of smoke. No past, no future. In his panic over Ismail, Gessen's younger, frightened self, newly resurgent, urged him to run into the forest and hide.

But he couldn't do that now. He was no longer little Anton, cowering in the dark, but a grown man whom others trusted with their lives. He rubbed his temples, trying to steel himself for what was to come. But first, he needed to do the one thing he dreaded most. Contact Mr Mahmoud and let him know his son was missing.

* * *

Darkness had fallen, with still no news. The police and Mountain Rescue had searched in an ever-widening radius across the mountain, but with mist and falling snow, visibility was poor all afternoon. Gessen could only hope the boy was on a train speeding towards the UK, alive and well, and not lying dead in the snow. When he'd telephoned Ismail's father earlier in the day, his heart heavy with dread, the man's personal assistant informed him he was on a plane to Cairo. She would relay the urgency of Gessen's message as soon as he touched down.

He forced himself to eat a few bites of his dinner, brought to him on a tray, though it had cooled now, with the fat congealed into grease. He stared into the fire. According to Keller's report, everyone was where they were supposed to be at the time Ismail went missing. But something niggled. *Vidor.* Might there have been an altercation? Vidor had attacked one man without provocation, why not another? Staff notes pointed to an ongoing tension between the two. Vidor complained, more than once, that Ismail sometimes knocked on the wall between their bedrooms at night, waking him from a deep sleep. When questioned, Ismail had vigorously denied doing anything so childish.

He straightened up and rang his Security head. 'Any word yet?'

'I'm afraid not.' Keller paused. 'You'll be the first to know when we hear something.'

Gessen glanced at the clock. Just after nine. It was going to be a long night, with sleep impossible. 'I need to see the Security log for one of the patients,' he said. 'Vidor K. Everything in the last forty-eight hours.' He dropped the phone and rubbed his eyes. Though Keller assured him that at the time Ismail vanished, everyone was accounted for, the log might provide the answer to a disturbing question. When Ismail went missing, where was Vidor?

27

The team from Mountain Rescue passed over the terrain for a second time, spreading out across the vast grounds of the clinic and into the surrounding valley. With their bright orange vests and helmet lamps flashing across the mountains, it was impossible to keep the search a secret. The patients were asking questions, and with Ismail pointedly absent from dinner, the staff couldn't feign ignorance for much longer. If he wasn't found by morning, Gessen would have to convene a meeting to give them the news. Nothing incited panic quicker than patients wondering amongst themselves if a terrible fate had befallen one of the group.

He entered the sculpture garden, wreathed in mist, and started when one of the statues moved. Frayed nerves and exhaustion were getting to him. He rubbed his eyes and blinked. Standing by the fountain, arms folded across his chest, Vidor gazed across the dark valley, where points of light flashed like panicked fireflies.

'There seems to be some excitement,' he said, his eyes fixed on a point in the distance.

'A search party.' Gessen stumbled on a loose stone. 'Someone from the village has gone missing. An older gentleman, apparently.' Even to his own ears, the lie sounded false. If he wasn't careful, he would start to babble. Should he ask Vidor if he'd seen Ismail since breakfast? But that would give the game away, and there was no sense in alarming anyone until they knew more.

'Does it happen often, people getting lost?' Vidor's voice seemed to echo in the dark.

'Not often.' Gessen hesitated. 'But the terrain in the mountains can be quite treacherous. Most of the walking trails are marked, but it'd be easy to lose your footing. Especially when the weather's bad. Or visibility is low.' As his voice faded, the silence felt like a weight. This year, already, nearly thirty people had died in the nearby mountains. Mostly hikers who'd wandered off the marked paths and plunged to their deaths, or skiers lost in the avalanches last spring.

Vidor stuffed his hands into the pockets of his coat and tilted his head back. 'Pity there's cloud cover. I've been tracking the lunar passage and if it clears up, we'll be treated to a glorious harvest moon tomorrow night.' He pointed to a distant peak. 'Pending a freak astronomical disturbance, it should rise right over there.'

'Yes, well, I'll leave you now.' Gessen gave Vidor a quizzical look before hurrying away. He paused once to glance back, but Vidor hadn't moved from his spot by the fountain. He checked his watch. Half past nine, and as the minutes ticked past, with still no word, he began to feel truly ill. The knot in his stomach tightened, and his skin felt feverish. In the privacy of his chalet, he flicked on the lights and sloshed brandy into a glass.

Normally, he waited until the weekend to indulge, preferring to keep his mind sharp, but he was sorely in need of fortification. The brandy burned his throat, but in a moment worked its magic, blunting his jangled nerves. He filled the glass again and carried it to the window. A flash of light in the mountains, followed by another, meant the search was still on. His body tensed as he waited for the phone to ring. Sipping his drink slowly, he counselled himself to breathe. When the call came in, he would need a clear head.

Fernanda, perhaps sensing his distress, rose from her bed in a corner of the kitchen and nosed around his feet. He absently stroked her head and gave her a biscuit before unfolding a detailed map of the grounds. A second printout contained a summary of the patients' movements in the past twenty-four hours. The scattering of coloured dots, accompanied by a time stamp, corresponded to each of the patients. In a single glance it was possible to follow Ismail's movements from the time he woke up to the moment he'd disappeared. Gessen picked up a pencil and attempted to connect the dots, as if it were a puzzle meant to be solved.

At seven that morning, Ismail was in his chalet, and at ten minutes past eight, in the dining hall for breakfast. He spent nearly an hour in the meditation hall, followed by a visit to the Zen garden, then back to his room. His last known location was a few minutes before two in the afternoon, where he'd been tracked close to the edge of the property, and near a copse of fir and spruce. A single wooden bench on a clear patch of land afforded a magnificent view to the west. A lovely place to take in the sunset, if one was so inclined.

That was the last dot. Then… nothing. As if he'd vanished into the air.

A quick survey of the other patients' movements revealed nothing unusual. Babette was in her chalet, then the swimming pool, followed by Movement & Meditation in the afternoon. He counted the dots in the meditation hall. Three. Along with Ismail, both Libby and Vidor were missing, but that wasn't unusual. Vidor came up with every excuse possible to miss M&M. Gessen traced the series of yellow dots with his finger. Vidor was in his room when he should have been at the session, where he appeared to have stayed until he left the chalet for dinner at six thirty. What time was it when he bumped into Vidor in the sculpture garden? He couldn't remember now. The terror of losing a patient had clouded his mind.

He finished off the brandy and massaged the back of his neck. Where could Ismail have gone? He switched off the lights in the chalet and peered at the dark shrubbery through the window and the jagged teeth of the mountains. In a moment of desperation, he began to pray. Not to the god he no longer believed in, but to whatever deities might be dwelling in the glades. *Please bring him back to us.*

    Alive.

28

'We'll be in the other room today.' Gessen ushered Vidor into the small adjoining room that was furnished with a single straight-back chair and the black leather couch. With still no news of Ismail, he'd had a sleepless night, reaching for his phone every few minutes to check that it was working. His eyes were gritty with fatigue. Even the effort to move the muscles in his face felt gargantuan. Up since dawn, he had again gone over the staff and patients' movements from the day before. Nothing seemed out of the ordinary, though it struck him as odd that Vidor had spent an unusual amount of time in his room.

'Perhaps we should cancel,' Vidor said, eyeing him intently. 'You're looking rather peaked.'

'No, I'm perfectly fine.' Gessen sat up straight. 'A little trouble sleeping is all.'

'Well, you'll be pleased to hear that I slept like the proverbial rock,' Vidor said, flexing his arms. 'In spite of having taken a long nap yesterday afternoon.' He breathed in through his nose. 'All this fresh mountain air knocks me right out.'

Gessen's smile felt like a grimace. He was in no condition to lead Vidor through a session. But until Ismail was found, what else could he do but continue as usual?

'Did they find that old gent who went missing?' Vidor twisted the ring on his finger.

'Who? Oh, yes. Safe and sound.' He forced himself to look Vidor in the eye, before asking him to lie down on the couch. Afraid he might crack at any moment, Gessen didn't want Vidor's keen eyes searching his face. Anyone with half an ounce of intelligence would see that something was wrong. At least in here, with Gessen safely seated out of view, while Vidor lay on the couch, he could hide from scrutiny.

'The clock is ticking, you know,' Vidor proclaimed as he stretched out. 'Tick-tock.'

Gessen's tongue, dry as an old shoe, cleaved to the roof of his mouth. What he wouldn't give to retreat to a dark corner and shut out the world. His phone remained mute. Ursula had promised she'd come to him the moment there was news.

'And which clock would that be?'

'The deadline for my grant application.' Vidor crossed his hands over his chest. 'I've designed an exciting set of experiments to study sensory processing in synaesthetes. You know, those unusual individuals, rare as unicorns, who can describe the colour of numbers or the shape of sounds? Crossed wires in the brain, so to speak. One of the many mysteries of sensory perception.' He laced his fingers together and closed his eyes. 'If I miss the deadline, it will be a tragic loss for my lab.'

Gessen said nothing. Today, of all days, he was not in the mood to be cajoled and manipulated into releasing his obstinate patient from the clinic. If Vidor only knew how serious his situation was, he might be more willing to cooperate. But there was still a risk in telling Vidor he could be charged with manslaughter – or worse. Once aware of the sword hanging over his head, Vidor could resort to all kinds of tactics to dodge responsibility for his actions.

After their last session, in the innocent time before Ismail's disappearance, Gessen had sent Vidor away with homework. He was to imagine himself as a young boy, still living with his

152

family in Budapest. Sift through his memories and take note of anything that came to mind. No filtering. Whatever came up, he was to write it down. Today, Gessen planned to follow up on that memory exercise with a session of free association. A deep state of relaxation often revealed a spate of interesting connections and long-buried events.

'Did you perform the exercise we talked about last time?' With the touch of a button, Gessen adjusted the blinds until the room was in shadow.

Vidor made a noise in his throat that Gessen took as a yes.

'It's strange,' Vidor said, after a lengthy pause. 'I hadn't expected to remember much, but the experience was fairly Proustian. So many things I'd long forgotten about bubbled right up to the surface.'

Gessen absently touched the phone in his pocket. *Still no news.* Blood from his pounding heart boomed in his ears.

'Odd that I could have forgotten this one particular memory,' Vidor was saying, 'because it frightened me terribly as a child. For months, I was afraid to sleep in my own bed. So, I would creep into my parents' room and stretch out on the floor, but they always woke up, and my mother carried me back to my room. She would help me check under the bed and in the cupboard, to prove there was nothing there.'

Gessen was all ears now. 'What was it that frightened you?'

'A strange man. I couldn't have been more than four at the time. Early summer it must have been, as my mother wanted to buy apricots to make a tart, and she'd brought me with her to the market. I saw the man stepping into a trolley car going in the opposite direction, but when we got to the market, there he was, standing by the butcher shop. So he couldn't have boarded that other trolley. Unless he was a magician – or had a twin.

'After the market, my mother and I went into a teashop with an ornate ceiling and chandeliers. She said they made the best anise biscuits in the city. While my mother poured the tea, I dropped my napkin on the floor. When I bent to pick it up, I saw the trolley man seated at the next table. He turned his head and grinned at me, flashing a mouthful of blackened teeth. His milky eyes reminded me of dead fish. I shrieked in terror, and babbled to my mother about a dead man. I could smell his decaying body and see the strips of skin peeling off him like dried paint.'

Gessen waited as the silence thickened between them. What an interesting story. A scary man, so telling in the details. Was this sudden outpouring of memory the result of Ursula's newest strategy? Suggesting to Vidor that he invent a fake childhood trauma to throw Gessen off the scent. A case of good cop, bad cop. An unsavoury tactic, Gessen believed, but at this point, trickery might be the only way to break the deadlock. And fake memory or not, buried in a lie was always a glimmer of truth. Even if the 'scary man' story was nonsense, it had come from the depths of Vidor's subconscious, where the real problem, yet to be revealed, lurked in the shadows.

'How frightened you must have been,' Gessen said, pausing to look at his phone. *Still no word.* 'Any idea who the man might be?'

The couch creaked as Vidor shifted his legs. 'My mother said no one was there. But I saw him, and I couldn't have imagined it, because I distinctly remember his smell. Like a rotting corpse.'

The tip of Gessen's pencil scratched the notepad. *Scary man, anise cookies, putrid smell.*

'It occurred to me,' Vidor said, slowly, as if trying to give extra weight to his words, 'that the sight of that man entering the hall in Copenhagen might have triggered my long-buried childhood memory. When I attacked that poor man – wholly unaware, of course – perhaps I was avenging my younger self against a similar man who'd terrorised me as a boy.'

Gessen suppressed a smile. Vidor's 'surprise epiphany' was straight out of Psychology 101. 'It's an interesting theory,' he said, with a note of gravity in his voice, 'and something I'd like to pursue in greater depth at our next session, when we'll attempt to get at the heart of what that man represents in your psyche. Age regression analysis might be just the thing for teasing out the details of that particular memory.'

His palms were damp with sweat. Still no word about Ismail. He checked his phone to be sure it was switched on.

Vidor sat upright and beamed.

How easy it was for Gessen to read his thoughts: *That Dr Lindstrom sure is a genius. A brilliant idea to tell Dr Gessen exactly what he wants to hear. All done and dusted. In a week's time I'll be back in Cambridge.*

It was time to burst his bubble.

'I hadn't wanted to show you before,' Gessen said, scraping back his chair. 'But I believe you're ready to see for yourself what happened in Copenhagen. With your childhood memories beginning to surface, the face of the man you attacked might remind you of someone from your past.'

Vidor's chin jerked up. No wonder he felt skittish, Gessen thought, as he eyed him closely. With unusual skill, he'd managed to sidestep any acknowledgment of the violent assault that had landed him in Gessen's clinic. Seeing that video would certainly come as a shock. It might even release the storm of pent up emotions sure to be lurking under the surface of Vidor's cool and courtly façade. And who could say where that might lead? He would have to tread with care.

Gessen beckoned Vidor to follow him into his office. 'I've got the video of the ceremony on my computer. Why don't we have a look at it now?'

29

The shriek of the telephone jolted him awake. As the news filtered through Gessen's brain, a darkness, terrifying as the shadow of a manticore, threatened to choke him, and the bitter taste of bile rose in his throat.

Ismail was dead.

Mountain Rescue had found him at the bottom of a deep crevasse not more than fifty metres from the clinic's northern boundary. His neck had broken in the fall. As soon as the local police and coroner were finished, they would strap Ismail's body to a stretcher and haul him up the mountain. Gessen had passed a restless night, slipping in and out of disturbing dreams. Twice he'd lurched from the bed to pray to whomever might be listening that the boy was found alive. Now, with the immutable fact of Ismail's death, he dropped his head in his hands.

With the clumsy gait of an accident victim in shock, he stumbled into the bathroom and splashed his face with cold water. Staring back at him from the mirror was his father's face, ravaged by cancer. Not his real father, a man he'd scarcely known, but the taciturn man who'd raised him as his own son, concealing Gessen's origins as his mother wished. It wasn't the cancer that killed his adoptive father in the end, however. Not long after he'd received the news that nothing more could be done, his car plunged off an icy road in the Dolomites. A timely accident. Or was it suicide? He would never know. Both fathers, long dead. Their disappearance from his life should have set him free, but such was not his fate. The two men lived on in his blood and bones. And ever since, he'd carried their ghosts on his back, and with them the long trail of the dead.

All he had left were his two surnames, one given at birth, the other later bestowed upon him, as if meant to wipe out the original sin. He'd seen those two names written together only once, on a memorial to the dead in a village in Baden-Württemberg. He'd come across it while walking in the Black Forest, not long after he discovered who he was. Stunned that a small village could furnish such an endless list of names, all snuffed out in the camps. As he read down the columns, he'd been startled to see, nearly side by side, the name he'd been given at birth, and the later one, *Gessen*, from his adoptive parents. A monstrous pairing. Together in life, joined in death. After falling to his knees, he'd vomited his lunch in the dirt.

And now, the reckoning had come. A patient under his care, a talented young man with a bright future ahead of him, lay bloodied and broken at the bottom of a ravine. He had failed before to ease a patient's suffering or to help them flourish. But not once had a patient died on his watch.

He dried his face and dragged a comb through his hair. The family must be contacted at once, and he would have to inform the staff and patients. With one of their number dead, and the police asking intrusive questions, the calm, healing atmosphere of the clinic would be torn to shreds.

* * *

Gessen jumped at the knock on his office door. Ursula slipped inside, looking as rumpled and miserable as he felt. Her skin was dull, and her hair bundled hastily in a ponytail. In her tired eyes rose a question she had no need to ask.

When he tried to speak, it came out as a croak. 'They've found him.' It wasn't necessary to say that Ismail was dead. The slump of his shoulders was enough. What next? He couldn't think what to do, other than to lie down in the dark and pray it was all a bad dream. Together, they would have to coordinate the news of Ismail's death, as well as cope with the ensuing fallout. As the clinic's director, he would inform the family, while Ursula told the patients, one by one, with Gessen providing any follow-up if needed.

As they huddled together in the grey light, they agreed for now to say it was an accident. But the patients would surely wonder how it was possible for Ismail to have wandered off. They might even start questioning the security arrangements and worry about their own safety. Or – worse – demand the freedom to wander about as they chose, regardless of the risk.

Had Ismail been so desperate to return to his studies, and the girl in England he wished to marry, that he'd endanger his life? A bitter taste rose in his throat. Too late to admit he'd been wrong to agree with Ismail's father that his son needed treatment. The boy had been mildly depressed, there was no question of that, but his earlier, half-hearted attempt at suicide was more likely an act of desperation than a sign of severe illness. Locking him away from his studies and the girl he loved was cruel medicine. With each passing day, Ismail must have felt the mountains closing in on him, and the walls of his prison driving him to madness. Escape, whatever the cost, the only way out.

A contest of wills between father and son. An eternal tale that often ended in tragedy. Oedipus. Zeus. Ram. Had he learned nothing from the exploits of the ancients he'd devoured as a boy?

After Ursula left, Gessen switched on his computer and pulled up the map of the grounds. A dotted red line indicated the electronic periphery of the clinic. Normally, if a patient crossed this boundary, clearly marked by a chest-high wooden fence, an alarm would sound in the operations centre, and a member of Security would rush to the site.

Somehow, Ismail had breached the boundary undetected. Was there a short circuit in the system? When his body was found, the digital monitor was still strapped to his wrist, though it appeared to have been damaged in the fall. In the twenty-four hours prior to his disappearance, Ismail's movements would have been tracked. Each position recorded on his personal log, along with his sleeping patterns, blood pressure, and heart-rate. With any luck, the data would provide some clues.

Gessen opened a window, but the bracing air did little to revive his spirits. He couldn't put it off any longer. First, he would speak to Ismail's bodyguard, and then inform the family. He picked up the phone and called Sendak. No response. With a twinge of apprehension, he summoned his head of Security.

When Walter Keller stepped through Gessen's door, his face was ashen. Losing one of their patients would have hit him hard, of course, but there must be more to it. With the bodyguard not responding to calls, something felt off. Could Sendak have played a role in Ismail's death?

In spite of the haunted look on his face, Keller's back was ramrod straight. 'He's gone, sir.'

'Who? The bodyguard?'

'Yes, sir. Must have slipped away as soon as we found the body of the boy. Afraid for his own neck, I imagine.' He looked past Gessen and squinted at the window. 'Considering the family who employed him.'

Gessen ran his hand through his hair. 'Do you think the bodyguard had something to do with the boy's death?'

Keller shrugged. 'Hard to say, but he's probably on a plane by now.'

Gessen cast around for the right words. Keller might be worrying about his own job as well. 'For now, it's business as usual. I don't want to upset the patients.' He glanced at his watch, conscious of time slipping away. He had a session with

Vidor in thirty minutes. Just enough time to get cleaned up. In Vidor's fragile state, it would be better for him not to know that a patient had died on Gessen's watch. Possibly lured to his death by the man hired to protect him. Highly suspicious that he'd slipped away. If he were innocent, why run?

Keller took a call on his phone. 'The police are here. They'd like to speak to you.'

30

The ground crackled with frost as Gessen cut across the lawn to meet the uniformed officers at the gate, a ruddy-cheeked young man with sandy hair, and an older woman whose face was impossible to read. His stomach lurched at the sight of them. Even as a child he'd feared the police. A holdover from the time he was a young boy living in a city of intrigue and secrets, where a man in uniform was something to fear. He couldn't remember who had taught him this, or if he was taking his cues from the wary-eyed adults around him.

The air was thick with impending snow, forecast for the afternoon. He shook hands with the officers and invited them through. Once inside the gate, they paused to look around, silently absorbing the vast sweep of the grounds, the manicured gardens and spacious chalets. He knew how it looked to outsiders: a fairy-tale village tucked away in a pleasant valley high in the mountains. Amongst the locals the clinic had acquired a rarefied reputation. Natural for them to be curious, but there wasn't much to see. Before he'd turned it into a psychiatric clinic, Les Hirondelles had been a typical mountain hamlet. One of hundreds, if not thousands, scattered throughout the Bernese Oberland.

Today seemed different though. Without a soul to animate the scene, even to Gessen's eyes, the clinic looked like a theme park, a facsimile of a charming, old-world Alpine village, overlaid with a sheen of fakery. He had instructed the staff to keep the patients occupied while the police were on site. Confined to their rooms or in a special session of group therapy. Ursula, still intrigued by Vidor's reaction to the abstract painting during their word association exercise, had assigned Vidor to another art therapy session with Isabelle. Skilled at plumbing the hidden depths of the psyche through art, Isabelle might succeed where he had failed. After the terrible business with the police was over, he was curious to see what Vidor might have produced.

The officers, Müller and Schulz, introduced themselves, and they stood awkwardly for a moment in the frigid air until Gessen led them down the stone path to the conference room on the ground floor of the manor house. Though bland and sparsely furnished in keeping with its function, it had a spectacular view of the mountains across the valley and provided a more appropriate place to bring them than his office.

'May I offer you a coffee?' Gessen said, as one of the staff stepped up to take their coats.

As the two officers exchanged glances, Gessen could sense what they were thinking. That this wasn't a social call, but it was a chilly day, so why not? 'I'll have a coffee,' said Schulz, the junior officer of the pair. His partner looked stern for a moment and then she softened. 'I'll have one too, if it's not any trouble.'

Gessen pressed a button by the door. 'Mathilde, would you bring us three coffees?'

While they waited, Schulz attempted some small talk. 'Nice set-up you've got here. *Sehr schön.* I grew up in the next valley over.' He gestured at the window.

Officer Müller pursed her lips and retrieved a notepad from an inside pocket of her jacket. Gessen tried to read her expression. They would have received the coroner's report by now. Did it mention this might be a suspicious death? He prayed not. An extended inquiry could go on for weeks. As far as he was concerned, Ismail's death was an accident. Suicide was the other possibility, though it seemed unlikely. Why would Ismail end his own life, when he was so desperate to be reunited with his beloved?

The only one at fault was Gessen himself. Any lapse in security rested squarely on his shoulders. After the investigation was over, he would reconsider his stance on securing the property with a high fence, though he hated the idea. This was a medical clinic, not a prison, and the patients' stays were voluntary. What would it do to their well-being if they had the impression they were locked in?

Even before he learned of his own family history, Gessen had a horror of closed spaces and locked doors, so he could only imagine what effect they might have on his patients. Far from home. Disoriented and vulnerable to whatever ailment had brought them here. What they needed most – and one of the selling points of the clinic – was the healing energy of the mountains and the illusion of wide-open space. No spirit can properly soar behind high fences, razor wire, and locked doors.

Officer Müller pointedly clicked her pen. 'Until additional information comes in,' she said, 'we're treating Mr Mahmoud's death as an accident. Suicide is also a possibility, of course, so it would be helpful to know something about Mr Mahmoud's state of mind in the days leading up to his death.'

Gessen had come prepared to the meeting, and he flipped open his diary to consult the relevant dates. 'The day before he went missing, Mr Mahmoud had a private therapy session with Dr Lindstrom at three in the afternoon.' He passed the diary to Officer Müller. 'I was away on other business and heading back to the clinic by train when Dr Lindstrom called to say that Mr Mahmoud was missing.'

Officer Müller glanced at the diary and made a note. 'Did Dr Lindstrom notice anything out of the ordinary? Perhaps he was agitated or upset.'

'I don't believe so. No more upset than usual.'

She raised her eyebrows. 'Can you be more specific?'

'Doctor–patient confidentiality, even after death, prevents me from divulging the details, but what I can tell you is that Mr Mahmoud had trouble accepting he was ill. He was not happy about being here. Our work together was hampered by his overwhelming desire to return to England.'

'What was stopping him?' Her eyes met his. 'If I understand the law correctly, no patient in this country can be kept against their will. Unless it's been shown they're a danger to themselves… or others.'

'That's correct,' Gessen said. 'But prior to admission, Mr Mahmoud demonstrated suicidal tendencies, and he'd threatened his father with bodily harm. Apparently, things were very heated between them, so they struck a deal. Mr Mahmoud, Ismail, would submit to six months of residential treatment at a clinic of his father's choice. If Ismail completed the treatment successfully, his father would release him from his obligation to take over the family business, which is based in Cairo. Ismail wanted to stay in the UK and study medicine. I believe there is also a young woman there he'd wanted to marry, but he never said much about that.'

Officer Müller tapped her pen on the table. 'Why did he need his father's permission to stay in England or to marry the girl of his choice?'

'That's not for me to say,' Gessen said. 'It was a family matter.' He sipped the last of his coffee, but the dregs were bitter on his tongue. He paused before continuing. 'It can be difficult for those of us brought up in the West to appreciate the importance other cultures place on family ties and dynastic succession.'

'Dynastic?'

'Mr Mahmoud is – was – the second son of a powerful family in the Middle East. When the oldest boy died in a car accident some years ago, the father assumed Ismail would give up his dream of becoming a doctor and step into his older brother's place. When Ismail refused, things grew ugly, and he made a half-hearted attempt to kill himself. He and I agreed that, as part of his treatment programme, he would keep his part of the bargain. Ismail was hoping that, after the six months were over, his father would come to his senses and allow him to choose his own path in life.'

Officer Müller jotted down a note on her pad.

Silence filled the room. Gessen looked up to see snow spinning down from the darkened sky. 'Though our primary focus is psychiatric treatment,' he continued, 'the clinic also functions as a place of refuge, a retreat for troubled individuals while they figure out how to live in the world.'

When Officer Müller met his gaze, it was easy for Gessen to read her thoughts: *Another playground for the idle rich. Wouldn't we all like to have such problems?* But he had no desire to explain that his clinic wasn't some upscale health resort for the wealthy bored. If they were interested in learning more about the history and philosophy of Les Hirondelles, they were welcome to pick up a brochure on the way out.

Officer Schulz cleared his throat. 'We understand that Mr Mahmoud had a private bodyguard who was posing as one of the staff.'

Gessen frowned. Who would have told them that? Were they already in contact with the family?

Müller cut in smoothly. 'We'd like to speak to him, as well as your head of Security.'

'Unfortunately, that will be difficult.'

The two officers stared at him.

'Our Security manager will be happy to speak with you, of course, but Mr Mahmoud's bodyguard has unfortunately vanished. No one's seen him since Ismail's body was found.'

This information seemed to animate Schulz. But Officer Müller didn't bat an eye. Instead they asked a few more questions. Did he think Mr Mahmoud could have taken his own life? Did he have any disputes or altercations with the other patients, or ever threaten to hurt anyone? The questions seemed routine, but a cold sweat soaked the skin under Gessen's shirt. The poor boy was dead. Accident or suicide, what did it matter now? Schulz cut in with a sharp tone that brought him up short.

'There's a third possibility.' His pen clattered on the table. 'He was murdered.'

Murdered? Gessen had shied away from considering that option, finding it unthinkable at first. Though of course it was possible. Even Walter Keller, as unruffled as they come, had broached the idea. Who would do such a thing, the bodyguard? 'What would be the motive?'

'Animosity, prejudice? A tussle over a woman, perhaps?'

Gessen shook his head. There was no woman who might fit the profile. Except, perhaps, for Libby. And who would be fighting Ismail for her attentions? The idea was ludicrous.

'He was in love with a girl in England.'

Office Müller broke in smoothly. 'Regardless, to get a full picture of the case, we'll need to speak to the staff. And the other patients, of course.'

And then there were five. The last thing his patients needed in their fragile states was to be grilled by the police about a possible murder. A bright young man whom nearly everyone seemed to like. He'd have Ursula put together the list of names, though one of them would have to be present during the questioning.

Why not start with Vidor? The police's probing might resolve his flicker of unease that Vidor might somehow be involved. As a housemate, he may have viewed Ismail as mildly annoying, but surely nothing that amounted to a motive for murder.

31

Vidor entered the conference room to find two police officers standing at the window. The sight made him uneasy. Two against one, an unfair match, though he supposed the police always worked in pairs. Ever since Gessen had shown him that odious video from Copenhagen – obviously a fake meant to frighten him – he'd been irritable and on guard, waiting for another trick to be sprung upon him. These officers could be another of Gessen's ploys to throw him off balance. With Ismail happy to play along in the conspiracy, only too pleased to put the screws on Vidor and make him sweat.

Behind the officers, the mountains were draped in a fresh layer of snow. One of Gessen's personal assistants, a petite woman with a cap of sleek black hair like a chickadee, brought in a tray of coffee and pastries.

The woman officer gestured to a chair. 'Please take a seat, Mr Kiraly. We'll try not to take up too much of your time.'

Time? He suppressed a sigh. All he had was time. Oceans and oceans of it. 'Please take all the time you need,' he said, giving the woman what he hoped was a winning smile. 'I have nothing but time, and little to fill it with. *Tempus rerum imperator.*'

'What's that?' The younger officer sat up straight, with all the earnest zeal of a schoolboy.

'Time: commander of all things.'

The boy noted it down. Another eager beaver. Vidor nearly groaned.

The woman cleared her throat. 'I understand you've been informed of the unfortunate death of Mr Mahmoud.'

'I have,' Vidor said. 'Though until today, I did not know that was his surname.'

'And why is that?'

'We use first names here only.' He paused. 'To protect our privacy.'

She raised her eyes to his, her pen poised. 'Did you know Mr Mahmoud well? I understand his room was next to yours.'

'It was, but he mainly kept to himself. I don't believe he spoke to me more than once or twice. This is a hospital, Ms…'

'Müller. Officer Müller.'

'Not a Club Med.'

She scratched something on her notepad. 'Could you tell me when you last saw Mr Mahmoud?'

Vidor considered this. Should he tell them that Ismail had made a point of rubbing him the wrong way and that he took special pains to avoid him? Better not. The sensation that prickled his skin whenever that annoying lad entered his orbit was too subtle to put into words. So was the vague sense of threat he felt at the idea of Ismail sleeping on the other side of his bedroom wall. The police might count it as a mark against him. Perhaps even wonder whether he'd had something to do with Ismail's disappearance. Preposterous, of course, but you never knew with the police, always so eager to point fingers at the innocent.

'Two days ago, I believe, was the last time I saw him. It might have been a Tuesday, or perhaps a Wednesday? Late afternoon. Around four, it could have been. Or five, though it's hard to say exactly.' He looked at his interlocutor. 'You may have noticed the absence of clocks.'

The two officers exchanged a glance. 'So, you and Mr Mahmoud were not on friendly terms?'

'I didn't say that.' He bristled. What were they implying? 'But I'm not here to socialise, and I don't make a habit of chatting with the other patients.' He examined a patch of abraded skin on his wrist. He must have scraped it yesterday when he slipped on the icy path. 'I'm supposed to be resting.'

Officer Müller checked her notes. 'One of the other patients said she saw you talking to Mr Mahmoud on the afternoon he disappeared.'

Vidor's head snapped up. Who would have told them that? 'Not that woman Hélène, I hope.' He tapped his temple. 'Mad as a hatter, that one.'

Officer Müller fixed him with a clear-eyed gaze, waiting for him to say more, perhaps even hoping to entrap him in a falsehood. Little got past this woman, that much was clear.

When nothing more was forthcoming, she closed her notebook. 'Thank you, Mr Kiraly. You've been very helpful.'

'Actually, it's Professor Kiraly,' he said. 'I'm a Cambridge don, and was recently awarded an OBE from Her Majesty the Queen.' He didn't want her thinking he was a drooling idiot with scrambled eggs for brains. 'Very sad, of course, what happened to that boy, but what could you expect?' He'd heard the rumours. 'Deeply depressed, apparently, and pining for some girl back in England. The young can be so impulsive, can't they? At that age, everything is so dramatic.' He briefly locked eyes with the younger officer. 'Are you familiar with the concept of *l'appel du vide*?'

The officer pursed his mouth.

'The call of... emptiness?' This from Officer Müller.

'I prefer to think of it as "void". The call of the void. It's an actual neuropsychological phenomenon,' Vidor said, warming to the subject. 'I'm sure Dr Gessen could enlighten you further on the psychology of it, but from a neurological perspective it describes the urge one gets, usually not acted upon, fortunately, when standing on a high platform. Or the side of a mountain. The seductive urge to fling oneself into open space. It's not a suicidal wish, more like a compulsion. Possibly tied to dopamine disturbances in the brain.'

Officer Müller's pen was poised in mid-air, as if contemplating whether or not to write any of this down.

'I feel it myself at times,' Vidor said, with what he hoped was a note of existential sorrow. 'It's particularly acute here, so high on the escarpment, and that vast bowl of empty space calling out to us, day and night. My solution is not to go near the edge. Perhaps young Mr Mahmoud felt, to his peril, inexplicably drawn to the call of that open space.' He looked from one officer to the other. At last, he had a captive audience. 'Or perhaps he simply lost his balance and fell.'

* * *

The snow was coming down fast, though more like shards of ice than downy flakes, and a bitter wind lashed the pines. Vidor welcomed the change in weather, the first real storm of the season to reach the valley, and a harbinger of what might be in store when the full force of winter arrived. Soon, the clinic would be cut off from the world. Subjected to the howling winds that shook the trees and scoured the granite outcrops. A reminder of how insignificant they all were, as they travelled through space and time on a whirling blue sphere, unaware of the meaning, if any, of their place in the cosmos.

In the English Fens there were often strong winds, but little in the way of snow. With the storm upon them, Vidor felt a surge of pleasure in the full force of the elements. As long as he was somewhere warm and dry, let it snow. Let the blizzards obliterate the landscape in crystalline fury. Surely, the clinic was equipped with a backup generator, though he could imagine the mayhem that might ensue should they be plunged into darkness and left to freeze like carcasses of beef.

His eye followed the path, nearly obliterated by the thickly falling snow, leading to the sculpture garden and out the other side. He'd never walked that far. Never felt the desire to explore the boundaries of the clinic. It wasn't as if there was anywhere one could go. At some point he would come up against the boundary line, where there was a chest-high wooden fence. Easy to breach if he was of a mind to escape the clinic's confines, though he'd been told upon arrival that such an attempt would set off an alarm. The day Ismail disappeared Vidor had seen the boy, looking furtive as he headed towards the entrance to the grove. He'd followed Ismail part way into the copse of dark firs before turning back, having lost interest in whatever intrigue might be at play. Possibly, he'd had an assignation with the English girl. Later, when questioned, he hadn't mentioned it, as it seemed of little account.

Perhaps, if Vidor had ventured a bit further, Ismail might still be alive. He could have shouted something, *Stay back!* Save him from that seductive force, *l'appel du vide*, that he knew only too well. It's why he chose to keep well inside the clinic's inner boundary, safe on solid ground. Once, as a cocky young lad, he'd vowed to climb to the very top of the Eiffel Tower, only to be paralysed by the height and the force of the wind buffeting the struts. Far below, the city called out to him. How easy it would have been to launch himself into that space, and to feel – for one glorious moment – the joy of Icarus aiming for the sun, before the loss of his wings and the final plunge to earth.

Hunching his shoulders against the wind and the sting of snow on his face, Vidor turned in the direction of his chalet. It would be quieter now with Ismail gone. The two officers must still be on the property, waiting out the storm. He could have told them he'd seen Ismail head into the dark copse of fir trees, but it seemed of no consequence now.

The boy was dead, and all the questioning in the world wouldn't bring him back.

32

Paris, France
November 1968

From the opposite side of the street, he studies the five-storey limestone building that matches the address a lady at the housing office scribbled on a piece of paper. He's been trying to move out of his student digs for weeks and this looks like as good a place as any. When he saw the notice of a room for rent tacked to a corkboard, his spirits lifted. Not only is he paying far too much for his tiny quarters in student housing, a cloud of depression hangs over him like a fog every time he enters the windowless room, no bigger than a monk's cell. At times he thinks he might die in there. His body rotting for months before being discovered.

This neighbourhood, on the other side of the Jardin du Luxembourg, is one of his favourite haunts. A new start after a rocky beginning. In the mornings, he could take the Métro to Odéon to attend his lectures and then walk back through the avenues of towering lindens and chestnut trees in the park, stripped of their leaves with the approach of winter, but in the spring, in dappled sunshine, it would be a delight to stroll beneath the rustling boughs.

He rings the bell and waits on the pavement until he is buzzed in. A woman with a tarnished brooch pinned to the lace collar of her black dress stands in the doorway of the anteroom. When he shows her the paper from the Sorbonne housing office, she gives him a suspicious look, but allows him to proceed to the back stairs, craning her neck to observe him as he makes his way to the second floor.

Before he can knock, the door swings open and a woman in a dark green dress and flowered apron greets him with a smile. 'Are you the boy from the Sorbonne, the one looking for a room?' He nods, and she beckons him inside. 'It's at the back of the flat.' She leads him through the front room where two girls are bent over their schoolbooks. Another, older girl is in the kitchen, stirring something in a pot with a long-handled spoon. 'These are three of my daughters,' the woman says, nodding at the girls. 'My two youngest daughters are very studious.' She smiles. 'Always with their noses in a book.'

He follows her down a narrow hallway that leads to the back of the flat. The room is modest in size, with a single bed and small chest of drawers. But it's the window that catches his attention. An amber light slants through the glass, and he steps closer to see that it looks over a courtyard. The branches of two lindens, with soft gold leaves going brown at the edges, almost touch the glass. It will be nice to wake to the sound of birds. He tells the woman it's perfect and that he can move in straight away. As they discuss the particulars, the slamming of a door is followed by someone clomping into the flat. 'My son,' the woman says, 'late as always. So, now you can meet him. He's in his last year at the *lycée*. So busy, we hardly see him these days.'

A handsome boy with light brown hair and clear grey eyes pokes his head through the doorway. '*Szia, mama.*' He frowns. 'Who's this?'

'Our new lodger. He's a first-year student at the Sorbonne.'

'Lodger?' His face darkens, and he turns abruptly on his heel.

'I'll be just a minute,' she says, and follows her son. The flat is small enough that he can hear everything they say.

'I don't want some stranger living here.'

'We talked about this,' the woman says. 'We need the money.'

'What about Katerina, where will she sleep?'

'With Rennie, of course. She's perfectly fine with it. And what does it matter? You're hardly at home these days. You'll never see him.'

Angry stomping, followed by a door banging shut. The woman bustles into the room. 'Sorry to leave you.' Her smile looks strained. 'There's a lovely light in here at this time of day, isn't there? If you think it will suit, you can move in tomorrow.'

33

Clinique Les Hirondelles
Saint-Odile, Switzerland
5 December 2008

A cold wind sliced through his skin as Gessen stepped onto the back terrace and scanned the sky for a break in the clouds. More snow had fallen in the night, and he gulped down his coffee, trying to shake off the frightening dreams that had plagued his sleep and left him flushed and feverish. His joints ached and his eyes felt hot and dry. If he were coming down with the flu, he would be no use to anyone.

Returning to the warmth of his kitchen, he punched Ursula's number into the phone and asked her to take over his patients for the day. Even if it wasn't the flu, he was in no shape to see anyone today. It was unconscionable that a patient had died under his care. That it was a promising young man with a bright future ahead of him was a tragedy.

Fernanda, always sensitive to his moods, crossed the floor to lean against his knee, and he reached down to stroke her silky ears. When he'd first dreamed of starting his own clinic, more than fifteen years ago, he would jot down notes, in the idle moments between patients, on his vision of an ideal psychiatric care setting. In those heady days of his relative youth, he'd imagined a high-class facility for healing the mind and spirit that lacked the look or feel of a typical clinic. No stark furnishings or clinically sterile patient rooms, and no visible barriers of any kind.

The place he imagined would reflect the beauty of its mountain setting. Natural materials and soft lighting. Gardens and landscaped grounds for the patients to stroll in. No locked doors or high fences. But in the aftermath of Ismail's death, he would have to reconsider his entire philosophy. Today, he would meet with his head of Security to discuss alternative means of securing the boundary.

An email from one of the house attendants popped up on his computer screen, informing Gessen of his resignation, effective immediately. Apparently, the man's mother had suddenly taken ill, and there was no one else at home to care for her. Home was a village in Slovenia, if Gessen recalled correctly. That the attendant was assigned to Ismail's chalet was mildly disconcerting. Was there a connection? Perhaps he felt responsible in some way, or was it something else? He had already been questioned by the police, so there was no reason to suspect anything was amiss. Gessen signed off on the request, and wrote a brief note wishing the man well, before sticking it in the outgoing admin tray for Mathilde to handle.

On the top of a stack of mail, a thick envelope from a law firm in Geneva stopped him cold. No need to guess what that might be. In a follow-up phone call from Ismail's father, after their initial heartbreaking conversation when he'd told the man his son was dead, Mr Mahmoud, deranged with grief, had bellowed into Gessen's ear, cursing him with a lifetime of torment and torture. Vowing to sue and shut down the clinic. He would follow Gessen to the ends of the earth, not stopping to rest until the man responsible for his son's death was behind bars.

Overwhelmed by a feeling of doom, he sliced open the

envelope with a penknife. *On behalf of Bélanger, Lacroix, and Moreaux*, we are writing to inform you that… It was indeed what he'd expected. He was being sued for gross negligence and wrongful death. Gessen dropped the letter on the desk and slumped in his chair.

A discreet knock, and Mathilde peeked through the half-open door. The alarm in her eyes spoke volumes. He must look a wreck.

'Sorry to disturb,' she said, 'but I found this in a stack of paperwork. It must have got lost in the shuffle, what with all the… ' Her voice faltered and she placed an envelope on his desk. 'Is there anything I can do?'

'Nothing, thank you. Except, perhaps a pot of coffee, if it's no trouble. I haven't slept since he went missing, you know.'

She ducked out and returned in minutes with the coffee and a plate of almond pastries. The single cup on the tray looked lonely, and he considered asking her to join him, though it wasn't company he wanted, so much as a reassuring pat on the hand. Someone to tell him all would be well.

'Do you need anything else?'

He shook his head and waited until he was alone before reading the lawyer's letter again. With less than an hour before his session with Vidor, he would have to wait until later to plan his next move. His lawyers would take care of the legal side of things, but they could do nothing to heal the blow to the clinic's exemplary record. Tainted with a reputation for negligence, who in their vulnerable state would entrust him with their care?

He poured himself a coffee and picked up the envelope Mathilde had left on his desk. The return address in Paris meant nothing to him at first, but then it came to him: the lady with the toads. He'd forgotten all about her. That he had been away from the clinic, chasing after ghosts, while Ismail hurtled towards his death, was a cross he would bear for the rest of his life.

He pulled out the letter and scanned the page… *a boy who*

lived with the Sovànys... no idea what he was called... student at the Sorbonne, I believe... Odd that Madame Sovàny would accept a strange boy, nearly a man, as a lodger, with her young daughters in the flat... Some kind of foreigner, though he spoke French well.

Tucked inside the letter he found three postcards from the Parc Zoologique, adorned with pictures of brightly coloured tree frogs, and other crawly things. *I thought of you when I saw these... aren't they gorgeous?* He shuddered and dropped the postcards in the bin. Such a remarkable woman, but he was afraid he'd opened up a can of worms, so to speak. For the rest of his days – or hers – he might become the hapless recipient of frequent mementos of her reptilian friends.

Gessen folded the letter and tucked it in a drawer. A male lodger with the Hungarian family downstairs. A foreign boy studying at the Sorbonne. The pieces seemed to slot together. All but one. If Vidor was the son of this family, when – and why – did he change his name to Kiraly? Had there been a family rupture of some kind? And the lodger. Was this Gessen's mystery boy from the Sorbonne? If Vidor and the lodger were friends, Gessen might have seen them together at a student cafe, and later confused one for the other.

What he didn't have was proof. He would need photos of the two boys, and evidence of a name change. A single, unbroken line that stretched back from Vidor Kiraly to Vidor Sovàny. Or another that split off at an angle, leading to the mystery boy with no name.

34

Vidor moved close to the hearth to warm his hands. The heavy damask curtains were drawn, shutting out the darkening sky and raging storm. With its walnut bookshelves, glass table lamps, and leather Chesterfields, the room could have been lifted, wainscoting and all, straight from a country house in Hertfordshire. On the low table by the fire, a silver tray of coffee and cakes beckoned.

They had met in this room only a couple of times before. Perhaps, with this latest invitation to have coffee together in the sumptuous atmosphere of the sitting room, the good doctor was finally prepared to treat Vidor as his equal. After all, he was a celebrated scientist and Cambridge don, not some slavering creature grubbing through the rubbish bins in a dark alley. The man captured on that odious video in Copenhagen, shouting and frothing at the mouth, was an unrecognisable lunatic, an aberration, that had nothing to do with him. Nothing could convince him that the video was anything other than a fake. A transparent ploy to frighten him into admitting he was ill. Hypoglycaemia and exhaustion were known risk factors for temporary psychosis. Gessen surely knew that. Chastened no doubt at having lost a patient due to his own carelessness, he might finally have come to his senses.

After the coffee was poured, Vidor waited for Gessen to

announce that he was fit as a fiddle and free to resume his position as chair of the Neurobiology department at St Catharine's. His heart skipped with joy. Surely, four weeks of playing by Gessen's rules was enough for him to admit the game was up.

'The cream comes from a local farm,' Gessen said, pointing to the silver pitcher, 'famous for its cheese and butter.'

Churned by elves, no doubt, Vidor thought. While the mountain folk clung to their outmoded ways, the twenty-first century nipped at their heels like an insistent terrier. He smiled at his own nonsense. The hope of being sprung from this penal colony at last was making him giddy. The fire crackled. The coffee was perfectly brewed. Vidor had settled into a soporific calm when Gessen's voice broke through his thoughts. Something about his teenage years in Paris.

A spasm of annoyance spoiled his mood. Had they circled back, once again, to the Paris of forty years ago? How many more hurdles did Gessen expect him to leap over before he was discharged? He gritted his teeth. 'I've told you everything I remember from those days.'

'Have you?' Gessen raised his cup to his lips. 'We've talked about your early days in Paris, when you were a schoolboy. We've never talked about your time as a pupil at the *lycée*, or about your decision to attend university in England.'

Vidor stood and walked to the window. He felt claustrophobic with the curtains shut, and pushed them aside to look out at the steadily falling snow. A winter landscape, gloomy, foreboding. In the distance he could just make out the Zen garden with its snow-covered topiary and the lamps lit against the gloom. A shadowy figure, lurking near the entrance, turned his face towards him before slipping inside the gardens. *Ismail*. He was alive.

It all made sense now. Part of the plot to force him to admit he was mad. *I'm onto you now*. As Vidor pressed his face to the glass, the boy caught sight of him and hurried away. Should he say something to Gessen? *No*. Better to keep it quiet and go along with whatever game the doctor was playing.

He returned to his chair and topped up his coffee. How to proceed? Tell Gessen the boring truth, or spice things up a bit to keep the man guessing?

'What's there to say? I went to school, did my homework, ran errands for my mother. When I was sixteen, I took a job at a grocer's, stacking shelves.' He smeared strawberry jam on a *gipfeli* and bit off a chunk of the flaky pastry. Lately, he'd developed a nearly uncontrollable craving for anything sweet. *Must be the mountain air*, Vidor mused. At home in Cambridge, he hardly ever indulged, but now he couldn't seem to get enough. 'I was never arrested, never tardy to class. An excellent student.' He dabbed his mouth with a napkin and gave Gessen a look of unrestrained exasperation. 'I had the most boring adolescence imaginable.'

'What about girls?'

'What about them?'

'Did you have girlfriends?'

Vidor snorted. 'I was too shy to have a girlfriend. No social graces at all. I didn't even kiss a girl until I got to Cambridge. And she was as shy as I was. Coke-bottle glasses, springy red hair. Valerie, her name was. One of only three girls in my advanced calculus class. And if you're planning to ask me about my sexual life, let's just say I'm a normal, red-blooded male. Everything in that department is perfectly functional.'

Gessen stood and poked the logs in the hearth, sending up a shower of sparks. When he returned to his chair, he opened a manila folder and extracted a glossy printout. 'Do you recognise anyone in this photo?'

Vidor barely glanced at the sea of faces before handing it back. 'No.'

'Take your time,' Gessen said, placing the photo on the table. 'No one looks familiar?' So, this was an ambush. The coffee and pastries, the chat by the fireside. A ruse to lull him into participating in his own demise. He pretended to scan the faces one row at a time. 'I don't recognise any of these people.' Gessen didn't blink. 'Though it might help,' Vidor said, 'if you provided some context.'

'It's a photo of the first-year international students at the Sorbonne, taken in 1968.'

Vidor tossed the photo on the table. 'I didn't attend the Sorbonne.'

'Duly noted.' Gessen placed the photo back in the folder. 'But did you ever attend any social events? Surely, you had friends who studied there?'

'Student parties were not my thing.'

'What about the boy in this picture, do you recognise him?' Gessen passed him another photo, a grainy blow-up, the resolution poor. A vein pulsed in Vidor's neck as he studied the blurred features of a boy with shaggy brown hair and sallow cheeks. Where was Gessen going with this line of questioning? What began as the gentle probing of past memories had turned into an interrogation.

'I haven't the slightest idea who this is.'

Gessen had moved to a writing desk a few paces away and was looking down at something. He glanced up at Vidor, then down again, squinting. Vidor craned his neck to see what was so fascinating. It appeared to be another photo of the shaggy-haired boy. He was desperate to get back to his room. It was too hot by the fire and perspiration broke out on his neck. He reached up absently and flicked his ear. When would Gessen announce he was free to go home?

But no such announcement came. Instead, Gessen was staring at him, pinning him to the chair with his eyes. Then he launched into a rambling soliloquy, about his own student days at the Sorbonne, and how exciting it was. The libraries, his teachers, the intellectual challenges. How he'd started out studying mathematics and philosophy before switching to medicine. Such heady days, those years of his youth when the fervour to scale the towers of learning was like a drug.

Vidor nodded along, rigid with irritation, wondering if

Gessen hadn't completely lost the plot. Perhaps he should check himself into his own clinic. The idea made him smile.

'I see my memories have brought you back to your own student days at Cambridge. In our next session, we'll explore that time in your life,' Gessen said. 'It will make an excellent starting point.'

A starting point? Vidor rubbed a painful spot at the back of his neck. 'But I thought…'

'That you were going home today?'

He squeezed his eyes shut, like a sullen child.

'I'm sorry to disappoint you.' Gessen's smile seemed to have morphed into a monstrous grin. 'But we have quite a long way to go yet.'

35

San Luis Obispo, California
6 December 2008

Dear Dr Gessen,

How strange to arrive home, after several weeks away, to find your letter waiting in the stack of mail gathering dust. As if travelling through decades of space and time, my brother's name fairly jumped off the page.

That you might have known my brother brings me great joy. Though I must correct you right away about his full name. Hungarian names can be confusing to outsiders, so allow me to explain: our family name (my father's surname) is Sovàny, not Kiraly. My brother Vidor's full name was Vidor Tadeas Kiraly Sovàny. Kiraly was my mother's maiden name. It was common, in those days, to give the mother's maiden name as a third name, in a nod to the maternal line.

Since you were somewhat cryptic about the nature of your inquiry, you should also know that just after he graduated from the lycée in Paris, my brother disappeared without a trace. There was an inquiry, but he was never found, and as time went on, our *poor Vidor was presumed dead. Evidence pointed to a drowning in the Seine. No foul play was suggested, but there were no witnesses – or at least none that came forward. He had just earned his baccalaureate and had gone out to celebrate with friends. My family could only assume that he'd had too much to drink, and fell into the river and drowned.*

A terrible shock. Our poor mother took to her bed for months. With no way to properly grieve, she found it impossible to live without knowing what happened. For a time, she was convinced he was still alive, and would spend all day wandering the streets, or standing at the window waiting for him to come home. At one point, we thought she might have to be institutionalised. She never believed he was dead. Though the other option, that he was alive and had run off, was even worse, I felt. Better dead than drive a stake through your own mother's heart.

Vida was our own dear boy – he was always Vida at home, never Vidor – the only boy in a household of women and much loved and petted. Though we couldn't make up for the absence of our father. We were refugees from the 1956 Hungarian uprising, and after helping us get to the Austrian border, my father turned back to join the resistance fighters in the capital. It was a terrible blow to all of us, but the unexpected abandonment affected Vida most of all. For months, he couldn't be consoled.

When Vida disappeared, I was the only child still living at home. My three elder sisters were either married or out of the house by then and had lives of their own.

I was very close to my brother and his sudden disappearance from our lives was a terrible shock. My sisters left home within months of each other, not long before Vida's disappearance, and in our diminished

household my mother was truly bereft. We'd had a
student lodger for a time, but he'd moved out by then.
So it was just my mother and me, drowning in our grief.

I'm not sure what else I can tell you about my
brother, but my sister Katerina still lives in Paris, and
she may be of more use to you. A sweet boy, he was,
and we had such hopes for his future. A glorious one,
I'm sure, if not sadly cut short.

Yours sincerely,
Mrs Renata Sovàny Thompson

Gessen folded the letter and added it to Vidor's file. So
there it was at last, the massive lie at the heart of Vidor's story:
that his father had lived in Paris with the family, after leading
them all to safety. When in fact, he'd abandoned his wife
and children at the border, obliging them to make their way
alone. This unexpected betrayal was likely the long-festering
psychic wound Gessen had been trying so hard to uncover.

Would it be impertinent, considering the family's tragic
loss, to ask her to send him a photo? At least the portrait of
the Sovàny family was coming into focus. But if his Vidor
Kiraly turned out to be Renata Thompson's long-lost brother,
Vidor Sovàny, it would be a fantastic coincidence. Even if
it were true, why would Vidor have changed his surname
to his mother's maiden name, and when? Before or after
his disappearance? It seemed horribly cruel to let his family
believe he had died.

In his years as a psychiatrist, Gessen had come across
many people who had spurned their families to make a new
start. But if that were Vidor's intention, why relinquish the
name of the man he claimed to hold dearly in his heart? To
escape detection and start a new life in England, free from
the mother and sisters who professed to love him? Or perhaps
Vidor unconsciously blamed his father for the betrayal at the
border. To a six-year-old, it would have seemed a monstrous
act to leave the family to fend for themselves.

He closed his eyes, calling up the image of Vidor raging at the man in Copenhagen. Though he'd been largely incoherent, a witness was able to identify two words in the stream of invective: monster and dead. Perhaps Vidor, in a break with reality, had confused a strange man with his father. And the voice spewing forth was that of a grieving and terrified young boy, shouting at the man who'd abandoned his family in their time of need. With Vidor blocking any attempt to uncover facets of his psyche, Gessen would have to get the information some other way. At least he had a lead on Vidor's original surname. If – and it was a very big 'if' – this woman's brother was the same Vidor who'd landed in his clinic.

That Renata Thompson's brother had vanished without a trace lent another twist to the story. If he'd intentionally dropped off the radar, the name change would cover his tracks. Armed with a new lead, Gessen could track down others who'd known Vidor Sovàny in Paris. Teachers, friends, neighbours.

But there was still the puzzle of the boy from the Sorbonne. Had Vidor stayed on in Paris after his disappearance? Living under the very noses of his family, after adopting a new name and foreign accent to throw everyone off the scent? While Vidor was looking at the boy in the Sorbonne photo, Gessen was sure he'd seen a flicker about the eyes, a certain tension. Faint, but it was there. The shape of Vidor's mouth, and the flare of his nostrils, were similar to those of the boy in the photo. And that funny tic with his ear. He'd noticed it happened when Vidor grew nervous or upset. Perhaps if he took the photos to Madame Joubert and questioned her again about the Sovàny family, she might shed more light on the mystery.

* * *

Ensconced in the plush armchair in his suite, blissfully quiet now that Ismail was no longer on the other side of the wall, Vidor gazed idly at the shifting clouds. His other housemate, the OCD chap, must be out, and he relished the feeling of being truly alone. Through the window he spotted Gessen hurrying through the main gate, a black travel bag slung over his shoulder. Off on another mysterious errand, or perhaps he was in search of a patient to fill the vacancy left by the boy's death. Egyptian, apparently, though Vidor would always think of him as a princeling from one of the oil-rich countries in the Gulf, where an accident of time and nature had bestowed the bewildered nomads with oceans of cash.

They were down to five now. How the clinic stayed in the black with so few patients was anyone's guess. The sight of Gessen leaving the grounds brought with it a sense of relief. Who knew how long he would be gone, but even if it were just a day or two, it meant a welcome break from the man's odious probing. Yesterday, at dinner, he'd found his schedule for today in an envelope on the table. A two-hour session with Dr Lindstrom in the morning, followed by another round of art therapy with Frau Olaru, or Isabelle, as she insisted he call her.

Why a man with a medical degree would promote such nonsense, he couldn't imagine. The idea of art therapy was patently absurd. Despite the surprising painting of a desert he'd made during his first session, he didn't believe that messing about with finger-paints like a preliterate child would reveal anything useful about the mysteries of the mind.

At least the art session with Frau Olaru would be amusing. Quirky and unconventional was not usually his thing, but he'd enjoyed his time with her. Besides, he needed a favour: to post a letter for him in the village. He suspected that his first letter, the one he'd sent to Magda, had been intercepted and opened. This new request for Magda's help was meant for her eyes only, and he didn't want to take any chances.

36

When he entered the breakfast room, Vidor was pleased to see Libby sitting alone at a table by the window. 'May I join you?'

She gave him a blank look. 'If you like.'

It wasn't until he started in on his plate of eggs and buttered toast that he realised she was particularly distraught. Pale and wan, with tear-stained cheeks. He hoped she wasn't crying over the Egyptian boy, though he'd long suspected the two of them had a special connection. Early birds, like himself, he'd come in to breakfast on a number of occasions to see them sitting at a corner table, their heads bent in conversation. Was she in love with him? Her eyes were definitely pink and puffy.

He should be upset, like everyone else, he supposed, even though the boy had harboured a malicious streak. After years spent in the thicket of undergraduates at the college, he could spot the bounders a mile away. It was a pity the boy had died, of course. Very sad for the family, indeed. But he was not sorry that Ismail was gone from the clinic. Vidor slept more easily at night now that the room next to him was empty. He hadn't been able to rest properly knowing the erstwhile Emirati Prince lay inches from his own bed, or had his ear pressed against the wall.

He lifted the pot of coffee. 'Shall I refresh your cup?'

'No, thanks.' She dabbed her nose with a linen napkin.

'Poor you.' He dared to pat her arm. He was old enough to be her father, so what harm could it do? He added a spoonful of sugar to his coffee and spread strawberry jam on a bread roll studded with poppy seeds, remembering, too late, he was trying to cut down on sweets.

'How are you holding up?' He gave her a sideways glance.

'How do you mean?'

'That poor boy's death.' He buttered another roll and sipped the coffee. Delicious as usual, though he suspected it lacked the full complement of caffeine. 'I could tell you had feelings for him.'

'I did not.' Her face flushed red. 'We were friends. Besides, Ismail was gay. Didn't you know? He was madly in love with a man back home.'

Vidor's hand jerked at the shock of this pronouncement. He stared at the splotch of coffee he'd spilled on the white linen. Not that it mattered, but he hadn't the slightest inkling. 'Back home. You mean in Egypt?'

'No, England. What made you think he lived in Egypt?'

Flustered, Vidor added more sugar to his coffee. 'I heard he was from there.'

She cut her gaze away. 'Why do you care all of a sudden? Ismail said you loathed him.'

Loathed? He'd found the boy annoying, but other than that, he certainly wasn't worth fussing about. He chalked up Libby's overheated emotions to the excesses of the young. But her words floated between them like a noxious cloud. Best to change the subject.

'I thought I'd take a swim today, work off some of this food.' He patted his belly. 'Have you used the fitness facilities? I hear the pool is very nice.'

She scraped back her hair. 'Better than those idiotic Movement & Meditation classes they make us do. What's that all about? Do they think we're stupid? Why not just call it Group Therapy and be done with it?'

In commiseration, he smiled at the frustration that so

neatly mirrored his own. 'But would you go to something called Group Therapy? I'd avoid it like the plague.'

Her smile, though sad, felt like a vindication of his poor attempt at humour. Over the rim of his coffee cup he made note of the slump of her shoulders and the blue smudges under her eyes. Impossible to imagine how such a girl, with everything going for her, ended up here. What existential tragedies could she have possibly suffered in her young life? Though it could be something organic, like anorexia. She was terribly thin, and her skin so delicate he could see a tiny blue vein beating in her temple. As far as he could make out, the only thing she'd had for breakfast was black coffee and two bites of toast. Wasn't anyone monitoring her food intake?

A shadow blocked the light. He looked up to see the German woman, Babette, making a beeline for the buffet. He hoped she wasn't planning to join them, but after she filled her plate, he was relieved to see her retreat to a corner table where she began to fork thick slices of sausage into her mouth. She was getting fatter and more choleric by the hour. It was an effort to drag his eyes away as she viciously tore into a hunk of rye bread. Gessen's patients were falling apart right in front of him, so where was he?

'I know we're not supposed to ask,' Vidor said, turning away from Babette, 'but since you know my story… it only seems natural.' Her eyes grew wary as if she guessed what was coming. 'What's a nice girl like you doing in a place like this?' He nearly reached out to pat her hand but stopped himself in time. Since arriving at the clinic, so many of his thoughts and actions seemed out of step, as if in constant struggle with a more enlightened version of himself. Perhaps all this probing into his early life had caused him to regress into a childish state.

She pushed her chair back, her eyes focused elsewhere. 'I have to go.'

'Shall we meet up later for a swim?'

Tears leaked from her eyes as she shook her head. 'I'm

sorry, I can't...' She gulped back a sob and bolted from the room.

Poor girl. He hoped he hadn't stuck his foot in it. The sound of that woman's monstrous chewing was driving him mad. What he needed was air. More than air. His desperation for a change of scene had reached a fever pitch. If he begged, perhaps Dr Lindstrom would agree to give him a pass to the village. It was the least she could do after thoroughly rebuffing his earlier and desperate plea to arrange for his discharge.

It would be his first outing from the clinic, and he'd been captive here for, what, nearly six weeks? Surely, he had earned the privilege by now. If he had to bring along a minder, so be it. Gessen had left them to their own devices. And while the cat was away, it was a given that the mice in his charge would get up to a little mischief.

37

Gessen emerged from the Métro to a sodden sky and rain-spattered streets. He'd packed his folding umbrella at the bottom of his bag and by the time he dashed across the boulevard to shelter in a doorway, his shoes and jacket were soaked. Madame Chabon was expecting him at two, and he was already late. Not a good start to what would likely be an awkward meeting. Forty years had passed since her brother Vidor disappeared without a trace, but the pain of such a shock never truly went away. The heart yearned for answers, or some sense of closure. But in this case, there was neither.

A tiny, birdlike woman in a dark red wool dress and high-heeled shoes opened the door to the fourth-floor flat. A cloud of fine white hair was swept back from her forehead, and her eyes, bright as pebbles, took his measure before she invited him inside. As he dripped on the parquet in her entry hall, he apologised for his lateness and the state of his clothes, but she waved it away.

'You are my guest, monsieur,' she said, showing him where he could hang his coat. She disappeared and returned with a bright turquoise hand towel to dry his hair. Awash with a pearly light, the high-ceilinged main room was plainly furnished. The dominant feature, a grand piano, in the far corner by the window, gleamed with polish. The faint whoosh of traffic filtered in from the street. On a bookshelf, a brass carriage clock ticked the minutes. Otherwise, it was silent, and the air filled with the weight of expectation.

She disappeared into the back of the flat and returned with a silver pot of coffee on a tray and a plate of oval buttery biscuits, the kind sold in those little shops in Brittany. He remembered them from the time he'd fled Paris and travelled to the Finistère, not long after he'd broken things off with Sophie. Since then, Gessen had never returned to that part of France. Even the smell of the biscuits brought back the familiar nausea, but he took one to be polite and placed it on the edge of his plate.

'What a shock it was to get your letter,' she said, pouring the coffee into white demi-tasse cups. 'When I was a girl, our family lived in this same *quartier*, not far from here. A few months after I married, I moved to Lyon with my husband, but after he died I returned to Paris. It was a stroke of luck to have found this flat. This neighbourhood has always felt like home to me. My three sisters moved abroad years ago, seeking their fortunes elsewhere. Strange, isn't it, how children born of the same parents can turn out to be so different from one another?'

Gessen perched awkwardly on a cream-coloured settee, while Madame Chabon reclined in the shadowy recesses of a yellow wingback chair. On the table between them lay a bulky portfolio with a faux leather cover stamped with gold lettering. It looked like a photo album or scrapbook, and he could hardly contain his excitement. Perhaps this was it: proof that this woman's brother, Vidor Sovàny, was the man known to the world as Vidor Kiraly. In which case, the young Vidor must have faked his death and adopted a new identity.

'So, you're a psychiatrist?' Madame Chabon tilted her head and fixed him with an inquisitive stare. 'How interesting.' Her face was lined and spotted with age, but the dazzling energy of the young girl she once was sparked in her eyes. 'I once considered training to be a psychologist, but I was a dreamy child and the thought of spending long hours with my nose in a book had little appeal.' She waved in the direction of the piano. 'Instead, I studied music and made my living as a piano teacher, like my mother. I suppose I was lucky to recognise my limitations at a young age, so as not to waste time chasing a dream that might never pan out.'

She turned her face to the rain-streaked window. 'Vida was the scholar in the family. Bright. Ambitious. Fizzing with energy. He was the light of my mother's life. But look where that got him. Soaring through the sky, too high and too fast. Like that boy in the Greek myth, what was his name?' She stirred her coffee with a tiny silver spoon. 'That was our Vida. Always chasing the sun.'

Gessen studied the shifting planes of her face as she talked, the interplay of light and shadow. He sensed she hadn't spoken of her brother in years. 'Tell me about him.'

Her lips twitched into a smile as she hesitated, but with little encouragement it all spilled forth. The flight from Budapest. The awful moment when their father turned back at the border. The refugee camp in Austria, and the early years of struggle after they finally settled in Paris. She became a second mother to Vida, while their own mother was away from the flat all day, working two jobs to keep the family afloat. In this household of women, their darling Vida was pampered and fussed over like a beloved pet. As he grew into adolescence, he increasingly resembled the father who'd disappeared from their lives and was never heard from again. Long presumed dead, it was as if the father had returned to life before their eyes. A popular boy, Vida excelled at school and had masses of friends. Not especially athletic, though he enjoyed kicking around a football on the playing fields. Everyone doted on him, and great things were expected of his future.

She paused and turned to the window. 'He did have his moods, though. Flashes of rage or periods of darkness, when he changed into someone I hardly recognised. I suppose, nowadays, you would call it depression.' She gave him a questioning glance. 'An anger turned inward, perhaps, at the father who'd abandoned him to a household of women.'

Gessen held still, afraid to move and break the spell.

'After earning his baccalaureate,' she said, looking down at her hands, ' he was all set to start at the University of Nantes in September. But then he…' her voice faltered, and her eyes grew misty. 'Then he disappeared.' She searched Gessen's face. 'Just like our father. There one minute, gone the next. As if…' She dabbed her nose with the handkerchief tucked in her sleeve. 'Do you believe in fate, Dr Gessen?'

'I do, actually.' He leaned forward and looked into her eyes.

'I still get teary when I think about it. Forty years ago, it was. But the pain is as fresh as if it were yesterday. Odd to think he'd be nearly sixty now if he had lived. No doubt with a lovely family of his own. When Vida hit his teens, the girls swarmed around him like bees. He could have had his pick of any of them, but now we'll never know what might have been. He's trapped in time, isn't he?' Her eyes sought his. 'Like any young person cut down too soon. He'll always be that bright and charismatic boy whose future was snatched away.'

She followed his gaze to the photo album on the table. 'I dug that out of a box in the cellar when I knew you were coming. The face of an angel, Vida had. Would you like to see some photos?'

38

With his pass from Dr Lindstrom clutched in his hand, Vidor felt a renewed vigour as he strode towards the main gate. His minder for the day out, a scrawny fellow with frizzy hair and spotty skin, followed close behind. If Vidor had a mind to flee, he could easily overpower him. But for the moment he was content to have the man believe he was as meek and obedient as a baby lamb. But once they reached the village, he would allow his instincts to guide him. The anticipation of this microscopic taste of freedom, a twenty-minute trip down the mountain by funicular to the small village in the valley, made his blood tingle.

The skies had cleared, though it was still too chilly and grey for anyone to be out on the grounds where the powdery snow was covered with a layer of ice. The high mountains all around them were cloaked in white and the the valley filled with snow. Pretty enough, he supposed, with its fairy-tale charm, though the thought of spending the winter here made him uneasy. Trapped in close quarters with the others for months. Cut off from civilisation by endless storms, and forced to fend for themselves like rats in a cage. His house attendant had assured him the clinic was well equipped to survive for weeks at a time with no need for outside assistance. A full larder and a backup generator, with plenty of fuel stored in an outbuilding, could get them through the entire winter, if necessary.

The attendant opened the gate and beckoned for Vidor to follow. His wrist monitor must have been deactivated. Otherwise, wouldn't it set off an alarm? They walked single file to the funicular, only to find no one about. Smoke curled through a blackened stovepipe poking through the little hut at the railhead. The driver must be inside, huddled by the woodstove for warmth. The attendant knocked and waited until a gnarled old man appeared in the doorway. He stared at them with rheumy eyes, a plug of tobacco stuck inside his cheek.

After examining the letter Vidor showed him with a suspicious squint he grunted for them to follow. Vidor and his minder climbed into the funicular and waited for the man to start up the engine.

'Good thing you got yerself a pass,' he said, 'or they'd come after you.' He snorted and tapped his nose. A veritable Charon to guide them across the Styx, the alcohol on the man's breath would knock over a mountain goat. Though it wasn't the underworld they were headed for, Vidor thought, with a flicker of excitement, but the real world. A kingdom without restrictions and rules. A marvellous land of clocks and calendars, with the regular arrangement of time, and normal people going about their business.

The funicular rattled and lurched as the cogwheel mechanism shunted them down the mountain. Vidor toyed briefly with the idea of doing a runner. Why go back to that nonsense when he could taste freedom in every breath of the pine-scented air? It might unleash a frantic chase down the mountain by the Swiss version of a SWAT team. But better to take a stand than wait for Gessen to let him go. With the tendrils of lassitude infiltrating his brain, any day now he would sink into a torpor, unable to summon the energy to speak or move. Gessen's insistent prodding and probing was herding Vidor down a dark passage he had no wish to explore.

If he didn't get away soon, inertia and rigor mortis might keep him here, a fly trapped in amber.

As the funicular ground through a gap in the trees, the branches of the pines smacked against the windows. Strange that he had no memory of coming up the mountain. Had he been unconscious at the time, or sedated? Dark thoughts scuttled through his head, as he questioned whether he had, in fact, agreed to be transferred here as Gessen claimed. And the business about attacking that man in Copenhagen. Most certainly staged, and the video a fake. Even the clinic might be nothing more than an elaborate stage set, and the other patients, actors. All in a ruse to extract information only he possessed. But what did they want? State secrets, or his special knowledge of the brain?

He was too smart for them, of course. Gessen would have anticipated that Vidor might guess it was a scam. That Egyptian boy must be in on it too. How could he be sure he was really dead? Where was the proof? Gessen's word was all he had. Wasn't it only yesterday, just before dusk, that Vidor had seen Ismail lurking at the edge of the Zen garden, partly concealed behind the boxwood hedge? It wasn't a ghost. When he looked up and saw Vidor at the window, the boy had taken flight and vanished into the trees.

Sweat soaked through his shirt. Blood beat in his neck. As he lurched from his seat to open the window for air, the attendant's head snapped up, mildly alarmed. But the windows were shut fast. *Air.* He clawed at the zipper of his jacket. He needed air. Darkness closed upon them as they entered a narrow chasm where water gushed through cracks in the rock, and pine branches scraped the window. By the time they finally ground to a halt, Vidor had pulled off his coat and hat. When the driver cranked open the door, he stumbled from the car and flung himself into the frigid air, gasping for breath.

The attendant stared at him goggle-eyed. 'Shall we go back? You don't look well.'

'No.' Vidor coughed and straightened up. 'I'm all right.' He clumsily patted the man's shoulder. 'Just a touch of… never mind. I'm fine.' And he was, more than fine, now that he was away from the suffocating pall of the clinic and once again in the bracing sphere of normal life. The contrast so great that only now did he realise how badly the atmosphere of the clinic had crushed his spirit, as if he'd been forced to live and breathe the fetid air under a bell jar. No amount of gourmet food and luxury accommodations could make up for that.

He stepped off the platform and headed into the village, a place he'd only glimpsed from the clinic's eyrie high above. A scattering of houses with steep roofs and painted shutters. A narrow road that snaked through the valley, hemmed in by pines. Up ahead, not thirty metres away, the red-and-white sign of the national railway shone in the grey light. Bless the industrious Swiss for building a railhead in the back of beyond.

As he hurried into the street, the hapless attendant in tow, he could sense the local villagers and shopkeepers turning their heads to stare at him. Wondering, perhaps, what flavour of crackpot he might be. Debilitated and dangerous, or merely deranged? There was nothing up the mountain but the clinic. Dressed in their standard-issue clothing, his status as a patient would be obvious to all. The jacket and trousers he wore, even his socks and underwear, were courtesy of Gessen, as if the man owned his very skin.

As they approached the station, a whistle shrieked, and the train pulled away from the siding. Exactly on time, surely, as the minute hand on the clock moved to 2.37. He closed his eyes and savoured the words, two thirty-seven. Too late to have given his minder the slip and make a run for it. Couldn't this one train, out of thousands in this clockwork country, be delayed for half a minute? Perhaps even the village and all its inhabitants were puppets under Gessen's control, with everyone conspiring against him.

He lingered in front of the departure schedule, his face bathed in the glow of the Christmas lights strung in the kiosk. With an hour to kill and not a cent in his pocket, there wasn't much he could do here. Would it be impertinent to ask the attendant for a few francs? Perhaps if he pressed his face against the bakery window, the red-cheeked woman inside would take pity on him and hand over a coffee and a pastry. But when he stuck his head inside the door and gave her a pitiable look, she shook her head and frowned.

Mist clung to the pines above the deep layer of snow. Frigid snowmelt gushed out through fissures in the rock and roared through a viaduct, draining the runoff from the mountain. Now that he was in the midst of it, the village seemed less idyllic than he'd imagined from the view above. Much of it lay in the damp shadow of the mountains, and the few desultory shops held little of interest. He shoved his hands in the pockets of his coat and bent his head into the wind. The attendant followed behind. Ahead, the high peaks of the mountains loomed. He passed a ski shop, a tavern, a kiosk. Hungry for news of the outside world, he scanned the headlines in French and German. No English papers, though hardly a surprise in this hamlet in the middle of nowhere.

Would there be an item on his disappearance? *Missing: Eminent Cambridge don. Believed kidnapped.* Or was he just a footnote now in the dusty archives of the university? No one was looking for him, as far as he knew. His coded letters to Magda had failed to induce his would-be rescuers to storm the clinic.

When he came out on the other side of the trees, the landscape opened up to reveal a farmstead halfway up the hill, where goats munched silage under a gloomy sky. Two children, bundled in bright parkas, sped past him on mountain bikes. No school today? Though it could be Saturday or a holiday. Stupid not to have noticed the date on the newspapers. At least he'd spotted the time on the station clock. Just the sight of those numbers had provided a calming effect. As if newly born, his arms and legs tingled, thin-skinned and raw. Thrust into a world he'd nearly forgotten. The freedom to do as he pleased, to go where he wanted, without being observed and monitored. How could he get back there? That seemingly mythical place he'd once inhabited, fast receding in the mists. Lost in the woods, indeed.

He crouched on the path and pretended to study a clump of mushrooms growing from a rotten stump. His mind urged him onward. *Run, run.* But where would he go? He glared at the attendant, who stuck to him like a burr. 'I'm still here. You can relax now.' The sharp wind froze the skin on his face and neck. He zipped his parka and spun on his heel, keeping his head down as he plodded back to the village. A long slog to civilisation, such as it was. For a brief moment he longed for the warmth of his room.

So much for his big adventure. That was likely Gessen's plan all along. Give him a day out beyond the gates to discover the truth: there was no 'out there' as opposed to 'in here'. Wherever you go, there you are. But Gessen was wrong, and his little plan had failed.

As he passed the news kiosk, a man emerged from the shop. Solid as an oak, his weather-worn brow creased in a frown as he stared at something in his hand. Dark green parka. Hobnailed boots. Vidor stopped in his tracks. That face... so oddly familiar, he'd seen it before. But where? His heart juddered as it came to him. His life-long nemesis, in the guise of the man from the prize ceremony. What was he doing here? How had he known where to find him? His wily, relentless foe, returning to haunt Vidor from his purported grave. He glared at the man's bent head and crossed to the other side of the street. When the man followed, Vidor quickened his step. Behind him, the hobnailed boots struck the pavement. *Clack, clack, clack.*

Panic gripped his throat. He darted across the street and quickened his pace. *The train station.* He'd be safe there. Vidor pivoted on his heel, but still the man followed. *Clack,*

clack, clack. His muscles tensed as he awaited the murderous blow to his neck.

The station hall was empty. Not the safe harbour he'd hoped for, but he crouched in the corner away from the windows and held his breath. No sign of the golem. He breathed out. But the door creaked open, and the man stepped inside, blocking the only exit as his eyes, aglow with the flames of hell, raked Vidor from head to toe.

'Stay where you are!' Vidor backed against the wall. 'Leave me alone.'

But the man advanced, his nailed boots ringing out as he crossed the stone floor. The sound was deafening, but Vidor refused to be cowed.

'You're supposed to be dead.'

But the man kept coming, his fiery gaze fixed to a point on Vidor's chest, as if seeking the exact spot to rip out his heart.

'Stay back.' Terror gave strength to Vidor's shaking limbs. The blood rushed to his face with the force of a volcano. With a cry, he leapt at the man's throat and knocked him to the ground. 'Monster. Traitor. Why aren't you burning in hell?'

The dark-eyed man, fiendishly strong, flung Vidor off like a sack of turnips. Two men in uniform burst through the door and pinned Vidor to the ground. *This is it*, he thought, *the violent death that had stalked him all his life*. Crouched in the shadowy cupboard in his bedroom. Lurking in the empty stairwell. Haunting the corpses, stacked like firewood, under the great city. The intricate dance of predator and prey.

And having pursued him across the infinite distance of space and time, Death had found him at last.

39

He opened his eyes to the dark. His head ached, and when he tried to sit up he fell back with a groan. A door opened, and a woman in a white smock appeared at his side. It felt like he'd been out for days. Skimming high above a blackened forest, tracing a path through the trees, where far below, in a grove of dark pines, an ogre crouched and waited.

Lights flickered overhead. The sharp odour of antiseptic stung his nostrils. As awareness slowly returned, Vidor blinked and tried to focus. Where was he? Not at home in Cambridge, or his bedroom in the chalet. This room was smaller, with pale yellow walls and acoustic tiles on the ceiling.

'Would you like to sit up?'

A sharp pain stabbed his temple. 'Where am I?' It came out as a croak.

The woman pressed a button on the wall to raise the bed. 'You're in the infirmary at Les Hirondelles. I hear you had quite an adventure yesterday.'

An adventure? What day was it? He closed his eyes. Sleep was all he wanted. A dreamless sleep. His brain stuttered with the effort of recalling the specifics of his life. Name, age, date of birth. What happened yesterday? What was today?

She glanced at the monitor above his bed. 'Your fever's down.' Her fingers were cool on his wrist as she checked his pulse. He tried to get a look at her watch, but the angle was wrong. As she handed him a glass of water, her smile was kind as she waited for him to drink. Dark hair, dark eyes. A quizzical tilt to the head, reminiscent of a flamenco dancer who'd once caught his gaze on the streets of Seville. But he'd never seen this woman before. Was he really back at the clinic or was this all part of a massive game of deception? Pulling levers and twisting dials, to entice him into believing their version of reality.

'Dr Gessen will be in shortly to see how you're getting on.'

He watched her go and closed his eyes. So, it was true. He was back where he'd started. Would he never escape the hell he'd stumbled into? Behind his closed eyes appeared the outline of a face. Dark hair, agate eyes, a cruel smile. That man in the village… He explored the painful bump on his head. He was the victim here. The man had attacked him first. Anything Vidor might have done afterwards was self-defence.

Those eyes. Staring out from a face altered by time, but the same cold and calculating eyes he'd known all his life. The furious glare and curled lip, studying his infant son with a clinical gaze. As if observing a particularly strange and disturbing insect. Staring, wondering, waiting. 'He's not mine.' The man's voice vibrated with rage. In the background, a woman wept. 'Whore! Did you really think you could pass off this pathetic worm as mine?'

'Vidor?'

A face, colourless as the moon. Dark holes for eyes. 'Vidor, can you hear me?' Fingers snapped in front of his face. *Go away.* So tired. They must have given him something to dull his nerves and muzzle his thoughts.

After passing through a vast dreamscape of shifting terrain and monstrous shadows, it was still dark when he once again opened his eyes. The blinds were drawn across the window and he lay in bed, stiff and sore, hardly daring to breathe, wondering what new tortures they had in store for him. When he raised his hands to his face, he saw that his ring was gone.

His mother's ring. A keepsake all his life, and now they'd stolen it from him. A rustling sound in the corner, like dried stalks of grass. The stale air of exhaled breath. He stiffened. 'Who's there?'

A shadow detached itself from the wall and moved towards him.

'Vidor?'

His heart thumped. Gessen. The blasted man was everywhere. All-seeing, all-knowing. Even now, sharpening his scalpel, itching to slice into Vidor's cerebrum, to burrow into the limbic system and pluck out his memories, one at a time. *Tell me about your father.* He groaned and turned away.

'How are you feeling?' He pulled up a chair and sat at the foot of the bed. 'Do you remember what happened?'

Vidor stared at the ceiling. 'I want to go home. Haven't you tortured me enough?'

Gessen switched on the bedside lamp. His eyes, obsidian in the dim light, shone with a keen intensity. Vidor squeezed his own eyes shut.

'If you're not ready to talk about it, would you mind, then, if I told you a story? We're never too old for stories, are we? And the best ones often have the power to change our lives.'

Vidor's leg ached, and he yearned to pull the bedsheet over his head. Never in his life had he so desperately wished to be alone.

'A long time ago,' Gessen began, 'there was a young boy who lived with his loving parents in a vibrant and beautiful city. He was the longed-for son, and from the time of his birth, he knew nothing but happiness. Spoiled and coddled by his parents and much older sisters, he thrived in the protective warmth of his family's love. Spending his days in the dappled sunlight of a courtyard garden, and his nights tucked up in bed by his mother, while listening to the classical music his father loved.

'A few weeks before his sixth birthday, he was awakened with great urgency and pulled from his bed in the middle of the night. Hurried into a black automobile and forced to huddle under a blanket, his heart beating wildly, as the car drove at great speed along the dark and treacherous roads through the mountains. It was one of the boy's starkest memories. Cowering under a blanket as the vehicle bumped and rattled through the blackness. The moonless night and hushed voices, the sharp, crystalline air.

'Many years later, he would learn the details of that night. How he had been taken from his home, under cover of darkness, to travel with his mother, ostensibly for a holiday, by ship and train and bus to the other side of the world. Their final destination was a village in Switzerland, across the Rhine from Baden-Württemberg. The boy was assured his father would join them later, but he never did. No matter how long he waited or how many times he asked, "When will he come?" His father never appeared on the doorstep, laden with gifts and wreathed in smiles as was his wont, and the boy was heartbroken. How could he feel otherwise, when his father was a kind and loving man who doted on his only son?

'Not long after the boy and his mother were settled in their new home, and he was enrolled in the local school, she failed to return from a trip to the market in the next town. He'd sat by the window until long after dark waiting for her to come. The two strangers, though friends of his mother's, apparently, who'd taken them in, looked upon him with pity. When he asked where his mother was, they said he was not to worry, and that he would see her soon.

'But the boy never saw her again. Nor his father, and it was understood he was not to speak of them. The people who raised the boy were not unkind, but having no children of their own, they often seem puzzled by what to make of him. When they left their home by the river and moved to another village, deep in the mountains, the boy wondered how his parents would find him so far away from where they had left him. At school, he used the surname of the people who'd taken him in. As the years passed, he could scarcely remember what his real name was, or the people who used to be his mother and father. All that remained was a photo, taken not long after he was born. His mother's thick dark hair falling across her cheek as she gazed at the child in her arms. His father's hand on her shoulder, looking straight into the camera, beaming with pride, as if to say, *See what we have made.*'

Gessen stood and pulled back the curtains. The moon was nearly full, and the ghostly light glazed the ever-deepening snow on the mountains. Beautiful but deadly.

'As the boy grew older,' Gessen continued, his eyes fixed on the highest peak, 'he looked for his parents everywhere. He was sure he spotted his father boarding a streetcar in Zurich or seated in the back of a passing taxi. And wasn't that his mother amongst the throngs of Saturday shoppers in the Bahnhofstrasse, pausing to look at shoes or handbags or bed linens in the plate-glass windows of the shops? With no proof of their deaths, how was he to know they weren't still alive? The trick was to stay alert, and to look for them everywhere. Harness the power of filial love to align the planets, until they reached the exact point in space and time when their paths would intersect.'

He returned to the chair by the bed.

In Vidor's drowsy state, the rhythm of Gessen's words had taken on the cadence of a well-rehearsed chant. In that strange state between waking and sleep, Vidor's mind left his body and floated towards the ceiling. A tranquil hideaway, under the eaves, where he might remain, suspended between the pull of the earth and the vacuum of space. Nothing in that liminal gap to disturb the peace and tenor of his mind.

'Even now,' Gessen said, the fading voice reaching Vidor from the other side of a distant shore, 'long after the boy grew up and learned what kind of man his father was. When he wants nothing more than to strip their shared DNA from his tissue and bones, he thinks he sees him at times, or someone who looks like him. Turning the corner of a crowded street.

Boarding a train. The scorched head and fiery-eyed gaze of a man burning in hell.'

A hush settled over the room. The only sound was Gessen's breath, synched in time to Vidor's own. 'The ties of blood and bone are not easily broken. Even in death.'

A long stillness followed. Was there a moral to this particular tale? Vidor turned his head away, trying to slow the urgent ticking of his heart.

'What I'm trying to say, Vidor, is that it might be helpful if you'd open your mind to the possibility you're being haunted by the shadow of another life. By someone, long hidden, who now wishes to make himself known.'

As Gessen's long monologue came to an end, Vidor could feel his mind, still unmoored from his body, being carried along on a deep current. Drifting above the ocean floor, wafting with the seagrass above the shifting sands. A shaft of sunlight pierced the murky water above his head. With little desire to swim towards the light, he clung to the seabed, feeling no sense of danger. Instead, a warm embrace and quiet murmur buoyed his spirits, as he felt the touch of a woman's hand. He drifted and dreamed, content to float for all eternity, until a vague threat, like a dark stain, blocked out the sun. A boy with a face like a hatchet emerged from the depths to taunt him. *You're not supposed to be here. You should have died.*

But he didn't die. *I did not die*, he shouted, though no words came. *I'm still here.* He gasped for air as he moved upwards through the murk, struggling towards the light.

40

Vidor was relieved to see it wasn't Gessen waiting for him, with his fangs concealed behind a false smile, but the welcome presence of Dr Lindstrom, dressed in a cream-coloured blouse and black skirt as if for a celebration. Had the Christmas holiday arrived, or was it already long past? While he'd been out, adrift in the liminal zone, time had lost all meaning.

She crossed the floor and handed him a glass of frothy liquid, the colour of a ripe peach. 'Try it,' she said. 'It's my favourite smoothie recipe. Loaded with vitamins.'

When he pronounced the drink delicious, she rewarded him with a smile. But as he settled into the chair her face creased with concern.

'What a fright you had the other day in the village.' She pulled her chair closer until their knees were practically touching.

'I asked Dr Gessen if I could take over your session today.'

The concern in her eyes made it difficult for him to look away.

'Just between you and me,' she said, lowering her voice, 'he can be a bit of a badger, don't you think? In light of your recent ordeal, I was able to convince him you might appreciate a more delicate touch.'

The scent of her cologne, reminiscent of a summer meadow, perfumed the air between them.

'Where do you want me?' he asked. 'On the couch, or perhaps in this chair?'

'The couch is better, don't you think? More comfortable for you.' She led him into the adjoining room and waited for him to stretch out, before covering him with a soft wool blanket. After lowering the lights, she settled in the chair behind his head.

'Now, I'd like you to close your eyes and take a few deep breaths. Not in your chest but deep in your abdomen.' She left the chair and placed her hand on his belly. 'That's right. Slow, deep breaths.'

When she moved her hand away, his heart lurched with a sense of inexplicable loss. How long had it been since he'd felt a woman's touch? His weekly forays into Magda's bed, always after dark, like a thief in the night, satisfied his physical urges to a degree, but did little to assuage his hunger for affection. But real affection required a vulnerability he was too ill-equipped to manage. Love offered, only to be withdrawn, would be the death of him.

'After I heard about what happened in the village, I was worried about you,' Dr Lindstrom said, her soft voice like music to his ears. 'That man who frightened you…'

Was that a catch in her throat?

'You've got to be careful with some of these mountain types. Living alone for months at a time. After what happened to Ismail, I sometimes wonder… well, never mind.' Her voice fell away. 'While you were in the medical bay, I was sick with worry.'

Behind him came the whisper of nylons as she crossed her legs.

'It might help if you could tell me about it.' Her breathing quickened. 'That man who threatened you. I saw him in the village once and immediately crossed to the opposite side of the street. Something in his face frightened me.'

'He was about to attack me, you know,' Vidor said, warming to his role as victim. 'He would have smashed my head on the floor like a pumpkin if I hadn't defended myself.'

She sighed in sympathy. 'I don't know why they let him roam around the village. But these mountain men think they own the place. As if anyone from outside is an intruder – or a threat.'

As Vidor listened to her voice, his breathing slowed of its own accord, and his limbs grew heavy. Was he naturally tired, or had she put something in that juice she gave him? Never mind. The floating sensation was pleasant, and her voice a soothing whisper in his ear.

'Tell me, did the man say anything to you? Had you ever seen him before?'

His lids fluttered, and he allowed them to close. 'Something about the eyes. Something...' As his mind drifted off, he struggled to stay awake. From a great height, he observed his own body stretched out on the couch, noting the shifting planes of his face and the laboured breath, as darkness descended like a veil.

'I saw him once before,' he said, his voice straining against the weight on his chest. 'In Paris. A long time ago. Cold wind slicing through my skin. Shivering in my thin jacket, feverish, ill. A man with a face like thunder stepped out of a cinema and frowned at the darkening sky. It was the man who'd been stalking my nightmares for years. He lit a cigarette and hurried away. I followed him. When he stopped at a kiosk to buy a newspaper, I caught a glimpse of his hands, and the familiar silver ring. I tried to call out, but no words came. Just before he stepped into a taxi, he looked up at me, but showed no sign of recognition. Only after he disappeared down the street did my voice return. I knew who he was and cried out. *Masakh! Khayin!* But it was too late. He was gone.'

* * *

Ten minutes into the video of Ursula's session with Vidor, Gessen nearly leapt from his chair. For a few seconds, Vidor's face and voice underwent a dramatic transformation. A brief spasm altered his urbane, middle-aged countenance into that of a terrified boy. A split-second change brought on while recalling the memory of a man stepping out of a cinema.

He would have to confirm with a translator, but he would bet anything that the words Vidor shouted were not Hungarian.

The question now was a matter of awareness. If a second identity lurked inside Vidor, did he suspect, on some level, that another persona, with a different name and history, shared his psyche? Had it been a conscious choice to reinvent himself as a Hungarian named Vidor Kiraly Sovàny, a boy who'd presumably died by drowning? Or was it an authentic case of dissociative identity? In his long career as a psychiatrist, Gessen had only come across one case of multiple personality disorder. A skittish young woman, badly abused by her mother as a child, had harboured four distinct personalities, or alters, one of whom was a middle-aged man named Roland with a craggy voice and dark sense of humour, who liked single malt whisky and unfiltered cigarettes.

His thoughts bounced from one possibility to another. But no matter how he labelled it, this glimmer of insight into Vidor's strange behaviour provided the evidence he needed to move forward.

He stood and walked to the window, but there was nothing to see but a thick covering of mist, with the high mountains lost behind the clouds. Only the second week of December, but all signs pointed to a bitter winter to come. The local Mountain Rescue would be busy this season. In the weeks since Ismail's unfortunate death, they had taken three other bodies off the mountains. Ismail's remains had been flown to Egypt for burial, and the civil lawsuit was working its way through the courts. At some point, according to Gessen's lawyer, he would be called to give a deposition, but he had no desire to think about that now.

He rang his assistant for coffee and jotted down a few notes, hoping to strengthen his case in favour of dissociative identity. Both judge and jury. *For the sake of argument,*

Gessen surmised, *let's say that two different men, the one in the village and the man at the awards ceremony, had triggered a painful childhood memory*. Not in Vidor's mind, but in the mind of his subconscious alter. Perhaps in the guise of the boy from the Sorbonne, who he could no longer think of as Milen. The name didn't sound right, but for this speculative exercise he would call him 'M'.

Those two strange men, under vastly different circumstances, had clearly triggered something in M. A memory so terrifying it manifested as a recurring trauma. But if Vidor's core persona was M, when had the transformation to Vidor Kiraly occurred? The other option, a dissociative disorder, or perhaps an extended fugue state, could mean that Vidor had acquired an alter that had nothing to do with his own life. What terrible traumas might he have suffered to cause his personality to split?

Returning to his desk, Gessen rewound the video to study it again, frame by frame, hoping to catch the exact moment of transformation. As he advanced the frames, a convulsion marred Vidor's features, followed by a flash of terror and a heart-rending cry. Just as quickly, the boy's frightened face vanished, to be replaced, a millisecond later, by Vidor's placid expression. As Ursula wrapped up the session, she looked straight into the camera and nodded. Vidor sat up and looked around him, befuddled, as if he'd returned from a long and complex journey through a barren landscape.

Who was he? Gessen had waited to open Bertrand's letter until he'd watched the video of Ursula's session with Vidor, but he reached for it now and slit open the envelope.

Chèr Anton,
I've held off writing to you until I had some news. It took some digging, as nothing is digitised from those years, and the archives are tucked away in a dusty annex. After calling around, I was able to get a copy of the registration forms for three students, one of whom could be your man. Fortunately,

a photo is stapled to the forms and, though much faded, might help you find what you're looking for.

Do let us know when you'll next be in Paris so we can find a time to meet. Eveline greatly enjoyed our evening together and sends you 'gros bisous'.

Bon courage,
Bertrand

He placed the copies of the student records side by side on his desk. How young the boys looked, with their earnest faces and shaggy brown hair. The first boy, Alejandro, was born and raised in Uruguay. On the second boy's file, a water stain had smudged the ink, so it was difficult to make out his country of origin. The first letter, A, was legible, though that hardly narrowed it down. Albania, Argentina, Algeria, Afghanistan, Australia? It could be any of those. The third boy, Zivko, was Yugoslavian.

Gessen turned back to the second file and studied the boy's eyes and the curve of his jaw. This one felt right, somehow, and when he saw the name, he smiled. Malik Sayid. Not Milen or Mikhail, or Miguel, but Malik. Somewhere, in the deepest recesses of his brain, he had always known the right name, but the memory, slippery as a minnow, had hovered tantalisingly out of reach. *Malik Sayid*. He leaned back in his chair and smiled again. Progress at last. He'd have to proceed carefully, but the moment had arrived. It was time to confront Vidor with what he knew.

41

Vidor stubbed his toe as he stumbled out the door and into the biting air, trying to shake off the effects of another bad night.

Ragged clouds, buffeted by the wind, sped through the high peaks. Snow had fallen in the night and was heaped on either side of the path that led to the dining hall. On a bench near the fountain, drained for the winter, he passed Hélène, bundled into a dark green parka, with a glossy, Russian-style Cossack hat pulled down over her ears.

'You're white as a ghost,' she proclaimed, as he drew closer. 'You haven't seen an owl this morning, have you? I saw a female just the other day, winging through the pines. A bad sign, you know. My eldest sister, may she rest in peace,' Hélène said, 'was quite the ornithomancer. A walking encyclopaedia of titbits about the meaning and lore of birds. I wonder if anyone spotted an owl just before that poor boy died. What was his name? But *you* look all right, so no harm done.' She tilted her head and examined him with a sharp eye. 'Too early for bourbon, but a strong cup of tea will fix you right up. Come with me.' She stood and looped her arm through his, careful not to jostle the Chanel bag, and steered him in the direction of the main building. He'd been hoping to avoid the place, not wanting to run into Gessen, but her grip on his arm was surprisingly strong.

'Nothing to be afraid of,' she said. 'It's the library we're heading to, not the dungeon in the cellar.'

'Dungeon?'

She tweaked his exposed wrist. 'What a scaredy cat you are.'

They entered through a side door and climbed a flight of stairs. The sounds of their passage down a long corridor were swallowed up by the thick grey carpet.

'Here we are.' She turned the knob on a heavy carved-wood door and led him into the room. Whatever Vidor had expected, it wasn't this. Mullioned windows, painted ceiling. The hushed atmosphere of a cathedral was created no doubt by the plush chairs and book-lined walls. Why had he never been in here before? It was like stumbling upon an Aladdin's cave, hidden behind a secret panel.

'Lucky for us we have the place to ourselves.' Her voice was brisk. 'You sit over there, while I ring for tea.'

The bossy manner was new. Was it thwarted maternal instinct that drove her to treat him like a truculent child? Vidor relaxed into a wingback chair near the fire crackling in the grate. It was all very bewildering, as if he'd been transported by magic to a country house in the Sussex Downs.

He'd been dimly aware there was a library on the grounds, clearly listed amongst the clinic's offerings in the patient information packet. But he'd preferred the sanctuary of his own room, rather than risk unwelcome contact with the other patients.

As Hélène fumbled in the depths of her bag, he turned away, expecting the worst, but what she pulled out was not a doll as he'd feared, but a glossy square of paper. 'I don't show this to just anyone,' she said, her voice dropping to a whisper. She unfolded the square and smoothed it out on her lap. 'These are my children. Well, two of the three anyway. Lucinda and Marcel, aren't they beautiful?' She passed him the sheet. 'Careful, it's quite fragile.'

The page had been torn from a magazine, a glossy tabloid

by the looks of it. *Tatler*, perhaps, or *Paris Match*, magazines he'd only seen when buying a newspaper at the kiosk. An advertisement, apparently, for a brand of high-end clothing, depicting a beautiful young woman with gazelle-like limbs and a cascade of sleek blonde hair, gleaming white teeth, green eyes. The boy next to her, leaping onto a pile of autumn leaves, boasted the cheekbones of a Greek god. Behind the dazzling pair, a blue sky framed the distant hills. Wealth, beauty, privilege. A glass-fragile world, easily broken. Look but don't touch.

Poor woman. What had gone wrong in Hélène's mind that she believed these two perfect specimens of the human form were her own children? A type of dementia, surely. And perhaps the rumours were true. Her child, or children, had died, and in her grief, she had projected their spirits onto the fashion models in a lifestyle magazine.

He handed her the page, worn and creased with age. 'Your daughter is the spitting image. And your son, what a charmer.' Getting trapped in the web of her delusions was the last thing he needed, and he sought an excuse to get away. Was he the only sane one amongst the bunch? But it was too late. A tea tray arrived, brought in by a woman who Vidor recognised as one of the staff from the dining hall. For the first time, he saw her as a person, rather than a nameless member of staff, and smiled as she set the tray on the table. 'Thank you, Miss…?'

'Kamila.' She smiled. 'Can I get you anything else?'

Her glossy black hair hung in a plait down her back, and her warm eyes were lively. For some reason, his vision today was sharper, his hearing more acute. Of course, Isabelle, his art guru, would take credit if he were to admit to his heightened senses. But that was nonsense, it had nothing to do with art. The film that had separated him from the world, dulling his senses, was indeed scrubbed away. But that was surely due to a change in medication. Or perhaps they'd replaced his daily tablets with sugar pills. That could only mean one thing: he was going home.

Hélène poured out the tea and passed him a cup. 'Try the lemon cake,' she said. 'It's a speciality of the house.'

The assertion blithely made, as if they were taking tea at a five-star resort and not a heavily guarded loony bin. But he accepted the offer. The cake was delicious and for a moment, he pretended he was in one of the private dining halls at St Catharine's. That when he was finished and the tea tray cleared away, he could gather his things and return to the hum and buzz of his laboratory, his students busily working on their research projects. Their journal club meeting set to discuss the most recent publications.

'Now, tell me what's going on with you,' she said, tapping him on the wrist with a manicured nail. 'From the look of things, you need to shape up and ride straight, or you'll be stuck here forever.'

Vidor was mystified by her change in character. A complete pivot from bonkers to bully in the space of a millisecond. He'd always thought her a harmless old thing, what with those bats in her belfry. Now, she was tart as a school mistress. Perhaps her meds had been changed as well.

Vidor's gaze skittered away from her piercing look. The silence stretched out awkwardly.

'You know, I've felt funny the past few days. Ever since I was attacked by that man in the village. I've been having strange dreams, and during the day I feel like I lose chunks of time. I'll look up to find the sun has gone down or that I've finished my breakfast, but I can't recall having eaten it.'

'What you need is to start facing your fears,' Hélène said, handing him another slice of cake. 'Get at the root of the matter. Face whatever it was that brought you here.' She met his eyes. 'Otherwise you'll end up like me, no longer the master of your own fate.' She sank into the depths of the chair until her face was in shadow.

The firelight gleamed on the emerald stones in her ears. Her hair, the colour of summer wheat threaded with grey, was freshly styled, as if she'd come straight from the beauty salon.

How long had she been a patient? Rumour had it she'd been here for years. At the thought of spending the rest of his life in this place, his heart jerked oddly, like a frightened creature struggling to break free. *No, absolutely not.* He would not end up like Hélène, forever locked in a gilded cage. He eyed the Chanel bag at her feet, and his panic evaporated. She was mad, of course, and only a crazy person would listen to a madwoman's advice. Even if her counsel made sense, he had no idea how to heal the so-called wound he was supposedly cursed with.

Was his ticket out simply a matter of baring his soul to Gessen and facing his fears? As for his psychic wound, did it really have something to do with his father? A man who'd abandoned his family to their fate. In his dreams, he sometimes heard the sound of a crying child. A plaintive cry woven into the wind on the days he remembered that the Earth was nothing but a ball of condensed gases, hurtling towards infinity.

'Talk to that nice Dr Gessen.' Hélène rooted in her bag for something, and he flinched, bracing himself, but she merely pulled out a tissue. 'He's not the enemy.'

42

Paris, France
April 1969

Stretched out on the bed, his philosophy book opened on his chest, he's too dreamy and distracted by the balmy air to read the required text for tomorrow's lecture. For weeks, he's questioned the choice of his field of study. His professors' lectures have grown tedious, even pointless, and he sits in the back of the lecture hall, fighting sleep, as the professor drones on about Kant and Descartes. Before the academic year winds down, he plans to transfer to the biology department.

Philosophy will remain a hobby, of course. A lifelong interest. But natural science will be his vocation. It has been calling out to him for weeks.

The door to the flat swings open, and his heart leaps. Rennie, returning home from school. But the clatter of shoes and laughter suggests she's not alone. Her sister, the next eldest, is with her and chattering excitedly about something. She's getting married in June, and flits around the flat, singing and giggling. Rennie, the youngest, is the most serious of all the daughters. Sometimes, when it's just the two of them alone in the flat, he can relax and let down his guard, rediscover his true nature, as they discuss their favourite books and films.

The sisters' voices float down the hall. 'I'm going to pop over to the shops,' Katerina says. 'Do you need anything?' He can't hear Rennie's reply, but if she's requested something it will be a pot of strawberry jam. At breakfast this morning, she'd been crestfallen to find the pot empty. 'It seems to be going fast, lately.' She giggles. 'I bet I know who the culprit is,' she sing-songs. He blushes. Is he eating too much? His board includes breakfast, but perhaps he is consuming more than his share.

His sweet tooth has only grown since coming to Paris, and he can't seem to get enough of those glass pots of *confiture*. Strawberry, especially. Though perhaps he should hold back a bit. Act more like a lodger than a member of the family. But the woman they affectionately call '*Anya*' has become a mother to him as well. Just last week she kissed him on the forehead as he came through the door, laden with vegetables from the market he'd offered to buy, and called him her *fogadott fiú*, adopted son.

What else but fate has brought him to this place that feels more like home than any he's known? Though the affectionate and light-hearted atmosphere is punctured at times with a darkness difficult to fathom. Friends from the old country, sipping tea in the front room as they murmur of lucky escapes. Not just from the Soviets, he's come to understand, but from an earlier, darker time before he was born. The time of the purges and the camps, of families vanishing in the night, never to be seen again.

He closes his book and steps into the kitchen, just as Katerina is heading out the door, and hastily retreats.

Rennie laughs. 'Don't be shy. Pull up a chair. You can help me peel the potatoes. Did you know that I'm a women's libber?' She cocks her eyebrow. 'All men should learn how to cook.'

He drops into a chair and gets to work, flushed with an

absurd joy at being a part of this family, even in the tiniest way. The son is a different story, scowling at the interloper in their midst, so he tries to stay out of his way.

The door flies open, and the family scion strolls in, his cheeks flushed from the spring sunshine, his hair tipped with gold.

His heart thumps. He knows it's silly, but he has a strange schoolboy yearning for this beacon of light. Though the son treats the family lodger like dirt, everyone seems to worship him, trailing in his wake, as if hoping to be blessed by a moment's regard.

The boy's face darkens. 'What the hell are you doing?'

He drops the knife. 'Peeling potatoes.'

'*Foutre le camp*! Get the hell away from my sister. She's not some random chick you can mess around with.'

He stands and ducks as the boy takes a swing at him. Rennie rushes over and whacks her brother on the arm. 'Are you crazy? Leave him alone.'

'I will not. Can't you see he's trying to seduce you?' The boy's sneer turns ugly, his voice menacing. 'I want you out of our flat.'

Sick at the thought of being tossed into the street like a mongrel dog, he wipes the boy's spit from his face.

'Today. If you're not gone by suppertime, I'm calling the cops.'

43

Clinique Les Hirondelles
Saint-Odile, Switzerland
17 December 2008

Ursula burst through the door, waving an envelope over her head. 'Wait till you read this,' she said. 'You won't believe it.'

She was gasping for breath as if she'd run all the way across the grounds. He took the letter, mildly alarmed by her flushed face. It was addressed to Dr Ursula Lindstrom, with the word 'confidential' written on the envelope in block letters with a red marker. Clearly impatient for him to read it, she perched on the arm of the chair.

As the contents of the letter sunk in, he met her gaze. It was sent by the former house attendant at Chalet Est, a man named Aleks, who had gone home to Slovenia in a hurry to care for his sick mother. Or so he said. But now it appeared he had another reason for leaving the clinic. In the time since his departure, his conscience must have got the better of him, and he now wished to confess. Apparently, Vidor had asked Aleks to help him with an experiment.

According to the letter, it went like this: Aleks would remove Vidor's wrist monitor, with the aid of a special device, and place it on his own wrist. He would then lie down on the floor of Vidor's bedroom and hold his wrist to his forehead and remain there quietly for thirty minutes. Vidor had told Aleks that he was a prize-winning brain scientist, and that he needed Aleks' help to prove a theory that people who lived in close quarters were able to synchronise their brain waves. *I realise, it was wrong of me*, Aleks wrote in a scratchy hand, *but it seemed like such a good idea and I didn't want to disappoint Mr Vidor*. He said I was doing him a great service in understanding the brain, and that he would mention my name in the article he published of the results.

Gessen looked at Ursula. 'Good grief.'

She shook her head. 'It gets worse.'

Only later did I realise I had helped Mr Vidor with his experiment on the day that Mr Ismail went missing. So, the reason I am writing to you is to tell you that the information on Mr Vidor's patient log is not correct. I don't think he did anything wrong, but ever since I left the clinic, it's been bothering me. I hope you will forgive me for not telling you sooner, and I am sending you this information now with the hope it will not change any facts about the day Mr Ismail died.

Gessen set his reading glasses on the desk. 'Why do you suppose he sent this to you, and not me?'

'I don't know.' She hesitated. 'Maybe he hoped I wouldn't say anything.' Ursula twisted the ring on her finger. 'But we'll have to inform the police now.'

'Not yet.' Gessen slipped the letter in his desk drawer and locked it. 'You don't mind if I keep this, do you? The date of Vidor's "experiment" could just be a coincidence, and there's no reason to suppose that he didn't spend the day in his room as he claimed. Even without his wrist monitor as proof.'

'But how can we—?'

'I'm not going to lie to the police,' Gessen said, cutting her off. 'But first I'd like to question Vidor myself. If he comes clean about the whole "brain-wave experiment", he probably has nothing to hide. If he doesn't…' His unvoiced thought hung in the air between them. Ismail's fall might not have been an accident.

* * *

Pellets of ice clattered against the window. Not yet three o'clock but the lamps were already lit. One of the dining room staff carried a tray of tea and biscuits into the room and set it on the table by the fire. Vidor eyed the buttery ovals topped with slivered almonds and caramelised sugar.

'Winter has come to stay,' Gessen said in an annoyingly cheery voice. 'The mountains cloaked in snow, the air shimmering like glass. My favourite season.' He passed Vidor the plate of biscuits. 'Do you ski?'

Vidor shook his head. He felt heavy and dull, like a tranquillised bear.

'I was in Paris recently,' Gessen said in what seemed like a complete non sequitur. 'A lovely city. After attending an interesting seminar, I met up with some former school chums. We talked about old times, as one does on such occasions. Laughing at the folly of youth and the wild dreams we once had. Our loves and our sorrows.'

'What is that smell?' Vidor pressed a napkin to his nose.

'Almonds and cinnamon, from the biscuits, I believe. Why, does it bother you?'

'No.' He hesitated. 'It's just that I'm not particularly fond of almonds. Poppy seed cake was what my mother used to make on Sundays. An old family recipe and a favourite of mine.'

Gessen raised his eyebrows, as if waiting for Vidor to expand on this particular memory. But Vidor had been feeling odd all day and was in no mood to oblige.

'My friends and I got to talking about our days at the Sorbonne as foreign students and how excited we were to be in Paris,' Gessen was saying as he nudged the plate of almond biscuits across the table. 'Somebody asked me if

I remembered this one particular boy. Very shy, he was. From somewhere in the Balkans, I believe. Or perhaps the Middle East.'

Vidor gave him a blank look.

'He was a philosophy student, and we had some classes together. Did I tell you I began my studies in philosophy before switching to medicine? At that age, I believed it was the great thinkers who had solved the problem of living in the world. Of course, I was wrong. My classmate had a change of heart, as well, apparently. When I inquired about him, I was told he'd left the university. I never thought anything about it, not for years. But after talking with my old school friends, I began to wonder what happened to him.'

During this rambling monologue Vidor experienced an odd sensation at the back of his skull. He shifted in the chair to look at the snow spinning from the sky. In the overheated room, the smell of almonds was nauseating. Sweat trickled down the side of his face, but when he thought about wiping it away, he couldn't move his arms. If he could just close his eyes for a minute… but when he did, the falling snow outside the window was replaced by the heat of a merciless sun, beating down from a copper sky.

As he scuffed along a narrow street, his leather sandals kicked up clouds of dust. In the distance, a slash of blue water gleamed on the horizon. His throat burned with thirst and he sought in vain a sliver of shade to rest in. As a plaintive call wafted through the air, shopkeepers covered their wares, and women hurried home through the streets, their straw bags filled with onions and mint, and raw meat wrapped in paper.

'Where are you now?'

The voice drifted towards him across a desert of space and time. The dusty street wavered and faded away. The blue water vanished. A man strode down the street. His black hair slicked back, his jaw clenched in anger. He ran after the man, but he was too weak to catch him. *Abi, entadr. Hadha ana.*

Father, wait. It's me. Without bothering to glance back, the man ducked into an alley and disappeared.

'Vidor? It's all right. You're safe here.'

The sun scorched his face, the stones burned his feet. He had forgotten to buy the onions and olive oil the old woman needed, and now the market was closed. Tears ran down his face.

'Vidor?'

He opened his eyes, rubbed the side of his head. *Where was he? Ah yes, the clinic.* The snow falling fast. And seated across from him, his nemesis Gessen, whose eyes bored into his very soul.

'I must have dozed off for a moment,' Vidor said. He brushed the crumbs from his lap. Had he eaten one of the biscuits? Perhaps they were laced with some kind of hallucinogen. He wouldn't put it past Gessen. Anything to trip him up. He rubbed his eyes. 'I haven't been sleeping well lately.'

'You seemed to have entered into a trance. Can you tell me what you saw?'

His head, heavy as a stone, threatened to pull him into the depths. 'Nothing. I saw nothing. But the heat… it was making me tired.'

'The heat?'

He frowned at the snow outside. 'Could we open the window? It's very warm in here.' When he looked at his hands, he did not recognise them. 'What day is it today, Wednesday, Friday?'

'Does it matter?'

'Yes,' Vidor said, shaking off his torpor. 'I need to know what day it is. The exact date and time. I can't…' His head spun, and he closed his eyes, hearing for a moment what sounded like billiard balls smacking together.

'It's Friday, 19 December.'

'And the time?' It was an effort to get the words out. 'I need to know the exact time.'

Gessen showed him his watch. 'In a few seconds it will be exactly 2.53 pm.'

Two fifty-three. That was the time? Two fifty-three. The laugh that burst from his throat came out like a bark. At last, he understood the absurdity of it. Man's ridiculous attempt to corral the movement of the sun inside the cogs of a wristwatch. Laughter bubbled up through his chest. Two fifty-three. What did it even mean in the unfathomable eternity of time? The puny lives of men. Brutish and short, indeed.

He absently flicked his ear. Gessen's eyes, keen as a ferret's, were riveted on Vidor's face. What was he looking at? Impossible to breathe with the air sucked out of the room, and he yanked at the collar of his shirt. His body quivered, and he gasped as he was swept – blessed relief – into the arms of darkness.

44

The only thing Vidor wanted was to be alone. But how to achieve a moment of solitude in this glorified hamster cage, where his every move was tracked and recorded? His own room should have been a refuge, but it was the first place someone might look. He would have to find a private nook to hide away in. Earlier, he'd taken breakfast in his room, desperate to avoid the clank of cutlery and furtive looks from the others. But he couldn't stay shut up here all day.

He crossed the room to look out at the gloomy sky and the grounds blanketed in snow. No one was about, but the skin on the back of his neck prickled as if someone was standing behind him. He spun around, but the room was empty.

All night he'd tossed and turned, plagued by strange dreams. From a narrow alley, a man with sun-bronzed skin and the yellow eyes of a raptor beckoned to him. The alley would provide a welcome shelter from the burning sun, but the man frightened him. Even within the chaotic flicker of his dreams he knew not to follow, that if he got too close, the man would yank him into the shadows and slit his throat.

When he woke, struggling for breath, he'd flung himself off the bed, tearing at his clothing, gasping for air, only to discover that during the night, someone had entered his room. Whoever it was had taken the polished stones from the brass tray on the dressing table and arranged them in neat rows of four by three, in the approximate order of the visual spectrum, beginning with the dark red jasper and ending with the amethyst, glowing violet in the morning light. The sandpiper painting was slightly askew. He'd counted the birds. Only nine. Where was the tenth? Where was the bloody tenth bird? He counted again, but the elusive creature had taken flight.

He squeezed his eyes shut. This infuriating nuthouse was driving him mad. Remaining closed up in his room all day felt impossible now. How could he? Not when he felt a presence near him and heard the whoosh of someone else's exhaled breath. Outside, the snow was piled up to the windows. What a fate to be buried here alive.

Escape was the only answer. But where? The pool and sauna would be crowded on a day like today, with everyone seeking the warmth and comfort of the pseudo-tropical heat. Saturday. He was sure of it. A minor triumph to know the day of the week. Something to cling to, a shred of sanity. With no sessions taking place in the Movement & Meditation hall, it was the perfect place to hide.

He pulled on his parka and hurried down the path, already cleared of last night's snowfall. Before entering the pavilion, he glanced back to check that no one had followed him. The meditation room was dark and smelled faintly of oranges. He hesitated before pressing the switch by the door. The fairy lights in the ceiling sprang on and winked at him like stars. From the stack by the wall, he took one of the cushiony mats, stuffed with dried grasses, and stretched out in the middle of the floor. If he squinted, he could pretend he was gazing up at the night sky in summer and breathing in the rarefied air of the high desert.

Vidor had never been to the desert, but as the darkness enveloped him like a warm cloak, he smelled the bitter tang of almonds and his body seemed to dissolve as it teleported to another land. A place with a burning sun and scorching sands swirling in the wind, scouring his skin and stinging his eyes. An excellent place to be alone, he imagined. Wrapped in a coarse wool blanket with only his eyes exposed, he would stare for hours at the shards of light above his head, scattered across the heavens, like bits of broken glass.

As his breathing slowed and the remnants of his dreams evaporated, it occurred to him that he could be his own healer. He didn't need Dr Gessen. In this moment, his mind was as clear as blown glass. He could go home now. That man in Copenhagen was perfectly fine. He'd barely touched him. The darkness pulled him in and from the void a woman's voice called to him. *Ana huna.* I am here. Go to sleep.

He held out his hand to touch her face. *Breathe in, breathe out.* It took him a moment to realise he had acquired an echo. With each breath, a second followed close behind. Someone – or something – was in the room with him. He tensed. It wasn't the woman urging him to sleep. She had fled. Could it be that the golem haunting his dreams had followed him here? But he wasn't dreaming, and he waggled his toes to be sure.

'Who's there?' His voice came out like a squeak, insignificant in the vacuum of space.

A whisper of fabric, a faint cough.

'I must have dozed off.'

An English voice. He blinked at the darkness as a form took shape on the other side of the room. 'Libby?'

'I'm over here.'

'Shall I switch on the light?'

'No, I like it this way. I'll come closer to you.'

A shadow fell across him as Libby placed her mat next to his and lay down on her back. 'I came here right after breakfast. It's like being in a cave, isn't it?'

The grass-filled mat rustled as she turned on her side to face him, so close her breath, smelling faintly of lemon drops, grazed his skin. Mixed with the meadow-sweet scent of dried grass, he had the odd sensation that he'd fallen through a hole in the earth and come out on the other side, in a land where summer reigned.

Her voice, when she spoke, was barely a whisper. 'I heard you went to the village the other day.'

He cringed. Was nothing confidential? It was too dark to see her face, but he could sense her brow was creased with concern. A point of light shone from her pupils, like a small woodland creature peeking from its burrow. In the tomb-like atmosphere, it was easy to picture what it would feel like to be dead, and for once the thought didn't frighten him. His spirit freed at last, while the atoms from his corporeal body returned to the earth from whence they came. How calm it felt to consider death in this place, with this girl beside him, when all his life he'd had a fear of dark places and a terror of dying. Damp grottos and train tunnels. Locked cupboards, prison cells deep underground.

Warm fingers grazed the back of his hand. 'You're shaking.'

He gasped as his mind returned to his body. 'No, I'm fine.'

She pulled her hand away.

'No, don't. It's… ' His cheeks flamed hot. 'It's nice to know that someone else understands.'

'Understands what?'

He sucked in his breath. 'The pain of living. The death of desire.'

For a moment she was silent. 'It doesn't have to be painful.'

He could just make out the ghostly outline of her profile, the smooth plane of her forehead and upturned nose. He took comfort in the idea that her whole life stretched before her like a field of wheat, shimmering in the sun. So, how could he possibly tell her that the sun-kissed grain transformed, at some point, into a minefield? You woke up one day to find that everything you loved was gone. He coughed and closed his eyes. 'I wanted to tell you before, but I didn't know how,' he said, crossing his hands over his chest. 'I think Ismail is alive.'

She gasped and bolted upright. 'Why would you say that?'

'I've seen him. Twice. The second time was just the other day, not long after the sun went down. He was lurking in a corner of the Zen garden and didn't see me. But he must have heard me coming for as I drew closer, he slipped away. I thought of calling out his name but… it seemed wrong to disturb him.'

Her voice was ragged with grief. 'It was a hallucination. Or one of your optical illusions.' She stifled a sob. 'I know he's dead. Dr Gessen told me he identified the body himself.'

'He could be lying.'

'And why would he do that?'

Her anger was like a slap in the face. It might be best to keep quiet about any further sightings. Something was going on, though, he was sure of it. Part of Gessen's plot to drive him to the brink of insanity.

She turned her head. In the dim light he had a vision of the older woman she would one day become. Accomplished, fiercely intelligent. Yet ever a free spirit, skimming lightly over the earth.

'You asked me earlier how I ended up here. If you still want to know, it's because I suffered some kind of amnesia after my friend died. She fell out the window at a student pub in Oxford. I'd begged her to go out that night, even though she wanted to stay in. If only she'd told me to piss off.' Libby sat up and hugged her knees. 'Three weeks later, when the police found me living in Bristol under an assumed name, I was admitted to the psych ward at a local hospital. After a couple of days, I finally remembered who I was, but I had no memory of travelling to Bristol, or the three weeks I'd spent there as a girl named Margaret. Turns out, I'd had something called a fugue state.' She tried to catch his eye. 'Even though I felt fine, my dad wanted me to come here to be treated by Dr Gessen. Apparently, that's one of his specialities.'

'Fugue states?'

'Anything to do with amnesia, I think.'

His heart thumped oddly. 'Funny how the brain works… Sometimes, I…' He hesitated, trying to formulate his thoughts. 'I've felt at times this strange sensation, that someone – or something – but not exactly me, had taken up residence in my body.' He smiled to let her in on the joke. 'Now you'll think I'm truly mad.'

When she said nothing, Vidor lay back and focused on the fairy lights, which once again had transformed into a sprinkling of stars in the vast reaches of space. In a gesture of solidarity, he reached out and briefly touched her wrist, grateful that she didn't flinch and pull away.

45

The chessboard was set up on the table by the hearth. Next to it, Gessen placed a tray with tea and a plate of those almond biscuits with the strange ability to transport Vidor to a different place and time. The scene was set. The only thing missing was the patient himself. Gessen turned to the window where the snow-covered mountains resembled great dollops of meringue. The glare was blinding, and he hastened to adjust the window shades.

In moments like these, waiting for his patient to arrive, he often grew dizzy at the monumental task ahead of him, and the complexity of the journey that had brought him here.

But here he was, driven by his compulsive need to help the suffering. After digging into the details of Vidor's past life in Paris, and compiling a meagre dossier on Malik Sayid, he hovered on the cusp of a hypothesis for Vidor's trouble. But even after viewing Madame Chabon's photographs of her brother, Vidor, the last taken when he was seventeen, it was difficult to say whether his patient, the grown-up Vidor Kiraly, was the same boy. The colour of the eyes matched, as did the slope of his forehead, but who at fifty-eight resembled their teenaged selves?

Somewhere along the wavy line stretching into the past, Malik Sayid must have played a part in Vidor's story. Had they been friends – or something more? A love sought and spurned. Perhaps Malik died in an accident and Vidor, in his guilt or anguish, had absorbed some of his friend's mannerisms. Gessen felt he was tantalisingly close to discovering the connection, but only Vidor could provide the final piece to the puzzle.

As if on cue, Vidor shuffled into the room, whey-faced and hesitant in his movements. Gone was the debonair strut and sheen of cultivated irony. Was he ill? Perhaps, in this more vulnerable state, like a newly hatched moth, Vidor would soften and reveal his true self.

'Please have a seat by the fire,' Gessen said. 'It will distract us from the weather.' With the speed of a freight train, a bank of clouds had rolled across the valley and the snow was coming down fast.

As soon as Vidor was settled, Gessen poured out the tea. 'If you don't mind my saying, you're looking rather worn out. Not sleeping well?'

Vidor's eyes swam as he attempted to focus on Gessen's face. 'Something keeps waking me at night, and I end up staring at the ceiling. Often till dawn.'

'Is something troubling you?' Gessen studied Vidor over the rim of his teacup.

A shake of the head.

'Strange dreams, perhaps?'

Vidor shifted in his seat. 'If I have dreams, I don't remember them.'

Gessen handed across the plate of almond biscuits, but Vidor grimaced and pushed them away. Like the last time, either the sight or smell of the biscuits seemed to sicken him. Almost as if Gessen had handed him a plate of uncooked snails. To give Vidor a chance to compose himself, he rose and closed the curtains, blocking out the elements. He dunked one of the almond biscuits into his tea and took a bite. Delicious. His chef had recreated a recipe he'd found in a cookbook on North African cuisine.

'In my second year of medical school,' Gessen said, as he topped up their glasses of peppermint tea, 'an interesting case, quite rare, was admitted to the Salpêtrière hospital. I didn't meet the patient myself, but his malady was described in detail during one of our lectures. The boy, just shy of his eighteenth birthday, had been suffering from stomach pains, and presented with a distended abdomen and significant weight loss. A CAT scan showed a mass growing in the boy's abdomen, just under the liver. His doctors thought it was a tumour, at first, but when they opened him up to remove it, they were shocked to discover that it was no ordinary tumour. The lump of tissue contained a spine and a rudimentary brain. Even vestigial fingers and eyes.' He studied Vidor's face for signs of squeamishness. But he didn't look uncomfortable, merely bored, as if counting the minutes until he could return to his room.

'What they found in the boy's body is called a *foetus in fetu*,' Gessen said, taking a sip of his tea. 'A parasitic twin, in common parlance. It's exceedingly rare. Worldwide, there have been fewer than two hundred recorded cases. The medical staff at the hospital were buzzing with excitement, as if an alien creature was growing inside the boy, though the reality was more prosaic.' He waited to see if Vidor would jump in with an explanation of his own. 'As it turned out, the boy's mother had been pregnant with twins, one of whom failed to develop. As the surviving twin grew, it enveloped the vestigial twin, which couldn't survive on its own without a functioning brain. But it continued to thrive, as a type of parasite, by attaching itself to the blood supply of the living twin.

'The boy, who was otherwise perfectly fit, complained often of disturbed sleep due to regularly occurring dreams in which he and another boy were trying to solve a complex puzzle. The boy knew that his companion in the dream was his twin. He even asked his mother if she'd given birth to two boys, and if one of them had died, because he could sense the spirit of this ghost twin inside him. She reassured him there had only been one child. But the boy was haunted by the sensation, both mental and physical, that he wasn't alone. That someone – or something – shared his thoughts. A psychiatrist diagnosed the boy as schizophrenic. But medication didn't help, and he continued to feel dogged by this other presence.'

A log in the fireplace collapsed into coals. The room had grown overly warm and Gessen considered opening a window. Vidor absently studied the skin on his palm. A picture of boredom.

'As a former student of philosophy,' Gessen said, 'I was just as fascinated by the metaphorical aspect of a parasitic twin as by the medical side.' He stood and poked the fire. 'What I'm trying to say is that it's not unusual to feel there's another being inside you, or a presence dogging your steps, even when you're alone.'

As Vidor turned to gaze at the fire, a ripple of life crossed his features.

'That's what I would like to explore with you today,' Gessen said, pressing on. 'The feeling that you're accompanied by another. It might help to explore who this being is, and what he might want from you.'

Gessen paused, afraid of spooking his skittish patient. They'd make no progress if the door was slammed shut.

'I have felt, at times, another presence,' Vidor said, shifting his gaze to the window. 'As you say, it's not uncommon, and a well-known neurological phenomenon. Probably a disturbance in the temporal lobe.'

Gessen bit into an almond biscuit and brushed the crumbs from his lap. 'Tell me about this other person. Does he talk to you, or leave you a message of some kind?'

'You mean like a note?'

Gessen suppressed a smile. If Vidor was playing this for laughs, he wouldn't give him the satisfaction of acknowledging his joke.

'Not necessarily. I was thinking more in the vein of strange disturbances. Like a ghostly figure at your side in times of distress, or finding things rearranged in your home, such as your books or papers.'

A spark flickered in Vidor's eyes. 'The tins,' he murmured. 'I'd forgotten about that.' He shook his head and smiled. 'I do the weekly shopping myself – don't look so surprised, and when I get home, I put the tins in a precise order, usually by type, with the labels facing front. But on a few occasions, I've opened the cupboards to find them all mixed up. I just assumed it was my housekeeper doing a bit of rearranging.' He fiddled with a button on his shirt. 'Obsessive compulsions. Or temporary amnesia. Is that what I have?'

'What do you think?'

Perspiration shone on Vidor's brow. Gessen cautioned himself to tread carefully. He nodded at the chessboard. 'Shall we have a game? You can be white.'

After Vidor made his opening salvo, Gessen picked up his bishop and made a move that was sure to be fatal, but it was important to let Vidor win this one.

They played in silence for several minutes, with Vidor keenly focused on the board. Gessen waited until Vidor had put his king into check before he leaned forward and tossed out the question he'd been waiting to ask for days.

'Tell me something,' he said, catching Vidor's eye. 'Does the name Malik Sayid mean anything to you?'

46

From his lookout in the turret, Gessen trained his binoculars on Vidor and Libby, bundled into identical grey parkas and red knitted caps, as they walked in the direction of the sculpture garden. Gessen required the patients to wear the red wool cap outside at all times in winter. Some resisted or complained, but it was easier to spot anyone who fell into a snowbank or got confused and wandered off.

Libby had her hands stuffed into the pockets of her coat and appeared to be deep in conversation with Vidor. Yesterday, when Gessen had asked him who Malik Sayid was, the response was abrupt, even surly. *Not a clue*. Was it Gessen's imagination that Vidor had become disoriented for several seconds before shaking it off? These signs, though vague, could point to something. But if this were truly a case of multiple personality, rather than an assumed identity, Gessen would have to force the second, less dominant personality, Vidor's alter, to show his face. Awakening olfactory memories with evocative scents was one strategy. The almond biscuits had seemed to elicit a minor change in Vidor's manner, and brought forth rambling memories of a desert city.

When Libby and Vidor reached the sculpture garden, they stopped in front of a bronze statue of a swan, where Libby flung her hands in the air and twirled in a circle. Her face was pink with the cold, her smile broad. She led Vidor to a smooth patch of snow and raised her arms over her head. In a single fluid motion she fell backwards onto the ground. Though the windows were nearly soundproof, Gessen could imagine the sound of her laughter. *Come on, give it a go.*

After a moment's hesitation, Vidor got down beside her and copied her movements, sweeping his arms in a wide arc and scissoring his legs. Snow angels. Libby was certainly an interesting girl to have come up with something like this. Vidor was such a tough nut to crack. A man who lived almost entirely in his head, seemingly oblivious to the body's capacity to hold onto pain. The Movement & Meditation classes had done little to help Vidor feel more grounded in his body, or to loosen the iron grip on his thoughts. But a fresh snowfall and a girl with a warm heart had done the trick. Gessen opened the window a crack to hear their laughter. Flat on the snow, moving their limbs in unison, they giggled like children. As their laughter rang out through the crystalline air, Vidor's face shone with joy.

After standing up to examine their creations, they clapped the snow off each other's backs. It was the first time Gessen had seen Vidor look relaxed and happy, and he couldn't help but wonder if this might be his first instance of spontaneous laughter in years. As he watched them head off in separate directions, Libby turned and waved at the turret. Did she guess he'd been spying on them? She couldn't possibly know he was up here. Cheeky girl.

Back in his office, Gessen plotted his next move. To prove his suspicions of a dissociative disorder, he would have to call the alter forth. In the case of an acquired – and repressed – identity, he would need to puzzle out when the one had become the other. According to Vidor's sister, their lodger Malik had moved out of the Sovàny home in April 1969, never to be seen or heard from again. Had he returned to where he came from, or moved to another city in France? He could easily have disappeared into the immigrant communities of a teeming city like Marseille. Perhaps with a new name. Impossible to trace.

If Vidor's true identity was indeed Malik Sayid, when had he become Vidor Kiraly? According to Katerina Chabon, by the time her brother vanished, and was later presumed dead, Malik had been gone from their lives for several weeks. With the anguish about the fate of their beloved brother and son, the family's one-time lodger would be a distant memory. Who would have given him a thought? Had Malik, after learning of Vidor's disappearance, devised a way to reinvent himself as a Hungarian? After which he slipped across the English Channel to begin a new life? But why bother to change his name and identity? Why not remain Malik Sayid?

The potential number of permutations made his head ache. He turned to the window and pressed his forehead against the glass. The falling snow, having started again, would soon erase Vidor's and Libby's snow angels.

Age regression therapy might provide some answers. If Malik was lurking in Vidor's psyche, a certain amount of poking around might ferret him out.

* * *

He tested the water with his toe before wading into the pool, blissfully alone. Vidor hadn't learned to swim until late in life, and not very well. As a child, he remembered splashing in the baths with his mother at the Gellert in Budapest, that glorious Art Deco confection that had lately become a mecca for tourists. Poor swimmer that he was, he still enjoyed feeling weightless when he floated on his back, and the delicious sensation of water sluicing over his arms and legs.

The door swung open with a bang, and a dark shape lumbered in. In the steamy air, Vidor couldn't make out who it was, but as the shape moved closer his heart sank. It was that wretched German woman. The one terrified of draughts, and whose eyes had a way of goggling at you like a flounder.

As she removed her robe, he turned his head away and doggy paddled to the far side of the pool. He could sense her staring at his awkwardness. But it wasn't his fault he'd never mastered the correct technique. Though his childhood city was full of thermal baths, and his mother fond of the water, the few times she'd tried to teach him he'd resisted. From the safety of the shallow end, he would watch her cleave the water in an effortless breaststroke, while he could barely stay afloat. The moment he stopped moving, he would sink straight to the bottom.

At the pool's shallow end, he hauled himself onto the green-tiled ledge and wrapped himself in a fluffy white robe with the clinic's name embroidered on the pocket. Tucked into an alcove off the pool area was a relaxation room with comfortable lounge chairs, potted palms, and a selection of lifestyle magazines. No news of the world, of course. Nothing to upset their fragile sensibilities. For all he knew, the world outside their little corner of Switzerland had been obliterated by a nuclear catastrophe, while their hardy band of six, now five, remained blissfully unaware of the carnage.

He lay back, arms over his chest, breathing in and out, as he listened to the slap of water against the sides of the pool. At the sound of vigorous splashing and the smack of bare feet on the tiles, he kept his eyes firmly shut as the chair next to him was scraped back. She snapped open a magazine and ruffled the pages with a noisy sigh. He tightened the belt on his robe and prepared to make his escape.

'Not disturbing you, am I?' Her smoker's voice grated on his ears.

'Not at all, I was just leaving.'

'Don't rush off on my account. I'll be quiet as a mouse.'

He closed his eyes and tried to run through his newly developed mathematical model for the signal transduction of neurotrophic factor in the brain. But her incessant sighs and annoying tsks jabbed at him like a raft of hot needles.

'Don't you hate these stupid ads? Look at this.' She

leaned across and poked his arm. 'All these beautiful young people, posing as a happy family. It's so fake. They're just models, yet we're supposed to believe this is some love-struck couple cavorting in an Alpine meadow with their perfectly behaved children. Crazy, yeah? It's these stupid ads that make reproducing seem like a good thing.' She leaned closer. 'Look, here's another one. A diamond is forever. Ha! Tell that to my ex. Can you believe he asked for my engagement ring back, after our divorce? Such an ass.'

Vidor's mouth puckered in horror. Every muscle strained to flee, but an unyielding force kept him pinned to the chair, as if they were two passengers trapped together on an aeroplane, with no possibility of escape.

She hauled herself from the chair. 'Look at this bruise on my leg,' she said, lifting her robe to reveal a well-larded thigh. High up near her hip bloomed a nasty patch of purple and green. 'I'm pretty sure it's cancer. Leukaemia probably. Bruises like this are a symptom, you know.' She pulled open her robe to reveal more flesh spilling from a too-small red bikini and pointed at the surgical scars criss-crossing the doughy flesh of her abdomen. Vidor flinched and looked away. What next? Was she going to pull out a breast and ask him to examine that as well?

'Look at these scars. Do you know how many surgeries I've had? And the idiot doctors say they can't find anything wrong with me. How can I have so much pain if nothing is wrong?' She flopped back into the chair. 'And they think I'm the one who's crazy.'

As his mind sought an escape route, it struck him that her accent wasn't German at all. If anything, it sounded American. In one of the Movement & Meditation sessions, hadn't she told some long-winded story of being forced to move out of her flat in Berlin?

'So what are you in here for?' She fanned her face with a chubby hand.

'I don't believe we're supposed to ask each other that,' he said in a chilly voice.

'Come on, I won't tell.' She winked and slapped his arm. Her mouth resembled a sucked lemon. Why not yank her chain and have some fun?

'I tried to kill my father and brother.' He said this with a straight face and solemn tone.

Her eyes widened in alarm, just as he'd hoped, and he bit his lip to keep from smiling. 'During an ill-fated family reunion. Such gatherings are best avoided, in my opinion. Too many people with axes to grind trapped in the same room drinking bad wine.'

He could practically hear her heart patter with excitement. She sat up and hugged her plump knees. 'What happened?'

'Oh, the usual family scrap,' he said, breezily. 'After my dear mother died, my father could barely wait a month to remarry. His second, much younger, wife is a ghastly woman, and the thought of her living in my mother's house and touching her possessions made me ill. The first thing she did was to toss all my mother's lovely things into a skip. And with my father's blessing.'

'How terrible.' Babette's expression was one of horrified glee.

'Indeed.' The humid air, suffused with the scent of eucalyptus and pine, was making him drowsy. 'We'd been estranged for years, my father and I, ever since his marriage to that woman, but then he was diagnosed with terminal lung cancer, so I travelled to the family home to say goodbye. But the moment I walked in the door, I knew it was a mistake.' He closed his eyes and pulled the cotton blanket up to his neck, preparing to doze.

'Don't leave me hanging.' She smacked him on the shoulder. 'What happened?'

He shifted away, regretting now his attempt to rile her up. 'The first thing I noticed was that there was nothing of my mother's in the house. The loathsome second wife was out,

246

so I had a chance to look through the rooms. Everything I'd known from my childhood had been stripped away. I shouted at my father that he had effectively murdered my mother. She died from grief, her heart broken by his endless affairs. The last with the woman who became his second wife. My hands moved of their own accord and wrapped themselves around his neck. I can still feel how his windpipe flattened under my thumbs.' Vidor raised his hands and made a choking gesture.

Her face was alive with excitement. *An actual, almost murderer.*

'My brother pulled me off just in time, but I took a swing at him and knocked him against the stone fireplace. I grabbed my things and fled the house, this time for ever, I thought, but when I arrived home, the local police were waiting for me outside my flat.'

She stared at him, wide-eyed. 'So nobody died.'

Clearly, she was disappointed by his little tale. 'Nobody died,' he said, with an air of sorrow.

A sharp line appeared between her eyes. 'So, you've never killed anyone?'

He frowned at her. 'Of course not. What do you take me for?'

She shifted her gaze to the window. 'I saw you with that other patient, Ismail, on the day he went missing. You followed him into that copse of trees near the boundary.' She narrowed her eyes at him. 'I didn't say anything to the police, but they might have guessed I was hiding something. So clever at reading people's faces, aren't they?

He felt a spasm of shock. What was she implying? Had he gone too far with his fanciful story, and now she took him for a murderer? He stared at her goggle-eyed. She was lying, surely. It was an attention-seeking ploy, nothing more.

A weariness descended upon him like a fog. Inventing this little anecdote for his own amusement had knocked the stuffing out of him. But where did it come from, this silly story of a father with a string of mistresses and a brother who always took his side? His own father, who'd disappeared from his life at the age of six, was presumably dead. He'd only ever had sisters, not an elder brother, though perhaps it had been a childish fantasy to want one. A rambunctious boy, it hadn't been easy to grow up in a household of women.

'Gosh,' she said, dropping her insinuations about Ismail and lying back in the chair. 'That's a whole lot worse than what happened to me.' She turned her head and coughed. A smoker's cough. He wondered if she'd been able to find a source of contraband cigarettes.

She picked at a scab on her elbow. 'I tried to kill myself.'
Who hasn't?

Where did that come from? Vidor had never tried to snuff out his own life. It must be this place. Probably half the patients here had tried to off themselves, including that boy Ismail, and now all of them, including himself, were blending in together.

* * *

Afterwards, when Vidor was safely back in his room, though sporting a mysterious bandage on his head from a tumble he'd supposedly taken by the pool, he tried to make sense of the past few hours. He had no memory of being attended to by a nurse, and he couldn't shake off the feeling of unease about the Canadian woman. For that's what she was, apparently, assuming she had told him the truth. Not German at all as he'd assumed.

He'd had to endure a full fifteen minutes of listening to her plaintive voice, veering into a whine on the high notes, before he could make his escape. Hailing from a remote town in Saskatchewan, she'd taken up with a German man who was touring the country on a motorcycle. An unplanned pregnancy was followed by a quickie marriage and a move to Berlin, after which she lost the baby. They struggled on for a time, until she caught him with another woman. Tears, anguish, divorce. She'd stayed on in Berlin and tried to make a life for herself, though she had trouble making friends and feeling settled.

Vidor had kept his eyes closed throughout this long lament, desperate to escape, but not wanting to anger her in case she questioned him about his actions on the day Ismail died. When he could no longer stand the note of complaint in her voice, he'd snapped. 'Why don't you go back home then?'

'Have you ever been to Saskatchewan?' Her voice was bitter. When he shook his head, the noise coming from her throat was like a strangled cat. 'There's nothing there for me but a mother who loathes me, and a father who's a drunk. I'd rather be dead than go back there.' She waved her hand over her body. 'And with all these strange illnesses I keep getting, and everyone saying I'm crazy, I'll probably die and get dumped in some unmarked grave, and that will be the end of my sorry, stupid life.'

Before he fled, he'd had a sense of impending doom, as though all the oxygen was being sucked from the air. How dare she insinuate he had something to do with Ismail's death? The Canadian woman's head had expanded and contracted like a balloon, before pulling free and floating up towards the ceiling. *What's happening?* A pain had stabbed his left temple. The water in the pool was the colour of blood. The last thing he'd heard was the sound of running feet, and someone calling for a doctor just before his head hit the tiles and he blacked out.

In the mirror, he examined the bandage on his forehead. A minor abrasion, apparently, though for all he knew he might have been subjected to an experimental procedure. Like his roommate, the OCD chap. How else to explain the bloody bandage on the man's head Vidor had spotted a few weeks back?

47

Gessen waved his hand over the chessboard with a flourish. 'I'm feeling in a particularly magnanimous mood today, so I'll let you be white.' He gestured at the outdoors where everything visible was covered in snow. The boxwood hedge and pines glittered like great dollops of ice cream, and the falcon sculpture was transformed into a snow cone. 'Isn't it stunning?'

He beckoned to Vidor to come through, but he seemed reluctant to step into the room.

'I woke with a terrible headache this morning,' he said, hanging back in the doorway. 'Must be from this bump I got yesterday.' He pointed to the bandage over his eye. 'Those tiles by the pool are dangerous. I think it's only fair to warn you that I might sue you for personal injury.'

Gessen let this pass. Vidor's skin was the colour of uncooked veal and his eyes were rubbed raw, as if he hadn't gotten a moment's rest in the night. 'Up until my little mishap, I felt in excellent form. I even swam a few laps in the pool.'

It was clear he had no memory of what preceded his collapse in the swimming pavilion. When Gessen questioned Babette, who'd witnessed the whole thing, she'd been quite voluble in her description of Vidor's condition, as if he'd taken some kind of turn. His face had contorted, and his eyes rolled back in his head. It could have been a temporal lobe seizure. Or a garden-variety migraine, perhaps, though Vidor hadn't mentioned any prior history. But such episodes seemed to be occurring more frequently. Babette was lucky he hadn't attacked her as he had the man in Copenhagen and the one in the village. Though she may have found the whole episode exciting, and a source of new symptoms to add to her long list of 'mystery ailments'. His patient for three months now, Babette's Munchausen's was proving particularly difficult to treat.

Vidor probed at the skin above his ear. Was he feeling something odd there? In rare cases temporal lobe seizures could result in violence. A possible diagnosis to add to the mix. He made a mental note to have Vidor undergo a seventy-two-hour electroencephalograph.

'I can give you something for the pain if you like.'

He shook his head. 'A nurse gave me some tablets that knocked it out. I'm still feeling woozy, but that will pass, no doubt.'

'A game is just what you need then,' Gessen said, 'to get your mind off things. We can have our session later, if you prefer, but a friendly round of chess will get the blood flowing to your brain again.'

Vidor perched on the edge of the chair, hands clasped in his lap, docile as a child. Gessen tried not to stare openly as he attempted to parse Vidor's state of mind. He looked befuddled and drained. Had something happened in the night? Another bout of sleepwalking or strange dreams? The frequency of nocturnal disturbances had shot up in the last few days. While exhausting for Vidor, it was a positive sign that his boundaries were beginning to dissolve. In this weakened state, his alter, if he were in there, was more likely to show his face. Tired, malleable, confused, Vidor might finally release the iron grip on his inner demons.

They faced each other across the chessboard. No fire was lit in the hearth today. Though Gessen normally relished the warmth and sound of a crackling fire, he didn't need the distraction. Now that he was closing in on Vidor's defences, it was important to stay focused.

Vidor moved his pawn in a classic opening manoeuvre. Gessen scanned the board, already several moves ahead. He checked his watch, hoping to reach checkmate in thirty minutes or less. Three moves in and his strategy seemed to be working.

Vidor swayed in his seat. 'What is that smell?' He wrinkled his nose as if faced with something putrid.

Gessen sniffed the air. 'Anise, I believe, with a dash of nutmeg and cardamom. Don't you like it? At this time of year, the housekeeper likes to place little sachets of her secret spice blend in all the rooms to put us in the mood for the holidays.'

'I thought you were Jewish.'

Gessen's chin tilted up in surprise. They'd never discussed religion before. Like most psychiatrists, he presented himself to his patients as a cipher, a blank slate upon which they could inscribe their own lives. 'Indeed, I am. A quarter Jewish, on my mother's side.' He paused to move his knight to f4. 'But that's never stopped me from celebrating Christmas at the clinic. Many of the patients miss sharing the holidays with their families. We keep it fairly secular, so as not to offend those of a different faith. And I'm sure you're aware that many – if not most – Christmas traditions pre-date Christianity. Evergreens, yule logs, sparkly lights. All pagan traditions meant to lessen the terror of the midwinter darkness.'

Vidor's gaze was fixed on the board, his expression dull, eyes unfocused. He plucked his queen into the air and moved it to a precarious position. Was he just going through the motions, or did he want to lose? Within two moves, Gessen had placed his bishop next to Vidor's king. 'Check.'

This seemed to have an effect. Beads of sweat formed on Vidor's brow. He frowned and shook his head, as if he'd never seen a chessboard before. He grabbed a pawn clumsily and moved it one square to the left. He sought Gessen's eyes. 'Is that a good move?'

Gessen's heart quickened. Something was happening. 'It's an

excellent move.' But Vidor's king was now wide open to attack. Should Gessen pretend he didn't see the mistake, or go in for the kill? Better do it now, while Vidor seemed to be under some kind of spell, as if his mind had come untethered from his brain.

With his bishop, he knocked over Vidor's king. 'Checkmate. *Sheikh mat.*'

Vidor's face paled. His pupils dilated.

'*Sheikh mat,*' Gessen repeated.

The words seemed to arouse Vidor from his stupor. 'Sheikh, what?'

'Mat. It's the Arabic version of the word "checkmate", a twist on the original Persian, meaning the king is dead.' When Vidor turned his face towards Gessen, his eyes had changed into those of a frightened child. 'I'm not dead,' he cried in a strangled voice. Bewilderment turned to accusation. 'You tried to kill me, but I'm still alive. *Ne me parle pas comme si j'étais stupide.*'

This last bit, in French… *don't talk to me like I'm stupid*, was uttered in the tone of a wounded boy. Gessen's heart flipped in his chest. He fought to keep his face neutral, not wanting to scare whoever this was back into hiding. Was it Vidor's alter, springing forth from some dark corner of his psyche? Or was this Malik Sayid, the boy he'd known in Paris, proclaiming his rightful existence? *So nice to see you again*, he wanted to say, but held his tongue. For several moments, in spite of his years of experience, Gessen didn't quite know what to do. He'd come across such cases in the literature, but each patient was unique, and nothing he'd read about would help him here.

'Would you like to lie down?'

'Why would I want to lie down?' he snapped. 'I feel perfectly fine.'

And just like that, Vidor's persona slotted back into place. *Damn.* He would have to find a way to coax the alter out of hiding again. Vidor's woozy state from the pain meds might have provided a doorway. Perhaps some form of deep relaxation would bring the alter back.

Gessen stood and beckoned with his hand. 'All the same, why don't you stretch out on the couch in the next room?'

Vidor pressed his knuckles against his temples. 'It's this damn headache. I thought it was gone, but it's come back with a vengeance.'

'Could be a migraine,' Gessen said. 'The best thing for that is to lie quietly in a darkened room.' He led Vidor into the adjoining treatment area and helped him onto the couch. After Gessen covered him with a blanket, he pressed a button on his desk that switched on the camera installed in the ceiling.

How long had Vidor's alter been lurking under the dominant personality? Had he emerged before, perhaps during times of crisis? Or had he remained hidden from view for years? Gessen would need more information to know what he was dealing with. It might be dissociation, a case of repressed identity, or even an extended fugue state.

That Vidor had felt agitated in Ismail's presence made sense now. He might have suspected that Vidor was not who he claimed to be. Whatever the case, Ismail's physical proximity could have triggered the slumbering alter to appear. If Vidor was indeed Malik, someone from Egypt, as Ismail was, might have detected a hint of common ancestry in Vidor's face. Or perhaps even goaded Vidor by tossing out a few choice insults in Arabic to see how he would react. If that were the case, there could be more behind Ismail's death than he'd first suspected. If Vidor felt somehow that the young Egyptian was a threat to his identity, even on a subconscious level, it might have been reason enough to get Ismail out of the way.

Gessen handed Vidor a glass of water spiked with a sedative. He looked at it with suspicion but drank it down. After dimming the lights, he had Vidor lie down and concentrate on his breathing, while looking at the mandala on the far wall. As Vidor's breathing slowed, Gessen retreated to the chair behind his head and led him through a relaxation exercise. As soon as Vidor reached a state of deep relaxation, the questioning could begin.

48

I was born in the early hours of January. Which day exactly, I do not know. But I opened my eyes and took my first breath on a night of bitter cold and a sky ablaze with stars.

I was one of twin boys. Later I learned that my mother had already given birth to seven daughters, two of whom had died in infancy, and was delirious with relief to have produced a son. After an arduous labour and the loss of a great deal of blood, my brother arrived first in the world. She thought she was done, but then I appeared twenty minutes later. My mother was too exhausted to push, and as I refused to be born, she thought I had died in the womb. When I finally slithered into the hands of the *darwisha*, pale as a worm and no bigger than a rat, no one thought I would live. My unschooled mother still believed in the old ways. Twins were a bad omen and she feared for our future. The *darwisha*, who'd acted as midwife, assured her she would take over my care in the coming days. If I died, it was the will of the gods.

My mother, a Bedouin woman celebrated for her beauty, had been sold as a young girl to my father in marriage.

Though she believed in the ancient gods, not in Allah, she would pretend to say her prayers to avoid my father's wrath. Entranced though he was by her beauty, my father, an educated man, was suspicious of her character. He hated the *darwisha*, a traditional healer whom he denounced as a sorceress.

I wouldn't suckle, so the *darwisha* dribbled the water from pieces of soaked bread into my mouth in a half-hearted bid to keep me alive. I did not cry like a normal newborn, so she feared I was infected by a malevolent spirit. As the weeks went by, and my twin brother grew into a fat bouncing infant, it became clear I was different in another way. My brother's skin was dark like my father's, while I was very pale, with strange grey-green eyes like a cat's. Paler even than my mother. As if I were a child of the northern steppes, and not sprung from the sands of the Arabian deserts.

Believing himself to be a cuckold, my father beat my mother till she was black and blue. Screaming that she was a whore. How else to explain the scrawny worm that clearly wasn't the fruit of his loins? He kept her up at night, shouting, beating her with his fists, hoping to pummel from her the name of her lover. It disgusted him to look at her, to look at me. After weeks of this terror, he forced her to decide: she must cast me aside or be banished forever. Did she want to be shunned as a harlot? She would end up in a brothel or on the streets. A filthy cur who opened her legs to any man who smiled at her.

I like to believe it wasn't an easy decision for her to give me up. I clung to that belief – I cling to it still – that it was torture for her to hand me over into the care of another. But that was my fate, to be given away to a childless old crone in a nearby village, who wasn't right in the head. But for the first six years of my life, she was the only mother I knew. If it hadn't been for a boy at school who took pleasure in taunting me, I would never have known that the woman I thought of as my mother had not given birth to me. Everybody but me knew that my real mother was a woman called Sahira, the Arabic word for enchantress. Famed for her beauty and green eyes, but burdened with a husband prone to jealous rages, who rarely let her leave the house, even in the company of a guardian.

A boy who lived in the dwelling next to mine – house is too grand a word for the hovel I was raised in – took me one day to the market town where my real parents lived and pointed her out. She was returning home from the souk, accompanied by the man I learned was my father. Blood from the package in her hand, a sheep's heart wrapped in paper, seeped through the cloth it was wrapped in. 'That's your mother,' the boy said, grinning like a jackal.

If it was true that the lady with the green eyes was my real mother, I wanted to be with her, not the old woman who treated me more like a goat than a son, insisting I sleep in the shed with the other animals. A disgusting place that smelled of dung, where I once woke to find a viper curled on my chest. After that, I would sneak off to the town as often as I could in search of my mother. My heart swelled when I saw her, and I would follow her through the narrow alleys of the souk. Though she'd borne many children and must have been nearly thirty by then, her step was quick as a girl's. Always veiled, the only thing visible were her eyes.

Usually, one of her older daughters was with her, or the boy who was my twin, Amir. She would tease him and ruffle his hair and hold him close as they moved through the throngs in the busy market. As they passed the tea stall, he would beg her to stop for tea and cakes. If I could be with my mother, I would never beg her for anything. But Amir was a young tyrant, the spoiled only son of a woman famed for her beauty, with hands so graceful they moved through the air like birds.

The first time he caught me following them in the market, I ducked into a carpet stall, but he tore after me and yanked my arm behind my back. Bigger and stronger, his face was twisted into an ugly scowl. Of course he knew who I was. I was the enemy, so losing sight of me might prove a fatal mistake. He spat in the dust at my feet. 'You should have been drowned at birth. Come near us again, and I'll tell my father. He'll throttle you like the filthy vermin you are.'

My father haunted my dreams and stalked my nightmares, with the eyes of a snake, seeking me in the dark. Once, when he caught me following my mother as he accompanied her to the market, he grabbed me and threw me to the ground, placing his foot on my neck, threatening me with exile to a notorious underground prison in the desert. The Dark Prince who gave me life, but would banish me, if given the chance, to misery and exile. Tormenting me to the ends of the earth, until I was dead.

* * *

After reading through the transcript a second time, Gessen placed his pen on the desk and rubbed his eyes. Was this the story of Malik Sayid, and evidence of a bona fide case of dissociative identity disorder, or was this tale of abandonment and terror simply a waking dream? Perhaps it belonged to someone Vidor knew as a child, or was drawn from a fable he'd read long ago? Since it was impossible to shine a light on Vidor's psyche, Gessen's only hope at solving the puzzle was to tease out the threads of his entwined personalities – if that's what they were – one careful step at a time.

49

Paris, France
23 December 2008

Dear Dr Gessen,
Ever since your visit to my home in Paris, when I
reminisced about my brother, Vida, so many memories
have come flooding back. Not just during the day
while I'm awake and pottering about the kitchen,
but in the darkest hours of the night, as well. Such
dreams that I haven't had in years have infiltrated my
slumber. And not just memories of Vida, but also that
student we took in for a short time as a lodger. When
you asked me about him, I could hardly remember
anything about that boy, as the tragedy of Vida's
premature demise crowded out everything else. But a
singular memory has come back to me, and it's a vivid
one. Though that boy – whose name I can't remember
– was older than Vida by a year or two, he seemed to
worship my brother, even to the point of copying his
gestures and slang.

He was an excellent mimic, that boy, and quite
a delightful person, actually, though painfully shy.
Rather anxious about doing or saying the wrong thing.

He arrived in Paris from a foreign country, though I can't say which one, and it was clear to me that he was desperate to fit into our way of life. One night when Vida had gone out with his friends, our young lodger moped about the flat, almost as if he'd been abandoned. I'm no psychologist, but it was obvious to anyone who looked that the poor boy had never received much affection or love.

Once, he seemed so bereft that I asked him to join me on the sofa while I watched a film on the television. Attentive as always, he made me a cup of tea and asked if he could do anything to help around the flat. Scrub the floors or run errands. Anything to make us happy. It did seem a little strange, this yearning to belong to our family, until he confessed this odd belief... that he and Vida were fated to meet, and that a power not of this earth had sent him to us. When I inquired how he knew this, he said it was a question of their names. Both Vida's and this boy's name meant, in their respective languages, the 'happy king'.

So strange, the memories your visit has unleashed! Almost as if the spool of time was rewound, and by merely closing my eyes, I can roam freely through the days and hours of forty years ago.

If you are ever in Paris and would like to meet again, do remember to call on me.

Sincerely yours,
Mme Katerina Sovàny Chabon

Gessen folded the letter and swivelled his chair to face the mountains. Avalanche warnings had been sent out earlier in the week, and some of the roads through the valley were closed as a precaution.

The happy king. Vidor Kiraly. Malik Sayid. Easy enough to confirm after a quick search online of the Hungarian and Arabic translations. Two boys, mirror versions of each other. It must have seemed to someone in Malik's fragile state a happy omen to have joined the household of someone whose name echoed his. A sign that it was possible to move forward in life, with the prospect of a bright future. To lay down the burden of the past and accept the mantel he'd been born with. The happy king. An admonition – or a benediction, depending on how he viewed his fate. And after the real Vidor disappeared, it might have seemed natural for a young man suffering from childhood trauma, and a disturbed sense of self, to step into the empty space left by the other boy's absence.

Perhaps Malik felt, in a convoluted way, that it was his duty to ensure that Vidor lived on, even if in a different form. To carry Vidor's legacy to the lofty heights he might have reached had he not disappeared into the roiling waters of the Seine.

And what of Malik Sayid? Who would miss him, who would notice or care if he were simply to disappear? A sewer rat, a bastard, rotten scum. A loathsome wretch from the colonies who dared to walk the streets of the shining city, the birthplace of Voltaire, Baudelaire, Renoir. What right did he have, born of an illiterate mother and a murderous father, to call Paris his home? But with the new mantle of a borrowed identity and the burnished pedigree of a survivor of Soviet oppression, he could walk with his head high, and construct the golden future that otherwise might ever be out of reach.

Gessen laid down his pen, his fingers cramped from trying to order his thoughts and determine the next course of action. As outlandish as it seemed, it all made sense. Only now he would have to prove it. If he came out and accused Vidor of being Malik Sayid, Vidor would surely laugh in his face – *show me the proof* – and challenge Gessen to a duel of wills.

50

Gessen shut the curtains against the darkening sky, only to open them again a moment later, after experiencing a discomfort at being shut in, though the room was cheery enough with the fire in the grate and the tea tray on the table. The Christmas holiday had come and gone with little fanfare, apart from a special meal on the day itself. Yet he felt the usual post-holiday let-down all out of proportion to what was, after all, just another day in the calendar.

For the first time in many years, since his early days as a practicing psychiatrist, Gessen experienced a flutter of anxiety before meeting with a patient. Now that he had documented proof that Vidor suffered from either a severely repressed or dissociative identity, it was time to inform him that this disturbance in his psyche was likely the cause of his violent outbursts. As a doctor, Gessen had an ethical duty to tell his patient what was wrong, to candidly discuss the reasons behind his diagnosis, and to present him with a treatment plan. But in the case of dissociative identity, the space between informing Vidor he had two personalities, unbeknownst to each other, and getting him to accept it was a yawning chasm he would need to bridge.

If it was a case of a wilfully repressed identity, Vidor was either a very good actor or a sociopath. If unconsciously repressed, it would take a skilful treatment strategy to break through Vidor's massively fortified ego defences. The revelation that he was someone else could lead to a catastrophic, and perhaps irremediable, breakdown. Gessen would have to tread carefully.

To complicate matters further, if this truly was a case of dissociation, it could be argued that it wasn't Vidor, but his alter Malik who was responsible for attacking both the man in Copenhagen and the local in the village. What these very different men might represent in Malik's mind, Gessen was determined to discover, not only to hasten Vidor's ongoing recovery, but also to prevent him from attacking other strangers in future. So far, the count was two, with one dead. Not to mention the ongoing, nagging suspicion that Vidor had played a role in Ismail's death. At least the man in the village had declined to press charges.

The deceased gentleman in Copenhagen was another matter. Unless Gessen could prove diminished responsibility, Vidor would be faced with a charge of manslaughter, or even murder. And few jurisdictions accepted a dissociative disorder as a mitigating factor in a plea of temporary insanity. Otherwise, it would be all too easy to say: 'Your Honour, it was my alter ego who made me do it.' Such a claim would not hold up in court.

* * *

Vidor entered the room, looking befuddled, as if he didn't quite know where he was, but then his expression cleared and he was the same courtly, self-possessed, and wryly humorous man Gessen had known since their first meeting.

After Vidor was seated, and coffee or tea offered and refused, Gessen waited a few moments, allowing the mood in the room to settle. Mathilde had placed a lit candle on the table, and the scent of orange blossoms filled the air between them. Gessen asked Vidor about his health and how he'd slept, but these were just delaying tactics. There was no getting around the fact he was obliged to impart difficult news. No patient wanted to hear he had a repressed identity or split personality. That he harboured more than one fully formed, and often vastly different, persona within a single mind, complete with different mannerisms, voices, and facial expressions. How Vidor would take the diagnosis was impossible to fathom. Denial would be the likely knee-jerk reaction. Or perhaps relief that at last a name could be pinned to his bewildering array of symptoms.

Gessen leaned forward and clasped his hands between his knees. 'We've made a great deal of progress together, haven't we, Vidor?'

'Progress?' He blinked rapidly, as if trying to dislodge a piece of grit from his eye.

'Yes. Since the unfortunate event that brought you here, you've made great strides. I know you found it difficult to talk about yourself, at first, or to allow me access to your memories.' He paused. 'It's not easy to let a stranger peer at our darkest secrets. But your trust in me and your willingness to take the first difficult steps on the road to recovery have led to important insights.'

Vidor's gaze drifted to the window.

'Wouldn't you agree?'

But his attention was fixed on something outside. Gessen turned to see what he was looking at, but there was nothing there. Just the usual jagged peaks, softened by a blanket of snow.

'I feel no differently than the day I arrived,' Vidor said. A muscle twitched in his jaw. 'Perhaps a trifle more rested and well fed, but as for my mood, or my personality, I feel the same as I always have.'

Gessen tried to catch his eye. 'Do you know why you attacked that man in Copenhagen, or the man in the village?'

'I haven't the slightest idea.' Vidor had yet to look directly at Gessen. 'Though in both cases, I'm convinced it was simply a matter of exhaustion and low blood sugar. Or perhaps a momentary disturbance in my frontal lobes.' He examined his fingernails. 'In all this time, we've never talked about the possibility of epileptic seizures as a mitigating factor.'

'Your EEG and brain scan in Copenhagen were normal.'

'A normal EEG in and of itself is not sufficient to rule out epilepsy,' Vidor countered.

'Have you ever wondered,' Gessen said, rising to close the curtains and shut out the mountains, 'why those two men? Or those particular occasions? I believe you have no record of previous incidents.'

'Of course I don't.' His face darkened. 'I'm not a ruffian.'

'What about the lapses in memory and the sleepwalking we talked about earlier? Or the feeling you once described of someone standing next to you, just behind your left shoulder. What do you make of that?'

Vidor shrugged. 'The brain shrinks as we grow older, and occasional memory lapses or quirks of proprioception are quite normal for someone my age.'

Gessen made a show of mulling over these assertions, before launching into it. 'I have another explanation,' he said, keeping his eyes on Vidor's face. 'I only suspected it at first, because it's quite rare. But all the evidence points to the same conclusion. And during our last session, the final clue fell into place.'

Vidor crossed his arms over his chest. He looked placid, even bored.

'While in a state of deep relaxation, you talked about your childhood. How you were born as a twin, and almost died, and were sent away to be raised by a woman in a nearby village. You mentioned what it felt like to watch your twin brother thrive under the care of your mother and sisters while you were cast aside. That your father was a monster who abandoned you to your fate as an outcast and a bastard, having accused your mother of having relations with another man, and insisting that you were not his son.'

Vidor removed a piece of lint from his trousers. 'Have you gone mad?' His thin smile looked pasted on.

'You have all the hallmarks of someone with a dissociative identity disorder,' Gessen said, keeping his voice steady. No need to antagonise Vidor any more than necessary. If he stomped out of the room in a rage, it might take weeks to reel him back to a place where he would listen to reason. 'Quite rare, but it's definitely legitimate. It's unfortunate that a few notorious cases have been misrepresented by the media. The condition typically arises after trauma as a protective mechanism. Childhood trauma in most cases.'

Vidor's face, cast in shadow, could have been carved from stone. 'I experienced no trauma as a child.'

'You lost your father at the age of six. I would call that a trauma.'

Vidor's chin jerked up, and the blood drained from his face.

He must be wondering how this fact had come to light, Gessen mused, having fought so hard to hide the truth of his father's betrayal.

'Many children lose a parent at a young age,' Vidor said smoothly, as if nothing were amiss. 'Are you telling me that all of them grow up to have a split personality?'

'Of course not. But on the face of it, it's a perfectly logical defence mechanism. The traumatised ego…'

Vidor held up his hands. 'Spare me your jargon. Where's your proof?'

Proof he had, fortunately, in the form of a video of Vidor narrating memories that belonged to the boy named Malik. But a stalling tactic might be a better way forward. Cornering Vidor felt akin to stalking a fox. Best to hunker down in the tall grass and let the quarry come to him. Later, if all else failed, he would show Vidor the video of himself as Malik describing his memories in French. But not today. If it was a true case of dissociative identity, it would come as a shock. But if Vidor was fully conscious of his deception, he would prevaricate and bluster. Or claim, for instance, that he was just having a bit of fun. If Gessen's tactic backfired, it could set Vidor's recovery back by months.

'Let's examine the evidence, shall we?' He retrieved Vidor's file from his desk and flipped it open. 'Periods of amnesia, and what you've referred to as sleepwalking, may not have been sleepwalking at all, but your other personality controlling your nocturnal habits. For example,' Gessen consulted the yellow pad, though it wasn't necessary. Such was the unusual nature of Vidor's case that every detail was etched in his mind. 'You've told me that there were a couple of occasions when, having gone to bed early and slept deeply, you entered the kitchen in the morning to find a half-drunk cup of cocoa on the counter, or an empty packet of biscuits. Yet, you've previously claimed not to have a sweet tooth and mentioned your dislike of cocoa. Perhaps, after considering the possibilities, you decided it was a simple matter of sleepwalking. A perfectly plausible explanation why you couldn't remember these activities when you woke the next morning.'

He flipped to another page in the file. 'A regression to a childlike state during times of stress could explain your hankering after sweets, but I believe my explanation is a better fit. In which case, you didn't go to sleep at nine o'clock at all. At that time your other personality would emerge. This other personality, more nocturnal than you, as Vidor, would make hot cocoa, eat a packet of biscuits, watch television, and perhaps go for a late-night stroll through the neighbourhood, before going to bed at one or two in the morning.

'It would explain why you might have felt tired the next day, even after an early bedtime, or discovered mud on your shoes when you remembered cleaning them before turning in. "Vidor" is a man of regular habits, who keeps a tidy home and eats dinner at seven and goes to bed at nine-thirty, while your alter is more slovenly. Perhaps, we might even call him angry or rebellious. He prowls the house at night or wanders the neighbourhood. Tracks mud into the front hall, leaves the television on and indulges in sweets, while Vidor has been cautioned by his doctor to watch his sugar intake.' Gessen waited half a beat. The air in the room had grown stale. 'How would you explain it?'

Vidor's mouth flattened into a thin line. 'What you're saying is preposterous. I am not two people. I am one person. Professor Vidor Kiraly, chair of the Neurobiology department at Cambridge University. Who happens, I readily admit, to suffer from bouts of tiredness and mild anxiety from time to time. Who occasionally sleepwalks at night. It's a known phenomenon, often exacerbated by stress, as I'm sure I don't need to tell you.'

'But let's say for the sake of argument that you did have a twin, or a double,' Gessen said, plunging on. 'Who would he be? Someone exactly like you, or your polar opposite? Someone capable, perhaps, of killing a stranger. A stranger he'd mistaken for someone else.'

'Killing a stranger…?' Vidor's expression was stony. 'I've done no such thing.'

'I'm afraid you have,' Gessen said. 'I refrained from telling you earlier because I didn't want the shock to interfere with your recovery.' Vidor's face had gone white. 'That man you attacked in Copenhagen suffered a severe head injury. Shortly after being taken to hospital he fell into a coma. Three days later, he died.'

When Vidor spoke his voice was flat. 'I am not responsible for that man's death. Nor do I have a twin, or have I ever entertained such an idea. Are we finished? I have a monstrous headache and would like to return to my room and lie down.'

51

Paris, France
May 1969

He spends all day at the Jardin des Plantes. The stale croissant
and bitter coffee he bought from a kiosk did little to quell
his hunger, and he wanders with an air of dejection into the
great hall of the Natural History Museum. The skeletons of
dinosaurs and mastodons rear above his head, and he consoles
himself with the thought that the lifespan of earth is finite, and
soon he will be dust. Along with all the other creatures who
have come before him. *Dead, mort, mayit.* Millions of years,
dead. That should be enough time to cleanse him of his sins.

A few minutes after four, he leaves the park to wander the
city. At least the air is balmy and the skies clear. Perhaps, as
the weather warms, he will take to sleeping on park benches,
anything to avoid the disgusting room he's rented in a slovenly
quarter after being tossed out of the Sovàny's flat. He misses
the lovely mother and sisters. The boy who's turned tyrant
doesn't merit a thought.

All he has waiting for him is the sour-faced drunk who
patrols his domain like an ogre, sometimes banging on the
bedroom door in the middle of the night. *Sale Arabe!* Filthy

Arab. The man can't get in, not when the door is barricaded with a chair. But loss of sleep and the terror of being murdered in his bed have worn him out. Some days he feels he's going mad.

His bursary ended with the school term, and his money is running out. He'll have to find a job for the summer. Cleaning floors, or schlepping carcasses at the butchers. It would be nice to get a gig on one of the *bateaux mouches* that cruise the Seine. Out on the water, and away from the streets, where he tramps alone day and night, perhaps he'll find a measure of peace.

He limps along the endless length of the Rue de Vaugirard, wincing at the throbbing blister on his heel, past throngs of students and housewives and businessmen enjoying the sun-kissed air. As he approaches a cinema, he slows to study the films on show.

A few people trickle out of the theatre with a desultory air and blink like moles in the light filtering through the lindens. A strange time to see a film, he muses, on such a beautiful afternoon. But perhaps, like him, they are desperate to escape their lives.

As he turns away, a man steps out of the cinema and tilts his head to look at the sky. In that instant, at 16:39 on 18 May 1969, the world as he knew it shatters into bits.

A man steps out of a cinema. He can scarcely breathe when their eyes meet for a tantalising second then flick away. With a grim set to his mouth, the man lights a cigarette and exhales the blue smoke into the air. He glowers as he looks at his watch. *Merde*. Spits on the pavement, walks away.

He follows. Sucking in air as his heart crashes against his ribs. When the man stops at a kiosk in front of the Pasteur Institute to buy a newspaper, he studies his profile. The aquiline nose, the flared nostrils, those agate eyes. How could it be? He's supposed to be dead. But there he stands, jaw clenched, rage oozing from his skin, very much alive. A familiar silver ring, intricately carved, glints on the man's finger.

There's the proof.

He's older of course. He hasn't seen that face for nearly ten years. But he knows that face as if it were his own. Every line of the cruel visage is etched in his brain. The voice thick with venom. That villainous madman who'd tortured his mother. He was supposed to be dead.

Blood pulses in his ears; his hands curl into fists. He longs to leap at the man's throat and squeeze until his eyes bulge in terror.

The man continues down the street, walking faster now. He follows, nearly running to keep up as the golem ploughs onward, weaving through the crowd, as if he senses he's being stalked.

He tries to close the distance between them without attracting attention. But the man is thirty metres ahead when he steps to the curb and hails a taxi. The look on his face is one of contempt. A dagger to the chest. His hands shake, he can't breathe. As the man reaches for the handle of the taxicab, he begins to run.

'Monster! Traitor! You're supposed to be dead.'

The man's chin jerks up and they lock eyes briefly before he steps into the taxi and speeds away.

He drops to his knees, gasping for air as the pavement spins and the world goes black.

Hours later, when he comes to his senses, darkness has fallen, and he finds himself in a neighbourhood he doesn't recognise. How did he get here? He touches the bloody cut on his chin. His palms are scraped raw. Tears spring in his eyes. So tired. He longs for home with the desperation of a child. That's all he wants, all he's ever wanted: to go home. But where? Where is that place? Not the land he's fled, or the flat with the mean drunk. Nor any place on the earth he can think of.

Katerina. So kind and sweet. She would take him in, he is sure of it, if only for one night. She'll make him a cup of tea, soothe his fears, assure him that everything will work out in the end.

But he can't go back. If he were ever to see her or Rennie again, he would tell them his story, the one that is etched in blood on his skin for all the world to see. An unwanted, bastard child, tossed in the gutter and left to die.

* * *

For days, he wanders the city, roaming the streets at night, sleeping rough, a wretched, loathsome creature, pustular and dirty, fit for nothing but the abattoir. Each evening, from midnight to the hour of the wolf, he walks along the river, trying to work up the courage to throw himself into the roiling brown waters.

Just after midnight, he stands on his chosen spot on the Left Bank. Beginning his journey at the tip of the Île de la Cité and heading west. Halfway to the Pont Neuf, he sees a scrum of rabble rousers. The lamplight glints off the hair of the boy in the center of the group, as he holds a wine bottle by the neck and dumps its contents on another boy's head. *'Plus de vin!'* he cries, grabbing a bottle out of yet another's hands. *Vidor*.

He hangs back in the shadows cast by the trees overhead and when the friends grow tired of their drunken revelry and disperse, Vidor continues along the river, talking to himself, or tossing back his head to howl at the moon.

He follows, keeping out of the light. It's clear his nemesis is very drunk, weaving amongst the trees and benches and stumbling on the cobbles.

Keeping ten paces between them, they pass by the Musée d'Orsay and come to a deserted stretch of the river. *Where is he going?* Vidor whirls suddenly and squints into the darkness. 'Who are you? Why are you following me?'

He holds back in the shadows, waiting for Vidor to

continue on his way. But the boy is two sheets to the wind and spoiling for a fight.

Stepping forward, Vidor holds up the bottle. 'Wanna drink?' But then his face changes when he sees who it is, tracking his movements.

'*Connard*. Bastard. What are you doing here? I told you to scram. Leave me and my family alone.' He slurs his words, sways on his feet.

'I just want to talk to you,' he says. 'I have no designs on your sister. I'd like to come back…' He almost says *home* but knows that would only enrage this surly lad looking for trouble.

The golden boy, master of the realm, stumbles towards him and swings, whirling comically when his fist fails to meet its target. That his adversary succeeds in evading the punch seems to enrage him. He stumbles and swings again.

Having nimbly avoided the attack, he decides it's time to flee. As his feet pound the pavement, certain he's being pursued, he hazards a look back, but no one is there. No one and nothing but the dark river flowing inexorably towards the coast. He steps close to the edge of the embankment and stares into the rushing water.

Has anyone seen him? If he returns to his room, it will mean waiting in fear for the police to arrive and take him away. Better to consign himself to the muddy waters than go on like this. He doesn't belong here, not in this city of emperors and queens. *Connard*. Bastard. For nine months he's been holding his breath, waiting to be found out.

The great river surges through the darkness. He closes his eyes, feels the damp spray on his skin. How easy it would be to jump.

52

Clinique Les Hirondelles
Saint-Odile, Switzerland
4 January 2009

At the sound of a knock on the door, Gessen dropped his pen and closed the file he was reading. 'Ah, Libby,' he said, when she poked her head through the doorway. 'Come on in. I've got a few minutes before my next session.' He stood and guided her to a chair. 'Ready to head back to uni?'

'More or less.' Her normally bright eyes were cast in shadow.

He followed her gaze to the window.

'More or less?'

'What I mean is, I wouldn't mind staying on longer.' She fiddled with a button on her cardigan. 'It's been such an eye-opening experience, and I'm grateful for the opportunity to observe real patients, and you and Dr Lindstrom at your work. I've learned more in six weeks here than I would from years in the library.'

He nodded to the bound report on his desk. 'I've already read your paper. You've done an excellent job.' He stood and passed it to her. 'I jotted a few notes in the margins. Have a look and let me know if you have any questions. I've also sent my feedback to your supervisor. I'm sure Dr Wakeford will be pleased with your efforts.'

Libby took the report and flipped through it. 'It's been a fascinating journey,' she said, tucking the report into her bag. 'I do feel badly, though, about pretending to be a patient. Especially with Professor Kiraly. He seems like a nice person, though I was struck by his pervasive air of sadness.' She brushed a strand of hair from her eyes. 'Have you found out why he attacked that man in Copenhagen?'

Gessen demurred. Surely, she knew he couldn't reveal the details of Vidor's case.

'I wasn't sure I should bring this up but...' She hesitated. 'Do you think he might have had something to do with Ismail's death? I got the feeling there was something... a bit off between them. A simmering animosity. Perhaps they fought. Or Ismail insulted him, and Professor Kiraly...' her voice trailed off. 'I'm sorry. I know you can't tell me, but I do hope I'm wrong.'

He stood and adjusted the blinds to block out the sun. It would be a relief to confide his own suspicions about Vidor's part in Ismail's death, but it would be unfair to unburden himself on a student who was already questioning her role in duping the others by pretending to be a patient. A fox in the hen house. He assured her she had played an important part in Vidor's recovery, and that the confidences from Vidor she'd passed on to him were things he would never have gleaned on his own.

'I realise it might have felt unethical, at times,' he said. 'Deceiving the other patients. But please be assured it was all in service to their healing. Professor Kiraly was able to open himself up to you in ways he couldn't with me, or Dr Lindstrom. You've made a tremendous contribution to his care.' Her eyes were troubled, and he held her gaze. 'Without your help, he wouldn't have made the progress he has.'

'So he's getting better?' Her face brightened. 'He's desperate to get home.'

'I know that. But sometimes, Libby, the life we're trying to get back to is just an illusion. The glossy carapace we create to conceal our inner pain. As you progress with your studies and begin to treat patients of your own, you'll find that much of our work entails stripping that carapace away.'

He laced his fingers together and regarded her with paternal sympathy, hoping she would take his advice to heart. Though he didn't want to belabour the point, she seemed reluctant to leave, as if needing something more. 'In humans, consciousness is both a gift and a curse,' Gessen said. 'We spend the vast majority of our time either agonising about the mistakes of the past or worrying about the future. Ever aware of our mortality, how do we construct a healthy life? How do we live, love, work when we know that obliteration awaits us at some unknown point in the future? Death might be decades away.' He paused. 'Or next week.' He had her attention now. 'Terrifying isn't it?' He tried to soften his words with a smile. 'It's no wonder we've invented all kinds of defences and distractions to avoid this one inescapable fact: that our time here on Earth is finite, and none of us gets out alive.'

'That's awfully gloomy. When you put it that way,' Libby said, with a nervous laugh. 'You'd think more people would put themselves out of the misery of waiting for the end.'

'Many do.' He hesitated. 'I don't need to tell you that.'

Her face blanched.

Of course, she was thinking about the brother who'd hanged himself. It was Libby who'd discovered the body when she arrived home from school. A shy and sensitive girl of twelve, just embarking on adolescence, the experience could have destroyed her. But that early tragedy had spurred her on to learn about the human psyche and fostered a desire to help others construct meaningful lives in the face of existential terror.

A shadow passed through Libby's eyes.

'What are you thinking?'

'Just that… I wish it wasn't necessary to lie to him about who I was. He only confided in me because he thought I was a patient.'

And not my spy. He leaned forward and met her gaze. 'We're all patients,' Gessen said. 'All of us. I myself have regular sessions with the analyst I've been seeing for years. Sometimes only two or three times a year, but when it's time to meet with her, and take my turn on the couch, I am reminded how fragile we are. Even those of us who pretend to have all the answers.'

When she didn't respond, he searched for something to give her solace. 'If you go on to qualify as a practicing psychotherapist, you'll find there are hard choices to make with every patient. Ethical dilemmas will come at you from all directions. I once had a patient whose mother died while he was in residential treatment. He suffered from severe depression and had attempted suicide twice. I made the very difficult choice to wait until he was stabilised before I gave him the news.'

'How did he take it?'

'Not well. He threatened to sue me for malpractice, furious I had denied him the chance to say goodbye or attend her funeral. But as his doctor, my loyalty was to my patient, not to a woman who was already dead.'

From the look on Libby's face, it was clear she would have told the patient about his mother.

'About three years later,' Gessen said, 'the man sent me a letter, thanking me for saving his life. He mentioned that every year on his mother's birthday, he would visit her grave to apologise for not being with her at the end. But also to tell her that I had rescued him from the depths of hell. I keep his letter in a file with the others I've received from patients over the years. They help remind me that some decisions, however difficult, turn out all right in the end.'

She stood and gathered her things. 'I should say goodbye to Dr Lindstrom. My train leaves at three.'

As he walked her to the door, he glanced at her profile, and was struck once again by the slight but distinct resemblance to Sophie. If they had married, as he'd wanted until fate intervened, they might have had a daughter like Libby. Fiercely intelligent, brimming with life. She sometimes appeared in his dreams, this fictional daughter, as a vibrant soul with a forgiving heart. Someone he would never meet.

'Let me know how you get on,' he said, walking her to the door. 'I see wonderful things ahead for you.'

When she was gone, he murmured the words he'd planned to say at the end of their meeting. But had changed his mind, finding them too heavy for the occasion. Of the oblivion that awaits us all, be not afraid. Stride boldly into the future.

Choose life.

53

'I would like to show you a video recording of one of our recent sessions,' Gessen said, as soon as Vidor was seated. 'It might come as a shock, but it will make it easier for your therapy to progress. Once you see for yourself that a second personality is residing in your psyche, your real treatment can begin.'

Begin? He thought they were finished. Vidor felt exposed, like a fox under a floodlight. What was on this video? Something embarrassing, no doubt. Footage that Gessen could use to humiliate him or as a form of blackmail. Knowing that a looming and ever-present threat hung over his head would ruin him.

'We need only watch a few minutes.' Gessen darkened the room and pressed a switch. A panel on the wall slid open to reveal a large screen. He clicked the remote control, while Vidor tensed in the chair.

On the screen his face appeared in close-up. The camera zoomed out to show his whole body, seated in an armchair. Gessen's shadowy profile was just visible on the left side of the frame. Gessen increased the volume until Vidor could hear the sound of his own breathing.

In the video, the shadowy profile spoke. 'I'd like to hear more of your story. Would you tell me your name?'

'Malik.'

'And how old are you?'

'*Dix-neuf.*'

Malik. Nineteen. What the hell was this? The voice in the video was deeper than Vidor's own, and he was speaking French. That was odd. He hadn't spoken French in years.

'Malik Sayid,' said the man in the film, who looked like Vidor in most respects, though some kind of transformation had happened. His expression was slack and frightened, his posture awkward. In the film, Vidor held a pencil in his left hand and scribbled on a piece of paper. Vidor frowned. He was right-handed and always had been.

In the video, Gessen asked, 'Can you tell me where you're from?'

'I'm from a place called Al Madinat Almajhula, a small city halfway between the mountains and the sea.'

Vidor reared up from the chair. 'What is this? Some kind of trick? More of your mind games? That isn't me. You've spliced my head onto someone else's body and altered my voice, like they do in films. Any half-wit kid with a computer can do the same thing.'

Gessen pressed pause. 'It isn't you, Vidor, you're right about that. But I assure you it's not a trick. I believe the person talking in the video is your alter, or other personality. At some point, not long after you moved to Paris to attend university, you met a boy named Malik Sayid. You may have been friends, or lovers perhaps, or even enemies. But I believe that this boy, Malik, played an important role in your life. I believe something traumatic happened to you, or to Malik, and that you somehow internalised his psyche, perhaps during a fugue state.' He waited a moment before going on. 'Does the name Vidor Sovàny mean anything to you?'

Vidor shook his head.

'He was a *lycée* student in Paris. Not long after he earned his baccalaureate in the spring of 1969, he vanished. Later, in the absence of a body or evidence of life, he was presumed dead by drowning in the Seine. How and when it happened isn't completely clear, but I have my suspicions.'

'You're mad.' Vidor's body felt heavy and dull. 'I'm leaving here today. With or without your permission.'

'Let's watch a few minutes more. You'll see it's not a trick.' He pressed the start button.

In the video, Gessen handed the man in the chair, who looked less like Vidor than a terrible imposter, a piece of paper and a pen. 'Could you write your name for me in Arabic, and a description of your family?'

The man wrote for several minutes before handing back the paper to Gessen who held it up to the camera. Vidor started when he saw the loops and swirls of the Arabic alphabet.

'I speak four languages,' he said stiffly, 'none of which is Arabic.'

'You might not speak Arabic, but Malik does.' Gessen extracted a file from a binder on his desk and handed Vidor a sheet of paper. 'This is what Malik wrote. Can you tell me what it says?'

The swirls and curlicues shimmered before Vidor's eyes. A child's scribble that meant nothing. He tossed the page on the table. 'Is this some kind of monstrous attempt to drive me insane?' He leapt from the chair and stomped to the door. 'We're all pawns in some elaborate game you've concocted for your own amusement.'

Gessen removed his glasses and rubbed his eyes. 'I realise this is difficult for you to take in, but the first stage in getting well is acceptance. Please humour me for a few more minutes. I'll play the rest of the video, to see if anything strikes a chord.'

In spite of the burning anger lodged in his throat like a fist, Vidor was riveted by the image on the screen. The man who was Vidor but not Vidor spoke in the voice of a shy and frightened adolescent. In excellent and nuanced French, he told the story of growing up in a dusty village. The searing days and freezing nights. How he was given away at birth. The person on the screen, man and child in turns, who was Vidor but not Vidor, spoke of how he'd dreamed of two things: that his father would die, and his mother reclaim him. But as he grew older and neither came to pass, he turned his face to a different horizon, towards the mythical city of Paris he'd learned about in school. He understood that if he worked hard, he might qualify for a scholarship to pay for his university fees in the great city to the north. It was a way out. A dream and a yearning for another world that softened the harsh reality of his circumstances.

* * *

Vidor jerked awake and rubbed his eyes. Had he been dreaming? He was startled to find himself seated on a chair. Across from him, a man with wiry black hair stared at him intently. He could have sworn he'd been running through a maze of streets, his worn sandals kicking up dust, and his heart beating like a captive bird in his chest.

'I must have fallen asleep.'

The man, whose name he now remembered – Gessen, Dr Gessen – looked at him kindly. 'Not quite, but we'll get to that later.'

54

Gessen waited until Vidor was safely escorted back to his room before reading again the letter he'd received that morning. Another nail, apparently, in Vidor's coffin.

Cambridge, UK
6 January 2009

Dear Dr Gessen,
I've been meaning to write to you for some time, but my life has been rather hectic these past few months, and in Professor Kiraly's absence I've taken on a number of administrative tasks in addition to my own research. The rest of my time has been spent trying to convince the Home Office to allow me to stay in the country. It was just last week that I finally received the welcome news that my visa will be extended for another year. Who knows what will happen when it expires, but for now I can rest easier and return my focus to my studies.
When Professor Kiraly won last year's Søgaard Prize, everyone was thrilled. It was a great achievement for him as an individual, but also a coup for the department and the university. There was much talk of him winning the Nobel at some point in the near

future. But after the prize ceremony in Copenhagen and Professor Kiraly's breakdown, some things came to light that made me question his contribution to the breakthrough which led to him being awarded the prize. Professor Kiraly received the award for his work on sensory processing, and communication between the cortex and thalamus. That's also the area that Hisham had been working on under the direction of Dr Tritter. It's not my own area of research, but it's similar enough for me to have known it was in direct competition with the work in our lab.

About a month ago I was looking for reprints of a paper Professor Kiraly authored, and in the bottom of his desk drawer, shoved in the back, I found one of Hisham's lab notebooks. Hisham mostly wrote in English, but this one had margin notes in Arabic. Quite a number, and many with exclamation points, so I take it Hisham was excited about some of his findings and wanted to keep them private. I don't read Arabic, and as far as I know, neither does Professor Kiraly, so I took the notebook to a Palestinian friend of mine who's a student in the Physics department. After he translated the notes, I was disturbed to find that much of Hisham's data provided the key to solving the last piece of the puzzle Professor Kiraly had been trying to crack in his own work.

I am not suggesting that Professor Kiraly stole Hisham's research. In the scientific disciplines, much collaboration is involved, and there is frequent sharing of data. However, such a coincidence, combined with the fact that the lost notebook had been mixed up with Professor Kiraly's papers seemed odd to me. Perhaps I suffer from an overactive imagination. Make no mistake, Professor Kiraly is a brilliant scientist, but the accomplishment he was recognised for may not be solely his. I have a meeting tomorrow with the Chancellor *to discuss my concerns. Though I can't predict how this meeting will go, he may suggest contacting the awards committee about a possible infraction. Worst case scenario, they might rescind Professor Kiraly's award, but I do hope it won't come to that.*

Kindest regards,
Farzan Rahimi

55

In the morning, Vidor was outraged to learn from Dr Lindstrom that he wouldn't be discharged as requested. How typical of Gessen to send a woman to do a man's job. What did Gessen think, that he'd attack him? Even worse, she had hinted that the police were interested in questioning him again about Ismail's death. Apparently, new evidence had come to light that pointed to foul play. Those words, *foul play*, straight out of a bad detective novel, were clearly a sign of an overheated imagination.

But two could play at this game. If Gessen was determined to hold him hostage here, emergency measures were needed. He might even have to take a hostage of his own. That Babette woman would certainly enjoy the drama, assuming her Munchausen's shenanigans weren't enough to attract the kind of attention she craved.

His mind skittered along a narrow precipice as he considered the possibilities. Storming out the main gate and boarding a train bound for the UK wasn't an option. Upon admission to the clinic, he'd handed over his passport and credit cards. He also needed Gessen to certify he had been mentally unstable at the time of the attack on that man in Copenhagen. Otherwise, he would be faced with an assault charge, or worse. Had he really died as Gessen claimed? Vidor can't remember now what he'd been told, though surely the man wasn't dead. Gessen only said that to frighten him. Sweat broke out on his neck, and he clawed at his collar for air.

On his way to his room, he spotted Hélène in her fur hat and dark green parka, making her way to the bench by the statue of swallows in flight. She might come to his aid, and he hurried to intercept her. 'Come with me,' he said.

She looked up, startled. 'Are you all right?'

His eyes darted about. Every fibre of his being urged him to run. 'I need your help.' He took her arm and steered her in the opposite direction of the main building and towards the far end of the property. He'd spotted an isolated chalet there once, hidden behind a dense stand of fir trees. He was certain it was empty. They could hide out in there until he figured out his next move.

If Hélène refused to help him, then drastic measures were called for. He could hold her hostage in the chalet, or threaten to burn it down, unless he was provided with passage home and absolved of all responsibility for the events in Copenhagen. He cursed the day he'd been given that award. It should have been the crowning pinnacle of his career, not the gateway to an unimaginable hell.

When they reached the chalet, he looked back to see that the trees had closed in behind them. The snow was piled high on either side of a recently cleared path that led to the door. The shutters on the front windows were fastened and no smoke rose from the chimney. All signs pointed to a vacant building. He hurried her up the front steps, dragging her by the arm. 'Ouch, you're hurting me.' Fear flashed in her eyes.

'I won't harm you,' he said, pushing her through the unlocked door and into a dim foyer. 'But I need to get away from here. I can't get Dr Gessen… he doesn't understand that I…' He grabbed the edge of a table and gasped for air. 'If I don't return to my life, I'll die here.'

'You'd better sit down.' She led him to a chair at the end of the hall. 'Try to breathe. You'll feel better in a minute.'

He didn't think he'd ever feel better, and certainly not in a minute. What a stupid measure of time. *Tick-tock*. In a minute there is time... for decisions and revisions... Was he going mad? His thoughts buzzed with the fragments of a poem he'd read long ago.

The front hall of the chalet was shadowed in darkness. There was a telephone on the table and he caught Hélène eyeing it. 'Don't touch it. Not until,' he coughed raggedly, 'I've come up with a plan.'

With snow piled up to the window ledges, and no wind, the chalet was eerily quiet. A perfect place to negotiate his release. He could fasten the shutters and barricade the door. Clearly no one had been in here for months.

'Do you mind if I turn on the lights?' Her voice had lost its tremor. Surely now, seeing how desperate he was, how impossible it was to remain here for another day, she would help him get away. Having been a patient for so long, Hélène must know more than anyone how it felt to be trapped, year in, year out, on this godforsaken mountain. A permanent psychiatric patient at the whim of whatever diagnoses and drugs that trickster Gessen might throw at you.

Without waiting for an answer, Hélène strode down the hall and switched on the lights in the kitchen and began to unload the contents of a straw bag on the counter. Eggs, milk, butter, bread in a paper sack. A bunch of carrots and a sack of potatoes. After putting away the food, she lifted a red enamel kettle from the hob and filled it with water.

'I don't know what's upsetting you, but I've always found that a cup of tea works wonders.' She rummaged in the cupboard. 'I have chamomile, peppermint, and lemon verbena. Or black tea, if you'd rather.'

While waiting for the kettle to boil, she set up a tray with a teapot, cups and saucers, and a blue-patterned bowl of sugar cubes. He was puzzled by all this activity and looked around in growing confusion. When he'd hustled her through the front door, he had the idea they were entering a disused chalet, or even a storage facility. It was too far away from the clinic's other buildings to house any patients, and the private residences of the staff were clustered around the sprawling manor house. He couldn't imagine what this was. Although as Hélène moved into the next room to turn on the lights and adjust the curtains, he noticed the window ledges were filled with plants. A piano stood in the corner. Two sofas, upholstered in a slate-grey fabric, faced a stone fireplace. On the walls hung reproductions of paintings one might see in a museum, except their quality was exceptionally fine, and the colours so exquisite, he sensed they weren't reproductions at all.

He passed his hand over his eyes, expecting the earth to crack open and swallow him whole. Gessen was right. He was mad as a hatter. What other explanation could there be to explain how reality had morphed into a slippery beast, impossible to grasp. When he opened his eyes, Hélène was carrying the tea tray over to the seating area in the living room. She placed it on a low table by the sofa and stooped to examine the mottled leaf on a lush green plant with waxy leaves. For a moment, he forgot all about his plan to hold Hélène hostage, though she made the perfect bargaining chip for getting him back to Cambridge.

She slapped her hands together as if wiping off dust. 'Why don't you have a seat, Vidor. You'll feel much better after a cup of tea. I've brewed a pot of the lemon verbena. It's very soothing, and perfect for a wintry day.' She poured out the tea and settled in the corner of the sofa. 'Come join me. I won't bite.' Her eyes shone with mischief.

As he sat beside her, it was easy to picture the excited young girl she once was, with her whole life before her. It occurred to him he didn't know a thing about this woman. Nothing but rumours and wild speculation. He looked around for the quilted Chanel bag with its supposedly gruesome contents, but there was no sign of it.

'What is this place?'

Hélène cradled the teacup in her hand. Her slim fingers looked naked without her rings. 'This is my home.'

'Your home? I don't…' It made no sense, unless she was eligible, as a long-term patient, for special privileges. Even if that were true, he couldn't believe any patient ill enough to be a resident here would be trusted with kitchen knives. Especially since the house was tucked away in the trees and out of sight of the clinic. 'You live here?'

'Yes. I live here.' Her eyes gleamed like a child with a long-held secret. With the sleeves of her sweater pushed up, her wrists were exposed. No monitor. He squeezed his eyes shut. Had she managed to cut it off?

'Vidor? Still with us?' She fluttered her fingers before his eyes. 'I thought you might have guessed long ago. Though given what the others say about me, it would be easy to think otherwise.' She sucked in her breath and let it out slowly. 'I'm not one of Dr Gessen's patients. I'm a private individual, and this…' she waved her arm to take in the room, 'is my home. It has been for many years, long before Dr Gessen came on the scene.'

His mouth dropped open. 'I don't understand. What about the baby who died, and the doll you carry around in that bag of yours?'

'Oh dear.' Her lips twitched into a smile. 'That's one bit of fun that got out of hand, I'm afraid. Actually, it was Anton's – Dr Gessen's – idea. When I sold him the property for the clinic, at a below-market rate I might add, we made a deal that I would not only be allowed to remain in my home, but also have use of the clinic's facilities during the periods I was here. In the early years, I wasn't here very often. Mainly a few weeks in summer and during the Christmas holidays, but three years ago, I sold my flat in Geneva, and this house became my primary residence. As I grew older, I began to see the advantages of having year-round access to the spa facilities and excellent dining.

'Dr Gessen felt it best to concoct an explanation for my

enduring presence here. So we came up with the story that I was a chronic patient who required extended care. From time to time, when I left the clinic to travel or visit my children, he would tell people, if anyone asked, that I had gone off to a specialist clinic in Germany, say, or France, for more intensive treatment.'

A wave of dizziness nearly knocked him flat. Hélène wasn't a patient? How was that possible, when all this time he'd thought… The deception was outrageous. What else was Gessen lying about? More than ever, he was sure he'd stumbled into the lair of a madman. Where left was right and up was down. Nothing he'd seen or heard while here could be counted on as real.

'You have children? But the picture of those models you showed me in that magazine. I thought…' He pressed his palms against his eyes. A dull ache beat at the back of his skull.

'You'd better lie down,' she said. 'You're positively green about the gills.'

They'd been speaking French, and it took Vidor a moment to realise she had switched to English. With an American accent at that. He dropped his head in his hands and squeezed his eyes shut. What was going on?

'You poor man.' She refilled his cup and handed it to him. 'There's no conspiracy. And I never actually lied to you, did I? Nor to anyone else, for that matter. People only see what they wish to see. When the others find me eating in the dining room or taking part in the meditation and bodywork classes, of course they assume I'm just another patient. Though one with special privileges, perhaps, as I'm not dressed in the clinic-issued clothing, and I'm allowed to wear my jewellery.' She paused, as if expecting him to interrupt.

'And that business with my Chanel bag…' She held up her hands and smiled. 'What can I say? It started out as a bit of mischief, to make me look like a genuine kook, but as things do, it got out of hand. Once the rumour spread that I kept a doll in there I believed was my dead child…' She tossed him a wry look. 'Yes, I've heard the story. It became so entrenched that I couldn't stop carrying the damn thing around. I'd dug my own grave, so to speak.'

He stood on wobbly legs and made an awkward circuit of the room, briefly touching a brass bowl, a glass vase full of lilies, and fingering the curtain fabric, before collapsing back on the sofa. He stared at her helplessly. 'I don't understand.'

'Would you like to hear my story?' She leaned back into the sofa cushions. 'It's a familiar tale, the world over. When it comes to love, we're all fools. None more foolish than a sheltered young woman eager to cast off the bonds of family, and hopelessly naïve about the ways of the world.'

He pressed his hands to his eyes. What was she going on about? Some fairy story she wished to tell him? He was in no mood to hear about a princess who lived happily ever after.

'I'm not sure whether anyone uses the word "heiress" anymore,' she said, fiddling with the gold locket around her neck. 'But that's what I was. You won't have heard of it, I don't imagine, but in the early years of the twentieth century, my grandfather founded a department store in the American Midwest. At the time, nobody thought much would come of it, but he was clever at business and within a few short years his store became hugely successful.

'My father later took it over, but when he died, rather prematurely at the age of fifty-two, the business was sold and the money left to me. A shrewd man, he included in his will a sternly worded letter encouraging me to use the money for the public good, and a warning to steer clear of fortune hunters. But I was a stupid girl of nineteen, cooling my heels at a finishing school in Switzerland, and desperate to break free from parental bonds.'

Vidor opened his eyes and squinted at Hélène. An American girl. An heiress. Such were her acting skills, he would never have guessed. She poured out more of the sweetly aromatic tea that brought back memories of a walking holiday in France. The bright lemon scent created a funnel in time he could pass through, and for a moment he was confused. Not sure anymore where – or who – he was.

'When word got out about my inheritance,' Hélène said, 'it didn't take long for the wolves to come sniffing at my door. The most persistent of these was an impossibly handsome and charming man, with sleek chestnut hair and beguiling brown eyes. You'd recognise his name if I told you, but I prefer not to speak of him. Some people claim you can summon the devil himself by speaking his name aloud, so let's not take any chances.' Her eyes crinkled. 'Anyway, we had a whirlwind romance, a lavish wedding, a glamorous honeymoon and parties galore. Of course I was too smitten and starry-eyed not to realise he had no money of his own. When the first of my three children was born, I wanted them to have the best in life, so no money was spared in raising them, though my Midwestern Calvinist heart quailed at the extravagance of our lifestyle. My father had drilled into me the idea that the two pillars of a good life were hard work and giving back to the community.

'I'm sure you can guess the rest.' She raised her hands in a gesture of weariness. 'He siphoned off most of my money. Fancy cars, yachts, women.

'After our children went off to private boarding schools in Switzerland, I tried to rein in his spending, but he counter-attacked by convincing some quack doctor I was crazy, and that he woke one night to find me standing over him with a butcher's knife. Not terribly original, but a time-honoured ploy men have used for ages to get rid of their wives. I spent some time in a psychiatric hospital, not this one, but a private clinic in the South of France. My children believed his poisonous lies and stopped visiting. We were completely estranged for several years, but I do see them now on occasion. That picture I showed you from a magazine. It wasn't the delusions of a madwoman. Those really are two of my children, though that photo is nearly fifteen years old. I scissored off the caption with their names and the bit about how they were the offspring of Count...' She made a sign in the air.

'Oh yes, I can see what you're thinking. European royalty, no matter how silly and outmoded, is catnip to a young American girl. I began life as Helen Roberts, but later transformed myself into *Hélène* at that finishing school in Switzerland, so I would sound more exotic. Anything was better than being plain old Helen Roberts from Cleveland, Ohio.' A shadow dimmed her eyes. 'What's that old saying? Be careful what you wish for.'

Vidor stirred from his befuddlement, as if passing through murky water, reaching for light and air.

'You're American?'

Her laugh rang out. 'Is that all you got from my story? I'd better wrap things up then. Here we go: fast forward several years, and Count – let's call him "Dracula" – and I divorced. By then most of the money was gone, so there was little to divide up, but I agreed to the divorce on one condition: that I was given sole ownership of this house and the property that came with it. It suited my needs perfectly. By that point I was so demoralised and beaten down, all I wanted was to hide away in this tiny village in the mountains and live out the rest of my days in peace.'

'When a psychiatrist named Anton Gessen showed up with fire in his eyes and began buying up the surrounding chalets to create his clinic, I resisted. No matter how much money he offered me, I made it clear I wasn't leaving my home. So we reached a compromise. I would stay on in this house, which was just inside the border of what would become the clinic grounds. To avoid questions from the other patients, I would pretend to be one myself. Heaven knows I had enough practice during the years my ex insisted I was crazy. For several years I've been acting the part, with nobody the wiser.' She raised her cup in a mock toast. 'Until now.'

Vidor's mind was electrified. If Hélène wasn't a patient, she was free to come and go at will. She might be his only chance to get away. It was now or never. With Gessen hinting that someone had pushed Ismail into that ravine, Vidor was sure the next step would be to accuse him of murder. He didn't kill that Egyptian boy. But who would believe him? The police would take the word of a doctor over a patient.

'I need your help.' He got on his knees in front of Hélène and took her hands. It didn't matter that she had played him for a fool. Not when she had the power to smuggle him out. His breath came in gasps.

'Do get up,' Hélène said, pulling her hands away. 'There's no need to panic. Anton isn't a bad man. His only concern is to help you get well.'

He lurched back. 'No! You don't know what he's been saying to me. He says I'm not who I think I am, that I was born as someone else, and stole another person's identity. Somebody who disappeared or died. He probably thinks I killed that person too.' His thoughts were spinning out of control. Hélène's face began to transform before his eyes. An air of menace filled the room like gas. Was she a spy? One of Gessen's minions in disguise? It was all a set-up. She had lured him into a trap. Spots swam before his eyes and he grabbed the table for support, but even in his confusion, he could see that she was frightened.

'Call him,' he gasped. 'Tell him I'm holding you hostage and won't let you go until I'm safely back in England.' He lurched forward and grabbed her arm. 'Call him, then pack your things. You're coming with me.'

'You don't want to do this.' Her eyes darted to the door. 'It will only make things worse.'

'Call him.' He hauled her from the sofa. She didn't resist, though he could see her mind was churning. *How to get away from this madman?* But he wasn't mad. He'd been perfectly fine until he'd been drugged and brought to this house of horrors against his will.

Her hand trembled as she picked up the phone. But when

she looked at him her eyes were sad. 'I need to speak to Dr Gessen. No, it can't wait. It's an emergency.'

Vidor wondered if this was a trick. Perhaps she had alerted the police instead. He grabbed the phone. 'Get Dr Gessen now!' But there was no one on the other end. Whoever answered had put her on hold. He pressed the phone to his ear. 'Hello? Get me Dr Gessen.' Sweat streamed down his face. His heart slammed against his ribs. Perhaps a massive coronary would end this misery, though death was not what he wanted. Life was what he longed for. His old life. Tears sprang to his eyes. How he yearned for his quiet house on Camden Road. Magda bustling about the kitchen, bringing him a cup of tea and slices of freshly baked bread topped with the perfect amount of butter. The buzz and hum of the lab, and the thrill of chasing data. The glorious tapestry of spring flowers in the lanes. *Home, home*. The plaintive cry reverberated in his soul. Once he got home, all would be well.

A voice sounded in Vidor's ear. 'Hélène? It's Anton, is everything all right?'

56

Vidor spoke into the phone. 'I've taken Madame du Chevalier hostage.'

'Madame who?'

Hélène shook her head. 'Not my real name. I made it up.'

What? He was being made a fool of. Everyone in on the joke, laughing at his gullibility. But once he'd broken the chains of his captivity, they wouldn't be laughing anymore.

'Hélène. I've taken her hostage.' He could hear Gessen's breath down the phone line. 'These are my demands,' he continued, pushing gamely on. 'A signed letter from you that I was not of sound mind when I attacked that man in Copenhagen. Certification that I am fit to resume my position at Cambridge, and full passage back to the UK. Today. I will not spend another night here.'

'Put Hélène on the phone, so I know she's all right.'

'She's perfectly fine. I won't hurt her. As long as you give me what I want.'

The phone went quiet for a moment, though Vidor could hear a faint buzz on the line. 'I won't give you anything,' Gessen said, 'until I've spoken to her myself.'

Vidor cupped his hand over the phone and turned to Hélène. 'No funny business.' He sounded like a gangster. When had he ever in his life been violent? 'Please, Hélène.'

He sought her eyes. 'You're my only hope.' He put the phone on speaker before passing it to her.

'I'm fine, Anton,' she said. 'But I think you'd better do what he says.' She met Vidor's gaze as she spoke. If she was trying to transmit a message, he didn't know what it was. He only felt relief that she seemed to be on his side.

'I'd like to speak with Vidor,' Gessen said.

After Hélène handed him the phone, he switched off the speaker and pressed the receiver to his ear. In the silence, Gessen's breathing made a shushing sound, like snow sliding off a cliff.

'Vidor? There's no need for you to take such drastic measures. Why not let Hélène get on with her day? We can meet in my office to talk things over.'

'No more talking. I've told you what I want. As long as you give me the letter and plane ticket, Hélène will come to no harm. If you don't…' Vidor sucked in his breath. 'Surely, you know I'm a desperate man. And since you believe my true nature is that of a killer, I wouldn't take any chances. What would it do to your reputation if an innocent woman died at the hands of a madman? A monster you unleashed.'

Hélène had lost the colour in her face. Was she afraid of him? Good. That would make his position all the stronger.

'Tell me what you want.'

Vidor felt a stab of joy, now that the tables were turned. 'The letters I mentioned. The return of my passport, five hundred francs in cash and two plane tickets to London. I will be taking Hélène with me as insurance. After the plane lands in London, she'll be released unharmed.'

As he listed his demands, the plan seemed clumsy and full of holes. At any time between the clinic's front gate and Heathrow, the police could swoop in. Though perhaps not. Gessen wouldn't want to put Hélène at risk. Vidor was harmless as a lamb, but if Gessen wanted to believe he was a murderous thug, let him go on thinking it. It would be an advantage in getting home.

'All right, Vidor.' Gessen's heavy sigh was audible. 'Though it's against my better judgement, I'll do as you ask. The important thing here is that Hélène comes to no harm.'

'You have thirty minutes.' Vidor hung up the phone.

Hélène turned her face towards him. 'Vidor.' Her eyes were the colour of an autumn meadow. An attractive woman even now, she must have been exceptionally beautiful in her youth. No wonder she'd been prey to fortune hunters and blackguards. Anger at the man who'd caused her so much suffering burned in his throat. Yet here he was, making things worse. Surely, she knew that, whatever happened, he wouldn't hurt her. He wasn't a monster. Vidor Kiraly, OBE, Cambridge don and prize-winning scientist, was not responsible for the murders of two people. It was outrageous to even think it.

Hélène lowered herself onto the sofa. She seemed calm enough, but when she lifted the teapot to fill her cup, her hand shook. 'What happens now?'

A spasm of fear squeezed his heart. Hélène's eyes were veiled. Could she see into his future? The roiling wave of disasters looming before him, one after another until the grave. He had a strange desire to clasp her knees and rest his head in her lap.

'Now, we wait.'

57

Hidden in a copse of pines, Gessen trained a pair of high-powered binoculars on Hélène's home. All was quiet. In defiance of Vidor's instructions, he had not come alone. Three seasoned members of his security team, dressed as maintenance staff, were staked out at key locations around the chalet.

He mounted the steps and pressed the bell. When no one answered, he tried again. *Had they already left the property?* His phone vibrated. Hélène. When she spoke, her voice was strained.

'He says you're to place the letter, travel documents, and passport on the mat by the door and then back away thirty metres.'

'Hélène, you're all right? He hasn't harmed you?'

'I'm all right. A little nervous, though.'

'Try not to worry. I'll do everything he asks. Just stay calm and…'

The phone went dead.

Gessen made eye contact with his head of Security and nodded. His own preference was to storm the house, but since that might endanger Hélène's life, they'd come up with a different plan. More complicated to execute, and with significant risks, but who knew what Vidor might do if he were cornered? Gessen placed the brown envelope with Vidor's passport, money, and travel tickets on the welcome mat by the door. The shutters were latched closed, but Vidor was almost certainly watching him from one of the heart-shaped peepholes carved in the wood.

Gessen walked backwards, holding up his hands to show they were empty. As he moved away from Hélène's front door, his mind raced to consider the best course of action. Good friends for more than ten years, but how they had fought in those early days, when he'd tried to buy Hélène out of her home. No amount of money could make her budge. She was a survivor, Hélène was. Always elegant and polite, even under pressure. He just hoped Vidor – or Malik – or whoever he was dealing with at the moment, would not do anything rash.

The door of the house swung open and Hélène stepped out. Clever man, Vidor. He must have suspected a sniper was lying in wait, with his head in the crosshairs.

Hélène looked straight at him and nodded before retrieving the packet of documents and money and slipping back inside. Now what? He waited in the freezing air for what seemed an eternity until his phone rang.

'Vidor?'

'It's Hélène. He says that the documents appear to be in order, and he wants to head into the village now. He's taking me with him, and he has a knife.' The phone was muffled, followed by the sound of scuffling feet and Vidor's voice in his ear. 'I won't hurt her,' he said, 'if you do as agreed. So call off your guards, I know they're out there. As soon as I've arrived back home in Cambridge, I'll let her go. If I see any sign of the police, I'm sure I don't need to tell you what could happen to Hélène. Do as I say, and all will be well.'

Gessen held up his hands and backed away. When he could no longer see the house through the trees, he turned and hurried to the main building, where he'd set up a situation room to deal with events as they unfolded. Two men from a private security company were positioned at the train station in the village. They'd been instructed to dog Vidor's movements, but not move in unless Hélène's safety could be assured. It was a tricky situation and getting Hélène free would be difficult. The best course, though he hated to do it, might be to allow Vidor to travel all the way to Cambridge, as requested, with one of the security team following behind them. Vidor wouldn't have seen the man before, which lessened the chance he would suspect he was being followed. Regardless, Vidor's plan was absurd. He must know that Scotland Yard would swoop in the moment Hélène was safe. If he were thinking rationally, that is, and it was difficult to believe he was. Or even to say who, exactly, was behind such an ill-conceived idea, that it would be possible to return to the UK and continue his life as if nothing had happened. Whether it was Vidor or Malik being driven by such delusions, he was heading towards a cliff.

* * *

Vidor pressed his eye against the peephole in the shutters. There was no one in sight, though he didn't trust Gessen's word that the place wasn't surrounded. How could he believe the man who'd kidnapped him from a hospital in Copenhagen? A man who'd manipulated his thoughts and tried to convince him he was a dangerous killer. And that he wasn't even Vidor Kiraly, but someone else. As soon as he was safely home in Cambridge, he would report Gessen to whatever medical board oversaw his activities. All this time, Gessen had been pulling the strings, but now Vidor had the upper hand.

Next to him, Hélène began to shake. Tremors ran through her body like electric shocks and her breath was coming fast. He was sorry to have frightened her, but there was no other way.

'Get your coat,' he said gruffly. A light snow had begun to fall, but the funicular ran in all but the worst weather, so there should be no trouble reaching the village. The thought of boarding the train to Geneva made his heart skip with glee.

If he was lucky, they would not pass through any tunnels. It wouldn't do to have a panic attack while making his escape, but he couldn't worry about that now. The important thing was to get home and back in the lab. For a brief moment he imagined the sound of his colleagues' applause when he walked into his first department meeting after so many agonising weeks away. He would feign surprise at the dinner they had arranged for him in belated celebration of the Søgaard Prize, the golden plum that neuroscientists the world over dreamed of holding in their hands. Now, one of their number, Vidor Kiraly, belonged to the blessed few. Next year, it would surely be the Nobel.

'Are you all right?'

He turned to see an attractive older woman looking at him with alarm. She looked familiar, but he'd momentarily forgotten her name. Ah, yes. Helen. The girl from Cleveland.

'What?'

'I've been calling your name, but you were off in a world of your own.' She hesitated. 'Don't you think it would be best to forget whatever plan you've come up with and let Dr Gessen continue your treatment?'

The frightened bird in his chest pecked at his heart. 'No. Put a jacket on. We're leaving now.'

While she gathered her things, he yanked out the phone wires. Not that it would help much, but it felt satisfying to destroy the only line of communication from the house. She returned with a handbag, though not the Chanel one with the doll, if it actually ever contained such a thing. It was still difficult to adjust his understanding of who she was. Or claimed to be. Perhaps the heiress story was all a lie, and she was indeed as crazy as the rest of them.

Hélène pulled on a warm parka and pushed her feet into fur-lined boots.

'Do you have your passport?'

'Yes.'

'Let me see it.'

She took it from her bag and showed him. *Grande-Duché de Luxembourg*. Luxembourg? The tangled layers of her story continued to mutate and grow.

'Good. Let's go.' With a length of washing line he'd found in a kitchen drawer, he tied her right hand to his left.

She winced as he tightened the knots. He was sorry to hurt her, but there was no other way. He slipped a fish knife, sharp as a razor, into his coat pocket.

Hélène paled at the sight of the knife. 'I won't use it unless I have to,' he said, with as much menace as he could muster. Desperate times called for desperate measures.

A final peep through the shutters satisfied him that the coast was clear. The snow had all but stopped and only a few flakes drifted through the air. He pushed her ahead of him out the door. No one was about, but through the trees he could sense several pairs of eyes watching him. He charged ahead and together they stumbled in the direction of the main gate.

58

Amongst the dense stand of trees not a soul was in sight. Where was everyone? The clinic must be in lockdown, with strict orders for everyone to keep indoors. By the time they reached the gate, Vidor's hands ached with the cold. When he turned the handle, it sprang open. So far, so good. Vidor sucked air into his aching lungs and hustled Hélène through to the other side.

'Stop, please.' She gasped in the freezing air. 'Let me catch my breath.'

'There's no time.' He scanned the horizon. 'We have to catch the train.'

The funicular was no more than fifty metres away, but it felt much further as Vidor hurried Hélène along. He was sorry to have involved her, but it couldn't be helped. Didn't she understand she was his only chance at freedom? In recent days, he'd begun to feel a certain fondness towards her, in spite of her loony ways, but that was over now. She would never forgive him, not after this.

The funicular operator stepped out of his hut, his weathered face impassive, though his black eyes swept their faces with an air of mistrust. He showed no sign of surprise at the sight of them, bound at the wrist, as they hurried towards him. Gessen must have warned him not to interfere. For the first time since his arrival at the clinic, Vidor felt in charge of his own fate.

The operator closed the doors and started the engine. Vidor held tight to Hélène's arm as they trundled down the mountain. The sound of the wheels grinding against the rails on the steep incline shredded his nerves. The twenty-minute ride felt like an eternity. At the bottom of the hill, the operator opened the door and stood aside, but before Vidor could step out, the man fixed him with a hard stare. Two coal-black eyes in a craggy face. '*Attention*, monsieur. This will not end well for you.'

Vidor felt a spasm of foreboding, as if the man were an oracle in disguise. But he squeezed his eyes shut and turned away. Don't panic. Just go. In the village, their train was just pulling into the station with a desultory wheeze. Eleven sixteen, on the dot. Only a few people waited on the platform. A sandy-haired man in a blue ski parka clutched the strap of a black carry-on bag, while another man hefted a snowboard on his shoulder. A woman in a bright red coat smiled at her two young daughters as she helped them board the carriage. Vidor and Hélène were right behind her.

Vidor eyed the two men who'd entered the carriage with them. The one in the blue parka looked out of place. Was it someone from Gessen's staff? He tightened his hold on Hélène's arm. It would take them a full hour to reach Montreux. Another hour and a half to Geneva airport, where they would board the flight to London. Plenty of time for things to go wrong. As much as he wanted to believe Gessen was a man of his word, Vidor was sure he would do anything to keep him from getting on the plane, at least with Hélène in tow. Perhaps, if he… the train jolted and slowed. The brakes squealed and they jerked to a stop.

Hélène, seated next to the window, strained to see along the tracks. This couldn't be a coincidence. Trapped like a rat in a hole. They must have stopped by order of the railway police.

The minutes ticked by. Vidor held tight to Hélène's wrist.

She was alert as a meerkat, poised to flee at the first sign of danger. His heart kept time with the clock, his breath stuck in his throat. But the engine started up again, and they began to move. When he relaxed his grip, Hélène shifted in the seat. 'I need to use the facilities.'

He stared at her and frowned. He hadn't thought of that. But now he'd have to untie their hands. It wasn't as if he could go in with her. 'All right. But I'll be standing just outside the door.' He struggled to loosen the knots. When she was free, she rubbed the red marks on her wrist. A pang of regret shot through his heart. What had he done? But it couldn't be helped.

They stood and moved awkwardly down the aisle. Vidor kept a firm grip on her arm. The train carriage was nearly empty, and no one looked at them as they passed. Not even the man in the blue parka, typing away on his laptop.

'Don't lock it,' he said, when they reached the end of the carriage. 'I'll be waiting right outside.'

He stood with his back against the door, surveying the passengers. He fingered the knife in his pocket, hoping he wouldn't have to use it. But she seemed to be taking an eternity. He knocked on the door. 'Hélène?' No sound but the whirring of the electric hand dryer. 'Hélène?' He rattled the door. It was locked. *Idiot*. Of course she wasn't coming out. What made him think he could trust her?

'Hélène?' When he slammed his shoulder against the door, it flew open, and he nearly fell inside.

She gazed at him levelly, her eyes sharp as flint. 'There's no need to panic. I'm not going anywhere. Obviously.'

Back in their seats, when he picked up the cord to tie their hands together again, she shook her head. 'I'll accompany you to London. But you're not tying me up.'

'I need your help.' He blushed at the desperation in his voice.

'Which you have. But if you hurt me, or I feel threatened in any way, I'll scream bloody murder.' She gave him a hard stare. Perhaps he'd underestimated her. Though if the story she'd told him was true, her lifetime of pain and troubles would certainly account for the steely determination in her eyes.

He stowed the length of rope in his pocket. 'If the weather is kind enough to cooperate,' he said, in a toffee-nosed accent. 'London can be very pleasant this time of year.'

She suppressed a smile, but he could read her thoughts. Mid-January? More likely it would be dismal. Damp and grey from the winter fog.

After arriving at Montreux without further incident, they changed for the train to Geneva Airport. Vidor studied the passengers. The man in the blue parka with the black carry-on boarded the train with them, which was a bit worrying, but the other one, the one with the snowboard, was nowhere to be seen. Vidor dared to feel a flicker of relief. Gessen must be playing it smart. Better to let him go, and why not? He wasn't a criminal. Whatever Gessen might believe in that lunatic imagination of his, he hadn't killed anyone. Once back in Cambridge, his time away in a remote mountain loony bin would make a good story for his colleagues. 'Nice facilities, but the clinic director is a bit of a nut job.' That's what he'd say at the pub he frequented on Fridays. The regulars would stand him rounds of drinks in a belated celebration of his prize and sing 'For He's a Jolly Good Fellow'.

Home, home. His heart fairly leapt with joy. His tidy house and garden. Magda's steady loyalty and affection. Both as housekeeper and – whatever it was they had – it was very pleasant indeed. If he had time, he would get her something at the airport as a token of his appreciation. A box of Swiss chocolates, perhaps. She would like that.

* * *

The departure hall was teeming with passengers, and he scanned the crowd. No sign of the man in the blue parka, or anyone he recognised from the clinic. They checked in for their flight without a hitch, though there was a moment when he thought Hélène might whisper to the ticket agent that she was being forced to leave the country against her will.

That neither of them had any luggage, not even a carry-on, elicited no surprise. The woman at the check-in desk merely handed over their boarding passes with a practised smile and wished them a pleasant flight.

They passed through security without incident. Mobs of vacationers, en route to their winter holidays, swarmed the departure hall. It would be raining in London. Or perhaps there might be a hint of winter sun. It felt like he'd been away for years.

Vidor checked the sea of faces. No one looked alarming. No beefy men in dark glasses with sidearms concealed under their suit jacket. At the departure board, he looked for their gate number. Their flight was on time. In a little more than an hour, he would be on the plane and nearly home.

***

A man next to Hélène on Vidor's left glanced at his watch. Dapper in a grey cashmere coat and cobalt tie, he tapped Hélène on the shoulder. 'Pardon me, but I believe you dropped something.'

'Did I?' Hélène peered at an embroidered handkerchief on the floor. 'Oh yes, I believe that's mine.' Vidor released his grip so she could bend to retrieve it, and in that moment, an arm snaked around his neck and snapped his head back.

'Hélène!'

But the man in the cashmere coat was leading her away. She looked back over her shoulder and gave him a sad smile. 'I'm sorry,' she mouthed. But it was too late, she had betrayed him, just like all the others. Stupid of him to forget about her phone. A quick text to Gessen would have been enough to torpedo his plans. It all happened so quickly. No one shouted or screamed. Two men in dark coats joined the man who had him in a choke hold, and together they marched him briskly through the crowd. Impossible to fight back. And what would be the point? He was the victim here, but they would drag him into a back room and treat him like a common criminal.

59

At the end of a long, brightly lit corridor, Vidor was handed over to a uniformed security guard. When he looked back, the three men in dark suits had faded into the crowd. The guard typed a code on the panel by a locked door and escorted him through. Vidor stopped short. It wasn't the barren room with grimy walls and tube lighting he was expecting, but some kind of high-class lounge. Two black leather sofas framed a polished glass coffee table. An enormous vase of lilies and red dahlias graced a table by the wall. Subterranean or high in the air, he couldn't say. Frosted windows let in a watery light, though nothing of the outside world could be seen.

The guard released his arm. Afraid of what might happen next, Vidor longed to curl up on one of the sofas and shut out the world. Would he spend the rest of his days in some grotty prison, at the mercy of hooligans and thugs? Whatever happened now was out of his hands. With his grand getaway plan reduced to rubble, his only wish was to close his eyes and succumb to the oblivion of the dead. A door clicked open, and a dark shape swam into view. Gessen, naturally. Who else could have orchestrated all this?

After a quiet word with the guard, who nodded and left the room, Gessen indicated one of the sofas. 'Why don't you have a seat, Vidor?' His eyes were kind. 'I can see you're very tired.'

Like a truculent schoolboy, Vidor allowed himself to be led to one of the sofas, where he dropped onto the cushions and closed his eyes. The other sofa creaked as Gessen settled across from him.

A knock on the door. He gazed dejectedly through narrowed lids, expecting to be hauled away in chains. But a uniformed man stepped inside, bearing a tray with two glasses, a plate of pastries, and a bottle of sparkling water. Vidor accepted the glass Gessen handed him and clutched it in both hands. So tired. If he could just close his eyes for a few minutes, all would be well.

'Is Hélène all right?' Vidor's voice seemed to come from a long way off.

Skimming above the surface of the known world, his mind floated untethered amongst the tangle of synapses, where each spark was orchestrated in perfect harmony. Thinking, feeling, seeing. Taste, touch, smell. What a wonderful machine the human brain was. If only the mind were so easily mapped...

'Vidor, can you hear me?'

As he tried to focus on the man across from him, it struck Vidor, for the first time, how much he and Gessen looked alike. Dark hair streaked with grey at the temples, eyes on the same spectrum of mossy green. If they stood side by side in front of a mirror, it would not surprise him to see they were of equal height and build. How odd to discover that he and his tormenter occupied two sides of the same, though slightly tarnished, coin.

He opened his mouth to speak, thought better of it. Tried again. What was the point of anything? When he finally managed to form the words, his voice came out as a croak. 'It's the end of the line, isn't it? My life is over.' His tongue felt strange in his mouth, and his face and hands not wholly his own.

'Why would you say that?' Gessen sounded genuinely upset. 'If you're suffering from a dissociative disorder, and I have every reason to believe you are, there are therapies that can help you.'

For a moment, Vidor considered going along with the good doctor's diagnosis, relieved at the thought of taking an easier path. But Gessen would catch on to him eventually, and they would end up right back where they were now.

'I don't have dissociative identity disorder.' He sat up straight and met Gessen's eyes. 'Though I've only just become aware of my particular affliction, if you wish to put a name to it, I suppose you could call it a case of severely repressed identity or perhaps dissociative amnesia.' He pushed away the empty glass. 'My flash of awareness occurred a few days ago, after waking suddenly in the night. It felt as though a glass bubble had shattered in my skull. Apparently, completely unknown to me, a different aspect of myself, the better part it would seem, has been locked away in the darkest and most primitive area of my brain.'

Gessen had grown still, his eyes fixed on Vidor's own.

'While some small part of myself, though very faint, like the signal from a long-extinguished star, has always known who I am – or who I was – I'd never thought to examine it properly. Nebulous signs would appear on occasion, spread out thinly over the years. Strange blackouts, bouts of lost time. Evidence of sleepwalking or eating foods I don't like. That other person, or persona, I suppose you would call it, had been killed off long ago, and once he ceased to exist, I never gave him a moment's thought. For nearly forty years, until the glass bubble broke, I had successfully erased, even to my own conscious mind, the person I once was.'

Vidor turned to look at the vase of blood-red flowers. 'It's not such a strange phenomenon, when you think of it. The suppression or even complete eradication of one's identity. It happens to everyone, doesn't it? When a boy becomes a man, the child he once was ceases to exist. The man in his fifties does not view the world through the eyes of a five-year-old. That child is gone, resting for decades, undisturbed in his grave. If not for your relentless probing and prying, the boy I once was, long dead, though at one time full of life and wondrous dreams, would have been content to remain in the dark for all eternity.'

'That's all very poetic, but…' Gessen gave him a puzzled look.

Had he not yet figured it out? Vidor inwardly scoffed. Not quite the genius he made himself out to be. He leaned back into the soft leather and closed his eyes. 'A long time ago, I began life as an illiterate boy from a poor village in a war-torn country. That boy, abandoned at birth and left to die, came from nothing and expected nothing from life, not even to survive. Until a kind foreign woman discovered he had a sharp mind and a knack for learning and got him enrolled at a local school. The boy worked hard at his lessons and excelled in his exams, all the while dreaming that he would escape one day to the gleaming city he'd read about in books. After many years of toil, not to mention struggling with the kind of loneliness and shame only an outcast endures, the boy grew up to become a world-class neuroscientist and Cambridge don, known to the world, of course, by a different name.'

He paused to allow Gessen a chance to speak, but for once the man had nothing to say. Vidor kept his eyes shut and tried to recall the sounds and smells of the souk in that long-ago village, the feel of warm stones on his feet, the scorching sands. Under the heat of the blistering sun, Vidor faded away and Malik raised his face to the light. '*Permettez-moi de vous présenter ce garçon mort depuis longtemps.* Allow me to introduce you to that long-dead boy.' Malik extended his hand and spoke the name given to him at birth, 'Malik Sayid. I believe the two of you might have met once or twice in your treatment room. But here he is properly, in the flesh, so to speak, though his essence grows fainter with the years and he could, at any minute, be forced into hiding again.'

The startled look on Gessen's face gave him no small measure of satisfaction.

'I'm sure you can piece together the rest of the story without my help. But first, let me assure you, in my defence, that I haven't been lying to you all this time. Until the other day, when I woke just before dawn with a terrible headache and noticed something odd about the paintings in my room. Nine sandpipers, instead of ten, and in the other painting, the camel caravan glittering on the horizon, clear as day. That's when I felt something shatter in my skull. Like a bolt of lightning from the sky, and it all came back to me. Who I was, and how I came to be the man known as Vidor Kiraly.'

His throat felt parched, and he drank down another glass of water. 'I suppose you have gleaned some hints from your hypnosis sessions, or truth serums, or whatever else you used on me. What you've been missing was the why and the how. Who and what were Malik and Vidor to each other? I can only surmise what you must have been thinking: split personality or delusional misidentification disorder. Excellent possibilities.' He shook his head. 'Neither of them correct.'

So tired. When would they allow him to sleep? 'I was hoping it wouldn't come to this,' he said, 'the unseemly baring of the soul.' He rubbed his eyes. 'A simple matter, or so I thought, to endure a course of treatment at your clinic, no worse for having done so, and return to my life as if nothing had happened. But that's not how it worked out. And here we are.'

'As if nothing had happened?' Gessen clasped his hands and leaned forward. 'Is that how you describe the events of the events of the past two and a half months? The man you attacked in Copenhagen is dead. You are a "person of interest" in the death of Ismail Mahmoud. And it is not yet clear to me what your involvement was in the drowning death of Vidor Sovàny.'

At the sound of that odious name, a chill coursed through his veins, and Malik stiffened. Was Gessen implying he was a murderer? 'I'm not responsible for anyone's death,' he said. 'I have no memory of my actions in Copenhagen. As for Vidor Sovàny, when he went into the Seine, he nearly took me with him. The next thing I knew, I was lying on the pavement, soaking wet, with a man asking something about a name. I thought he wanted to know the other boy's name. "*Vidor*," I said. "Well, Vidor," he replied, whacking me on the back as I coughed up a mouthful of water. "You had a pretty close call. Most people that fall into the river never come out again."

'*Vidor*. To my addled brain, the name sounded right. The next thing I remember was being on a Channel ferry chugging through the dark. I was wearing one of Vidor's jackets and had his passport in the pocket of my jeans – Vidor's jeans. No idea how I got them. Perhaps I went back to the Sovàny's flat while everyone was asleep? I was sick with nausea and my head ached so badly I believed in that moment that Vidor, trapped in limbo, had managed to possess my body so he could torment my soul. That would be my penance: forced to embody his malevolent spirit, a fate I had no wish to endure.

'Only after several days, exhausted by confusion and misery, did I realise it was my ticket to freedom. As Vidor, I could start over in a new country, shed my old self like an unwanted skin. Abandon the wretched Malik to the churning waters of the Seine. A stain on his family since birth, who would miss him?'

Malik's mouth had gone dry, and he could scarcely speak. 'It wasn't until later that I discovered what a dangerous bargain I'd made. To sell one's soul to the devil... there's always a price isn't there? Vidor is stronger than I am... With each passing year, more of my essence is chipped away, and it becomes harder to resist him. Only in the dark of night can I gather enough strength to assert myself, but it's just enough to rebel in a minor way against his basest impulses.'

60

Outside the frosted windows, it had grown dark, though it was impossible to say how much time had passed. Malik seemed to have drifted through varying stages of waking and sleep. At some point, someone had wheeled in a table laden with dishes of food. He had no appetite, but nodded when Gessen offered him a plate.

'Do you want to know what tipped me over the edge?' Malik asked, his voice heavy with fatigue. 'The dark fissure in my life that ultimately brought me to you, and to this particular place and time.' The sight of the food, some kind of fish in saffron sauce, turned his stomach. He stretched out on the sofa and closed his eyes. 'It's a story as old as time, though not a pretty one.

'Once upon a time, a naïve young man fled his wretched beginnings to start a new life in a fabled metropolis. The loftiest of all cities, where the great thinkers of Europe had trodden on hallowed ground: Voltaire, Descartes, Rousseau, Sartre. To walk those same streets, to breathe the rarefied air, was all he'd ever wanted. What our young man did not understand, however, despite the bloodshed and turmoil from which he'd fled, is that once he set foot on the sacred ground of his dreams, he would be viewed as an alien creature, someone to be despised and feared.

'One day, not long after he arrived, the boy was invited to have a drink at the cafe table of three young women. International students, just like himself, embarking on the great adventure of their lives. He readily accepted, anxious to belong, even accepting a glass of wine though he'd never touched alcohol before. He was so enamoured of his beautiful new friends that when asked where he came from, he readily named the place of his birth. What he didn't expect, what he could not have imagined, was what happened next. Two of the girls looked shocked and instantly rose. Terror was stamped on their faces as they rushed to get away. In his mind, he was an innocent young boy, eager to embrace the riches of life that had long been denied him. But to those girls, he was… what? A white slaver, a terrorist? An evil creature intent on slitting their throats the moment they dropped their guard. Even after all these years, their fear and disgust has remained with him. A constant companion, never fading.

'Spat on in the Metro, cursed by cab drivers, it became clear that the city of Rousseau and Voltaire was not for the likes of him. To survive, he learned to stay in the shadows and keep his head down, though sometimes during lectures when the greats of Western civilisation were discussed, he wanted to shout at his professors, "Why do we not learn about Al-Khwarizmi, the great mathematician and astronomer? Or Ibn Sina, Avicenna, the brilliant Persian physician upon whose works modern medicine was built?" Those great men, and many others, dismissed as nobodies and forgotten in their graves, all because they happened to worship a different god or wore a turban on their head.'

Gessen had yet to move a muscle, afraid to disturb the rush of memories he'd waited so long to hear. The mystery of how Malik's emotions had hardened into stone, so many years ago, was at last coming into view: *feel nothing, reveal nothing, let no one in*. Now, with nothing left to lose, he tossed with abandon at Gessen's feet the bone he'd been chasing for weeks.

'In that terrible frame of mind,' Malik continued, lying back and closing his eyes, 'I wandered the streets, feeling like pond scum, wondering if it wouldn't be better to pack up and leave the city for good. Not knowing of course that, a few days later, I would be drawn into the Seine by the sadistic boy who'd been trying for months to annihilate my very soul.

The sun streamed through the bright green leaves as I walked and walked, not knowing where I was headed. When I turned a corner, sick with despair and weak with hunger, I looked up to see a man coming out of the cinema.' He paused. 'A man came out of a cinema. Such a simple thing. But not in this case.'

He opened his eyes and looked at the ceiling. 'That man was my father.'

Malik gave Gessen a sad smile. 'All this time you've been anxious to meet the man himself, and here he is at last. Exhibit A: The man who betrayed his own people, during the war of independence, in an act of despicable treachery. Villages razed to the ground, countless innocents slaughtered. The man who terrorised me as a child. The man I was told had died when I was twelve.'

He examined Gessen's face, hoping for a flicker of disgust, or even surprise, but Gessen's eyes, etched with deep lines at the corners, showed only sorrow. Perhaps he had guessed long ago. As the two men faced each other, Malik – or was he Vidor now? – couldn't help but wonder how far they had travelled. Having lost track of the game, what had become of the king? Was it check or checkmate? *Sheikh* or *sheikh mat*? Dead or alive, what did it matter? In his soul where it counted, he had been dead for a very long time.

As a pain stabbed his temple, he squeezed his head between his hands, and a wave of nausea knocked him flat. Someone – or something – grabbed him by the throat and choked him with an iron grip. As the walls closed in and he struggled to breathe, a shadow fell upon him and everything went dark.

* * *

The journey home was a blur of green and white and grey. Above ground and below, he passed through a maze of tunnels, black as pitch, but they had lost the power to frighten him. How strange that such gloom, deep underground, could bring him moments of peace. He yearned for nothing more than to lie down in that darkness and sleep for eternity.

No such luck. Jostled by the train and delirious with exhaustion, he remembered hearing, or thought he'd heard, a voice coming at him in a series of waves. Fragments of a story told in a circular fashion. The tale of a father, not his own, who'd harboured a monstrous evil in his heart, and an unquenchable thirst for death. So he wasn't alone, even in this.

Days had passed, or so it seemed, by the time he was jostled awake to find himself guided through a tall iron gate both familiar and strange. Helped by a kindly man with moss-green eyes, he was led to a wooden house with the steep roof and carved shutters of a cottage from a fairy tale. The room contained a wide bed and an armchair patterned in green and gold. A brass bowl held an array of polished stones. Amethyst, jasper, lapis lazuli, malachite. Their pleasing colours and shapes gave him comfort. Someone helped him out of his clothes and into bed, but rather than sleep, his thoughts slid free. Gliding down rivers, scaling mountains, soaring like a falcon above a dry and desolate land of ochre and umber, barren as the moon.

My name is Ozymandias, King of Kings; Look on my works, ye Mighty, and despair! Nothing beside remains. Round the decay of that colossal Wreck, boundless and bare, The lone and level sands stretch far away.

When at last he woke, hours, days, or weeks later, his mind was once again clear. On the table by the bed, someone had placed a travel clock. The sight of it should have made him happy, but he felt nothing as the minutes ticked away. *Time.* What did it matter now?

Lying next to the clock was a faded photo. Where did it come from? He remembered the doctor handing him something as he boarded the train. A small square of cardboard. He held it in his hands and stared into the eyes of a boy in a pair of grubby trousers, cut off at the knee, squinting in the sun. No matter how many times he'd tried to vanquish that small boy, desperate to be seen, he travelled with him always. How many hours, how many years, had that boy been swimming against the tide? Asking nothing more than to be seen and heard, as he struggled to break free.

Malik looked around and recognised the room by the paintings on the wall. A seascape with sandpipers. A camel caravan shimmering in the desert. Brighter than he remembered, nearly incandescent. He counted the birds. Only nine, not the ten as he'd once believed. Or had he only dreamed the presence of the extra bird? He couldn't recall seeing the painting in the daylight before.

A pale sun streamed through the crack in the blinds. It was all coming back to him, the life he'd had, and the one he'd cast away. He slipped his feet into a pair of fine wool slippers and circled the room with his eyes half closed, arms crossed over his chest in an attitude of supplication.

Voyage autour de ma chambre. A journey around my room. Though small, the space contained magnitudes, capable of holding the infinite reach of his thoughts. Past, present, and future. As the sun grew brighter, he began to weaken, until it was impossible to hold back the malign force of that other being, fighting for his soul. The daylight grew, until Malik felt his arms and legs being moved like a puppet, compelling him to inscribe a circle on the floor. Three full revolutions was all it took.

When he stopped turning and opened his eyes, Vidor looked at the paintings and smiled. Ten sandpipers, and the camel caravan was gone. Now that Malik had been forced back into hiding, at least for the moment, he knew exactly what to do.

61

Gessen had waited until Vidor, still in the guise of Malik, though it was difficult to say, was safely aboard the train to Saint-Odile, in the company of two attendants from the clinic. Only then did he feel free to catch his flight to Copenhagen to discuss Vidor's case. He wasn't quite sure what to tell the authorities, though his goal for now was to buy Vidor more time. With Gessen's original diagnosis in tatters, proving diminished responsibility in the death of Mr Nielsen would be difficult, if not impossible.

Then there was the lingering issue of Vidor's involvement in the death of Ismail Mahmoud. When questioned, he'd denied following Ismail into the copse of trees, even though Babette had later confessed she'd seen him. Had Vidor simply blacked out, or transformed somehow into the persona of Malik? Perhaps everything he claimed was a lie? If new evidence implicated Vidor in Ismail's death, what could Gessen say in his defence? The fact that Vidor had tricked an attendant into removing his wrist monitor now flashed like an omen through the fog. And yet, after all this, Gessen still didn't know what he was dealing with. Was Vidor – as Malik – someone to be pitied, a victim of the lingering effects of his childhood trauma, or was he a man with an unwavering mission, fully cognisant of his actions as he plotted a well-calibrated agenda of revenge? The man in Copenhagen mistaken for his monstrous father, and Ismail for the hated brother he'd tried so hard to leave behind.

As he boarded the plane and stowed his bag under the seat, he felt oddly relieved to have shared with Malik some of the details of his own torturous history, even if it meant crossing a sacrosanct boundary to unburden himself to a patient. If nothing else, it might appear to an outsider as a macabre form of one-upmanship. *You think your father was a monster? Well, listen to this.* Before today, he'd not told his story to a single soul. Even Sophie, his oft-mourned love, had been spared. What would have been the point in tainting her with the horror of his father's crimes? Malik Sayid might be one of the very few he'd met in his life who understood the cost of dragging a monstrous inheritance behind him.

Though saying the words out loud would do little to relieve the crushing weight of his legacy, and the horrific acts perpetrated by his father. The man who'd given him life was none other than the commandant of a notorious Nazi concentration camp in Poland. Fuelled by his allegiance to a murderous regime, a man who'd orchestrated the deaths of some 900,000 men, women and children. Rounded up like swine, stripped of their dignity, gassed like vermin.

And Gessen's mother. How could she have stood by such a repellent creature? As a half-Jewish woman, registered as a *Mischling*, the Nazis' insidious label to keep non-Aryans from government positions, how was it possible she could stand by as her own people perished? Those photos he'd found in his father's desk as a child and been so charmed by. It was only later he understood that the eyes of the children were dead. Clouded by the foregone knowledge of the future that awaited them, as the clock ticked the minutes to the end.

When he, as little Anton, had first opened his eyes, it was to the tremulous purple blossoms of the jacarandas lining their quiet street on the outskirts of Buenos Aires. Five years earlier, his father had deftly eluded his fate at Nuremberg by changing his name and boarding a passenger ship, with his pregnant wife and daughters in tow, to start a new life in South America.

Of all this, Gessen knew nothing for years. Two days after his father was plucked off the streets and extradited to Germany, his mother fled with her son to Switzerland where she later left her six-year-old boy in the care of friends. Bewildered by the sudden loss of his parents, he'd been fed all kinds of lies by his adoptive family, that his father passed away from illness, and his mother died of grief.

It was only later, while looking for his mother's wedding ring to present to Sophie on bended knee, that he uncovered the horrifying truth. For months afterwards, he'd teetered on the edge of shock and horror, his innocence shorn away in a single blow. The loving father's mask stripped off to reveal the sadistic grin and bloodstained hands.

Dearest Sophie. How he'd loved her. So much so that the kindest thing was to send her away. What type of devil would wish to burden a wife – or a child – with such a past?

In forty years, he'd found nothing to ease the pain. While the months in Asia, locked away in a Tibetan monastery, had provided a small measure of solace, he'd emerged to find that nothing had changed. The ghosts of the past would always be there, waiting to greet him wherever he went. The money he donated to a charity in Poland for survivors of the Holocaust did little to assuage his grief. No amount of self-recrimination, or good deeds, had the power to raise the dead.

* * *

Gessen lifted his travel bag from the overhead rack, ten minutes before the train pulled into the tiny station at Saint-Odile. He was anxious to get home after the onerous trip to Copenhagen to argue Vidor's case, but the journey through the mountains seemed to take longer than usual. Each time he looked at his watch, the minute hand had scarcely budged.

Darkness had fallen hours ago. Nearly nine o'clock and the patients would be in their rooms, the library and swimming pavilion shut, the clinic closed down for the day.

When he'd spoken to Ursula after landing in Geneva, she assured him everything was fine. Vidor had chosen to take the evening meal in his room, but he seemed in good spirits. The other patients were where they should be, and all was quiet. 'It's so pretty right now,' Ursula said. 'The snow-covered chalets would look right at home in the window of a pastry shop.'

'You'll miss it when you're gone.'

'I will.' Her voice was tinged with sadness.

No more needed to be said about that. He told her he'd see her shortly, and after cutting the connection, he muted his phone and closed his eyes.

As he entered the funicular and waited for Thierry to start up the engine, he rested his head against the seat. Tomorrow, or the next day, or whenever Vidor felt ready, they would begin again. He had managed to buy a little time with the public prosecutor in Copenhagen. Enough time, he hoped, to gain additional insight into Vidor's case. In his heart, he suspected there was little he could do to save Vidor (and Malik, of course) from the consequences of his actions, triggered by a long-buried rage. But that wouldn't stop him from trying. If he failed, Vidor would be arrested and tried for the wrongful death of Mr Nielsen. In the meantime, he faced some probing questions from the police about Ismail.

It pained Gessen to accept he would have to face all of this alone. When he'd finally asked Ursula about her plans, she had told him, not without regret, that she planned to marry in the spring and move to Bern with her husband to set up a private practice of her own. They'd made a good team over the years and finding someone to take her place would not be easy.

As they lumbered through the trees and slid through a narrow gap in the ravine, he sniffed the air. Was something burning? He stood and craned his neck to peer through the dirty window. A streak of orange glowed above the treeline and a column of smoke billowed towards the sky. Something was wrong. He urged Thierry to move faster, but the old funicular was agonisingly slow. He checked his phone and saw that Ursula had rung him four times. When he tried to reach her, she didn't pick up.

Frantic now, he grabbed the door and attempted to wrench it open, but Thierry clamped him by the arm. It was insanity to dash out into the dark, but he had to get to the clinic fast. One of the chalets must be on fire. How had it happened? Was anyone hurt?

The moment they jerked to a stop, he yanked open the door and began to run. Smoke was thick in the air. On the other side of the bank of trees, flames crackled and spat. He tried ringing Ursula again, but dropped his phone when he caught sight of her running towards him, her hair streaming loose.

'It's Vidor. He's in the tower.'

Gessen unlocked the gate, and she stumbled into him, gasping for breath. There was a fire in the library. He must have started it and then locked himself in the tower.

'And the others?'

'Everyone else is safe. I had Jean-Claude evacuate all the patients and staff to the swimming pavilion.' She touched his hand. 'Fernanda's okay. It was her barking that alerted Security. She must have sensed something was wrong. Hélène's taken her in.'

He grabbed her arm and together they ran up the path. As they burst out the other side of the trees and the manor house came into view, Gessen stopped short, then dropped to his knees. The whole building was in flames. Great sparks flew upwards to the starless sky. He raised his arm to shield his face from the heat.

'We have to get him out.' But the words died in his throat. Far too late to do anything. Vidor must have doused the place with the diesel fuel stored in the cellar for emergencies. As the heat grew and the inferno roared, the windows in the tower shattered and shards of glass rained to the ground. Flames leapt out, greedily licking the air. He sank into the snow.

'Why did he do it?' Gessen's words were lost in the roar of the fire.

Revenge, retribution, annihilation? They would never know.

'I sat with him in his room while he ate dinner,' Ursula said. 'He seemed subdued, but…'

The flames leapt higher and Gessen looked away.

'He asked after Hélène,' Ursula said, her voice catching in her throat, 'and we spoke for a few minutes of trivial things.' She started to babble, and he squeezed her hand. 'Then he wished me a happy life. Before I left, he asked me to count the number of sandpipers in the painting on the wall. When I told him there were ten, he smiled. 'Just as I thought,' he said, before lying down on the bed and closing his eyes.'

Huddled next to him in the snow, she shivered. 'What made him do it?'

Gessen shook his head. The man, a chimera of two psyches, who'd fought every attempt to parse his thoughts and character, would forever remain a mystery. Perhaps he could imagine no other recourse. Unmasked as an imposter, his life and career destroyed. Accused of one count of murder. Possibly responsible for two more. Trapped in a web of his own creation, Vidor had left no avenue for escape. Transforming himself back into Malik Sayid, a wounded young man, imprisoned in time, was impossible. The other option, moving forward in disgrace, stripped of his academic credentials and everything he'd worked for, meant a life sentence of ridicule and pain.

Unless… a disturbing thought came to him as the cinders rained down. Unless Vidor started the fire as a cover for his escape. No identifiable remains would be found in a conflagration of this magnitude.

Sheikh mat. The king is dead.

How simple it would be for the man to disappear into the void where no one would find him. The chance to start anew must have been too seductive to ignore. *L'appel du vide*. So easy to answer the call, and having consigned both Vidor and Malik to the flames, why not drag Gessen with them into the fire? After reducing to ash the life's work of the man who'd destroyed him, he would rise from the flames like a phoenix and create a new life.

What better revenge than this, for daring to disturb the mysteries of the mind?

62

Zurich, Switzerland
21 May 2009

From the window of his office on the eastern edge of the city, Gessen looked up at the sound of a passing car. His new suite of treatment rooms was located on a quiet, tree-lined street with little traffic, though he had yet to get used to the sound of tyres on the macadam. The office was small, with just enough space for himself and an assistant, and a view of the distant mountains, so there was some consolation in that. He'd moved into the building a week ago, and rather than sleep in his office, he'd also rented a furnished flat nearby while he looked for something more permanent.

After the fire had razed much of the clinic to the ground – only the swimming pavilion and two of the chalets were left untouched – he had no other recourse but to transfer his remaining patients to another facility. Hélène was staying on in her home, fortunately spared from the fire, and had gladly offered to keep Fernanda with her until he was settled. He missed the dog to an absurd degree, even though he understood she was likely happier in familiar surroundings.

She was getting on in years and the move to the city might be too much for her.

The insurance company were dragging their feet on paying the claim, having declared they were not legally obliged to pay since the fire had been ruled as arson. Gessen could take the company to court, but his lawyer said the fees would be costly and he would likely lose. Even if he were to win, he didn't have the heart to rebuild in the same location. The view and isolation had been ideal for a certain kind of individual, but perhaps it was time to find other ways to help his patients heal from their troubles, while living in the world.

The lawsuit from Ismail's father was settled out of court, and a great deal of money paid out by Gessen's insurance company. A pointless exercise, he felt. All the money in the world wouldn't bring Ismail back, nor ease his guilt and pain from the loss of such a vibrant young man. As for Hisham, another promising young student, and possibly one of Vidor's victims, an email from Farzan Rahimi had informed Gessen of his fate.

During the spring thaw, a body had washed up on the shores of the Cam, several miles north of Cambridge. Forensic evidence revealed that it was Farzan's friend Hisham, the student from the rival group in Vidor's department, whose lab notebook was stolen. He'd been dead for several months, if not longer. Drowned, apparently, following a blow to the head. The man in Copenhagen, Ismail, Hisham. Possibly Vidor Sovàny. A quartet of death's in Vidor's wake. How many, Gessen wondered, had come before?

After he'd dealt with the authorities and provided support and job placements to the shell-shocked staff, Gessen, bewildered and exhausted himself, hadn't known quite what to do. 'Take some time away,' Hélène had urged during the few days he'd stayed in her home and been too busy with the police and paperwork to grieve what he'd lost.

Uncertain of how to move on from the wreckage, he'd followed Hélène's advice and made a pilgrimage to Jung's former residence in Küsnacht, now a museum, seeking the great man's counsel. While walking along the lake, he was reminded of Jung's injunction on how to approach the second half of life. By ignoring the script of his youth and beginning again.

Startled by the sound of a door slamming shut in a gust of wind, he turned to study the framed painting that hung on the wall near his desk. It was the second painting created by Vidor – or possibly Malik – in his art therapy session with Isabelle. Two dark figures, one in sunlight, the other in shadow, faced each other on opposite sides of a deep ravine. In the distance, barely visible, a lone creature, perhaps a bird, or some mythical beast, hovered on the far horizon. A message or story Gessen has yet to decipher. But one day it would come to him, if he looked at it long enough, and with an open mind.

Having confronted – and survived – the prophecies of that long-ago fortune teller, who'd warned him about a dark knight, a gold ring, a monstrous secret, it was time to lay the past to rest.

High time, indeed, for a change.

But it wasn't until he arrived at Zurich airport and scanned the departure board that he'd decided where to go. A flight for Buenos Aires was departing in two hours. Coincidence or fate? On impulse, he'd bought a one-way ticket. It was time to discover, or rediscover, the place of his birth. How long he planned to remain there was impossible to say, but enough time, he hoped, to pacify the panicked yearning in his soul. Normally attuned to his own moods and desires, everywhere he turned in recent months had seemed like a dead end. The catastrophic loss of his clinic, the sole pillar around which he'd constructed his life, had left him adrift in place and time.

Perhaps, by strolling through the streets of the Argentinian city, he might reconnect with the child he'd left behind, and learn to forgive himself for the sins of his father he'd been helpless to prevent. *Though our lives are an accident of birth, our fate is in our hands.* A sentiment he repeated often as a form of solace. *We do not choose our parents, or the debt they've bequeathed us. But we can, if we choose, create something better and finer from the ash heap of the past.*

* * *

Two weeks later, back in Zurich and refreshed in spirit, if only marginally wiser from his rendezvous with the past, a stack of mail awaited his attention. Gessen made an espresso from the little machine he'd purchased in a local shop and savoured the rich taste as he flipped through the envelopes. A letter from abroad sent to Les Hirondelles contained a postmark from a month ago. It must have languished in the post office in Saint-Odile until someone thought to forward it to his new address in Zurich. After reading the letter, he opened the window wide to let the spring air blow through the room, pausing for a moment to study the faces of the pedestrians in the street.

There was no sign of a furtive, middle-aged man slipping around the corner. But for the rest of his days, Gessen would be on the lookout for a spectral figure with a watchful air. Holding his breath in anticipation of a sign from his mysterious double, hovering in the wings, waiting to be king.

* * *

Astrid I. Olsen, MD, PhD
Committee Chair, Søgaard Prize for Excellence and Innovation in Neuroscience
Copenhagen, Denmark

15 May 2009

Dear Dr Gessen,
Regarding your letter of 21 January 2009, I was very sorry to learn about the unfortunate passing of Vidor Kiraly.

How terrible to hear he perished in a fire at your clinic in Switzerland. In my capacity as chair of the Søgaard Prize Committee, I am writing to you in connection to some disturbing information the Committee received at the end of last year. I would have contacted you earlier, but we first wished to undertake a thorough investigation of the allegations made against Professor Kiraly.

A few months ago, I received an anonymous letter that was posted from London. The author of the letter suggested that key data supporting the ground-breaking research published by Professor Kiraly's laboratory may have been stolen from another research group at Cambridge.

Having awarded Professor Kiraly with the highly competitive Søgaard Prize for the research in question, the Committee was duty-bound to investigate. We take accusations of impropriety and theft very seriously, and so created a sub-committee to explore the authenticity and ownership of Professor Kiraly's data, fully aware that rivalry between scientists is not uncommon, and that the anonymous letter may have come from someone with the intention of stirring up trouble.

I will spare you the details of our lengthy inquiry into this matter. Suffice it to say, we left no stone unturned, and have regretfully corroborated the allegations of data theft. Following a unanimous vote, the Committee has formally rescinded the prize awarded to Professor Kiraly at Rosenborg Castle in October of last year. We are currently considering other scientists to nominate as a replacement.

Our efforts to recover the prize money have been complicated by Professor Kiraly's death. Our attorneys have recently learned that the prize money of one million euros was transferred from Professor Kiraly's account at Barclays Bank in London to an unknown location. Most likely to an offshore account. We learned of the transfer when Professor Kiraly's housekeeper, a Mrs Magdalena Bartosz, came forward to confess that she received a letter from Professor Kiraly in December. Inside the letter was a sealed envelope addressed to Kiraly's bank manager that she was instructed to hand deliver. She claims not to know what was in the letter, but we can only surmise it was instructions for the transfer. The bank has informed us that, in the absence of convincing evidence of criminal activity, they will not breach their policy on the confidentiality of international transfers.

So, it seems that the money is gone, and unless Professor Kiraly speaks to us from the grave, we have given up hope of any chance to recover it.

Sincerely yours,

Dr Astrid I. Olsen

Acknowledgements

I am indebted to the many people who assisted in the making of this book.

My brilliant agent, Charlotte Seymour, for her continuing support and enthusiasm, and the entire team at Andrew Nurnberg Associates.

The talented crew at Legend Press in the UK, with a special thanks to Lauren Parsons for her keen eye for language and instinctive feel for what makes a good story.

Rosie Jonker at Ann Rittenburg Literary Agency in the USA for looking after my interests on the other side of the pond.

Jason Donald and Amy Butcher for insightful suggestions on an early draft of the manuscript.

Shamala Hinrichsen, Ginny Rottenburg, and Allie Reynolds for their always cheerful camaraderie and writerly friendship.

And finally, to the kind librarian, whose name (alas) I have long forgotten, for introducing an eager young reader to the wondrous stories of Vladimir Nabokov.